Roses

Author and Cover Photo by K & R Photography
Front Cover Design by Abby Welch

ISBN (Print): 9781735909202
ISBN (EPub): 9781735909219

Library of Congress Control Number: 2020918877

Published in Raleigh, NC

Roses

RUTH ANNE CREWS

To Anna Sanders, for starting this journey with me
To Samantha Nelson, for editing the first complete draft of this book
To Grandaddy and Paw Paw, who taught me to pursue my dreams
To Mama, for your unending support

And most importantly to the Author and Perfecter of my faith, who put this story in my heart and gave me the desire to write it.

Chapter One

"Welcome to Schaeffer!" Rett Johnson could feel the eyes of every single girl in the room on him, but he was somewhat used to that feeling. It had been like this ever since he started college. In high school, he had been able to fade into the background for the most part, but at Schaeffer University, things were different. He was not sure why, but he guessed it was because girls were more serious about getting married.

This was his second year being a Welcome Leader for a group of new freshman. The weekend before classes started, Schaeffer hosted a couple days of activities to get the incoming freshman introduced to the university. When Rett had first gotten his group list and started reviewing the students' names, information, and photos, he was shocked to see someone on it from Albany, Georgia. His mentor had mentioned he knew someone in the incoming class, but Rett hadn't expected the person to be in his group—much less be a beautiful girl. He hadn't been able to get the blonde girl out of his thoughts for the last two days. He watched for her as the group filed in, she was even more beautiful than her picture.

"You ready?" Claire Thompson, his partner for the weekend, interrupted his thoughts and field of vision. Rett nodded, knowing she going to start introductions. "Hey, everyone!" Claire said, raising her voice to get the students' attention, "Welcome to Schaeffer! Say your name, where you're from, your major, and something you're looking forward to about being in college. I'll start. I'm Claire Thompson. I'm a senior. I grew up in Lima, Peru, as a missionary kid. I'm a secondary education major, and I'm excited about all of you being here."

"I'm Rett Johnson from Dallas, Texas," Rett followed. "I'm a junior theology major, and I'm excited about interning with a youth group here in Jackson this year." He waited as the freshman continued the introductions. He was making eye contact with the people talking, but his eyes kept drifting back to the blonde from Albany, Georgia.

"I'm Kate Adams. I'm from Albany, Georgia." She looked at Rett, and their eyes locked for a second before she looked away. "I'm a secondary education major, and I'm excited about making new friends."

"I'm Caroline Drews from San Antonio, Texas," the girl with short brown wavy hair sitting next to blonde said, taking her turn. "I'm a secondary education major, too. I'm excited about being away from home and not having to answer to my parents constantly." Everyone laughed, but Caroline was serious. It was hard being the youngest—there was a reason she had picked a college in Tennessee. Plus, she had a flair for the dramatic.

The group finished introductions and went over the schedule for the day. Rett had hoped for a chance to talk to Kate, but he was running out of time to get to the chapel.

"Claire, it's time for worship. I have to go," Rett reminded her. He was leading worship and needed to get there before everyone else.

"Got it; go on," Claire told him. He took off for the chapel as she finished giving the group their instructions.

* * *

"Was it just me or was Rett staring at me?" Kate asked Caroline as they walked to the chapel.

"Oh yeah, that boy couldn't take his eyes off you. Don't complain; he's beautiful!" They laughed and caught up the rest of the group.

Claire was making sure everyone was with them. "Y'all are the education majors, right?" Caroline and Kate both nodded. "Do you know what you want to teach?"

"Spanish," they both said at the same time and looked at each other.

"Shut up. Quiero enseñar Español también," Claire said in perfect Spanish, telling them how excited she was to be student teaching in a Spanish classroom that year. When they walked into the chapel, Claire noticed a sign with their group number on it on a row towards the front. Rett had saved them seats.

"Make sure you leave room for Rett," Claire reminded them. Thanks to Caroline, Kate found herself next to the empty seat on the end of the row. There was something about this guy. He was gorgeous, that much was obvious. He was a theology major and interning at a church, so he had to love Jesus. And he also happened to play the guitar and sing. There seemed to be quite a few reasons to like him.

Rett sat down next to Kate and mouthed "hi" as the service started. A smile spread across Kate's face, and Rett saw the sparkle in her eye. Up close, Kate's blue eyes were the color of the ocean. Rett wanted the service to end so he could talk to her. He found he even had to resist the urge to put his arm around her or hold her hand. Rett chastised himself; he was acting crazy. He did not even know this girl, but he certainly was developing a crush on her.

"Kate, right?" he asked after the service ended and they walked to their night activities. She nodded. "Rett Johnson. Nice to meet you." He extended his hand, and she shook it.

"Nice to meet you, too," Kate laughed. It was a sound that Rett knew he would always treasure.

"You're from Albany, right?" Kate's head turned sharply, and she stopped mid-stride.

"Wait, you know where Albany is? Not the one in New York, right?"

"Yep! I'm very close to a family in Albany. Do you know Joshua and Hope King?" Rett laughed at the confusion on her face. This was obviously not a normal question for her.

"Oh my gosh! Hope told me she knew someone who was a student here. Crazy! I can't believe you're my Welcome Leader." Kate suddenly remembered the conversation she had with Hope on her last Sunday at church. It had been surprising when Hope had come looking for her just to tell her she knew a student at Schaeffer.

"It's definitely a little crazy. I'm looking forward to getting to know you, Kate," Rett smiled as Caroline walked up.

"I'm looking forward to getting to you know you, too," she responded, and he turned to talk a couple of the guys in the group.

"What was that?" Caroline asked, and Kate filled her in as they walked away. "He so likes you. Of course, my first friend is going to have a boyfriend within a month instead of me," she groaned. Her dramatic air and expressive eyes made Kate laugh.

"I don't know about all that, but if he asked me out, I wouldn't say no. I think I'll talk to Claire about him and get my sister to do some recon for me. Or at least get her to talk to Hope," Kate said.

As the night wore on, Kate and Caroline played board games with their new classmates and listened to people embarrass themselves by singing karaoke. Kate was fine just listening, but before it was over, she had let Caroline talk her into singing "Popular" from *Wicked*. As silly as it was, she was thankful for new friends who encouraged her to come out of her shell.

***

"Why are you calling me? You're supposed to be enjoying your first weekend of college," Emmie Wren Thomas, Kate's older sister, answered the phone on Saturday night.

"I need—"

"I guess I was right, Schaeffer is just too far. I'll call—"

"I'm trying to talk to you!" Kate did her best to remain calm.

"And I'm trying to tell you that you can come home, there is no shame in that," Emmie Wren said.

"I don't want to come home, Sissy."

"You don't?" Emmie Wren sounded surprised. "Then why did

you call me?"

"Because I need intel."

"Oo, who am I Facebook stalking?" Emmie Wren was in her element.

"That's not exactly what I meant, but you're welcome to do that too," Kate laughed.

"Wait, what?" Emmie Wren was confused.

"The Schaeffer student that Joshua and Hope know? He's my Welcome Leader." Kate swallowed. She knew where this conversation was going to go.

"He?" Emmie Wren repeated.

"Uh huh," Kate nodded, forgetting that Emmie Wren couldn't see her.

"Is he cute?"

"That's one word for it," Kate laughed.

"And what word would you use?"

"Gorgeous," Kate said without thinking.

"Well, then," Emmie Wren laughed. "I take it you want me to talk to Hope in the morning?"

"Yes, please! Because, um, I think he might like me." Kate bit her lip.

"What?! Geeze, Kate, way to bury the lead," Emmie Wren laughed. Kate had a way of glossing over the big stuff sometimes.

"Sorry," Kate said. She was distracted thinking about Rett again.

"What's his name?"

"What?"

"The gorgeous guy who might like you—what's his name?" Emmie Wren asked.

"Oh, right. Rett. Rett Johnson," Kate smiled.

"Got it. I will talk to Hope in the morning."

"Thank you, Emmie Wren. I really appreciate it."

"This is what sisters are for. So, tell me about Rett," Emmie Wren pushed.

"He's from Texas. He's a theology major, and he wants to be a youth minister," Kate said.

"Of course, he does." Emmie Wren's eye roll as almost audible. "At least you know he loves Jesus."

"That's true. Let me know what Hope says," Kate said.

"Hang on; Sky wants to talk to you," Emmie Wren sounded apologetic as she handed the phone off to her husband.

"I've just heard bits and pieces, but be careful. The last thing I want to do is drive seven hours to beat some guy up when he breaks your heart."

"I will keep that in mind." Now it was Kate's turn to roll her eyes. Her brother-in-law could be overprotective. As thankful as she was to have brother-in-law like Sky Thomas, he was just too much sometimes.

***

"Where did all these people come from?" Kate felt overwhelmed with everyone back on campus for the "Welcome Back Party" on Monday night. Welcome Weekend was officially over, and the new freshmen found themselves in the midst of a crowd of upperclassmen. Thankfully, Claire had told the girls in their group that if they needed someone to help navigate the crowds, they could hang out with her.

After dinner, the girls were heading to a concert Schaeffer was hosting when Kate got caught in a crowd of upperclassmen greeting each other. As she tried to catch up with Claire, she tripped over a crack in the concrete and lunged into one of the upperclassmen— Rett, who just happened to be standing there. His arms steadied her before she could fall.

"Thanks," she said laughing, "I'm such a klutz."

"No, these sidewalks can be rough. I wanted to talk to you for a minute, though," Rett smiled, biting back a laugh.

"Yeah?" Kate could not help but smile, even if she was still a little shaken up.

"I was wondering if you would want to get coffee sometime this week. I'd really like to get know to you better."

"Yeah, I'd love to," Kate answered, hoping the disbelief was not evident on her face.

"Good! Thursdays are best for me because of my schedule. Is that okay with you?"

"Yeah. I have class until two, though." As they made plans, she started to feel slightly more confident.

"Two at Abri then?" This was working out better than Rett had hoped.

"Perfect."

"Let's exchange numbers so if either of us are running late or whatever, the other will know," Rett said, trying to act casual.

Kate giggled at his attempt to get her number. "If you want my number, all you have to ask. I already agreed to get coffee with you." Kate batted her eyelashes.

"Kate, could I have your number?" Rett asked directly.

Kate paused a minute like she was thinking about it. "Okay, fine," she huffed and then laughed. He handed her his phone and Kate put her number in. "Text me."

"Rett! How was your summer?" a guy called as Kate walked off.

"What happened to you? You were right behind me and then you were gone," Caroline said when Kate caught up with her and Claire again.

"Upperclassmen—well, and Rett," Kate laughed. "I got caught in a crowd. Then I tripped, Rett caught me, and asked me to get coffee."

"What?" Claire was clearly shocked. "Well, look who Superman decided to ask out. I guess the weekend is over, so you're not technically in our Welcome Group anymore."

"Superman? You have a date with Superman?" Caroline exhaled. "He would pick you."

"Superman? Who's going on a date with Rett?" A guy with mousy curls walked over and hugged Claire.

"It's not a date, it's just coffee," Kate piped up, feeling a bit defensive in front of a guy she had never met.

"Yeah, Rett's been to coffee with a lot of girls—including me when I was sophomore—but it's mainly to get them to leave him alone. He's never asked anyone on an actual date. But maybe you can change that," Claire teased.

"Seriously?" Caroline's dramatic eyes were huge.

"Oh, wow," Kate said. "Thanks for warning me." She felt even more overwhelmed.

"That's what I'm here for," Claire laughed. "By the way, this is my boyfriend, Stephen."

"Nice to meet you," he nodded to the girls. "Everyone's over by library. Do you want to walk over there?" he asked Claire.

"Sure! Girls, do you want to come?" Claire said, but Kate and

Caroline could tell she was just being nice.

"Thanks, but we can hang out with some other freshmen. Thanks for everything! We really appreciate it," Caroline told her. Claire nodded, walking off with her boyfriend.

"You ready for this?" Kate looked at her new friend.

"Let the adventure begin." Caroline pulled Kate alongside her as they looked for familiar faces in the sea of college students.

Chapter Two

"I don't know if I can do this," Kate said to Caroline as they walked to the library on Thursday. The coffee shop she and Rett had agreed to meet at was inside, and being in full view of other students made her even more nervous.

"Oh, would you stop worrying? It's just coffee. Plus, we both know Rett couldn't take his eyes off you during Welcome Weekend. I know it's nerve racking, but take it one day at time. Besides, you look good. I did an excellent job picking out that outfit," Caroline affirmed, flipping her hair. Kate smoothed out the gray t-shirt she was wearing with jeans and her favorite turquoise sandals. A colorful scarf completed the look. Caroline was the perfect stylist.

"You did. Thank you. Okay, I will see you at dinner." Kate took a deep breath and walked in the building that housed both the library and Abri, where she was meeting Rett. He was already sitting at one of the tables in the back, and there were a few other students sitting around the cafe. She could feel the nerves bubbling again, but she heard Caroline's reminder that it was just coffee. "Hey," she said as she walked over and set down her bookbag. "I hope you haven't been here long."

"This is my favorite place to study," he shrugged, closing his computer. "Do you want something?"

"I'm not really a coffee drinker but I'd like a chai latte," she said.

"I'm sure that will change by the time you graduate. But chai it is. I'll be right back."

"Rett, you don't have to do that," Kate half-heartedly tried to stop him.

"I want to," Rett said getting up from the table. Kate tried to not let herself get carried away by the simple fact that he was paying. She reminded herself it was just coffee, and he had done this lots of times before—at least, according to Claire he had.

"You okay? You seem nervous," Rett asked Kate when he got back. She was picking at her fingernails and looked distracted.

"It's just . . . Well, Claire said that you do this a lot. Take girls out to coffee, I mean. Not that I'm not flattered or excited to be here, but I'd really just like to know if this is a date or if you just like coffee or—" she rambled.

"Kate," Rett reached across the table for her hand, stopping her words. "I don't say this to brag, but girls tend to find me attractive. And sometimes, those girls can be aggressive and forward. In order to get them to leave me alone, yes, I get coffee with them. But you are different."

"I am?" she squeaked.

"Yes. You didn't come after me. I asked you here because I'm interested in you." Rett smiled, and Kate felt herself relax.

"How do you know Joshua and Hope?" she asked, hoping to turn the conversation in a more comfortable direction.

"Joshua's my mentor. He used to go to my church in Texas. He's been in my life since I was about nine, and he was actually the one who led me to the Lord when I was eleven. And Hope I've known forever. She babysat for us."

"That's awesome! Joshua actually officiated my sister's wedding last year. She thinks the world of Hope."

"Sister, huh?"

"Yeah, she's pretty awesome. Emmie Wren's my hero. I've been following her around my whole life. She's five years older than me and married to her high school sweetheart." Kate giggled. "What about you? Do you have siblings?"

"I do. I have two younger sisters. Rachel is a senior in high school and Abbie is a freshman. We like to call Abbie my shadow. When I'm home, she likes to be near me. Always has."

"That's sweet."

"Most of the time," Rett laughed. "No, I love her. I wouldn't have it any other way."

"I bet you take being a big brother very seriously," Kate leaned back in her chair.

"I do. Between me and my best friend, who is basically my brother, they are probably never going to date," Rett said, and Kate burst out laughing.

"Oh really? Because my brother-in-law has said the same thing about me, but here I am. I mean, I know this isn't a real date, but you get the point," Kate caught herself, and covered her face with her hands.

"Your brother-in-law is clearly protective."

"He's been dating my sister since I was ten, so he's basically my older brother," Kate explained.

"Wow!"

"Yeah, they started dating when Emmie Wren was sophomore in high school and he was senior. They broke up for about year while they were in college and were engaged forever—like almost two years. Now, they are happily married."

"I'd like to hear that story sometime," Rett smiled.

"But not now?" Kate laughed.

"No, because today is about getting to know you."

"Well, I'm an open book. What do you want to know?" Kate swallowed, this was really happening.

"What do you like to do for fun?"

"I'm a big reader. I love being outside. I've played soccer since I was, like, three so that's a big part of my life. Or it was."

"Both of my sisters play soccer. Abbie's really good—like could play in college good."

"Wow, that's awesome. I went to a little teeny tiny school, so no one even knew who I was. Sky played baseball at Alabama, though, and tried to talk me into playing in college. But it wasn't for me."

"Sky?" Rett questioned.

"Sorry, my brother-in-law."

"Ah, that was my guess. So, why wasn't it for you?"

"Because I want to actually be able to focus on school, and there was no way I could do that and play soccer. Not that someone can't both; I just can't."

"I get it; school is important, and you have to do what is best for you," Rett's smile relaxed Kate's nervousness.

"What about you? What do you like to do for fun?"

"I play a lot of basketball with my friends, but if I'm not studying, I'm normally hanging out with middle school and high school students."

"You really want to be youth minister, don't you?" Kate cocked her head, remembering how he had introduced himself during Welcome Weekend.

"I do. I love teenagers. I feel like most people only expect teenagers to do dumb things and act out, but I know that if you push them, they can do just about anything. Joshua influenced my life when I was their age, and I want to have that same impact on other teens," Rett gushed.

"I can tell you've spent some time thinking about that." Kate bit her lip. "My life goals are not that concise."

"I didn't say that was my life goal; I just think that's the first step."

"What is your life goal then?"

"I want to be a senior pastor," Rett sighed. "It's a long story for another time."

"Well, I look forward to hearing it." Kate couldn't stop smiling. "I want to teach high school Spanish. My Spanish teacher made an incredible impact on my life. She's the reason I fell in love with Spanish, and her example made me want to teach."

"You want to be around teenagers too?" That fact somehow made her even more attractive.

"Yeah, I do. Most people think I'm crazy, but that's who I am," Kate shrugged. They spent the next few hours continuing to get to know each other. When Kate's phone buzzed, she suddenly realized what time it as. "I should probably go. I'm supposed to meet Caroline for dinner."

"I didn't realize how late it was. Next week?" his smile reached all the way to his eyes.

"Sure. Same time?" She bit her lip.

"Yep. I really enjoyed this time with you, Kate."

"Me too. See you later!" Kate picked up her backpack and walked with Rett out of the library. Once he was out of sight, she darted for the cafeteria.

"So?" Caroline was waiting on her outside.

"Girl. He. Is. A. MAZE. ING!" Kate exclaimed. She was grinning and giggling; she could not help but be a little dramatic with her most animated friend.

* * *

As Rett drove to his apartment, the conversation with Kate played in his head. Everything she said about herself and her laugh—Kate's melodic laugh—echoed through his soul and warmed his heart. She was genuine and kind. Her ocean blue eyes sparkled when she talked about things that excited her, like her sister and teaching. Rett had been waiting for the right girl, and he was pretty sure he had found her. He wanted to talk to Joshua first and get to know her a little better before setting his plan in motion, though. He prayed for Kate and about moving things forward with her as he fixed dinner.

The next morning, Rett woke up and read his Bible, just like he had for the past six years. He called his mentor at 7:30 am. After their normal morning banter, Joshua brought up Kate.

"Can I ask about Kate now that you've gotten coffee with her?"

"Sure. It went really well. She's special," Rett said vaguely. He couldn't figure out how Joshua already knew about their coffee date, so Rett was going to keep his mentor in suspense a little longer.

"Glad to hear it. Are you going to see her again?"

"We're getting coffee again next week. I take it you know her sister."

"I do. Emmie Wren and Sky are great. I know that she and Kate are very close. She asked Hope about you on Sunday," Joshua said.

"That's how you knew!" Rett exclaimed.

"Yep. I'm happy for you, Rett. Kate seems like a great girl."

"I think so, too," Rett smiled.

"You really like her, don't you?"

"I think so. I do want to get to know to her a little better before I commit to anything serious, though."

"Are you going to date her—I mean, really date her?" Joshua asked him.

"I think so. I really think so. I've never felt like this."

"Felt like what?" Joshua wanted him to define his feelings so that Rett would able to understand why he was attracted to Kate and what he liked about her.

Rett was silent for a few minutes before he finally said anything. "I don't think I can put words to it yet. I haven't spent enough time with her."

At least Rett was honest about the situation. The two men talked until 8:00 am when Joshua got to his office. Rett hung up, his mind spinning. Joshua was always good at giving him lots to think about. He fixed his coffee, unable to shake thoughts of Kate and how their potential relationship could affect his life plan. He didn't have class, so he headed into the church for a little while to see if he could get anything done on his lesson for Sunday school. But with everything Joshua had said, he was sure all he was going to be thinking about was Kate. This was certainly new for him, but it was what he had been waiting for his whole life—or at least he hoped it was.

Chapter Three

"Hey Kate?" Rett somehow seemed both nervous and sure at the same time as he reached across the table for her hand. They had spent the last four Thursdays together, and he was finally ready to begin an adventure he had been praying about for a long time. "I'd like to take you to dinner tomorrow night. What do you say?"

"I'd love to," Kate grinned. She hugged him before heading to meet her friends for dinner. She was giggly and excited when she found them and announced that she was going on an actual date with Superman.

* * *

"I did it. I asked her out," Rett told his roommate and best friend, Nathan Daly, when he got back to their apartment.

"Wait, let me get this straight. You asked a girl out on an actual date?" Nathan was shocked.

"Don't sound so surprised. I like this girl."

"I know, but you are so dang picky. I wasn't sure it was ever going to happen," Nathan laughed.

"Glad to know that my best friend has such great confidence in me," Rett kidded as he slapped him on the back.

"I'm just glad you finally decided to ask a girl out on a real date," Nathan said, still dumbfounded.

Rett heard the reply as he looked up the phone number for a florist. He wanted to buy roses for his soon-to-be girlfriend and officially launch his plan into motion. The plan centered around an idea he, Nathan, and Joshua had talked about a long time ago. Though it was just an idea then, Rett had latched onto it. The plan included giving a woman twelve bouquets of red roses with an engagement ring coming on the twelfth rose of the twelfth bouquet. Each bouquet was supposed to come at a significant moment. Rett had never actually set the plan into motion before. He had never even come close to setting it into motion, for that matter. He could hardly wait to see Kate the next day and for her to officially be his girlfriend.

* * *

"Hey, Claire!" one of the RAs in the resident life office called out to her.

"Hey! What's up?" she stuck her head in.

"I just didn't expect to see you in the freshman dorm and wanted to say hi."

"I'm glad you did. One of the girls from my Welcome Group has a date with Rett Johnson tonight, and I came by to help her get ready."

"Rett's actually taking a girl on a date?"

"Yep," Claire laughed.

"What's her name?"

"Kate Adams," Claire answered as she started to walk out.

"Wait! Those roses are for her," the RA called as she motioned to the bouquet sitting on the desk opposite her.

"I'll take them up." Claire grabbed the vase and headed to Kate's room. Knocking, she announced, "Delivery!"

"Oh, my word," Caroline gasped. "Not fair!" She took the bouquet and set it on Kate's desk as Kate finished her makeup. "Here," Caroline handed her the card with a tiny pretend pout.

"1. Your laugh. 2. The fact that I've already turned you into a coffee drinker. 3. I really hope you'll be my—" Kate froze, unable to finish.

"Girlfriend? Is that what it says?" Caroline grabbed the card out of Kate's hand. "Ah!" she squealed.

"Looks like Superman found his Lois Lane," Claire said happily. "You got a good one."

Kate just stood there in shock. Rett Johnson, the guy who had never asked a girl out on a date, was asking her to be his girlfriend. She sucked in a breath and let out a small squeal before turning back to her friends to finalize her outfit. She had to be dressed before she could say yes! The girls decided on a floral sundress with a woven belt. She accessorized with a white cardigan, pearls, and the same turquoise sandals she had worn the first time they got coffee.

"Let's pray. You look like you need it," Claire observed. She put a hand on Kate's shoulder, and the three girls prayed together. "Heavenly Father, I pray that you calm Kate's spirit and let her enjoy this night with Rett. Help them both to honor you in how they treat each other. In your name we pray, amen."

"Thank you," Kate sighed. She let out another breath as her phone dinged with a text from Rett letting her know he was outside. "Well, I guess it's time to go see my boyfriend," Kate giggled, and she walked out to meet him.

Rett's nervousness faded when he saw Kate's beautiful smile, perfectly straightened blonde hair, and the sundress that hugged her curves in all the right places. "Wow! Kate, you look beautiful!"

"Thanks. You don't look too bad yourself," Kate beamed, noticing his khakis and light blue button down that made him look even more handsome. "And thank you for the roses."

"You got them?" he grinned. "What did you think?"

"They are gorgeous! I can't believe you got me roses on our first date." She didn't say anything about the card, though. She wasn't going to let him get away with not actually asking her in person.

"Yeah, well, I figured it was worth it for my girlfriend," a smile widened across his features as he said the word.

"Girlfriend, huh?" Kate bit her lip, pretending to look doubtful.

"If that's okay with you." Rett couldn't stop smiling. She had gotten her first bouquet of roses, and they were headed out on their first date.

"It's more than okay, now that you've actually asked," Kate assured him as her phone started ringing. "Sorry, I forgot to put it on sile—" Her words stopped when she saw Sky's name. "This is my brother-in-law. He never calls. Hey," she answered, stepping aside with a feeling of dread.

"How soon can you get home?" Sky tried to sound calm, but the first words out of his mouth sounded urgent.

Kate instantly froze; something was wrong. "Sky, what's going on?"

"Emmie Wren got into a really bad wreck on her way home from work. She's in the ICU." Kate started to cry as Sky pleaded, "Come home." She worked to hold herself together as she hung up.

"What's wrong?" Rett asked gently.

Kate took a deep breath so that she'd be able to speak before turning to Rett. "I need to go home right away. My sister was in a car accident. I'm so sorry." She was amazed at how steady her voice was.

"Yes, you definitely need to get home," Rett sighed. This was not how the night was supposed to go. "Can I pray for Emmie Wren before you go?" Kate nodded. She was worried she was about to start sobbing. "Dear God, I pray that you would be with Kate and her family has they face the hours and days ahead. We pray that you will heal Emmie Wren. Give Kate your peace and comfort, and may she always remember that you heal the brokenhearted and bind up their wounds. In Jesus' name we pray, amen." He hugged her, asking, "Let me know when you make home? I'll be praying for your family."

Kate walked back inside the dorm and made her way back to her room, trying to process what was happening.

"Kate?" In a daze, she nearly passed Caroline in the hallway, but when she looked at her, her eyes were full of unshed tears. "What happened? Where's Rett?" The tears overflowed as Kate broke into sobs and tried to explain what happened. "Let's go get you packed." Caroline walked Kate to her room and helped her pack a suitcase, surprisingly calm for one prone to adding drama to her own life events. She definitely wasn't going to let Kate drive the seven hours by herself. She called Claire to let her know what was happening and to Caroline's shock, Claire insisted on coming with them.

"Kate, are you ready?" Caroline asked. Kate nodded and grabbed her bag. For the moment, she had managed to get her emotions somewhat under control. They got in Caroline's car and drove over to Claire's dorm. "What's your address?" Caroline asked Kate as she pulled up the GPS in her car.

"We'll actually go straight to the hospital," Kate said, googling the address on her phone. "417 3rd Avenue West, Albany, GA, 31701." Caroline put the address into the GPS and they waited on Claire to get in the back seat.

"Ready?" Caroline asked as she slid in.

"Ready," Claire said. "My one request is that we get some food before we get on the road." Caroline agreed, and they went through a drive-thru before getting on the interstate. Kate said she wasn't hungry, but they ordered something for her anyway.

They were barely on the road when Kate's mom, Emily, called. "You're coming home, aren't you?" she asked her youngest daughter.

"You really think I can just sit at school when Sissy's in the ICU? Of course, I'm coming home." Kate didn't even try to stop the tears.

"I'm glad you're coming. It's bad, Katie. There's a possibility she won't make it." Emily used the name only her family and closest friends used.

"Mama," Kate sobbed, "Claire and Caroline are with me; we're just getting on the road."

"Be safe and pray. I love you."

When Kate was off the phone, Claire started praying, "Holy Spirit, we come before you and ask that you will comfort your daughter in a special way. She's hurting and needs your peace that everything will be okay with her sister. Give her strength to be able to deal with this situation with grace. We love you. In your name we pray, amen. John 14:27 says, 'Peace I leave with you; my peace I give to you. I do not give as the world gives. Do not let your hearts be troubled. And do not be afraid.'"

"Thanks, Claire. I needed that," Kate managed to get out. "Okay, I need something to jam to. I don't want to cry the whole way." Caroline laughed and turned on Taylor Swift. They jammed for a while, and Kate eventually ate the food they bought her. Each of the girls took a turn driving. Even Kate had pulled herself together enough to drive once they got through Birmingham. She headed straight for the hospital when they got to Albany just after 3:00 am. Kate called her parents, and her dad said he would meet them in the lobby. She texted Rett to let him know they had made it safely and woke her friends up.

"Hey girls, I'm Charlie," Kate's dad introduced himself when they met up with him. "Thanks for driving with Kate." They all walked to the waiting room together. Kate saw her mom and scanned the room for Sky, but she quickly realized he was with Emmie Wren. All three girls got visitor badges from the nurse on duty, and Emily offered them the seats next to her as Charlie disappeared into the ICU.

He returned a few minutes later. "Katie, Sky said you can go back."

Charlie led her to Sky and Emmie Wren. Sky hugged Kate, and she sat down in the chair next to Emmie Wren's bed. She could not believe all the cords and wires that were connected to her sister. Thankfully, the beeping of the heart monitor was constant reminder that she was still alive. The tears returned as Kate realized just how dire the situation was. She couldn't the find the words to say, and when she tried to open her mouth, nothing came out. Sky, who had been leaning against the doorframe, walked over and bent down in front of Kate.

"Katie, look at me." He took both her hands. "I know it's hard to see her like this, and I know you're scared. But you have to pray and believe that everything is going to be okay. I know in my heart of hearts that Emmie Wren is going to pull through this. I just have a peace about it. But if God has decided this is it for her, I'll be okay with that too, eventually." He was strong, no doubt, but he began to tear up, too. "I want to yank all those wires out because I can't even touch my wife. Katie, be strong for me. Can you do that?"

Kate nodded and wiped the tears from her eyes. If Sky could say those things, maybe she would be able to as well. She composed herself while she spent some time praying. She hated this. Her sister was dying, and there was nothing she could do about it.

When she couldn't take any more of staring at Emmie Wren, Kate walked out to the waiting room and snuggled up next to her dad. She was exhausted and worried. She had not even told her parents about what had happened with Rett.

It could wait until morning.

Chapter Four

"Rett? You're not supposed to be here." Nathan was surprised when Rett walked through the door, a mere twenty minutes after he left. "Wait, did she turn you down?"

"Her sister was in a car accident so she's going home," Rett explained.

"And you didn't go with her?" Nathan stared at him.

"We've only been dating for five minutes. No, I didn't go with her." Rett sat down on the couch.

"Should we pray? I feel like we should pray." Nathan could see how worried Rett was.

"Thanks—hang on, this is Joshua," Rett said, picking up his phone.

"You answered, so I take it you know about Emmie Wren's wreck?" Joshua asked.

"I do. Kate is on her way home," Rett said.

"Well, if you need somewhere to stay you are welcome to stay with us."

"I'm not with her," Rett answered, beginning to regret his decision to stay behind.

"Really?" Joshua sounded surprised.

"Really," Rett said.

"If you change your mind, the offer stands," Joshua said. "I gotta go, but I'll update you later."

"Thanks, Joshua, for everything." Rett hung up, and Nathan prayed for Emmie Wren.

"What do you want to do?" Nathan asked.

"Distract me. Let's watch something." Rett settled on the couch, and they found a movie. But Rett was restless and couldn't seem to sit still even after Nathan ordered pizza for their dinner.

"I wish you would just go," Nathan finally said.

"You think I should?" Rett asked doubtfully.

"I don't know what you should do, but you've walked from the couch to the kitchen to your room about ten times in the last thirty minutes," Nathan answered, rolling his eyes.

"You're right. I'm going to go." Rett stood quickly, packed a bag, and got ready to leave. Nathan landed him a cup of coffee and told him to be safe. After a quick prayer, Rett settled in for the long drive ahead of him. He called Joshua at about three when he was exhausted, and he finally pulled into the hospital at 6:00 am.

Joshua had told Rett how to get to the waiting room they were in, and as he entered, he immediately saw Claire and Caroline asleep on one of the couches. He looked around until he spotted Kate, who was asleep on a man he figured was her dad. He was watching Rett, so Rett introduced himself before settling down on the other side of Kate, already wishing he wasn't in a hospital. But this is where Kate and her family were, so this is where he would stay.

* * *

Kate woke up thinking, *Where am I?* Then she remembered: she was in the hospital because Emmie Wren had been in a car wreck. She had fallen asleep next to her dad. But when she looked up, the first person she saw was Rett. "What are you doing here?" she asked in total shock.

"You were upset and I was worried about you, so I drove down to be sure you were okay," Rett reassured her.

"What time is it? How long have I been asleep?"

"It's almost noon, but you clearly needed sleep."

Worry masked Kate's face again, and Rett just wanted to make everything go away. "The doctors just checked in with your parents and Sky. She's still hanging in there," he let her know. "Do you need anything?"

"I'd love something to eat. I'm starving," Kate said with her stomach growling. Rett offered to get food, but Charlie told him that Emily's friends were on their way. They were sure to bring enough food to feed the whole floor. Kate walked into the bathroom to try and freshen up.

"Katie, I'm glad your friends are here," Emily said, following Kate into the bathroom for a moment alone with her daughter. "And Rett—he's something special for sure."

"I know. I can't wait for Emmie Wren to meet him," Kate sighed, trying not to give up hope.

"And she will. You have to remember that our hope comes from

29

God, who is in control." Emily hugged her. "Go on. Go see her now that you've had a chance to rest."

Sky was asleep in a chair next to the bed; Kate couldn't imagine how hard this was on him. All she could do was listen to the beep of the machines keeping Emmie Wren alive and let Sky sleep. There was no telling how exhausted he was. But when a nurse walked in a few minutes later, Kate knew he would want the latest update. She bumped Sky to wake him up before darting out of the room.

"Katie," Sharon Williams, one of her mom's friends hugged her when she walked back into the waiting room. As Kate's dad had predicted, she had brought plenty of food for them all to enjoy. "Haleigh Nicole wishes she could be here, but she's stuck at UGA this weekend." Sharon passed along the text Kate's high school best friend had sent her.

"I know; she let me know that she's praying, too. I miss her," Kate sighed. It was hard going to different colleges, but they were each already on their way to making new friends. Kate introduced Claire, Caroline, and Rett to the women who had come to pray over her sister. They were some of the most influential women in her life. The whole group enjoyed the food the women had provided, talked, and prayed until Sky appeared in the doorway.

"She's awake," Sky said with the twinkle back in his eye. "They're running tests, but things are beginning to look up." Kate made it to him first. They hugged and waited on the doctor to come with more information.

"Emmie Wren is going to be okay," the doctor announced as soon as he entered the room. "It was a long night, and she's got a long way to go, but she's going to pull through. We're working on getting her moved into a regular room. Y'all can see her then." He motioned to everyone behind Sky, since Emmie Wren had only been allowed a few visitors so far. Sky thanked him, and they waited with relief and renewed faith for Emmie Wren's recovery.

* * *

"I love you. I love you so much," Sky repeated as he kissed his wife.

"I love you, too. And I want to see Katie. She's here, right?" Emmie Wren whispered. Sky reminded her not to wear herself out before going to get Kate. As soon as Kate walked into the room, tears started to flow.

"Emmie Wren," was all that she managed to get out.

"Katie, I love you," Emmie Wren said, looking her little sister right in the eye.

"I love you, too, Sissy. I'm just glad you're okay," Kate smiled through her tears. Things were going to get better. "Want to meet my friends?" Kate's eyes sparkled with excitement. Emmie Wren nodded, and Kate pulled everyone in.

"Emmie Wren, this is the famous Caroline," she introduced the brunette.

"It is so nice to meet you," Emmie Wren said. "I've heard lots about you."

"All good I hope," Caroline's eyes got wide.

"Of course," Emmie Wren said, laughing. Her sister had been right about the drama in those eyes. "And you must be Claire."

"Yes. I'm so sorry that this happened to you. I'm praying for you," Claire said.

"Thank you; that means a lot," Emmie Wren said. "And thank

you for taking care of my sister."

"Of course," Claire smiled.

"I'm sure I don't need an introduction, since Hope said you were asking about me?" Rett teased, eyes twinkling. He had not let go of Kate's hand.

"So, are y'all—"

"Official? Yes," Kate leaned into his shoulder for a second. "We were supposed to have our first date last night, actually. But I'm just glad you're going to be okay."

"Me too," Emmie Wren said.

"Can we pray for you?" Rett asked.

"I would love that," Emmie Wren said, closing her eyes as Rett led them all in prayer for her recovery.

"Thank you, Rett," Sky said when Rett finished. Sky had walked in along with the girls' parents during the prayer. They all talked for a few minutes until Emmie Wren started to get tired. Then they cleared out of her room to let her rest.

"I know you're worried about your sister, but she's going to be fine. Go home; get some real rest," Emily told Kate. Then she turned to the other girls. "I know Kate is not leaving until Emmie Wren is out of the hospital, but we do not expect any of you to stay that long. Still, our home is open to you."

"Caroline and I are going to head back in the morning. I have a couple tests next week that I can't miss," Claire said. "Thank you for your generous hospitality."

"I'm staying as long as Kate needs me, but I'm staying with Joshua and Hope King," Rett explained.

"How do you know the Kings?" Emily cocked her head; this was new information for her.

"They went to my church in Texas before they moved here. Joshua's my mentor. He's been in my life since I was nine," Rett explained as they all got ready to leave. As the girls went to get some dinner, he headed to the King's house. It had been too long since he had seen them.

* * *

"Rett!" Hope exclaimed as she opened the door. "Honey, Rett's here! Come in, come in!" she gushed.

"Rett, you're just in time for dinner." Joshua slapped him on the back. "I'm glad you finally got to come to town. It's been too long. This is Jessie," Joshua announced, motioning to the little girl with black hair bouncing in her booster seat.

"And this is Helen," Hope added, patting her bulging stomach. Rett smiled. He was so glad to be with them for the first time in almost five years. "Jessie, can you say hey to Rett?" Jessie smiled and waved. "Well, that's a start. Give her time," Hope told him.

"She's precious. How old is she again?"

"She just turned two. Hope is due to have Helen mid-December. How's Emmie Wren?"

"She's awake and out of ICU. They are expecting her to continue to improve," Rett answered, sounding hopeful.

"How long are you staying?"

"As long as Kate wants to. I know she's going to want make sure that Emmie Wren is okay. I think we'll probably stay all week. Is that alright?"

"EJ, you know you are *always* welcome here," Hope assured him, calling him by the name his parents did. After dinner, Hope got

Jessie ready for bed while Joshua and Rett settled onto the couch.

"Kate is your girlfriend now, right? Officially?" Joshua asked.

"Yes, as of last night."

"Are you ready for this? I mean, really ready?"

"Joshua, I've never liked a girl like I like Kate."

"You know you're going to have trust her if this relationship is going to go anywhere," Joshua said. Rett rolled his eyes; he should have known this conversation was coming. "Rett, I'm serious," Joshua added.

"I know. I know I have to tell her, and I will in my own time. We have only been dating two days. We haven't even been on a real date yet," Rett reminded him, flustered.

"Just making sure you know what is coming down the road," Joshua shrugged, backing down. "Did Jessie go down okay?" he asked, turning to Hope as she returned.

"Asleep before I finished reading the story." Hope sat down on the couch. "I know you're exhausted, but we're so glad you're here." Joshua echoed the sentiment and showed him to the guest room. Rett collapsed onto the bed. It had been a long couple of days, and he was glad to finally be in a bed.

Rett meet Kate at Generations Baptist Church the next morning. She loved having her boyfriend beside her at the church she grew up in. They sat with Joshua and Hope, enjoying the music and Pastor Eddie's sermon on the faith of Abraham. When the service was over, Kate got ready to go to Sunday school.

"Are you coming with me?" Kate asked.

"Not this time," Rett responded mysteriously. "I'm going to hang out with Joshua. Come find me later." Kate walked off as Joshua and Pastor Eddie joined Rett.

"Eddie, this is Rett Johnson—the guy I've been telling you about. He's a junior at Schaeffer University in Tennessee," Joshua introduced him to the senior pastor of Generations. This church was where Rett hoped to work one day, and if Joshua had anything to do with it, he would. Rett met most of the staff that morning and tried to remember everyone's names. "Are you and Kate going to have lunch with us?" Joshua asked as they waited on Hope and Kate to get done with Sunday school.

"Of course," Rett nodded as Kate walked over.

"What's happening?"

"Lunch with the Kings." Rett wrapped his arm around her. "Speaking of lunch, where are we going?" The two couples landed on Longhorn, and they headed out.

"How's school going, Kate?" Hope asked after they ordered.

"It's good! I've made some great friends, and classes are going pretty well. They are harder than I thought they'd be, but I like them."

"Good, I'm glad. Didn't a couple of your friends drive you home?"

"Yes, they were great. I was in a total panic when I got the call about Emmie Wren. I'm so thankful for them—and for this guy." She elbowed Rett who just rolled his eyes.

"You're my girlfriend, Kate. I wasn't going to let you be on your own. I know how important your sister is to you." Rett squeezed her hand.

"Speaking of Emmie Wren, we should probably get back to the hospital soon." Kate didn't want to rush lunch, but she was anxious to get back to her sister. Emmie Wren might be out of the woods, but she still had a long way to go before she would fully recover.

Kate felt like she knew Rett a little bit better once she had seen him with Joshua. It was easy to see how close they were, and it made her realize she wanted to meet Rett's friends, too. Even though they had been meeting for coffee every week for a month, they hadn't really had much time to hang out with other people.

"Thank you for lunch; we so enjoyed it." Rett hugged his mentor.

"Of course! I hope you'll be able to come back to church tonight. Sunday nights are always special."

"Me too; it will just depend on how Emmie Wren is doing." Rett knew that was the truth.

"How was church?" Emmie Wren was waiting for Kate when she walked in.

"It was good. Joshua and Hope treated us to lunch," Kate said smiling. "I think Rett loved being with Joshua all morning."

"You really like him, don't you?"

Kate stifled a giggle. "You have no idea. Rett is wonderful. He . . . well, I never imagined he would be willing to come to Albany and stay until you're out of the hospital. He is so romantic, and he's one of a kind. Emmie Wren, I can't wait for you to get to know him," Kate gushed. Emmie Wren just smiled and shook her head. "What?" Kate felt her face turn red.

"You've got it bad. I can't wait to get to know him. So, he's staying?" Emmie Wren asked, but before Kate could answer, Rett appeared in the doorway.

"Kate, would you like to go back to church tonight?"

"Sure," she nodded as he ducked back out. "Yes, he's staying." She enjoyed the afternoon with sister, glad she was starting to seem more like herself.

That night, Pastor Eddie preached on Colossians, and Kate and Rett spent the rest of the evening with the Kings. Throughout the week, Rett was glad to get to spend some time with Joshua, Hope, and sweet Jessie. He and Kate spent a lot of time at the hospital each day, where Emmie Wren was steadily getting better. On Tuesday night, Rett took Kate to a restaurant called Baja for their first real date.

"I'm glad we're finally getting to do this," Kate said when Rett picked her up. "It hasn't even been a week, but with everything that has happened with Emmie Wren, it feels like forever ago that we were supposed to have our first real date!"

"It does, but I'm glad, too. You look beautiful. I'm glad that dress made it into the suitcase," he added, smiling. She was wearing the same thing she had on Friday night when their plans were interrupted by Sky's phone call.

"It's about the only thing that did," Kate laughed. Her laugh warmed Rett's heart; he loved the sound of it. Both Sky and Joshua had suggested the same place for dinner, so they took their advice and headed to Baja. It was great decision—the perfect place for their first date. Kate was thankful for all the time they had spent together already; it made everything less awkward. They talked and laughed their way through the meal. As they left the restaurant, Kate said, "Thanks for tonight; it was just what I needed."

"You're welcome. I'm just glad our first date is behind us." Rett pulled in to the hospital to drop Kate off. "See you tomorrow, Katie."

She smiled as she got on the elevator and realized that he called her the name her family used.

"You look beautiful," Emmie Wren said.

"Rett and I finally had our first date."

"Oo la la," Sky laughed from the corner.

"Shut up," Kate and Emmie Wren said at the same time, laughing. They talked for a little while before Kate stepped into the bathroom to change.

"Better?" Sky asked as she emerged in sweats and a t-shirt.

"Much more comfortable. How are you today?" Kate asked, turning to Emmie Wren.

"Better. I'm so ready to get out of here, but they're saying it will probably be Friday before I can leave," Emmie Wren sighed. She was a nurse, so she understood why they were keeping her, but she was getting restless. Kate stayed with Emmie Wren that night so Sky could get some real rest.

"I wish he would go on back to school, but I know he won't," Emmie Wren told her sister. "I'm going to be fine. They're taking great care of me. Honestly, I'm surprised he actually went home at all tonight, even with you here."

"I'm sorry. I know it's hard. Sky is just worried about you. I mean—I'm still here, aren't I? And we're not even married." Kate winked and Emmie Wren laughed.

Kate filled her sister in on the details of her relationship with Rett as they fell asleep. They had talked about everything, sure, but it was all over the phone. It was different being together in person. The sisters were extremely close, and it was finally Kate's turn to gush about a boy. She had very vivid memories of when Emmie Wren brought Sky home for the first time. She had watched her sister fall in love, and now it was her turn—or at least, she really hoped it was.

Sky woke Kate up the next morning. They talked for a few minutes because he wanted to know all about Rett, too. Sky and Rett had gotten to know each other a little, and Sky seemed to approve of him, which made Kate's heart soar. She had always valued Sky's opinion, especially when it came to guys.

"Is Rett coming to get you?" Emmie Wren asked after the nurse left the room.

"No, I look awful. Mom is supposed to be taking me home around noon. Rett will get me from there at about three, and we're spending the afternoon together. I know he wants to go to church tonight to see the Wednesday youth service."

"I can't believe you've only been dating for a few days," Emmie Wren laughed. She was happy for her sister, but she knew that they were definitely in the honeymoon stage where everything seemed perfect. The sisters were laughing when Emily walked in.

"I have missed hearing that sound," Emily smiled. There was nothing better than the laughter of her daughters, especially when it was coming from a hospital room. She brought lunch, and they all ate before Emily took Kate home.

* * *

The next two days passed more quickly than any of them expected, and Emmie Wren was released from the hospital on Friday. They family had a celebratory dinner that night, and Rett and Kate headed out Saturday morning.

"Thank you for this week; it meant a lot to me." Kate squeezed Rett's hand before she got out of the car to walk into her dorm.

"I'm just glad Emmie Wren's okay," Rett smiled.

"Me too." Kate opened her door. "See you later." She waved as she got her bag and walked to her room. She texted Caroline to let her know she was back and slumped onto her bed. A few minutes later, when Caroline walked into her room, Kate was shocked to see the bouquet of roses her friend carried.

"These are for you. Rett apparently had them sent to me so you would have them when you got back." Caroline set the second bouquet of roses on the desk and rolled her eyes. "I was this close," Caroline sighed, holding her thumb and pointer finger close together.

"No, you weren't," Kate laughed, pushing her.

"A girl can dream, can't she?"

"Not when he's my boyfriend!"

Chapter Five

"Kate's coming, right? I still can't believe y'all have been dating for a month and I haven't even met the girl the yet," Nathan complained.

"Yes, sorry about that. You'll finally get to meet my Katie. She's pretty great," Rett apologized. "Please tell me this isn't going to be a big party." He leaned his head back hopefully. He did not like that Nathan was making a big deal out of his twenty-first birthday.

"No, it's just Patrick and possibly his flavor of the week, Houston and Lynne, and Mariah, of course," Nathan told him.

"Good, because I don't want to overwhelm Kate. You and Patrick are enough," Rett insisted, rolling his eyes. Someone knocked on the door, and when Rett opened it, he was surprised to see Kate standing there.

"Happy birthday! I know I'm early, but I wasn't sure how long it would take me to get here," Kate said, hugging him.

"You look beautiful. I kind of wish tonight was just me and you," Rett confessed.

"Twenty-one is a big deal, Rett. Besides, I haven't gotten to meet your friends yet," Kate replied, batting her eyelashes.

"Let me fix that! I'm Nathan Daly, the best friend," Nathan said, appearing from behind Rett.

"Nathan! Oh my gosh, it's so good to finally meet you." Kate took in the six-foot two guy with dark blonde hair and piercing blue eyes. "I feel like I know you already," she commented.

"Pizza's here!" A dark-skinned girl with long black hair walked in carrying four pizza boxes. "Happy birthday, Rett!" she exclaimed as she hugged him. Kate watched the exchange, feeling very cautious of this girl. She knew Rett liked her, but he always turned heads—and this girl was stunning.

"Hey Nate." The girl hugged Rett's best friend, too, before turning to Kate. "You must be Kate. I'm Mariah Knowles," she introduced herself.

"It's nice to meet you," Kate answered, but she was completely confused as to who this girl was. Before she could ask, the door opened again.

"The party can start. I'm here!" The big voice belonged to an equally big guy with short brown hair and a contagious smile.

"You're ridiculous, Patrick. Remember, this night is not about you. It's about Rett," Nathan admonished as he rolled his eyes. They all hugged as a couple walked in.

"Happy birthday, Rett," the guy with glasses and a beard greeted him. "I'm Houston," he said, turning to Kate. "And this is my girlfriend, Lynne," he introduced the red-head with vibrant smile. Kate was thankful for Houston's quick introduction. Were all the girls Rett hung out with this beautiful?

"You must be Kate. I'm so excited to finally meet the girl who actually got Rett to go on a date." Lynne looked serious for a second as she considered Kate but then laughed as she caught Mariah's eye. "Rye!" she called. Mariah walked over. "Have you meet Mariah yet?"

"Briefly," Kate smiled. She needed more information on this girl. "Are you dating Nathan?" Lynne started laughing uncontrollably.

"No, no, no. We are just friends," Mariah denied the suggestion. "Friends, nothing more."

"They are 'just friends,' but we all know they are going to end up together," Lynne said when she managed to stop laughing.

"I doubt it," Mariah protested. "I'm planning doing the Journeyman program when I graduate, so I'll be gone for two years."

"Journeyman?" Kate had no idea what Mariah was talking about.

"It's two-year program through the International Missional Board where you go serve as a missionary somewhere overseas. I'm hoping to get placed in a Spanish-speaking country because I'm basically fluent."

"That's really cool! I didn't know anything like that existed. I love Spanish, and I want to teach someday. You'll have to help me; I'm not as good as I'd like to be."

"Anytime," Mariah smiled brightly. In spite of her reservations, Kate knew she had just made a friend.

"Do you speak Spanish, Lynne?"

"No. I took French, but I'm awful. I'm an English major. I don't have to worry about languages any more, praise the Lord. But more power to ya," Lynne smiled, and Kate laughed.

"English, huh?" Kate wanted to keep the conversation going.

"Oh, Lynne is a total bookworm. English is the only major for her," Mariah explained. It was easy to see how close they were.

"I love to read; I want to be an editor, but we'll see what God has planned. Houston's going to dental school when he graduates, so I have no idea where we will be."

"That's cool. How long have you been dating?"

"Too long," Lynne smiled. "Almost three years. We started dating in high school, when I was junior and he was senior."

"High school sweethearts," Mariah rolled her eyes.

"I think it's sweet," Kate smiled.

"At least some one around here appreciates it." Lynne hip checked Mariah.

"I appreciate it; I just don't want it in my face all the time," Mariah teased back. "So, you're dating Rett?" She turned back to Kate.

"Yes, I am. He's wonderful, and I'm really excited to finally be meeting all his friends."

"He's been talking about you since the beginning of the semester, so we're glad to finally meet you, too," Lynne giggled as Kate blushed bright red. "Let me give you the lowdown. Obviously, you know Rett. He and Nathan are attached at the hip. They've been best friends forever and can read each other's minds, I swear. Nathan is the jokester; he can make anyone laugh and is the best at diffusing tense situations.

"We all kid Patrick about making everything about himself. He does like to be the center of attention, but he is one of the most generous people you will ever meet. He wants to be college professor, and he's going make a great one. We have to find him a girl, though, because Lord knows he is having too much fun dating around at the moment.

"Somehow, Houston is the quiet one in this group, which I normally never say about him, but with Nathan and Patrick around, he definitely is. He loves to have a good time but is very committed to his studies."

"How did they all meet?" Kate asked when Lynne took a breath.

"They were suitemates," Lynne said.

"What about you, Mariah? How do you fit into all this?" Kate tried to act casual as she asked.

"Nathan and I had class together last year and became really good friends. He invited me to hang out with them. Now Lynne and I are roommates."

"Thank you, Nathan," Lynne exclaimed, high fiving Mariah. "Oh crap," she muttered as Nathan walked over.

"What are we thanking me for?"

"Nothing," Mariah said, a little too fast.

"So, Kate," Nathan started, raising an eyebrow and moving until he was standing in between Mariah and Kate. Clearly, he intended to replace the girls' conversation with one of his own.

"Seriously, I hate you right now," Mariah griped as she tried to move. But Nathan kept moving with her.

"You're going to grill me, aren't you?" Kate crossed her arms, prepared.

"You're the only girl Rett's ever dated, and I need to make sure you're not going to hurt him. That's what best friends are for, right?"

"I would never. Just ask me what you want to ask me; I have nothing to hide." Kate knew he was being protective, but she was thankful to know he had close guy friends like Nathan. She answered all the questions Nathan asked her, and he came to his conclusion.

"Well, Katherine Joy Adams, I have no objections to you dating Rett."

"Good, because I'll let you in on a little secret," she leaned forward and whispered in his ear. "I have no intention of letting him get away." Kate knew she had won his approval as a smile spread across Nathan's face.

The group spent a fun night watching a movie and eating tons of popcorn. Kate enjoyed getting to know Rett's friends and how they all interacted.

"I'm tired. It's been a long week," Lynne said when the movie was over. "Happy birthday, Rett!"

"Happy birthday again," Houston echoed as he stood up. "Hoops tomorrow, right?"

"Thanks. Right. Bye Houston. Bye Lynne." Rett opened the door for them.

"I'm gonna head out too. See you tomorrow, and happy birthday." Patrick swallowed Rett in a hug before he left. "Bye, Kate. It was nice to meet you."

"You, too!" A thought popped into Kate's mind as the party broke up, but she decided to wait until she and Rett were alone to speak it.

"I have to go; I have to work in the morning," Mariah sighed. "Kate, it was so nice to finally meet you. I'm sure I'll see you around soon. Happy birthday, Rett." Mariah walked out, and Nathan headed to his room. Kate and Rett sat down on the couch in the sudden quiet.

"Thank you for everything tonight," Rett began. "Having you here was amazing. It's been the best birthday yet," he told her as he brushed the hair off her face.

"I'm so glad. I had a lot of fun. And, um, does Patrick have a girlfriend? Because I think he and Caroline would be great together," Kate brought up the thought she had earlier.

"No, he doesn't. But really? You think so?" Rett said pensively. He seemed to be really considering it. "We don't need to meddle, little matchmaker."

"I am not a matchmaker!" Kate defended herself, only to start laughing. "Ok, maybe I am. But I really like your friends. Can we please do more stuff with them?" Kate asked.

"I would really like that. I'm glad you finally got to meet them," Rett said. The party had been great. His friends loved her, and he hated that she had not been introduced to them earlier. Rett did not want her to leave. He wanted to kiss her and tell her that he loved her, but he knew that it would be a bad decision; it was just too soon.

"What?" Rett realized he was staring at Kate when she gave him a funny look. To cover his tracks, he shared part of what he was thinking. "How did I get so lucky?" he asked, his finger tracing her jawline.

"No, I'm the lucky one. I'm dating Superman, after all."

"Superman? I don't know how true that is, but I'm flattered," Rett laughed.

"Claire said you were harder to get a date with than Superman, so we've been calling you that for a while now. I guess I've never actually said that to you in person." Kate laughed, too, as she told him the story behind the nickname.

"She said that?" Rett scoffed.

"Yes, Superman, she did." Kate's eyes sparkled.

There were a lot worse thing she could call him; he would answer to that any day. "Katie, can I kiss you?" Rett asked as he as leaned in.

Kate pulled back and bit her lip. "I don't think I'm ready yet." She did want to kiss him, but she wasn't actually ready to take that step.

"I know I should probably already know this, but have you ever been kissed?" Rett asked cautiously. They were comfortable enough with each other to talk about this, but he knew there was wisdom in being careful about how they did.

"Yeah," Kate answered. "I dated this guy for a while during my junior year of high school. He was jerk, as it turns out, but I can't do anything about it now. I promised myself that the next guy I kissed—it would mean something. What about you?" Rett just looked at her. "Rett?"

"Our kiss will be my first." Rett was not surprised by the look on her face.

"You know you can have any girl you want, right?"

"But I won't want any girl; I want you, Katie." Rett's eyes locked with hers, and Kate started to rethink the whole kiss thing for a minute.

"Rett." Kate didn't know what to say, so they just sat together in silence for a few minutes, wrapped in each other's arms. "Thank you for a wonderful night. I had a great time," she finally managed, getting up from the couch and breaking the spell. "Happy birthday, Superman." Rett stood to hug her and see her to the door, thankful she had found the courage to move first.

She headed back to the dorm and went straight to Caroline's room. When she got there, she dramatically collapsed on the floor and announced, "I'm dating Superman. I'm really dating Superman."

"What in the world are you talking about, Drama Queen? Wait—you kissed him, didn't you?" Caroline's expressive eyes got huge and her voice went up an octave.

"No, but we came pretty close. We had an awesome conversation, and he told me that I am the only girl he wants." It all came out as a bubbly giggle.

"And you didn't kiss him? What is wrong with you?" Caroline playfully slapped her, laughing. "How did you get him, again?"

"I've been wondering that myself all night. I like him so much," Kate sighed.

"You think you might even—"

"Yes," Kate interrupted.

She couldn't let Caroline finish.

She couldn't go there,

Not yet.

Chapter Six

"I have something I need to talk to you about," Rett began, biting his lip. Thanksgiving break had snuck up on them, and Rett was soaking up all the time with Kate he could. "I've been putting this off because I didn't want to tell you, but before we ever met, I applied to spend the spring semester in Israel. I leave January 15," he said.

"Really? Rett, that's awesome!" Kate threw her arms around him.

"You're okay with it?" Rett looked stunned; this was not the response he expected.

"Yeah! I mean, I'm going to miss you terribly. But come on, it's Israel. I'm a little jealous, if I'm being totally honest. Tell me about the trip," Kate said.

Rett began to explain that he would be taking courses with Israeli students in English. It would be an opportunity for him to learn about a new culture and explore Israel.

"You better send me lots of pictures. I can't wait to hear all about it." Kate was grinning.

"I don't deserve you," he whispered, his voice changing as his hand rested on her cheek.

"What are you talking about?" Kate shook her head.

"Don't worry about it."

"Rett, what's wrong?"

"Nothing. We'll talk about it later." Fear flashed through Rett's eyes, but Kate decided not to ask him about it yet. She did not want to ruin their last few moments together before they went their separate ways for Thanksgiving break. "Goodbye, Kate." Rett pulled her into a tight hug.

"Bye, Rett." She stood in his embrace for a long time. She was going to miss him—not just next week, but while he was in Israel. Though she was excited for him, that trip was coming sooner than she cared to admit to herself.

* * *

"It's crazy to think that we're almost done with our first semester of college," Kate said as she and Caroline got their stuff together after going through security at the airport. It was nice that their flight times were so close. Even if Thanksgiving break was only a few days long, she was going to miss her friend.

"It's been fun, though. What are you going to do with Rett being gone all semester?" Kate had told Caroline about Rett's news on the drive to the airport.

"I don't know. I haven't fully processed that fact yet," Kate sighed. "I'm just glad I have another week and a half with him when we get back."

"I'm sure. Well, this is where we must part. I have to get to my gate." Caroline hugged her best friend.

"See you Monday," Kate said as they went their separate ways. She got to her gate to wait and pulled out the bag of notes she'd been working on for Rett. She wrote a couple more at the gate and as she flew to Atlanta and again on the second flight to Albany.

"Welcome home!" Emmie Wren pulled Kate into hug when she made it off the plane at the Albany airport.

"I'm so glad to see you," Kate said, and they walked out to her sister's car. Kate was glad to see her driving with confidence. After the accident, she was afraid Emmie Wren would be too shaken to get behind the wheel of a car for a while. But three months' time seemed to have healed her of any fear.

The girls met Emily for lunch, and Kate went home with her mom. Thanksgiving week was a quiet affair in the Adams house. They had the typical meal for lunch on Thursday and then headed out to get a Christmas tree from the local lot they had been getting trees from for as long as Kate could remember. With the tree strapped to the roof of the car, the whole family headed home to decorate it. It was fun night of family time and traditions as they got the house ready for Christmas. This was always one of Kate's favorite times of year. Friday was spent finishing up the decorations at the Adams house, and Saturday, Kate helped her sister get things ready at her and Sky's house.

"Do you really have to leave tomorrow?" Emmie Wren asked as they worked.

"Only if you don't want me to fail my classes," Kate laughed.

"Dang it." Emmie Wren shook her head.

"It's only a week and half," Kate reminded her sister.

"That's good news. For the record, I still don't like you going to college seven hours from home," Emmie Wren said. Her sister had chosen to stay home to get her nursing degree, but Kate knew God had her at Schaeffer for a reason.

"You continue to remind me of that." Kate rolled her eyes. She was thankful for her time at home, but she knew she had to finish the semester well—and say goodbye to Rett.

* * *

The week and a half between Thanksgiving and Christmas pasted too quickly. Kate spent as much time with Rett as possible since he was leaving for Israel in January. She would not see him again until he got back in May. On their last day before Kate headed home for the break, they exchanged Christmas gifts.

"I know it's cheesy, but I won't see you for almost six months, and I wanted you have something to hug when you missed me," Rett said as she pulled a teddy bear out of the bag he gave her.

Kate hugged the bear and said, "Thank you. I got you something for while you're gone, too." She watched as he opened his gift.

"It's perfect! Thank you." Rett flipped through the photo album full of pictures of their adventures from the semester and thumbed through the notes she had written him. He had at least one for every week of his semester abroad. "I'll put them up in my apartment in Israel so I can see your face every day," Rett grinned.

"I'm going to miss you so much," Kate cried, falling against his chest.

"I'm going to miss you, too," Rett said as he tilted her face up towards his.

Kate waited, but there was no kiss. She opened her mouth to say something about the fact they hadn't kissed yet—and to remind him that he was going to be gone for a whole semester—but no words came out. After a few minutes of silence, she finally said, "I'm tired. I don't want to go, but I need some sleep before I drive home." Yet she couldn't seem to get herself off the couch.

"Katie, don't forget that if you need anything next semester, you can always call Nathan or Patrick." Rett wanted to say that he loved her and to kiss her, but he could not. Somehow, it still felt like it would be too soon.

Kate finally managed to force herself off the couch and out the door. It was going to be long few months, they both realized.

Nathan walked into the living room when he heard the door shut. "I'm an idiot," Rett said without looking at his roommate.

"I mean, I know that, but why are you an idiot this time?" Nathan asked.

"I didn't kiss her. I'm leaving for an entire semester, and I didn't kiss her."

"You're the biggest idiot of them all," Nathan replied with a sad laugh. At the moment, Rett couldn't find it in himself to disagree.

Chapter Seven

"Hey Katie!" Rett's face filled her computer screen in mid-March.

"I'm so glad to see you," she exclaimed. It had been almost two weeks since they had gotten to talk, between both of their schedules and the spotty internet Rett was dealing with. "I miss you so much."

"I miss you too. I'll be home before you know it," Rett assured her. He told her about his adventures that week and the friends he was making in Israel. Kate loved to hear about his time over there. "Are you going to Nathan's birthday thing?" he asked as he wrapped up his narrative.

"Yes, and I'm taking Caroline with me."

"That'll be good. Do you know what happening? Nathan wasn't sure."

"Yeah, it's just a simple get together at the apartment," Kate answered, glad he hadn't asked more about Caroline going. She still wasn't sure about how he felt about her matchmaking schemes. "Nothing big."

"Good. I sent you Nathan's gift. It should be getting there tomorrow. Be on the lookout for it," he instructed.

"You're ridiculous, but I will look for it."

They talked for a few more minutes before he decided it was time for him to go to bed. Even though it was only mid-afternoon for Kate, he was eight hours ahead. "Good night, Katie."

She got to work on her homework, only to be interrupted a few minutes later by Caroline. "You're sure it's okay for me to go to this party with you on Friday?"

"Oh my gosh, Caro, stop. Yes! I talked to Mariah, Lynne, and Nathan. Even Rett thinks it's good that you're going with me. You'll be fine." Kate was tired of having the same conversation, and she didn't want the fact that she had other motives Caroline knew nothing about to slip out.

Caroline asked about the party again at dinner with Mariah and Lynne. "Seriously, if you ask again, I'm going to slap you," Mariah answered half playfully, half out of frustration as she got up to take her plate to the trash.

"You're Kate's best friend. Why couldn't you come?" Lynne reminded Caroline.

"Because it's Nathan's party, and we're not close."

"What does that have to with price of tea in China?" Lynne rolled her eyes.

"Let's get out of here, please," Kate pled before Mariah could sit back down again. "I can't listen to Caroline worry anymore."

"You're coming, and that's the end of it. Got it?" Lynne looked at Caroline, one eyebrow raised.

"Got it," Caroline nodded, eyes wide.

"Good. Now, what would you say to froyo? I could use a longer study break," Lynne asked the girls. They all readily agreed and piled into Lynne's car. "Rye, what's the plan for Nathan's party?"

"Chill, just a game night with everyone. Nate didn't want anything huge. He actually didn't want to do anything with Rett being gone, but 21 is a big deal." Catching herself, Mariah looked at Kate in the rearview mirror and asked, "How are you handling Rett being gone?"

"I miss him so much," she answered immediately. "I mean, I hate him being gone, but he's having a great time, making friends, and learning a lot," she clarified. "We got to talk today, and he was telling me about exploring the temple mount. I'm kinda jealous, really. It seems like a great trip. Just a lot of emotions."

"So cool! He's getting to walk where Jesus did and really experience it," Caroline sighed longingly.

"I want to go Israel," Mariah whined.

"You just want to travel," Lynne laughed as she pulled up at the froyo place.

"Exactly! Preferably somewhere I can speak the language, though," Mariah announced. The girls paused their conversation to fix their frozen yogurt and find a place to sit.

"I'm so excited about us all living together in the fall," Lynne grinned. It had all come together rather quickly, but they were excited about it. They even managed to find an apartment in the same complex where the guys' apartments were.

"I know it's going to be great," Kate grinned. "It will be so nice to able to walk to Rett's apartment."

"Tell me about it. I'm so ready to be closer to Houston," Lynne sighed. "I don't know how you're handling Rett being gone for three months, because I could not do that with Houston."

"Yeah, well, let's not forget that Rett and I have only been dating six months. And we haven't even kissed yet," Kate groaned.

"Everyone operates on their own timeline. You haven't seen Rett since December. I'm sure if he were here, things would be different," Lynne reassured her as she put a hand on Kate's knee.

"See, that's what I've been telling you! Just wait until he gets back and this will be a totally different story," Caroline said.

"I agree. That boy is smitten with you. After not seeing you for five months, he not going to be able to keep his lips off yours." Mariah pursed her own lips and nodded knowingly. Kate was suddenly uncomfortable with all the attention on her and her relationship with Rett.

"Okay, okay, enough about me and Rett. Rye, do you need help with anything for Nathan's party?" she asked, changing the subject.

"If you want to come with me to pick up the cake, that would be wonderful."

"Sure, I'm in," Kate laughed.

"I hate to have to break this up, but I have let this study break go on for too long. I do actually have a test tomorrow," Lynne sighed, and the four girls headed back to campus. "Thanks for the study break, ladies. See you on Friday," Lynne called as Kate and Caroline climbed out of the car.

* * *

"What did you get?" Caroline asked, seeing the package Kate was carrying as they met up to walk back to their dorm after class on

Friday.

"It's Nathan's birthday present from Rett," Kate told her. "I'm kinda hoping there is something in here for our six-month anniversary, too."

"Knowing him, it wouldn't surprise me at all," Caroline laughed.

"Lynne's picking you up, right? I mean, I'm going to go with Mariah to get the cake soon, otherwise we could go together."

"Yep," Caroline answered, finally seeming more happy than anxious about the party. "I'm excited to meet all these guys you keep talking about."

"Me too!"

Kate and Caroline went their separate ways to their rooms. As soon as her door was closed, Kate sat down to open the box from Rett. Sitting on top was a note addressed to her. She carefully opened the envelope and pulled the note out.

Dear Kate,

I'm missing you so much, but Israel is incredible! I can't wait to see you again and celebrate six months in style. But until I get to see you in person, I hope you'll wear this necklace and think about me.

Until I see you, Rett

She reached into the box and pulled out the smaller of the two gifts—a jewelry box with her name on it. Inside was a beautiful necklace and a note declaring that it had been hand made in Jerusalem. The necklace boasted a delicate silver cross, and Kate immediately slipped it around her neck and snapped a picture to send to Rett. Then she pulled out Nathan's gift and wrapped it while she was waiting for Mariah.

"You're sure Patrick's coming?" Kate asked when she was in the car with Mariah.

"Yes," Mariah answered, rolling her eyes. "Wait, why do you care if Patrick's there?"

"I just want him to meet Caroline," Kate shrugged, trying to sound nonchalant. "I really think they'll hit it off."

"Caroline and Patrick?" Mariah didn't seem to agree with her, but then her face changed. "Oh! Actually, I can see how they'd work together," Mariah said. Kate looked at her, confused. "She's just not the type he normally dates. But she's definitely the type he could marry," Mariah laughed.

"What?" Kate was even more lost.

"When I met Patrick, he was dating a girl who was more like Caroline—fun, a bit dramatic, but a real friend. But ever since they broke up, he's been dating girls just for fun, nothing serious. Most of them have been either super clingy or way over-the-top," Mariah explained. "He is such a flirt. What's your plan?"

"I'm introducing them and letting the magic happen on its own," Kate asserted. She was sure she just needed to get them into the same room.

"You're confident." Mariah tried not to scoff too much before changing the subject. "Did Nathan's present from Rett get here?"

"Yep, got here today. What do you think my about present?" she showed off her necklace.

"It's beautiful! Rett did good."

"He sure did." Kate couldn't stop smiling.

The girls finished at the grocery store and headed to Nathan and Rett's apartment. "Hey ladies," Nathan smiled, letting them in and taking the bags of groceries from their hands.

"Happy birthday!" they chorused as they set about getting things ready.

"Kate, have you heard from Rett lately?" Nathan asked.

"Yep, I talked to him on Tuesday, and I'm expecting a text any minute now. Have you?" she asked.

"I just did. He said something about a birthday present?" Kate raised the gift in her hand. "That dude, I swear." Nathan shook his head. "Did he at least send you something for your trouble?" She showed him her necklace.

"I'm so ready to see him. Do you know when he's getting back? He's being all coy with me," Kate sighed.

"I'm working on it. I plan on us going to pick him up from the airport, but just know it is probably going to be a last-minute thing." Nathan's eyebrows shot up in warning.

"I can handle that," Kate smiled

"He will be home back soon." Nathan patted her shoulder.

"I hope so; it's been too long," Kate sighed.

"Listen, I know he's your boyfriend and all, but this is longest Rett and I have been apart since we met a *long* time ago," Nathan huffed. "If you think it's long, multiply it by like ten for me."

"Having separation anxiety, huh?" Mariah called from the kitchen.

"He's my brother, okay. I'm allowed to have separation anxiety. And being in this apartment by myself is not helping anything."

"Yeah, how are you functioning right now?" Laughter filled Mariah's voice.

"I spend a *lot* of time at Paddy and Houston's. This place is too quiet with Rett gone," Nathan admitted. Getting ahold of himself, he realized they girls had taken over his apartment while they had been talking. "Hey, what can I do to help set up?"

"Nothing," Mariah assured him. "This is your party. Relax; we've got it handled."

"You really didn't have to do this."

"You're turning 21 and Rett's gone and you're lonely—clearly someone had to remind how to have fun. Besides, you made Rett have a party," Mariah reminded him.

"Yeah, because I needed an excuse to meet Kate," Nathan shot back defensively.

"Alright then, Kate's trying to set up Patrick and Caroline, so do it for them," Mariah shrugged.

"You're trying to set up who now?" Nathan spun on his heel to address Kate.

"My best friend, Caroline, and Patrick," Kate answered, staring daggers in Mariah's direction.

"Patrick? Patrick Whitfield?" Nathan arched an eyebrow and examined her expression carefully.

"Yes. I think he and Caroline would be good together," Kate said as casually as possible, moving out of Nathan's reach as she did so.

"I'm going to tell you something not a lot of people know," Nathan said in a warning tone. "Patrick's last girlfriend broke his heart when she dumped him when we were sophomores. It seemed to come out of the blue, and he's never really gotten over it. He's gone on a few dates here and there, but he doesn't want to seriously date anyone until he's sure he can see a future with her. I'm sure you think it'd be fun for Caroline to be a part of the group, but don't get your hopes up."

Kate swallowed and nodded, but deep down, she was still sure it would work.

The girls finished getting everything set up. As Nathan pulled out a couple games he wanted to play, Lynne and Caroline walked in with Houston on their heels. "Happy birthday!"

"Where's Paddy?" Nathan asked Houston. He had assumed the roommates would arrive together.

"I don't know. He's been gone all day. I'm sure he'll be here soon. He's planning on coming; we talked about this morning," Houston assured him. "In the meantime, happy birthday, and welcome to 21. Nice of you to finally join us," he teased with a smile.

"Shut up," Nathan shot back. "With all the girls around, I'm not the baby of the group anymore."

"Nope, that title goes to me," Kate announced with a flip of her hair, and everyone laughed.

"There's food, and Nathan pulled out some games," Mariah announced, getting the party started. "What do you want to play first?" she asked the birthday boy.

"Let's wait on Paddy," Nathan said to the general agreement of the group. They were talking and hanging out when the door opened about twenty minutes later.

"Nathan, dude, sorry. Stupid group project. I'm not going to be able to stay forever, either, because I have a paper to finish." Patrick sat down at the table between Kate and Caroline. "Hey there, Kate. How ya holdin' up without yer boy?" He had put on his best Texas accent to try to make her laugh.

"I'm fine; I just miss him. Patrick, this is my friend Caroline. Caroline, this is Patrick," Kate introduced them, hoping her plan would work.

Nathan picked Catchphrase for their first game. They played girls versus boys, and even though the guys were a man down, they still managed to win. "Can we play Catan?" Houston asked excitedly when they tired of Catchphrase.

"Sure, you're on!"

Nathan's competitive side came out, and he really seemed to enjoy his birthday party after all. Kate enjoyed herself, too, but it made her miss Rett even more being with all his friends. When they finished the game, Houston and Lynne cleared out, and Patrick and Caroline made their way to the couch to continue the conversation they had been having. Nathan, Kate, and Mariah were left to clean up.

"Do you think they know we're here?" Nathan asked, nodding to the two on the couch as he handed Mariah a plate to dry off.

"No way," Kate sighed dramatically. "I'm so ready to go, but they are in their own little world."

"Hot date?" Nathan cocked his head.

"Yeah with my Spanish book." She rolled her eyes. "Say something please," she begged Nathan, nodding again to Patrick and Caroline. "I don't want to interrupt them."

"Paddy, I thought you were leaving early," Nathan spoke up.

"Best laid plans," Patrick shrugged and started laughing.

"Sorry; I didn't mean to keep from your paper," Caroline smiled, her hand on his arm.

"Don't be! You were great distraction. It's due Wednesday. What do you say I take you out on Thursday?"

"That would be great," Caroline answered, hugging him before she walked out the door with Kate and Mariah.

"So?" Kate asked the minute the door shut behind them.

"We have a date Thursday," Caroline squealed.

"Well, it worked," Kate crowed as she and Mariah high-fived.

"What worked?"

"My plan to get you and Patrick together," Kate grinned mischievously.

"Are you serious? I don't even know what to say to you right now. Part of me is thrilled, and the other part wants to slap you." Mariah erupted in laughter. "But thanks," Caroline said, joining in the laughter.

"So much for leaving early," Patrick shrugged again on the other side of the door.

"It was worth it though, right?" Nathan asked.

"Beyond worth it. She's great," Patrick grinned. "I'm excited about her, like I haven't been in long time. Happy birthday, Nathan! But somehow, I feel like this party benefitted me more than you," he joked.

"Thanks, Paddy," Nathan said glumly as he sat down on the couch.

Patrick wished he hadn't been so lighthearted. "Are you okay?" he asked.

"I'm just missing Rett. It's weird for him not to be here."

"I know, but he'll be back before you know it," Patrick smiled. He wanted to cheer Nathan up, but wasn't sure what else to say.

"Sorry to be such a downer," Nathan sighed.

"Nate, your best friend is across the world and missing your birthday. It's okay to miss him. I miss him, too. Maybe you should talk to Kate. She's probably the only person who misses him like you do," Patrick reminded him.

"I have," Nathan answered, trying to perk up enough to let Patrick know his attempts were helpful. "Thanks for the pep talk. Go write your paper so you can take Caroline on that date." Nathan nudged his friend out and shut the door. It was strange to be the apartment alone, and he wasn't sure he would ever get used to it. He missed Rett's calming presence—and his weird habits, like taking showers at 3:00 am when he was stressed. The two had been inseparable since they met when they were six. Now, to be apart for so long was beyond weird.

Nathan opened the present Rett sent with Kate. Inside, he found an olive wood domino set.

Happy birthday, Nate!
It's still strange that we are celebrating your birthday apart. I'm glad to know that Mariah is making a big deal out of your birthday since you made a big deal out of mine. I hope it's a great one. I'll see you when I get back. It will be here before you know it.
Miss you, Brother.
Rett

Nathan smiled as he closed the note. All that was left now was to find out exactly when Rett was getting back. There was no way he and Kate were going to miss showing up at the airport to greet him.

***

In spite of papers and exams, Caroline and Patrick talked every day until their date. By Thursday, they were both ready for it. Kate was sitting on Caroline's bed while she tried on clothes for the evening.

"Are you sure this looks okay?" Caroline looked at herself critically in the mirror.

"Caro, you have tried on everything in your closet. That dress is perfect." Kate collapsed backward onto the bed. She was tired of looking at outfits. "Ugh, you are such a perfectionist." Caroline twirled in a blue and white chevron dress with sleeves that came to her elbows. She decided to keep it on, since at that minute, Patrick texted her to let her know he was outside. "Have fun!" Kate laughed as Caroline walked out to meet Patrick.

"Hey," Caroline smiled at the guy who was leaning against the hood of his car, looking calm, cool, and collected.

"Ready?" He opened the door for her.

"Yeah," she answered as she bit her lip nervously. "What are we going to do?"

"Dinner and movie good with you?" Patrick asked.

"Yes, that sounds like a good plan to me," Caroline said as she got in his car. They spent dinner getting to know each other and laughing a lot. After dinner, they headed to the movies.

When Patrick finally brought her back to campus, he walked her to the door of her dorm. There, he stopped and looked down at her. A smile spread across her face as Caroline gave the slightest of nods. Patrick pulled her close, leaned down, and brought his lips to hers. As the kiss deepened, Caroline pulled back first.

"Thanks for tonight. It was perfect." Caroline had a grin on her face. "See you around?"

"Of course. I had a lot of fun. In fact, this was best first date ever," Patrick said.

Caroline walked straight to Kate's room. "Tell me everything," Kate said as she patted the spot next to her on the bed.

"I don't kiss and tell." Caroline's hand flew over her mouth.

"You kissed him! On the first date?" Kate playfully shoved her.

"Yes!" Caroline squealed. "It was the only way to end the perfect date."

"I can't believe you kissed on the first date. I've been dating my boyfriend for almost seven months, and we haven't kissed yet," Kate teased, but she shook her head in frustration at the same time. They were in the middle of debriefing Caroline's date when Kate's phone rang. She wouldn't have answered it but she had been playing phone tag with her sister all day.

"I have some news for you," Emmie Wren declared immediately. She sounded happy, so Kate didn't worry about what her sister might say.

"What would that be?" Kate waved her hand to silence Caroline, who was humming, still on a high from her date.

"You're going to be an aunt," Emmie Wren announced without fanfare.

"You're pregnant?" Kate screamed, jolting Caroline out her trance. "Oh my gosh, when are you due?"

"September 19."

"Yes! I'm going so spoil that baby. I'm so excited for you! And for me," she laughed. "I'm going to be an aunt!" September was shaping up to be an exciting month, between her anniversary with Rett and now a new baby.

If only Rett would get home.

Chapter Eight

"What are you doing?" Nathan's call came a week before finals in May.

"Attempting to study," Kate answered as she closed her books with a sigh.

"Well, stop. Come outside and get in the car." Nathan hung up. Kate was confused, but she walked outside where Nathan waiting on her impatiently. "Get in. We're leaving," he insisted.

Fully trusting Nathan, Kate got in the car and asked, "Where are going?"

"To pick up your boyfriend." Nathan put the car in drive, but Kate was in shock. Rett was not supposed to be back until Monday.

"You're serious?" Nathan nodded, and tears started filling Kate's eyes. "I'm so happy right now."

Nathan smiled as Kate wiped away the few tears that escaped. "There are markers and poster board in the back if you want to make a welcome back sign."

"How did you find out that Rett was getting back early?" she asked, reaching into the back seat.

"I'd tell you, but then I'd have to kill you," Nathan winked as Kate worked on the sign. She shot a quick text to Caroline to let her know what was going on, since they were supposed to study together later that day.

* * *

Rett took a deep breath as his plane landed. He was glad to be back in the states and one step closer to Nathan and Kate. He just needed to rent a car and drive to Schaeffer. It had been a long day of traveling, but it was worth it. As he gathered his things to get off the plane, he imagined what it would be like to see his girlfriend for the first time since December. Thankful he had already gone through customs at JFK, Rett finally made it off the plane and headed for baggage claim. When he spotted a sign with his name on it just before baggage, he froze. He was not sure what was going on until Kate's arms were around him.

"Welcome home," she said, but Rett didn't hear her. His hand touched her cheek, and he pulled her face towards his until his lips touched hers—something he had wanted to do since he the day he met her. Kate's hand moved up to the back of his neck as she leaned into the kiss. For a moment, they weren't in a crowded airport; it was just the two of them.

"People are staring," Nathan griped, pulling them back to reality.

"I'm so glad you're home," Kate laughed before stealing another kiss.

"Yeah, me too." Rett and Nathan hugged.

"Just one question: how in the world did you know I was getting here today? I thought I would surprise you two, not the other way around!" Nathan just laughed. This was one secret he was taking to the grave.

They got Rett's luggage and headed for the car with Rett's arm around Kate. At the pleading look in Kate's eyes, Nate sighed, "I'll be the chauffeur so you two don't have to split up." She and Rett climbed into the back seat and cuddled up. Rett talked about his trip between stealing kisses from Kate. In return, Nathan and Kate filled him in on everything that had happened over the semester while he was gone.

"Where would you like to go to dinner?" Nathan asked after a while.

"Chick-fil-A," Rett said without hesitation. Nathan pulled into the one in near Schaeffer's campus. "I'm so glad to be back."

"How long are you staying?" Kate asked as they walked in to the restaurant.

"I'm riding home with Nathan, so what—a week?" Nathan nodded, and they ordered. They were just about to sit down when Patrick walked in.

"*Paddy!* It's been too long!" Kate loved seeing Rett reconnect with his best friends.

After a fun dinner, Nathan and Rett dropped Kate off at her dorm. "I'm sorry; I'm exhausted," Rett apologized. "But I promise, all day tomorrow, I'm yours."

"I'm just glad you're back." She kissed him, a long, deep, and slow kiss before she walked into the dorm and straight to Caroline's room. "*Finally*," Kate excitedly squealed.

"He kissed you, didn't he?" Kate nodded as she jumped on the bed next to her.

* * *

Kate was at Rett and Nathan's apartment at 9:00 am the next morning. Nathan handed her a cup of coffee while they waited for Rett to get up. At about ten, he emerged from his room and collapsed on the couch with his head in her lap.

"Good morning, beautiful," he greeted her. "What do you want to do today?"

"I don't care. I just want to be with you. I only have a week before you go to Texas, and then I won't see you again until August."

"About that." A smile spread across his face as he sat up and looked over at Nathan. "I'm not spending the summer in Texas; I'm spending it in Albany." Nathan rolled his eyes; Rett was too romantic for his own good.

"Rett, don't play. My heart can't take it," she chided as she put a hand on his chest.

"I'm not. I'm interning with Andrew, the youth pastor at Generations," he smiled. Kate grinned as tears formed in her eyes and she caught the big grin on Nathan's face. "Katie," Rett said as he pulled her in close, "I'm not going anywhere." He kissed the top of her head, her forehead, and finally her lips, which made Kate relax.

"I'm sorry I'm crying; I'm just so relieved." Kate wiped the tears from her eyes. "I can't wait to spend the whole summer with you."

"It's going to be a great one," he insisted. "I just know it."

Chapter Nine

"I can't believe you're finally getting to spend the summer in Albany," Nathan said as they got on the road. Rett had been talking about going to Generations since Joshua and Hope moved when they were sixteen. "I'm glad I get to spend a little bit of time with you, too," he admitted. While he was excited for his best friend, he'd miss their summer together. The guys took turns driving to help make the fifteen-hour trip more manageable.

Along the way, Rett called Kate a couple of times; he was definitely ready to see her. She invited him and Nathan to join her family on the lake the next day. As he accepted, he felt his best friend's eyes boring holes into him. "See you tomorrow, Katie. Bye." He hung up and asked "What?" without even bothering to look at his best friend. He knew the expression that was on Nathan's face.

"You know what."

"Nathan, I will tell her. I just don't know that on the phone is the best timing. Tomorrow in front of her whole family is probably not the way to do it, either," Rett said. Nathan punched his shoulder and rolled his eyes. The rest of the trip passed uneventfully. They got dinner in Birmingham and pulled into Albany just before midnight. Joshua and Hope were still awake to greet them.

"Hey guys! Nathan, oh my word, it's been too long," Hope exclaimed as she opened the door for them. "I'm glad y'all are here!"

"Rett! Nate! So glad to see you." Joshua rounded the corner and mentioned, "I think I heard Helen."

"I'll check on her," Hope offered and disappeared. Joshua offered the two men food and drink, which they turned down. They talked for just a few minutes before Joshua showed them to their room and handed Rett a key to the house. Rett and Nathan were exhausted, and both fell asleep quickly.

* * *

The next morning, Rett surprised himself with how well he remembered the route to Kate's house. After all, the only time he'd been there before was to pick her up for Wednesday night service the week of Emmie Wren's car accident.

"Dude, you didn't mention that she *lives* on the lake." Nathan's eyes were wide when they pulled down her driveway.

"Oh yeah. Last time it wasn't really something we talked about. I spent more time at the hospital and the church than I did at her house," Rett responded, distracted as he checked the text from Kate letting him know that the family was on the boat dock.

"I'm so glad you're here!" Kate met them in the yard.

"Me too." Rett kissed her. "I've missed you."

"Don't worry about me," Nate piped up. "I'm not as interesting as the boyfriend." Kate laughed and hugged him; he always knew what to say to lighten a serious moment. "Are we tubing?" His eyes lit up at the sight of the boat and tubes as they made it to the dock.

"Mom, Dad, Emmie Wren, Sky—this is Nathan," Kate introduced Rett's best friend. "Nathan, this is my family: my dad, Charlie; my mom, Emily; my sister, Emmie Wren; and my brother-in-law, Sky."

Nathan shook his head. "I didn't realize I was going to be meeting everybody. Dude, I don't know how you did this when you had only been dating for a day!" Nathan pretended like he was nervously shaking about meeting her family. Kate and Nathan had spent the past semester building a friendship, and she saw him as brother— sometimes older, sometimes younger depending on the mood he was in. That day, Nathan was in rare form as an extreme extrovert who had been cooped up in the car with the same person for fifteen hours the day before.

"Okay, Nathan you are going to be riding on the tube with Sky," she said. "Rett and I will take the other one." Nathan eyed Emmie Wren, sure she would want to ride with her husband, but she just patted her stomach. She was barely showing, but there would be no tubing for the mom-to-be. She handed him a life jacket, and he jumped on the tube without another word.

Kate turned around to find Rett buckling his life jacket over his shirt, "Rett, it's hot. Aren't you going to take your shirt off?"

"The sun loves my skin; it's just easier with a shirt on." Rett was thankful she couldn't see the look that Nathan gave him. This just wasn't the right time or place for the conversation Nathan kept bugging him to have with her.

They enjoyed their day on the lake. Nathan had more fun than anyone and only fell off the tube twice. He kept them all laughing as Rett watched Kate with her family, thankful to be a part of the fun. The day ended with Charlie, Sky, Rett, and Nathan grilling burgers and frying sweet potato chips. They all ate around the pool, and Kate thought about how excited she was to spend more Saturdays like this as she rested in Rett's arms.

"Emmie Wren, when are you due?" Rett asked.

"September nineteenth." Emmie Wren glowed with excitement. They spent some time talking about the baby and debated whether it would be a boy or a girl. Around 8:00 pm, Rett and Nathan got ready to leave.

"Sorry we have to go," Nathan said, standing up. "We have barely seen Joshua and Hope, and I'm only going to be here a week." Kate walked with them to driveway, and Nathan gave the love birds some time to themselves. "I'll be in the car," he said with an eye roll.

"This day has been perfect. I had so much fun," Rett said as he kissed her. "I'm so glad I get to spend the summer with you."

"I don't want you to go yet," Kate sighed, sinking her head into his chest.

"I'm just going to Joshua's," Rett laughed. "I'm not even leaving town, and I'm going to see you in the morning. Tell you what—I'll call in the morning to wake you up so I'll be the first person you talk to in the morning."

"I like that idea," Kate grinned. "Ok, I guess I'll let you go." Kate kissed him once more as Nathan honked the horn. "Mr. Impatient," she laughed.

"He's just jealous. He can wait a few more seconds." Rett's hand ran up the back of her neck, and he brushed his fingers through her blonde hair. As he kissed her, Kate's hands ran through his beautiful hair. Finally, he pulled away, smiled, and got in the car. Kate stood watching as he backed down the driveway before she headed back to the pool to rejoin her family.

"Is Nathan the one who took care of you the whole semester?" Emmie Wren asked, and Kate nodded. "All those stories make so much more sense now," Emmie Wren laughed.

* * *

"Good morning, beautiful. Get up!"

"Five more minutes, handsome?" Kate asked groggily.

"You don't want to be late for church," he admonished her before hanging up to get ready himself. When Kate eventually dragged herself out of bed, she had a feeling they had just started a new tradition.

She got ready and headed to church, finding a spot between Rett and Hope. The service was good; Pastor Eddie was teaching through Galatians. During Sunday school, Rett went to help with the youth, and Nathan went with Kate to the college and career class. After their lesson on John 15 and abiding in Christ, Nathan and Kate walked outside to wait for Joshua, Hope, and Rett. Hope walked out first with Jessie and Helen.

"Are you joining us for lunch, Kate?"

"Yes! I think I get to hang out with y'all all day," Kate answered, reaching for five-month-old Helen.

"You are going to be a great aunt," Rett observed, walking up behind Kate as she bounced Helen on her hip.

"Thanks; I'm ready. Too bad I have to wait until September." Kate fought the urge to kiss him. Nathan, Rett, Hope, and Kate talked until Joshua walked up about ten minutes later.

"Daddy!" Jessie ran and was scooped into Joshua's arms.

"Sorry; that took longer than I thought it would. Where are going for lunch?"

"Moe's!" Jessie squealed, and Joshua agreed.

Nathan, Rett, and Kate walked to Rett's car. Rett opened the passenger door for her, but before he could walk off, she pulled him close and kissed him. Rett grinned as he got the car started. Nathan just laughed and shook his head. He knew Rett still had something to tell her, but he couldn't deny that they were great together.

They pulled in to Moe's just after the Kings. Jessie kept them laughing all through lunch, and they headed to Joshua and Hope's for the afternoon. Once the girls went down for their naps, the group talked about plans for the week and about what Nathan would be doing since he was not flying home until Saturday. Kate and Nathan would be hanging out most days, since Rett's internship started first thing the next morning.

"I guess it's going to be you and me this week," Nathan nudged her.

"Yep, just like all semester," Kate laughed. "I'll try to find something fun for us to do. Maybe Sky will join us, too." Kate thought including Sky would be good for Nathan since Sky was on summer break. Nathan and Rett both seemed to like the idea, so she promised to talk to Sky that night. She even texted her sister to see if she could spend the night with them.

"Daddy," Jessie said sleepily, emerging in the doorway. Joshua walked over to pick up the two-year-old. She rested on his chest as Helen began to cry. Hope got up to feed and change the baby, but not before kissing Jessie on the cheek.

"Did you have a good nap?" Nathan asked Jessie, who just

responded with a nod.

"She's always shy right after she wakes up," Joshua explained as Jessie clung tightly to his chest. "Kate, do you have big plans for the summer?"

"Not really; just hanging out with Rett and my sister, helping her get ready for the baby." Kate leaned against Rett.

"I'm sure it will be a great summer," Joshua said. "And if I know your man, he has something special planned for you."

"I hope so, especially since I have a birthday coming up," she hinted, looking at him. He just shook his head; he wasn't giving anything away. "You're ridiculous, you know that? No hints at all?" She shook her head.

"Yet you put with him," Nathan laughed. A smile spread across Kate's face, and Rett kissed the top of her head. She grinned and relaxed into his chest.

The friends all enjoyed a couple hours of rest before church that night. After church, Kate found her sister and Sky. "Hey, you're spending the night, right?" Emmie Wren hugged Kate.

"Yes, but do you mind if we run by the house? I don't have anything with me," Kate grinned. Emmie Wren shook her head; it was classic Kate.

Nathan, Kate, and Sky spent the week hanging out exploring Albany while Rett jumped into his internship at Generations. The trio spent time downtown at Turtle Park, the Aquarium, and Chehaw, but they ended up spending the most time on the ball field just throwing a ball around. Nathan and Kate went to the youth service on Wednesday night, and they spent every evening at the Kings with Rett. She was going to be sad when Nathan left on Friday, but he had an internship waiting on him in Dallas.

"I can't believe it's already been a week. I don't what I'm going to do without you around this summer." Kate hugged Nathan before the boys left take him to the Atlanta airport.

"You'll be fine," Nathan laughed. "Keep this one line in for me," he added, elbowing Rett.

"Always," Kate laughed.

"Two minutes, Rett," Joshua called as he got in the car.

"Have fun this weekend." Kate kissed him.

"I will. See you Sunday!" As he got in the car with Joshua and Nathan, Kate waved good-bye, thankful that Rett would be around for the whole summer.

Chapter Ten

"She's almost ready," Emmie Wren announced as she opened the door. "Kate! Rett's here," she yelled back through the house, and Rett thanked her. Kate appeared in the kitchen in a blue dress the same color as her eyes.

"You look beautiful." A smile spread across his face. "Happy birthday," he added, wrapping her in a hug.

"Thank you." She pushed up on her toes to kiss him. "See you later, Emmie Wren," Kate giggled as she and Rett walked out to his car. "Are you going to tell me where we're going yet?"

"Not until we get there," Rett laughed. Kate had been trying to get him to slip and tell her the details of her birthday date since Rett got to Albany, but he never cracked.

After they drove for a few minutes in contented silence, they arrived at Henry Campbell's, the nicest restaurant in town. "Rett," she breathed. She wasn't expecting this.

Rett helped her out of the car. "E. Johnson, reservation for two," he told the hostess once they got inside. She seated them, but all the while, Kate had a confused look on her face. "You're wondering where the 'E' came from, aren't you?" Kate was shocked he could read her mind so easily. "Rett is short for Everett. E."

"Ok, but why did you use 'E' instead of 'R' for the reservation?"

"Because there was already an R. Johnson on the list for tonight," Rett shrugged as they were walked to their table.

"This place is too nice. This where Sky took Emmie Wren for dinner the night they got engaged," Kate whispered as they got situated.

"Think of it as a catch up for all the dates I missed while I was in Israel." He was fighting off laughter at her discomfort.

"Rett—"

"We're here. You deserve all the best things. Enjoy it," Rett cut her off.

"Thank you." She got the hint to drop the subject. They ordered, and the conversation turned to how his internship was going and the youth group at Generations. When dinner was over, they decided to get dessert at the frozen yogurt shop next door.

"Thank you so much. I thoroughly enjoyed tonight," Kate said when they got back in the car. Truthfully, she was a little thankful to be out of the fancy restaurant where she couldn't seem to stop thinking about engagement rings.

"Who said it was over?"

"What?" Kate was confused as he pulled the car into a parking spot at the local YMCA.

"Okay, we're here. C'mon. If we don't hurry, we'll be late!" Rett opened the door for her, and they walked into a room with about seven other couples. An older couple stood toward the front.

"Everyone, fill in and come to the front," the woman said. As Rett and Kate joined the rest of the group at the front of the room, she realized what they were doing.

"Ballroom dancing, Rett?" Kate was grinning from ear to ear. Rett knew he had made the right decision. She was thrilled. Their first lesson included the proper hold and the box step for the waltz. They laughed through the whole lesson, and Rett had to get help when he couldn't stop stepping on Kate's feet.

"That's it," the teacher said. "You have to let him lead, sweetheart." The teacher looked at Kate, who nodded and stepped back into hold with her boyfriend. After another half hour, they moved together much more fluidly.

"That's wrap for tonight. Great job, everyone! See you next week," they were dismissed at the end of the lesson.

"Well, that was more fun than I thought it was going to be," Rett admitted, kissing her.

"It was great! Thank you. This has been the most wonderful birthday," Kate told him.

"I'm so glad." Rett liked seeing her like this—happy and with him.

"How long are the lessons?"

"Six weeks," he said.

"Thank you, Rett, for everything." Kate kissed him as she got out of the car. She was not the least bit surprised to see a bouquet of roses sitting on her dresser when she got inside and texted Rett to thank him for the third bouquet before calling Caroline.

"Happy birthday, Kate!" Caroline said before Kate caught her up on the details of her day.

"So, um, I think I'm falling," Kate fumbled.

"Say it, Kate," Caroline demanded.

"I'm falling in love. I love Rett, Caro. I love him," Kate said for the first time.

"What happened tonight?"

"He took me ballroom dancing for my birthday. It was perfect. This summer has been amazing, and it's only just begun."

"I bet. I'm kinda jealous, though. Patrick and I aren't going to see each other at all over the summer."

"Sorry," Kate said.

"It was mutual decision, mainly because I came home to San Antonio and he stayed at Schaeffer," Caroline reminded her. "But I'm glad you're happy, Kate."

"Me too. I love him; I really do," Kate said once more. "Thanks for letting me you tell me you, since I can't tell Rett yet."

"He does love you. You know that, right?" Caroline knew exactly what Kate was afraid of.

"Why doesn't he say it then?"

"I'm not Rett, Kate; I can't tell you that." Caroline let out a sigh. "But I know he does. I can see it. I know you can, too. That has to be enough for you until he does say it." Kate could feel tears stinging her eyes.

"What if he doesn't?" Kate knew she sounded ridiculous even as she asked the question.

"He will. Just wait on him," Caroline assured her. "I hope you feel my hug through the phone. Give him time, Kate. He's worth it, and you know it." Caroline wished she could be with her best friend, especially when Kate started to cry. "I wish I could give you a huge hug! Shoot, I have to go, but call Emmie Wren, please. She'll tell you the same thing."

As soon as Caroline hung up, Kate dialed her sister. Emmie Wren came over as soon as she heard the sorrow in Kate's voice.

"Why is this so hard?" Kate said through her sobs.

"What?" Emmie asked, holding her sister.

"Love," Kate said.

"Love? Katie, are you serious?" Emmie Wren questioned.

"Yes, and I'm scared to death." Kate's voice quivered.

"Rett loves you, Katie. It is written all over his face. Let him be the first one to say it."

"How long did it take Sky to say it?" Kate's head rested on her sister's shoulder.

"Just the right time amount of time. I knew I ready to say it, too. Rett is his own person and has his own challenges. You have to let your relationship unfold in its own way, too. It's yours—not mine and Sky's or anyone else's. Look at me." Kate lifted her head to look at her sister. "Rett is crazy about you and is trying to figure all this out himself. Give him time; he'll come around," Emmie Wren encouraged her as she let her cry everything out. "I promise, he will."

"I know, but why doesn't he just say what we are both feeling?"

"Because he's a boy and boys are dumb," Emmie Wren said definitively. Finally, Kate started laughing. Her sister had a point.

* * *

"Where did this summer go?" Rett pulled Kate close. It had been a fun eight weeks in Albany, a summer Rett knew he would remember forever. He loved working at Generations, and spending the summer with his mentor was nice bonus. His time with the youth group taught him a lot about what it would mean to be a youth minister, more than his internship in Jackson. It made him even more excited about life after graduation and the possibilities that were in front of him. Andrew, the youth minister, had become a good friend, too, and Rett knew he would be a resource for years to come.

"Don't go. Please, don't go." Kate had tears running down her cheeks. It was hard to believe their summer had ended. It had been so wonderful, especially after a semester apart, and even after eight weeks, she wasn't ready to let him leave again.

"It's only two weeks, Katie," Rett assured her. "Then we'll be back at school, and everything will be normal again."

"I know. I'm going to miss you though," Kate sighed as she fell against his chest. "Don't go?" she tried one last time.

"I have to, but I'm going to miss you, too. Bye, Katie." It was only 7:30 am as Rett got in his car to start the drive home to Texas. Kate was in his rearview mirror, tears streaming down her face.

"I love you," he said, even though he knew she couldn't hear him.

Chapter Eleven

"Are you sure being a Welcome Leader is the best idea?" Kate and Rett were moving her into the apartment with the rest of the girls.

"Oh, my word, you are worse than Nathan." Rett shook his head.

"I don't have to worry you about falling for some new girl?"

"That would never happen," he laughed as he kissed her.

"Stop making out and help please," Mariah griped as she put down a box. "I realize that you discovered the joys of kissing over the summer, but we are trying to get moved in, and we can't do it if you two keep kissing all the time."

"Dang, task master," Rett laughed. "Come on, before we get yelled at again." Rett picked up the boxes he had been carrying and moved them into the room that was going to be Kate's. Once all the boxes were situated, the guys started moving in the furniture.

"I think we got a little more than we bargained for," Houston said after the third time they moved the couch, trying to find a place for it that made all the girls happy.

"Thank you, sweetheart," Lynne cooed, kissing his cheek.

"Yeah, we ordered pizza for everyone to say thank you," Mariah announced, which made the guys happy.

"Thanks again for helping," Kate said, setting out plates for everyone.

"Of course! I'm glad you're closer this year," Rett answered as he kissed her again. "And you know you have nothing to worry about with me being a Welcome Leader, right?"

"I just have to give you a hard time," she smiled. "I know you only have eyes for me. But please, don't let those freshmen ogle you too much."

"I will do my best," he assured her.

"Oh, Kate, he's too good looking for his own good. That's a little much to ask of your boy here," Nathan kidded as he slapped a hand on Rett's shoulder.

Rett rolled his eyes. "Nate, you're not helping."

"They can't be any worse than the teenagers he works with at church," Kate admitted.

"You'd be surprised," Nathan said.

"Yes, but this time is different because I actually have a girlfriend."

"You're not wrong," Nathan shrugged. "Well, if you have any cute ones, send them my way."

"You're terrible." Kate shook her head.

"I'm serious," Nathan replied.

"No, you're not." Mariah plopped down on the couch next to Nathan.

"And how would you know that?" Nathan cocked an eyebrow.

"Because if you were going to ask someone out, it would be me."

Mariah's comment seemed to suck all the air out of the room.

"If I remember correctly, I asked you out. And you turned me down—multiple times," Nathan reminded her with a hint of ice in his voice. Kate looked at Mariah, who was grinning mischievously.

"We would kill each other," Mariah shrugged.

"That's for dang sure," Lynne laughed, and it released the tension in the room.

"Here's to all being in the same apartment complex." Houston raised his pizza slice, and everyone else followed suit.

"Here's to a great senior year," Rett added.

"No, not okay," Kate flinched.

"What's not okay?" Patrick laughed.

"Senior year! I don't like to think about everything changing." Kate set her pizza down and pulled her knees into her chest.

"It's okay, we've still got plenty of time to spend together and make memories," Rett reassured her, pulling her close.

"I have a feeling this year is going to hold a lot of memories," Patrick commented.

"I like that idea." Caroline kissed him.

"The first of many nights like tonight," Mariah observed, relaxing again. "I'm so glad to be in this apartment instead of that stuffy dorm."

"Same here," Lynne smiled. "This year is going to be awesome."

"It sure is." Houston kissed her and pulled her into a tight embrace. Everyone was enjoying being back together and getting the girls settled. It was hard to believe that the boys only had one year left. No one was really ready for the boys to graduate, but it was coming faster than any of them cared to admit.

"First day of sophomore year. You ready for this?" Caroline asked as they headed to campus the next morning.

"Yes. It has to be better than being a freshman who knows nothing on the first day," Kate smiled.

"Truth. I'm just glad I have you to do it with."

"No one else I'd rather do this whole college thing with," Kate replied, hugging her. "Let's do this."

They headed into their first class of the semester.

Together.

Chapter Twelve

"Give me a hint?" Kate batted her eyelashes at Rett a few weeks later.

"We're going somewhere Saturday," Rett grinned as he kissed her. "Gosh, you're beautiful."

They were about two hours into their drive to Albany. Emmie Wren was going to have the baby any day now, and they were headed down in hopes of being there for the birth. To top it off, Rett had a surprise planned for their one year anniversary on Saturday. He was just praying Emmie Wren wouldn't have the baby that day. Kate had been pestering him for information, and now that they were trapped in a car for seven hours, she was using all her powers. "Don't change the subject, no matter how beautiful I may be," she kidded.

"Katie, it's a surprise for a reason. I'm not telling you anything else," he insisted, and Kate turned with a light huff toward the window. "Final call: girl or boy?" he asked, changing the subject again. They had been talking about Emmie Wren's baby since they left the school.

"Fine. Girl, final call," Kate said.

"Boy."

"You're just trying to be different from me, but what do you say we make this guessing game a little more fun?"

"What are you thinking?"

"If I'm right, I get to find out one surprise of my choice—ahead of time."

"Only if I have the right to veto it."

"You're going to have to tell me eventually."

"*If* you get it right," Rett grinned. He had no idea what he would want if he won this little wager, so he told her he would think about his answer. They fell into easy conversation, and Kate was amazed at how quickly the drive flew by. She was thankful for time alone with Rett. It been a crazy start to the semester, and she had not gotten a lot of quality time with him.

"You ready to be an aunt?" Rett asked as they took pulled into Albany.

"Yes! I'm so excited! That baby is going to be so loved," Kate giggled with excitement.

"That's for sure. I just hope that the baby comes while we're in town."

"Me too, because otherwise this was very long drive for a first anniversary trip." They both laughed, and Rett knew she was right. As excited as he was for their plans tomorrow, he did hope the baby came this weekend.

"Please tell me your mom is going to have dinner ready, because I'm hungry," Rett complained.

"You're the one who decided to drive straight through, mister. But yes, dinner will be ready." Kate rolled her eyes; Rett could be so stubborn sometimes. They pulled into her driveway and walked straight to the table for dinner.

"Thanks for waiting us." Kate hugged her parents.

"Of course! How was the drive?" Charlie asked, sitting down at the table first.

"Long but not too bad," Rett said.

"Any word on when Baby Thomas is going to make an appearance?" Kate asked.

"Hopefully anytime now," her mom laughed. "Your sister is threatening to ask to be induced if the baby doesn't come this weekend."

"Induced?" Kate asked.

"For the doctor to give her medicine so the baby will come," Emily explained, and Kate nodded. They spent the rest of dinner talking about the baby.

"Thank you for dinner; it was delicious," Rett said, excusing himself from the table. "I'm sorry to eat and run, but I'd like to get to Joshua's at normal hour."

"You're fine. Thanks for bringing our girl home," Charlie said.

"Of course," Rett replied as Kate followed him out. "Nine in the morning, be ready."

"Got it." She kissed him. "I can't believe it's been a year."

"Me neither. See you tomorrow, Katie." Rett got in his car and headed to Joshua and Hope's for the night.

* * *

"Happy anniversary, beautiful. Get up; I'll be there in forty-five minutes."

"I'm up, handsome. See you then," Kate dragged herself out of bed so she would be ready when Rett pulled up at 9:00 am. She loved hearing his voice first thing in the morning each day. Once she was dressed, she told her parents bye and asked them to call her if Emmie Wren went into labor.

"What's the plan?" Kate asked as soon as Rett opened the car door for her.

"You'll find out." Rett wasn't going to give in to her charms, even today.

"Rett, please?" Kate batted her eyelashes.

"You can't do that to me," Rett begged, looking at her helplessly. "I would tell you anything you want, but I can't. It would ruin everything." She acquiesced and was quiet for most of the hour long drive.

"Do you know where we are?" he asked as they pulled into a small town.

"I think so," Kate grinned. "Thomasville?"

"Yes," Rett answered as they found a parking spot and headed toward the main stretch of downtown. "I wanted this day to be fun for both of us," he explained.

When they walked into the town square, Kate's jaw dropped. There had to be thousands of books lining the sidewalks, and there were dozens of people milling around looking at them. She had never seen so many books.

"Rett! What is this?" Kate had the biggest grin on her face.

"This is a book auction," Rett answered. He knew he had made the right decision. She was elated—happier than Rett had ever seen her. Kate was soaking it all in as they looked at book after book. They walked over to table and both spotted it the same time—a tattered old copy of C.S. Lewis' *The Screwtape Letters.*

"You like C.S. Lewis?" Rett asked as they both reached for the book.

"Like? Lewis is my absolute favorite. *Mere Christianity* is at the top of my list," Kate told him.

"He's mine too, and this has to be in my top five," Rett said as he motioned to the book.

"These are for sale, but the big book auction isn't until four. Here's the list of books that are being auctioned off," the person standing behind the table said as he handed them a list of books.

"In that case, I'll take *The Screwtape Letters.*" Rett paid, and they continued to talk about their favorite Lewis books as they looked around the square.

After a while, they walked into a clothing store. "If you find something you like, let me know," Rett told her; he wanted her to have something special to wear for that night. Kate smiled and headed into the dressing room with a few options. She was about change when her phone rang.

"*What?!* We're leaving! Tell Baby Thomas to wait on us!" Kate ran out of the dressing room. "Emmie Wren's in labor!" Kate squealed as she pulled Rett out of the store. She ran to the car, calling for Rett to keep up the whole time. Kate was bouncing up and down when Rett finally made to the car. He dramatically acted like he was out of breath.

"You're ridiculous," she cried. "My sister is having her baby! I can't miss it!"

"I know! Calm down," Rett laughed, unlocking the car. But when he sat down in the driver's seat, more emotions than he was ready for hit him full force.

"Rett?" Kate felt the air in the car change.

"It wasn't supposed to happen this way!" Rett hit the steering wheel as he sat unmoving behind it. "Sorry. I am thrilled, really. I just had our whole day planned, and I was going to tell you that I love you, but now it's ruined."

"What did you say?" Kate's heart was in her throat. Slowly, Rett turned to face her.

"I love you, Kate," he repeated, resting his hand on her cheek.

"I love you, too." Kate kissed him before he finally put the car in drive and headed to the hospital. She couldn't stop smiling as Rett took her hand. They were quiet as they drove, neither wanting the moment to end. When they pulled into the hospital parking lot, they both got out of the car and decided to wait a minute before going in.

"I love you, Katie," Rett said again as Kate rested with the small of her back against the hood of the car.

"I love you," she answered, kissing him until she was out of breath before pulling back.

"Let's go inside before you're the one in there in nine months," Rett laughed. Kate gasped and slapped him in the ribs so hard he doubled over. "Sorry," he gasped. "I love you, though."

She rolled her eyes and dragged him into waiting room where her dad and some of Emmie Wren's friends were waiting. "Any news?"

"Not yet." Charlie patted the seat next to him. "I'm sorry the hospital is becoming a normal place for y'all to spend this day of the year."

"It's okay. At least this time it's for something happy." Kate leaned against Rett's shoulder, and he kissed the top of her head, thankful that she always saw the good in any situation.

They talked until Sky walked in and announced, "It's a boy!" The whole room erupted with excitement. "His name is Kaden Daniel." Sky beamed with pride.

"When can we see them?" Kate wanted to know.

"Soon," Sky promised and disappeared again. A few minutes later, Emily came out and told Kate, Charlie, and Rett to come back. "Here he is," Sky was holding Kaden when they walked in, and Kate reached for him.

"He's perfect, Sissy," she said when Kaden was in her arms. "Hey Kaden, I'm your Aunt Kate."

"He loves you already," Rett noted, standing behind her. "He's precious."

"Thank you both. I'm sorry he took over your day," Emmie Wren half-heartedly smiled. Kate and Rett spent the next hour with Kate's family, Kaden, and various friends before deciding to go to dinner to finish celebrating their anniversary. Rett dropped her off at her house with the promise that he'd be back in an hour. Kate dug a new dress out of her closet and changed. She curled her hair and was almost ready when her phone lit up with a text.

"Hey, sorry, I have three more pieces to curl," she apologized as she opened the back door. "Wow, you look—and roses, Rett," she kissed him. "There's a vase under the sink in the kitchen," she called, heading back to the bathroom to finish her hair.

"Kate?" Rett set the vase with the bouquet on her dresser a few minutes later.

"Well, what do you think?" she asked, stepping out the bathroom and spinning for the full affect.

"You are absolutely beautiful," Rett grinned. "You ready?"

"I am." She kissed him and grabbed her purse, taking a look at the fourth bouquet of roses from Rett on their way out. "I'm sorry this day didn't go the way you planned."

"Me too, but my mom has always told me that babies have their own timetables. I guess Kaden proved that today."

"He's really cute though," Kate laughed. "You won, by the way. You have to think about what you want for real now."

"I have no idea," Rett conceded, shaking his head. "I'm not worried about it."

"Okay. Where are we going, by the way?" Kate noticed they were headed in the opposite direction of the restaurants in town.

"Americus. Joshua and Hope gave me a suggestion for a restaurant since the original plan of Jonah's didn't get to happen," Rett said.

"We were going to go to Jonah's?" Kate pouted at the missed opportunity.

"Yeah, but there is no way we were going to make that reservation with the day we had. Plus, Thomasville is farther than I thought," Rett explained, and Kate had to agree with him.

"It was fun while it lasted, though. I hate that we didn't get to finish your day. That book auction sounded really cool."

"At least we got to look around for a little while. Thomasville is definitely a neat town."

"They do a Victorian Christmas thing there every year. Emmie Wren and I have been going since she could drive. It's one of my favorite traditions."

"That sounds like fun. Is it just you and Emmie Wren?"

"It just depends on the year. Sometimes, it's just us. Sometimes, Mama and Daddy come with us. Sometimes, Sky makes an appearance," Kate said.

"Someday, I hope I get to go with you."

"I would love that." Kate reached for his hand. They drove the rest of the way to the small town of Americus with random bits of conversation between songs on the radio.

"Rosemary & Thyme? I've never heard of this place," Kate commented as they got out the car.

"Joshua said this was where he took Hope for their anniversary last year, and they loved it," Rett said.

"Joshua and Hope have been spot on with their suggestions so far," Kate laughed as they walked into the restaurant. "So, I'm expecting great things."

"Me too," he laughed as they got seated.

"I just want you know that even though this day has not been up to perfect Rett standards, I have loved every minute of it. And I love you."

"It has been a fun day. And not everything has to be perfect," Rett said. Kate snorted and picked up the menu. "It really doesn't it."

"Uh huh," Kate knew his standards better than that.

"So, um, my parents have been bugging me about meeting you," Rett said after they ordered.

"I would love to meet your family," Kate smiled brightly. "When are you thinking?"

"Thanksgiving is when my parents suggested. I know it's the next time you're supposed to come home—"

"You have spent so much time with my family, but I haven't gotten to meet yours yet."

"Yeah, well, between being in Israel for a semester and then interning at Generations this summer, there hasn't really been a time to go to Texas," Rett said.

"Thanksgiving seems as good a time as any to meet your family."

Chapter Thirteen

"Is Nathan's class over yet?" Kate complained as they waited on Nathan so they could head to the airport.

Rett laughed. "There he is. You're cute when you're frustrated, though."

"Shut up," she joked back as she kissed him. "I'm trying not to freak out." To be honest, she was nervous about meeting his parents. Rett rolled his eyes, knowing she was worrying about nothing.

As they got settled on the plane, though, Rett could tell that she was still uneasy. "Look at me. My parents will love you because I love you." Rett kissed the top of her head and put his arm around her to reassure her. She knew he was right. Her parents loved him; there was no reason for his parents not to love her. She put her head on his shoulder and fell asleep before the plane even left the gate.

Rett watched her sleep as they flew and ran his fingers through her blonde hair. She was perfect, and his parents were going to love her.

"Do your parents know that you haven't told her?" Nathan whispered.

"Can we not talk about this about this now?" Rett was annoyed that his best friend would interrupt this perfect moment to nag him again.

"I'll take that as a no," Nathan rolled his eyes. "But thanks for letting me have the window seat." They were silent for a while. Rett knew he had to tell her, but it had to be in his own time, in his own way. Just as Nathan was about to say something, Kate stirred, and he shut his mouth. When she didn't wake up, Nathan finally said, "Look, one more warning and I promise I'm done I'm talking about it on this trip. I just don't want you to blow this. But if you don't trust her, you definitely will."

In the end, Rett knew Nathan wanted what was best for him. But he couldn't help snipping at him, "Thanks for the vote of confidence."

"It's more than that and you know it. You love her, but you are acting like you don't trust her. That's a dangerous combination."

"Nate," Rett sighed.

"Okay, I'm done. But eventually you're going to have to tell her," Nathan said before throwing his hand over his mouth and crossing his heart.

Rett nodded and laughed. He was thankful for Nathan. He had been there through everything, and Rett knew he would be there for years to come.

Kate didn't wake up until the wheels hit the runway in Dallas. "Welcome to Texas, beautiful." Rett kissed her, and a smile spread across her face.

"Your parents are picking us up, right?" Nathan asked, as the plane pulled into the gate.

"I think that's the plan."

"Wait, you don't know even know who's picking up us from the airport?" Kate rolled her eyes. "Classic." She shouldered her bag and stepped into the aisle. Boys—she would never understand them, especially Rett and Nathan. They got off the plane and headed to find whoever was there to get them.

"It's my parents, which is what I thought," Rett said when they got to baggage claim. Nathan pointed out a man in jeans and cowboy boots and his arm around a woman with dark hair and a big grin on her face. But Kate knew they were Rett's parents before Nathan said a word—no reason, no explanation, she just knew.

"EJ," Rett's dad had a deep Texas accent that was evident even though he only spoke two letters.

"It's good to see you, Dad," Rett said as he hugged him. "Hey, Mom. This is Kate. Kate, this is my dad, Dale, and my mom, Esther. Where's Rachel? I thought she was flying in today, too."

"She is. Her plane lands in just a few minutes," Esther smiled.

"Where's Abbie?" Nathan looked around for the sixteen-year-old who was normally Rett's shadow. Kate noticed his parents exchange a look.

"She's a got big project due next week that she's trying to finish up," Esther sighed, but Kate thought it might be more than that.

"But still, this is first time Rachel's home, right?" Rett questioned, and his dad nodded. "That seems out of character for Abbie."

"She's still adjusting to being the only one home. It hasn't been easy," Dale told his son. "Especially since you and Rachel both decided to go to college so far from home."

"She never said anything," Rett lamented.

"I'm sure she's just being dramatic. You know how Abbie can

be," Nathan tried to reassure everyone. "Finally! What took you so long?" Nathan said exaggeratedly as a girl with shoulder length black hair and olive skin walked over to them.

"Oh, you know, I was just in the air." The girl rolled her eyes, and Nathan just shrugged.

"That's no excuse," Nathan admonished, biting back a laugh.

"Whatever!" She slapped him, and he hugged her. "Gah, can't take you anywhere. Seriously, Rett, how do you put with him *all the time*?"

"I don't know, I just do," Rett laughed and pulled in her for a tight hug. "Rachel, this is Kate."

"Oh my gosh, I totally forgot you were coming!" Rachel squealed. "I'm so excited to finally meet you. Rett doesn't shut up about you."

"I'm excited to be here," Kate replied, hugging the girl.

"I thought Abbie was coming?" Rachel looked around.

"She decided to do schoolwork instead," Nathan said casually.

"What? That's stupid, why would she——" she paused and looked around before meeting her mom's eye.

"What is going on?" Rett asked.

"Don't worry about it, EJ," Dale patted his shoulder. "Everyone ready? Did any of you check a bag?" A chorus of no's sounded, and they headed for the car.

"Abbie's not thrilled I'm here, is she?" Kate whispered to Rachel as the guys loaded the luggage. Rachel just shook her head, casting a glance at Rett. Kate sighed. She knew something was up with Abbie.

"I'll explain more when we get home," Rachel whispered back.

"Kate, I feel like we already know you. But still, tell us about your family," Esther said as they got on the road. Kate laughed, reaching for Rett's hand as she told them all about herself, her family, and her relationship with Rett.

During a break in the conversation, Rachel cut in. "Okay, we have all week to get to know Kate. Can I tell you about school now?" she asked, clearly desperate to be able to talk.

"Why you? I could have things to say too," Nathan shot back.

"Are you dating that Mariah girl yet?" Rachel asked, a cocky look on her face. Kate leaned into Rett, trying to stifle her laugh.

"No, but—"

"Then no one cares." Rachel's sassy side was coming out.

"Oh yeah, we're going to be good friends," Kate laughed. The rest of the car ride was spent talking about their semesters. Kate listened, watching Rett and Nathan; she loved their relationship. As she listened, she watched out the window and saw the city of Dallas fading behind them. When Nathan started talking about a concert they had gone to in Nashville a few weeks before, Rett caught her eye and smiled. Kate wondered what he was thinking and why his dad was calling him "EJ." He had seemed oddly distant since they met up with his parents, but maybe he was thinking about Abbie's absence.

"Welcome home," Esther said as they turned off the highway. Kate was amazed at the scene that unfolded before her eyes—acres of land with a beautiful, tan brick, two-story house in front of them. They drove behind the house, made a few more turns, and pulled up to a smaller tan brick house.

"Thanks for the ride." Nathan got out of the car and pulled his bag out of the back before they headed back to the first house and unloaded the car. Kate smiled. She hadn't realized just how close the boys were—physically, anyway. Growing up that close together explained so much about their relationship, like why they were basically brothers.

* * *

"I'm gonna need your help this week," Dale said as they walked in to the house.

"I know, Dad," Rett laughed. "Plus, I don't think Nathan would be too happy if I got out of chores and he didn't." Rett's eyes sparkled with laugher. Kate watched the interaction; she knew he was close to his dad, but she was glad to be able to see him interacting with his parents up close.

"Abbie! We're home," Rachel called. "I'm going to check on her. I'll back in a minute."

"Take your time, Rach," Esther patted her shoulder. "Welcome to our home, Kate! EJ, show her to the guest room."

"Thank you," Kate said as Rett grabbed her bag.

"I'm sorry about Abbie. I'm going to check on her in a minute. Are you okay?" He kissed her before pushing a door open.

"I'm sure it will be fine. But yes, I'm wonderful. Your parents clearly love you, and Rachel is awesome. Plus, I think I understand a little more about your relationship with Nathan now that I've seen how close you live." Kate couldn't stop smiling.

"I love you." Rett shook his head before kissing her. "I'm going to change and help Dad. I'll see you at dinner."

"I love you, too." Kate watched as he walked up the stairs and disappeared around the corner. She decided to get settled and started to unpack her backpack. A couple minutes later, there was a knock on her door. She turned to see Rachel standing there. "How's Abbie?"

"Surprisingly, actually working on a school project," Rachel said in disbelief. "But Abbie's been having a hard time. She's a bit of a drama queen, and being the only one at home is taking a toll on her. Plus, she's lived her life as Rett's shadow, so I don't think she knows how to handle Rett having a girlfriend."

"What about you?" Kate asked.

"Rett doesn't shut up about you, like, ever. I feel like we are already friends because of it. I almost came to Schaeffer for fall break, but I got invited to go home with a friend at the last minute. Honestly, I had a hard time deciding what to do because I wanted to meet you so badly."

"He never told me about that," Kate mused.

"Because we didn't want to get your hopes up. But I'm coming soon. I'm so much closer now that I'm in Birmingham," Rachel grinned. "I miss him. It was hard when he left. Everything about the house changed, so I get where Abbie's coming from somewhat. But it's different with her, and now that I'm gone, too—" she trailed off.

"Hopefully, she'll come around. Now, I feel like I should go help your mom with dinner?" Kate's eyebrows raised.

"Look at you, already trying to earn those brownie points. Let's go." Rachel pulled her into the kitchen.

"Is there anything I can do?" Kate asked.

"A girl after my own heart. Rachel, where's Abbie?" Esther asked.

"Still working on that project," Rachel shrugged.

"Sorry about her," Esther sighed, setting Kate on potato dish.

"It's okay. Change is never easy." Kate was trying to stay optimistic, and they fell into easy conversation as they got dinner ready. Kate and Rachel were becoming fast friends, and Esther enjoyed seeing their interactions; it was easy for her to see why Rett had fallen for Kate.

"Wash up and sit down. Supper will be ready in five minutes," Esther said when Dale and Rett walked through the door. "EJ, will you go get your sister?"

"Yes ma'am." Rett quickly washed his hands and headed upstairs. They had just finished setting the table when Rett reappeared with a girl who looked a lot like Rachel. With her black hair pulled up in a high ponytail, it was easy to see that if it were down, it would have hit far below her shoulder blades. Unlike Rachel's brown eyes, Abbie's were blue, and she looked a little more like Esther than Rachel, who seemed to favor Dale. "Abbie, this is Kate."

"Hey Abbie! It's so nice to finally meet you," Kate greeted the teenager with a bright smile.

"Hi." Abbie gave a half-smile and sat down. By her interactions throughout dinner, it was easy to see that Abbie was frustrated by the fact that Kate was there. It wasn't anything drastic, but she definitely avoided talking to Kate or Rett directly.

"Abbie, would you help me clean up?" Esther asked as they cleared the table.

* * *

"Grab your coat and meet on the back porch in five," Rett whispered in Kate's ear as they put their plates in the sink. She nodded and ducked out of the kitchen wordlessly, pulling on her favorite Alabama sweatshirt—one she stole from her sister. "Ready?" Rett was his normal blue coat holding a blanket and a flashlight.

"Did you talk to Abbie?" Kate reached for his hand as they walked off the porch.

"Yeah. I can't figure her out right now. I think she just needs more time," Rett sighed. "But other than Abbie, thoughts so far?"

"I understand why you love this place, and your parents are wonderful. Plus, Rachel has already decided that we're friends," Kate laughed. "But I do have one question."

"And what would that be?" Rett was pretty sure he knew what was coming.

"Why do your parents call you EJ?" Kate said. Rett swallowed; this was his moment.

"I figured you were going to ask me about that. My parents are basically the only people who call me EJ," he started as they rounded a corner between two fields. Rett spread the blanket out, and they sat down. "I've debated when and where I wanted to tell you this." Kate waited, curious as to where the conversation was going. "This feels like the right place. This is my favorite spot in the world. Out here, I can think and breathe in a way I can't other places. I've spent a lot of time out here praying and seeking God." He lay back on the blanket, and she put her head on his chest, looking up at the stars glittering in the night sky.

"It's beautiful," she whispered.

"Right? The stars shine brighter here than they do anywhere. I like to think it's why my dad named the place Star Bright Ranch. But in truth, he named it that mainly because my mom's name, Esther, means star," he laughed.

"That's sweet," Kate commented. "Your parents clearly love each other."

"They do. I've wanted what they have for a long time." He paused. "Their love is a stark contrast to what I had modeled for me as love when I was younger." Kate bolted up, searching for his eyes in the pale moonlight.

Rett sat up and took both her hands. "I know I should have told you this sooner, but I was adopted by my parents on my ninth birthday. I was placed in their care a while before that."

Kate opened her mouth to say something but thought better of it. Rett may have waited to tell her all of this, but he was at least opening up now. This was his story; he could tell it how he wanted to.

"When I moved here, my whole life changed," he continued. "Everything I knew was suddenly different, and I wasn't always the easiest kid to be around. About a week after I got here, I started telling my parents that they couldn't call me Rett. My biological mom called me that, and I insisted that they weren't my real mom and dad." He inhaled, shuttering at the memories of his earliest days with the Johnsons. "They decided to call me EJ instead. It worked so well that it stuck. Through all of the transition and struggles with fostering and adoption, Joshua got involved in my life. My parents were desperate for help, and someone at church gave them his name. He started hanging out with Nathan and me. From the day I moved in, Nathan and I clicked. We've kind've been a package deal from the very beginning."

"Rett, I—I don't really know what to say. Wow." Kate fell against his chest. He held her for a moment, playing with her hair as they enjoyed the crisp night air and the beautiful stars, each lost in their own thoughts. "What's so special about this particular spot?" she asked as they lay back down on the blanket.

"When I was younger, Nathan and I would come out here because it's far enough from the house that you feel like you're out of reach but close enough that Mom and Mrs. Susan, Nathan's mom, could see us." He pointed across the field, and she could see a light in a window at Nathan's house. "As we got older, it just became our spot. We would come out here to talk, cut up, and pray. The week Joshua and Hope got engaged, he brought us out here and talked to us about praying for our future wives and what it meant to pursue a girl's heart. He gave us some examples and ideas for what a romantic, godly, and proper pursuit could look like." Kate couldn't see his face, but she could hear the smile in his voice as he continued. "There was one idea in particular that I latched on to. I decided that when I found a girl I was ready to pursue and walk towards marriage with, I would put the plan into action." Rett said. Then it seemed to Kate that he suddenly changed the subject. "You know that I had coffee with a lot of girls before you. I had never actually gone on a date with any of them, but there is actually something I've given you that no other girl has ever gotten from me, either."

"And what would that be?" Kate already knew she was his first kiss, so she was wracking her brain for what he could possibly be talking about.

"Roses." Rett sat up, bringing Kate with him. She drew in her breath. "You've gotten four dozen roses from me. You know that, right?" Rett cocked his head.

"Yeah," she answered slowly. "But I don't understand what that has to do with this conversation."

"I'm getting there," Rett laughed. "That idea Joshua gave me out here—the one I decided to use when I found the girl I was going to be in a relationship with? It involved twelve bouquets of a dozen roses. Each bouquet would symbolize an important moment or memory. At the end of my plan, I would propose to this girl by giving her an engagement ring along with the twelfth rose of the twelfth bouquet."

"Rett, are you saying what I think you're saying?" Kate's heart was in her throat. She loved the flowers, of course, but she hadn't known how much they really meant.

"I can't think about my future without you in it," Rett answered, pulling her a little closer.

Having her here, in the place he had spent so many nights praying for the girl he would give roses to, it just felt right.

In fact, it felt like home.

Chapter Fourteen

"Kate?" Someone knocked on her door the next morning.

"Come in," Kate chirped. She was sitting on the bed with her Bible and journal out, a coffee mug half-full sitting on the bedside table. Her mind was still reeling from her conversation with Rett the night before.

The door pushed open and Rachel walked in. "Whatcha reading?"

"Philippians one. It's helping me reflect on how God is continuing the work He started," she answered, reaching for the cup of coffee. "What's up?"

"Dad and Rett are almost done with morning chores, and then I think we're going riding. Just thought you should know."

"Thanks." Kate finished what she was writing and set about getting ready for the day. She pulled on jeans, boots, and the flannel shirt she had packed. She deftly swept her hair back into a French braid and finished by putting on powder, eyeliner, mascara, and some lipstick.

"Did you do that yourself?" Rachel asked when Kate walked into the living room.

"Do what myself?" Kate adjusted the flannel shirt, feeling slightly uncomfortable.

"Your hair!" Rachel gasped. "I have tried to figure out how to braid mine so many times, but my arms get tired halfway through."

"I've been doing it forever, but I'll braid yours later, if you want," Kate shrugged. She had mastered the skill when she was in middle school, so she didn't think much of it.

Rachel, however, was practically bouncing with excitement at the idea. "I would love that! Maybe Abbie will let you do hers? I will warn you, if she does, hers will take forever because her hair is so long," she laughed.

"Is she going riding with us?" Kate wondered where the youngest Johnson might be.

"No, because that would require her to be around you." Rachel rolled her eyes, and Kate got the feeling it had been sore subject between them that morning. "But Nathan's coming."

"Nathan makes everything more fun," Kate commented. "What do we need for today?"

"We're going to do a picnic lunch, so I need your help grabbing what we need for that." Rachel started bustling around the kitchen. She pulled out sandwich fixings for Kate to put together while she cut up some fruit. Then they packed it all into a bag and headed to meet the boys in the barn.

"No Abbie?" Rett asked, only half-surprised to see only one of his sisters.

"Nope, she's studying," Rachel answered with exaggerated air-quotes.

"Well, she better make a one hundred on that project with all the work she's doing on it to avoid you," Nathan laughed.

"Agreed," Kate high-fived him.

"Her loss," Rett shrugged. "I know you haven't ridden a lot," he said, turning to Kate, "but this is the best way to see Star Bright."

"And it's fun," Nathan added, bumping her shoulder.

"Let's do it. I can't wait to explore," Kate giggled.

"Sweet! This is Silver." Rett guided Kate to a white and gray horse. "She is about as gentle as they come. Let me help you up." Rett got her settled on the horse while Nathan and Rachel did the same. He showed her what to do before getting up on his own horse. "Ready?" Rett pulled his horse away from the fence.

"Giddyup," Rachel laughed as they headed out. Nathan and Rachel took the lead as Rett's horse fell in step with Kate's. He pointed out various sites along the way.

"This is my favorite spot," Rachel called a while later. Kate pulled her horse up to Rachel's side.

"Wow! This is beautiful." They were at the top of a ridge with a valley below them. A stream ran through it.

"It's incredible. This is actually the edge our property," Rett smiled.

"We used to camp out here all the time when we were younger," Rachel said.

"Yes, and it was always in the middle of the summer. Kasey hated every second of it," Nathan laughed.

"Kasey?" Kate questioned.

"My sister. Sorry, I guess I've never actually used her name around you before. You'll meet her tomorrow. She and her husband will be there for Thanksgiving," Nathan explained. "Okay, you ready some intense trail riding?"

"He's kidding. It's open spaces until we stop for lunch." Rett rolled his eyes.

"Race ya," Rachel called to Nathan, and they took off. Kate started to ask Rett about Rachel and Nathan's relationship but thought better of it.

"What?" Rett asked.

"Just something for me talk about with Rachel later. I love being here, by the way. I like seeing you in this space."

"I'm glad. I don't get to come home often, but I miss it."

"I can see why. This place is just—wow," Kate breathed.

"And I like having you here." Rett reached for her hand. "But we do need to head on," he said after a beat. "I have the lunch bag, and you know how Nate gets when he doesn't eat." They met up with Nathan and Rachel at the lunch spot, which was a picnic table by a small stream.

"What took you so long?" Nathan was sitting on a rock with his feet in the stream.

"How's the water?" Rett helped Kate off the horse and pulled down the lunch bag.

"Cold," Rachel laughed.

"Nah, you're just a wussy."

"Stop trying to get me riled up. It's November! The creek is freezing." Rachel set about getting lunch ready as Rett bent down and stuck a hand in the creek.

"Nate, you're insane. That water is way too cold." Rett flicked the water on his hand at his best friend.

"It's refreshing." Nathan threw his head back with dramatic flair.

"Just come eat," Kate commanded, rolling her eyes. "Tell me about Thanksgiving. I don't really even know who all I'm going to get to meet. I was too focused on your parents to worry about anyone else."

"You're cute." Rett kissed her.

"Get a room," Rachel teased. "But Thanksgiving is really chill around here. It's just our family and the Daly's. Oh, Gran and Gramps are coming too."

"They are? Since when?" Rett wanted to know.

"Abbie said they want to meet you, Kate," Rachel grinned.

"Abbie said?" Rett looked at his sister.

"We talked last night while you took Kate to the field," Rachel sighed. "She's just scared of losing you, Rett. She feels like Kate is stealing you from her."

"It sounds to me like you need to spend some time with her alone," Kate said.

"Katie—"

"No, Rett. I am the little sister in my family. I know what it's like to feel like someone is trying to take your sibling from you. She just needs your reassurance that nothing has changed between you. But you can't do that if I'm around. Spend some time with your sister. I'm sure Rachel and I can find something to do tonight, right?"

"Of course!" A smile spread across Rachel's face. Turning to Rett, she whispered loud enough for everyone to hear, "I like her! Don't screw this up."

"I keep telling him the same thing." Nathan cocked his head, and Rett was reminded that he still needed to tell him about the conversation he and Kate had the night before.

"He's doing pretty great, so far, if I say do so myself." Kate bit her lip.

"Good to know." Rett kissed her temple.

They finished up lunch and let the horses rest a bit longer before heading back. As she got settled back in the saddle, Kate said, "Tell me about your horse."

"This is Rebel," Rett answered. "He got here about the same time I did, and we bonded. Dad says we share a lot of the same personality traits. I think that's why he named him Rebel," Rett laughed. Kate just shook her head. Seeing Rett here, hearing him compare himself to a horse named Rebel, made her realize there was still a lot she didn't know about him.

* * *

"What would you say to dinner and movie tonight?" Rett leaned against Abbie's door frame.

"With you and Kate?" Abbie rolled her eyes.

"Just me," Rett smiled.

"For real?" Abbie's face lit up.

"Yep. I'm ready when you are. I even got out of evening chores for you," he winked, and she ran into his arms.

"You're the best. I'll be ready in ten minutes." Abbie was jumping up and down with excitement.

"Okay; I'll meet you downstairs. Bring your license and I'll even let you drive."

"Best brother ever!" Abbie cheered as she rushed into the bathroom.

As soon as Abbie was ready, they headed out. "I've missed you," she admitted the minute they stepped out of the house.

"I've missed you too, Shadow. I can't believe you're driving. This is weird," Rett laughed as he got into the passenger seat of the car.

"Do you have to call me that?" she cringed.

"You've never complained before. Why now?" Rett asked, stiffening for the barrage he worried was coming.

"Because I'm sixteen, not six," Abbie rolled her eyes.

"You're all grown up now, huh?" Rett relaxed, and Abbie just shook her head. "But seriously, tell me what's been going on with you. How's school?"

"School is school. I'm just ready for soccer season. I'm in this weird lull between club and school seasons."

"When does that start?" Rett asked.

"We start practicing in February. I could not be more ready."

"I bet. Kate played soccer in high school. Her intramural team at Schaeffer even won last year," Rett said.

"You were doing so well," Abbie sulked, pursing her lips.

"If you actually tried, you would like her," Rett pushed back.

"Did it ever occur to you I just don't want to try?" Abbie shrugged.

"Wow! What is your deal?" Rett knew Abbie was upset, but he didn't expect her to be totally stubborn and indifferent.

"I just don't understand why you would rather spend time with her than spend time with me."

"Is that what you think?" Rett sighed; Kate had been right.

"Yes! You never come home. After you went to Israel, you spent the whole summer with her. We barely got to see you! And then first time you do come home, you bring her with you," Abbie spat.

"There is so much wrong with that statement, it's not even funny. Plus, I don't know how you could ever think I wouldn't want to spend time with you."

"But you brought her with you."

"Because I wanted Kate to meet my family—which, by the way,

includes you." Rett was trying not to let his frustration show.

"Can we talk about this when I'm not driving?" Abbie turned on the radio, and they drove the rest of the way to the restaurant in silence.

When they were seated, Rett tried again. "Can we talk now?" Rett asked, glancing up from the menu.

"You're not going to let this go, are you?" Abbie sighed.

"Me? You're the one that is refusing to spend time with my girlfriend," Rett groaned.

"Why are you so upset right now?"

"Because I love Kate, and I plan on spending the rest of my life with her, but my little sister—who I love! —isn't even trying to get to know her."

"You're going to marry her?" Abbie let the menu fall against the table.

"That's the plan," Rett grinned. "I think that's the first time I've actually said it out loud."

"You're really going to marry her?" Abbie repeated.

"I'm 22. Kate and I have been dating for over a year. It's not like we're going to get married tomorrow. But yes, once Kate graduates, I fully expect that we will get married," Rett explained.

"You—you—what is happening?"

"I love Kate, and it would make me really happy if you tried to get to know her instead of shutting her out."

"Sorry. I'm still processing the fact that you're planning to marry her." Abbie shook her head and picked up the menu again.

"Are you okay?" Rett asked after the waiter took their order.

"I don't like the fact that she is taking you away from me."

"She's not taking me away from you," Rett smiled sympathetically.

"But you spent the summer with her instead of being home."

"I spent the summer interning at Generations and hanging out with Joshua. If anything took me away from you, it was my desire to serve God," Rett explained gently. "It was perk that Kate was there, but I didn't choose her over you. I would never do that."

"You wouldn't?"

"You're my sister. There is no way I could choose someone over you."

"Really?"

"Abbie Jane, I love you. You are important to me," Rett assured her.

"I love you, too," Abbie sighed. "Um, can we start over?" She bit her lip, a half-smile appearing on her face.

"I would like that a lot."

"There's a part of me that still doesn't want to like her, but I guess if you're going to marry her, I kinda have to, don't I?"

Rett laughed; Abbie was too much sometimes. Kate had been right—they just needed some time together.

* * *

"Can I join?" Abbie knocked on Rachel's door.

"Kate's in here, you know that, right?" Rachel sat up.

Kate shot Rachel a look as Abbie walked into the room. "Yeah, I know," Abbie answered. "Rett and I talked. I owe you an apology. I can be a bit of a drama queen, and Rett, well, he's my best friend. I panicked because everything about my life is changing, and I took it out on you. I'm sorry. Can you ever forgive me?"

"Of course! It's never easy when someone new comes into your family," Kate answered, immediately reaching to hug her. "It's not easy being the little sister."

"You're a little sister?" Abbie questioned.

"I am," Kate laughed. "My sister is married. When she got a boyfriend, it was hard for me. So, I understand more than you know."

"And now?"

"I love him. I actually spend a lot of time with them both. He makes my sister happy and loves her well."

"What does that mean?" Abbie plopped down on the bed.

"It means that he does his best to love her like Christ loves the church," Kate explained. It was something her dad told her when Sky and Emmie Wren had started dating. The conversation was one she would never forget; it had shaped how she approached dating. She wanted a guy who led with grace and encouraged her relationship with the Lord—both of which she had found in Rett. Her dad had reminded her and Emmie Wren that marriage is supposed to reflect the gospel to the world, and love is a choice you have to make daily, especially on the days when it feels the hardest.

"Does Rett love you that way?" Rachel asked, pulling her knees into her chest and interrupting Kate's thoughts.

"He does. He works very hard to keep Christ at the center of our relationship. We pray together and talk about things the Lord is teaching us," Kate grinned. She was so grateful for the way Rett loved her, and it was nice to be able to say it out loud.

"Do you think you're going to marry him?" Abbie asked, earning a gasp from Rachel.

"I'd really like to. I love him—a lot. He's everything I ever wanted in a guy. I can tell you that we are definitely headed that way."

* * *

"Where's Kate?" Nathan asked as he joined Rett in the field.

"Hanging out with Rachel—and hopefully Abbie," Rett said.

"I take it things went well with Abbie tonight then?"

"They did. I think telling her I am going to marry Kate helped a lot."

"You told her what?" Nathan blinked. It was first time he had ever heard Rett actually say that he intended to marry Kate.

Rett shot Nathan a sideways glance as he casually continued, "Kate's gotten four bouquets, but I should probably just go ahead and give her the next one. I mean, she handled the fact that I am adopted so well."

"You told her?" Nathan was getting hit from all angles.

"Yeah, well, Mom and Dad call me EJ, and she wanted to know why," Rett grinned.

"I'm proud of you," was all his best friend could manage.

"Thanks. I told her about the roses, too."

"You did?" Nathan wasn't sure how to handle all this information.

"It just felt right. With Kate, I feel like I'm home," Rett said with confident smile.

Nathan couldn't argue with that. There were very few people Rett felt at home with. Now that he could officially add Kate to the list, he wasn't quite so worried about Rett blowing it up. He had already made the first step in telling Kate his story.

Chapter Fifteen

"Mama! When are Gran and Gramps getting here?" Rachel asked the next morning.

"Any minute," Esther answered, and they immediately heard the door open. "That's either them or the Daly's."

"Well, where is this Kate I've heard so much about?" a voice boomed from the hallway.

"Gramps! Gran!" Rachel ran to the hall and hugged them both. "Rett isn't quite ready yet, but this is Kate," she said as she walked them into the kitchen to introduce them to the blonde standing beside her mother.

"You're real pretty. Rett did good," Gran observed with a thick southern accent.

"Thank you, Gran. I think so too," Rett beamed as he walked in. He kissed a blushing Kate on the cheek and hugged his grandparents just before Nathan and his family walked in.

"I didn't miss any drama, did I?" Nathan whispered in Kate's ear when he hugged her.

"You're awful," Kate slapped him, laughing. He introduced Kate to his parents, sister, and brother-in-law. Before she even had a chance to catch her breath from all the introductions, everyone was pitching in to get Thanksgiving dinner on the table.

* * *

"Bedtime, if you want to go Black Friday shopping in the morning," Esther reminded Rachel. "Kate, you are more than welcome to join us. Abbie, are you planning to come?"

"Are you crazy? That doesn't sound fun at all. I will be staying here," Abbie laughed.

"I would love to go," Kate said. She had never really been a Black Friday shopper, but she looked forward to the chance to bond with Rett's mom.

Esther opened her door way too early the next morning. "Kate! Rachel! We're leaving in fifteen minutes!" Kate climbed out of the bed and nudged Rachel, who groaned and sat up. They had stayed up way too late talking the night before, and Rachel had fallen asleep in Kate's bed. As Rachel trudged upstairs to her room, Kate pulled on jeans and a sweatshirt and put on little bit of makeup before heading to the still-dark kitchen. Somehow, Rachel was right behind her. "Ready?" Esther handed them both a cup of coffee, and they walked out the door.

They were in line at Target at 4:30 am for Black Friday shopping. "Over here!" Esther yelled to two women after they had been in line for about five minutes. "Kate, this is my sister, Ruth, and my sister-in-law, Sophie," she said, hugging each woman in turn.

"It's nice to meet you," Kate smiled. "I'm Rett's girlfriend."

"You're the Kate then. It's nice to meet you, too," Ruth, the taller of the two, said. Kate blushed, thankful it was still dark outside.

"Aunt Ruth is harmless. Aunt Sophie is the one you have to worry about," Rachel whispered before greeting her aunts.

"No Abbie?" Sophie asked.

"Nope. She told me I was crazy and that she was going to sleep in," Esther laughed.

"She's not wrong," Ruth said, winking. The ladies talked about their strategy for when the doors opened. They were very organized and managed to hit Target, Old Navy, and Macy's before ten. Then the women took a short break for coffee and breakfast before heading to Wal-Mart for a couple hours. Rachel and Kate talked and laughed all along the way. Shopping turned out to be quite the friendship-builder for them.

"My boys are so picky. It feels impossible to pick presents for them! Was Rett like that when he was younger?" Ruth was looking for a video game for her sons.

"Was? You've met my son, right? He's as picky as they come," Esther laughed, and Kate couldn't help but agree. When Ruth finally found the right game, the group left Wal-Mart to head to Kohl's and then lunch at The Twisted Root Burger. Finally, they made the rounds at the mall before heading back home.

"Did you have fun?" Rett asked as Kate sat down on the couch. She nodded and curled up next to him. "I'm so glad." Rett kissed the top of her head as Kate's eyes closed. She was exhausted and quickly dozed off in the comfort of his arms.

"She did good keeping up with us today," Rachel laughed. "I

could tell she wasn't used to the aunts' shopping pace, but she put on a brave face."

"Katie." Rett shook her gently, and she groaned. "Go take a nap," he said. She didn't have to told twice as she made her way to the guest room and collapsed on the bed.

"You ready, EJ?" Dale walked into the living room a few hours later.

"Will you tell Kate where we are?" he asked his mom and sisters.

"Sure! I'll make sure she knows that you left and are never coming back," Rachel deadpanned.

"Go! The sooner you get back, the sooner we can decorate the tree." Esther shooed him out the door behind his dad. "Rachel, will you get your sister and wake Kate up? We need to get things ready for the tree." Rachel hopped up to do what she was told. Fifteen minutes later, all four girls were in the living room, moving things around and pulling out Christmas decorations.

"Where are Rett and Mr. Dale?" Kate asked.

"Cutting down our tree," Esther smiled. "There is a grove of fir trees on the property, and they cut one every year."

"Did you order the pizza?" Abbie asked.

"There's a couple in the freezer. Can you handle that for me?" Esther asked. Abbie nodded and headed to the kitchen. The pizzas were almost ready when the men arrived with tree and set it on the stand. The traditions with Rett's family were definitely different than hers, but that did not stop her from enjoying getting the house ready for Christmas.

* * *

"Was your first trip to Texas as bad as you expected?" Nathan asked on their way through security. The rest of the trip had passed quickly, they could barely believe they were already headed back to Schaeffer.

"What? I didn't expect it to be bad," Kate laughed. "I loved it."

"You still gonna keep this guy around?"

"Yeah, he's not so bad," she teased back, leaning in so Rett could kiss her. Kate found a seat at their gate, and Rett settled in next to her. He was thankful she put up with him and Nathan. Any girl who was going to be in his life for the long haul would have to get along with his best friend.

As soon as they got home, Kate was greeted by all three of her roommates. "Those are for you," Mariah announced, pointing to the bouquet of roses sitting on the table.

Kate pulled out the card, which simply read, "Five."

Five down,

Seven to go.

Chapter Sixteen

"What are you and Rett doing for Valentine's Day?" Caroline asked as she and Kate walked to class. Christmas had come and gone, and the spring semester was kicking into high gear. Kate didn't like to think too far into the future, when Rett would graduate and their relationship would become long distance. But she was excited for Valentine's Day, which was just around the corner. It was the first one she and Rett would celebrate in person, since he had been in Israel the year before.

"You really think that boy is telling me anything?" Kate scoffed. Rett loved to keep big dates a secret.

"Sorry; I forgot who I was talking to." Caroline rolled her eyes.

"Are you going out with Patrick?" Kate asked gently. She never knew how to handle their relationship.

"He hasn't mentioned yet, but I'm going to be ticked if he doesn't take me out. It's Valentine's Day, for crying out loud!" She exhaled as they walked into the classroom, their conversation cut short by the start of the lecture.

"Do you really think Patrick will brush off Valentine's Day?" Kate asked after class.

"No. It's not in that man's nature to brush off anything that will that will make him the center of attention." Caroline rolled her eyes.

Kate could tell Caroline was exasperated, but she wasn't sure what to do about it. "Things with you and Patrick are…?"

"Fine," Caroline answered. "Look, I get that you don't understand our relationship, but Patrick's not Rett, and I'm not you. I like him. He makes me happy, but we don't have to spend every waking hour together. We have plenty of time, too. Patrick's going to be here for two more years, so there's no reason for us to be super serious right now," she explained.

"Okay. It's just—"

"I like Patrick and Patrick likes me. We're dating. He's my boyfriend, even if he does get on my nerves sometimes. It's that simple. You don't have to be weird about it. Not everyone's relationship looks like yours and Rett's," Caroline said.

"I know that," Kate laughed, and Caroline shook her head.

"Do you have any ideas what Rett might have planned?"

"I stopped trying to figure things out a long time ago. It's not worth it, because I will never actually get it right," Kate said. "That man; I love him so much."

"You definitely got a good one," Caroline said. "I'm going to head to the library to get some work done." She slipped off, and Kate headed to spend the evening with Rett.

"Can I ask about Valentine's Day? Or is it a surprise?" Kate asked as they waited for dinner to come out of the oven.

"It's a surprise, but I think you will enjoy it. It's something we've talked about doing for a while." Rett kissed her as the timer went off.

"Sounds like a plan. I'm just glad we get to spend it together this year." Kate helped him get dinner on the table.

"Me too," Rett smiled. They sat down just as Nathan emerged from his room.

"I see how it is," Kate joked. "You will come out for food, but not otherwise when I'm around?"

"I wish! I'm knee-deep in my senior thesis, and I have to have an outline, complete with sources, to my professor by the end of the week. I wish I could hang out, but I can't—not if I actually want to graduate," Nathan sighed.

"Yikes; that sounds like torture," Kate said.

"It's the best," Nate groaned sarcastically. "This semester is going to kill me."

"Last one, though! You can do it," Rett reminded him.

"Don't remind me," Kate winced.

"Sorry. I know you're not handling this whole change thing well." Rett kissed her temple.

After an enjoyable dinner together, Kate helped him clean up the kitchen. "Thanks for today. I needed it," she as she gathered her stuff.

"You are always welcome here." He pulled her close and kissed her.

"I love you. I'm excited for Valentine's Day next week," she smiled, content with his arms around her after a simple, perfect afternoon with her boyfriend.

* * *

"Happy Valentine's Day, beautiful," Rett woke her up.

"Happy Valentine's Day," she repeated, sleepily.

"You up?" Rett asked through the phone.

"Yes." She pulled herself into a sitting position.

"I will see you this afternoon. What time do you get done with class?"

"Two," she groaned.

"I will see you then." Rett hung up, and Kate got ready for class. She was full of nervous excitement and kept watching the clock, just wanting the school day to be over. She was distracted all through her Spanish class that afternoon and managed to botch the simplest conjugations.

"What is wrong with you?" Caroline asked as they walked out of class.

"It's Valentine's Day! I just want to spend it with Rett, not be in stupid class," Kate answered dramatically. "I'm going to get ready for my date. I will see you later." She practically skipped to her car, eager to get ready for the afternoon and evening with her boyfriend.

* * *

"Hi." Rett stood in the doorway of her apartment looking even more handsome than normal.

"Happy Valentine's Day," she answered, kissing him. "Am I dressed okay?" She spun in her jeans, boots, and sweater. It was hard to get ready for a date when she didn't know what they'd be doing. With Rett, it could be anything from a trail ride to a fancy restaurant.

"You are dressed perfectly," he assured her. "Ready?"

"Let's go!" She grabbed her purse and her gift for Rett. "Are you going to tell me anything?"

"We're exploring Cypress Grove Park, and I even packed us a picnic," Rett grinned.

"Finally! For record, it's the best Valentine's date you could have picked." She leaned over and kissed his cheek. They drove the fifteen minutes to the park, and Kate couldn't stop smiling. They spent the afternoon wandering around under the trees, talking and laughing.

"This place is amazing!" Kate didn't even care that it was little colder than she would normally have liked.

"You seem happy," Rett observed. He had noticed that she was smiling a lot.

"I'm with you in this incredible park! Why wouldn't I be happy?" She turned to look at him full on.

"You're right. I just hate it took so long for us to get here," he answered, kissing her.

"We're here now," she said, smiling again. "But you have to promise me we will come back in the spring." He nodded enthusiastically as they started looking for a spot to have their picnic. As they enjoyed the dinner Rett had packed for them, they exchanged gifts. Kate got Rett a new Bible. Since Christmas, he had been hinting at wanting one he could take notes in. Rett got Kate a copy of the newest book by her favorite author.

"Thank you; this has been perfect." She kissed him as they sat in the car watching the sunset.

"Oh, this date is not over yet. I have one more surprise up my sleeve," Rett laughed.

"Of course, you do." She shook her head. He was too much for his own good sometimes. To end the day, they spent a couple hours exploring the local bookstore before heading back to campus.

"I'm so glad I got spend this day with you," he told her as they stood outside her door.

"This day has been perfect. Thank you," she sighed as she kissed him. "Would you like to come in and hang out for a while?"

"Unfortunately, I have a paper to write and a test to study for." Now it was Rett's turn to sigh.

"Lame, but I understand. Good luck," she smiled, watching as he got into his car. It had truly been a perfect Valentine's Day. Kate had halfway expected roses because this felt like a special moment, but Rett obviously had different ideas about the milestones of their relationship. Kate had faith that Rett had a plan. Besides if everything went according to that plan, the next bouquet would put them halfway to getting engaged.

Chapter Seventeen

"I have some news for you," Rett told Kate as they sat on the couch in his apartment in early March. He eyed her sideways as he said, "I have a job interview."

"You're serious?" she gasped, and Rett nodded. "That's awesome! I want to know everything." Kate was thrilled for him even before she knew the details, as usual.

"That church in Atlanta, the one Joshua and I have been talking about? They want me to interview to be their youth minister," Rett explained. Kate was in shock; she didn't know what to say, but she was so happy for him. When the words wouldn't come, she leaned in and kissed him—the only way she knew to convey the things she was feeling.

"I'm going to miss the first few days at the beach though," Rett said apologetically.

"You're getting a job—the one you have been talking about for months, in fact. A couple days of a beach trip is not a big deal in comparison. This is your future we're talking about," Kate reminded him.

"I know. I just wanted you to know," Rett laughed, and Kate shook her head. "I kinda wish the job was at Generations though, if I'm being honest."

"You still think that's where you'll end up?" Kate pulled her knees into her chest. Over the summer, they had talked a little bit about Rett's dream to work at Generations.

"That's the goal. I would love to work there, and I really think I will someday. There's just not a spot for me yet. Plus, I'm super young," Rett said.

"A little experience always helps. This church is smaller, right?"

"Yes. It's a newer church, and I would be their first youth minister," Rett explained.

"That's so cool! Personally, I'm glad it's not Generations right now, because I don't want you that far from me," Kate admitted, leaning across the couch to kiss him.

"Seven hours would definitely be rough," he acknowledged. "Thankfully, Atlanta is closer."

"Thankfully," Kate laughed. "But speaking of the beach trip and spring break, do you know what the plans are? I can't get much out of Lynne."

"I just know we're going to her beach house. I don't think there are many plans past that. It should be a fun week. A chill week," Rett said, hesitating just a bit at the end.

"You know something." Kate narrowed her eyes.

"I don't know what you're talking about," Rett insisted.

"Fine, keep your secrets," Kate huffed.

"Now, kids, no fighting," Nathan chided, walking into the living room.

"We're not fighting, Rett just won't tell me what's happening next week," Kate informed him.

"That's because it's not his place to tell you," Nathan said, which earned him a death glare from Rett.

"Not his place—wait, Houston's proposing next week, isn't he?" Kate stood up in her excitement.

"I can neither confirm nor deny," Nathan said, crossing his arms.

"Fine, be that way. Are you going to look for jobs in Atlanta too?" Kate asked Nathan, changing the subject and settling back down on the couch.

"Yep! I have already applied for a couple jobs," he answered, settling into his usual chair. "Rett wouldn't last two days without me."

"Try the other way around," Rett chuckled.

"Whatever. Right now, I'm just ready for spring break." Nathan rolled his eyes.

* * *

"Aren't the boys supposed to be here by now?" Caroline propped herself up on her elbow, looking at the other three girls laying out on the beach.

"They just got here. They are dropping their stuff at the house, and they'll be here soon," Kate answered without opening her eyes.

"How do you know that?" Lynne turned to look at her friend.

"Rett texted me." Kate didn't understand what the big deal was. She was usually the one anxious to see Rett, but the girls were enjoying their time on Jekyll Island, just laying out and exploring Driftwood Beach a few streets over from Lynne's house. The guys would get there when they were supposed to.

"I haven't heard from Houston." Lynne looked at her phone for the hundredth time in two hour span they had been sitting on the beach.

"Lynne, chill, he was the one driving. He couldn't text. They will be here soon." Mariah rolled her eyes. The girls had been fine the last few days without their boyfriends, but now that they were on the island, it seemed to be the only thing they could think about.

"Do you think they'll be able to find us?" Caroline asked Lynne.

"Oh yeah. Houston knows this is my spot," Lynne assured her. He had been coming to her family's beach house since high school; he would know just where to find her.

"See, I told you I could find them!" Houston's voice reached them at that exact moment, and Lynne jumped up to greet her boyfriend. Caroline was on her heels, eager to find Patrick. Mariah turned to Kate, who still lying on her towel with her eyes closed.

"I think she might be asleep," Mariah told Rett as he squatted down next Kate.

"Katie," he whispered.

"I was almost sleep," she groaned, "But Lynne and Caroline kept me awake worrying about when you were going to get here," Kate said sitting up.

"Hello to you too," Rett laughed.

"Hi. I'm glad you're here," she smiled, kissing him. "How was the interview?"

"Really good. I'm supposed to hear something by the beginning of next week," he grinned.

"You sound confident," Kate said as he sat down next to her.

"I am. But we'll see what happens. Are you enjoying spring break?"

"It has been glorious. I love Jekyll," Kate said.

"Have you been here before?"

"Yeah. It was our spring break spot for a while when Emmie Wren was in high school," Kate explained. They spent the afternoon enjoying the beach. Kate and Rett sat on her towel, talking and laughing. Nathan and Patrick found a frisbee to throw, and before long they were all splashing in the water and throwing the frisbee around. Lynne's mom had a seafood dinner ready for them when they got to the house. They finished the night off with a movie, glad to all be together at the beach on spring break.

* * *

"Hey, Lynne, let's go for a walk." Houston reached for her hand Friday evening.

As soon as they walked out of the house, Patrick stood up. "Okay, people! We have twenty minutes," he announced, and the group started getting the house ready for a surprise engagement party while Houston and Lynne walked down to Driftwood Beach.

"This place is my favorite," Lynne hummed as she leaned into Houston's shoulder.

"Mine too. Do you remember our first trip here?" he asked.

"Of course, I do. How could I forget prom and our first kiss?"

He laughed. "Do you know where we're going?"

"Driftwood Beach. We have made this walk too many times too count," Lynne giggled. "But something about tonight feels special."

"You have always been able to read me. I could never pull off surprises like Rett does," Houston teased, bumping into her shoulder.

"It's a good thing I hate surprises," Lynne reminded him as they walked out onto Driftwood Beach.

"I guess it's a good thing this isn't one." He stopped next to a big pile of driftwood and dropped down to one knee.

"What are you doing?" Lynne knew what was coming, but it still took her breath away. "Houston. Oh, my word, this is really happening."

"You are my best friend, and I can't imagine my life without you in it. Almost five years ago, I kissed you on this beach for the first time, and I knew this was where I needed to do this. Lynne, I love you. Will you marry me?"

"Yes, yes! The answer will always be yes," she squealed, bending down to kiss him as he stood up. "I love you." She stared at the ring sparkling on her finger, a simple round diamond on the band.

"We're engaged," he whispered, resting his forehead against hers.

"You did good. You did real good." She kissed him, and they enjoyed a few minutes to themselves before walking back to the house. "This doesn't feel real," Lynne laughed.

"Oh, it's real. I just dropped a bunch of money on that engagement ring. It's definitely real," Houston said.

"Whatever; you're thrilled. You get to marry me."

"You're right, future Mrs. Singletary," he replied, his eyes sparkling with excitement as he looked up ahead.

"What are you up to now?" Lynne narrowed her eyes but took his hand as they rounded the corner.

"You didn't think I would really propose at the beach over spring break—with your parents and our friends all here—without planning a little something else, did you?" he laughed, pulling her along as they approached the house.

"Congratulations!" everyone shouted as the newly engaged couple walked in the door. They had decorated with a "She said yes!" banner, and Lynne's mom made cookies. They spent the next couple hours celebrating Houston and Lynne. Lynne's mom had even made a slideshow of pictures from their relationship.

As the girls lay in bed that night, Mariah spoke up, "I can't believe you're really engaged."

"You're not allowed to leave for your Journeyman adventure until after my wedding," Lynne said. "I need you to be a bridesmaid."

"I think I can make that happen," Mariah answered. "As long as your wedding is pretty close to graduation."

"We've been talking about Memorial Day weekend for a while, so as long as we can get the church then, that's when it will most likely be," Lynne said.

Kate wondered what it would be like to be that stage, prepping for marriage. Lynne knew exactly when she wanted her wedding to be because she and Houston had already talked about it.

"You know, you and Rett will probably be the next ones to get engaged," Caroline whispered, reading her thoughts as Lynne and Mariah continued to talk about wedding details.

"Not for a while. I've only gotten five bouquets of roses," Kate said.

"What?" Caroline's dramatic eyes were wide with confusion.

"I'm going to get twelve bouquets before he proposes." Kate tried to keep her tone casual, but Caroline was giddy with excitement at the new information.

"And how to you know this?" she demanded.

"He told me," Kate shrugged. She put Caroline off with the promise to explain later. Tonight was about Lynne, not her. Yet as she rolled over and went to sleep, she couldn't help but think Caroline was right.

She and Rett might be the next ones to get engaged.

Chapter Eighteen

"Are you really graduating?" Kate asked. Finals were over, Rett and Nathan's families were in town, and even Joshua and Hope were on their way. It was almost time for Rett to start his job as the youth minister of a small church in Atlanta. As excited as she was for him, graduation also meant that he wouldn't be just around the corner any more.

"I think so," Rett laughed as he kissed her. "I can't believe how fast these last few weeks went by. I love you," he added. He knew Kate was the best thing that had ever happened to him. He did not want to be five hours from her, but she still had two years of school left, and there was nothing he could do about that.

"Are you packed and ready to move?" Dale asked.

"Pretty much," Rett reassured his dad. "The girls have been a huge help."

"Well, I'm glad we won't have too much to do," Esther said as they walked into the apartment. Kate recruited Rachel to help her with the last few things in the kitchen while Esther and Abbie finished up in Rett's room.

The apartment was just about packed and they were loading the trailer when they heard, "Need some help?" as Joshua and Hope pulled into the parking lot.

"About time you got here!" Rett hugged his mentor when he got out of the car.

"Kate, I don't know how you make that drive all the time. It's killer," Hope complained, hugging her.

"Tell me about it. Where are the girls?" Kate asked, looking around for the Kings' two daughters.

"At home with my parents. They would be going crazy about now," Hope said laughing. "Definitely not the trip for them. Oh, my word," she exclaimed, seeing Rett's sisters for the first time. "Rachel? Abbie?" The girls both hugged her.

"I'm glad I finally get to see y'all again! It's been way too long," Rachel said. It was the first time the Kings had been reunited with the two Texas families since they left for Georgia six years earlier. Once the apartment passed Esther and Susan's inspection, the whole group headed to dinner, thankful to be together again.

* * *

"You ready for this?" Nathan asked Rett on their way to campus the next morning. It was graduation day, and Rett was nervous and excited all at the same time. Really, he just wanted the ceremony to be over. He was excited about the new phase of life he was walking into and couldn't wait to start his job.

He and Nathan were already dressed in their graduation robes, so they headed to the gym. They found their seats and impatiently waited through the speeches and the pomp and circumstance for their names to be called.

"Everett James Johnson," the dean of the college called. Rett walked across the stage and shook hands with the president of the university while his proud family and girlfriend cheered.

After the ceremony, Rett took pictures with his friends, family, and Kate. "You did it! I'm so proud of you," Kate exclaimed, kissing him.

"It's crazy," Rett answered, shaking his head. "I can't believe Nathan and I are about to move to an apartment in Atlanta and start our jobs."

"I don't want to think about being at Schaeffer without you," Kate pouted.

"I won't be too far. You'll be fine. I, on the other hand, am still not sure how I'm going to handle this summer with you being in San Antonio."

"You'll be fine," she parroted back to him, and he just laughed.

* * *

"Let's do this," Rett smiled as they loaded up the cars the next morning. Everyone headed out together. They laughed and talked the whole way to Atlanta, making such good time that they were able to get the cars unloaded before tracking down some lunch. The majority of the afternoon was spent getting Rett and Nathan settled in the apartment.

"Sorry you got roped into helping with all this," Rett apologized to Kate as he handed her another box of kitchen stuff.

"It's fine, really. I'm just glad there are lots of people to help so that it actually gets done," Kate laughed.

"It would have gotten done…"

"Yeah, in like six months," Kate teased, shaking her head.

"She's right, you know," Nathan said as he walked out the door to get another box. It was a full effort to get the boys settled as much as possible before it was time to go.

"Thank you for all your help here," Rett said to Kate as she got ready to leave with the Kings late that evening.

"Of course! It was only fitting, since I helped pack your apartment in Jackson. I hope you love Atlanta and have the best first week of being a youth minister. I'm so proud of you," she reiterated with a genuine smile.

"Thank you. I love you." He kissed her.

"I love you too," she replied, both of them knowing just how much they would miss one another.

* * *

"What are you plans for this summer?" Hope asked Kate as they got on the road.

"I'm headed to San Antonio to teach ESL for six weeks with Caroline," she answered.

"Wow, that's awesome!" Joshua said.

"I know! I'm really excited about the opportunity. I think it will be good for me—help improve my Spanish and my teaching skills," Kate explained.

"I'm sure it will be," Hope smiled. They talked about her trip for the majority of the ride back to Albany. The Kings helping Rett move had been such a blessing, as it allowed Kate to come straight home before she headed to San Antonio.

"See ya later," Kate said as she got her bags out of the car. The Kings waved as they pulled out of the driveway and Kate opened her back door. Her parents were glad she was finally home, but Kate was most anxious to see Kaden. Her nephew would be so much bigger than the last time she had seen him! "When am I going to see Emmie Wren and Kaden?" she asked immediately.

"Tonight! They are coming over after church," Emily said, and Kate grinned. She worked on unpacking and helped with dinner. Finally, they heard the door open.

"Katie!" Emmie Wren called as she walked into the kitchen with Kaden on her hip.

"Emmie Wren!" she hugged her sister and immediately took Kaden. "Stop growing, okay? You're too big." Kate poked his chest and spoke a high-pitched voice, telling Kaden all about how wonderful and handsome he was.

"You got Rett settled in?" Sky asked, greeting his sister-in-law as he followed his wife into the room.

"Yeah. Having everyone there was big help." She sat down on the couch with Kaden while Emmie Wren and Emily set the table. She hated being so far from her nephew. He babbled as the family talked about Kate's plans for the next few weeks.

* * *

"First day! You ready?" Rett called to Nathan as they both got ready for their first day of work.

"Yep, I'm excited about it. See you tonight," Nathan called back over his shoulder as headed out the door and to his job at an advertising agency. Nathan spent the first few hours in meetings and making sure he had everything he needed to get into the building. There were specific offices he'd need access to, as well. He felt overwhelmed, but he was glad to finally be at work.

At lunch, Nathan's boss and some of his co-workers took him to their favorite restaurant. Then the afternoon began with Nathan's first client meeting, which lasted a few hours. He mostly observed how the team worked, and everything went great. He felt ready to get started on their campaign. The team he was working with spent the rest of the day splitting up their responsibilities and setting deadlines and expectations for the job. When the clock hit five, Nathan breathed a sigh of relief. He had survived his first day of work.

* * *

"Welcome, welcome," Jason, the lead pastor at The Well, greeted Rett when he walked in. "We are so excited you're here!" He showed Rett around the church, introducing him to other staff members as they went. Rett could hardly believe the day had finally arrived; he was starting his ministry.

"You're the new youth minister, huh?" A built blonde guy who looked more like a surfer than a pastor walked into Rett's office.

"That would be me, Rett Johnson," he introduced himself.

"Chad Borshkin, I'm the discipleship pastor, which basically means I'm in charge of all the groups around here." The guy extended his hand, and Rett moved to shake it. "Careful with the hands; they're the money makers," Chad cautioned as they shook.

"Excuse me?" Rett cocked an eyebrow.

"I've got an audition for commercial this weekend," Chad said, as though it were an explanation. "Well, see you around."

Rett stood there stunned, unsure what to make of the guy. Something told him they were going to be friends, though. All in all, Rett's first day was a great one that even included getting to meet a few of the students in his ministry. The way he saw it, this job was the first step into the rest of his life.

And the future was looking really bright.

Chapter Nineteen

"Just who I was looking for," Chad bellowed, sitting down next to Rett at the welcome table in the youth room.

"Hey Chad, what's up?" Rett said. Nathan, who had decided to attend Rett's church and help out with the youth, had also heard a lot about Chad over the last few weeks. His mouth fell open.

"My sister-in-law is going to be town this weekend, and there is no way I can manage by myself with those two sisters for a long weekend." Chad blew out a breath. "So, I was hoping you could come over Monday? We can hang out and grill. My sister-in-law's single," he added, nudging Rett.

"Grilling sounds fun, but I've told you, I have a girlfriend. She is going to be in town this weekend, though. If you're okay with me bringing her, we'd love to come." Nathan cleared his throat loudly. "And if you're trying to set your sister-in-law up, Nathan's single," Rett added, clapping a hand on Nathan's shoulder.

"The more the merrier! I'll text you the address." Chad grinned and flashed his signature white smile. "Mission accomplished," he muttered to himself as he walked off.

"So that was Chad. You have to meet him in person to really understand, I guess. Wow!" Nathan let out a low whistle. "That was Chad," he repeated, blinking a couple times. "I think I was blinded by the light reflecting off his teeth. I didn't know they could be that white."

"Right? It's like in the commercials when people have a glimmer on their teeth," Rett laughed. He'd been trying to explain Chad to his best friend for two weeks.

"Yes! That's it! It's like I heard an actual ding when he smiled," Nathan laughed back. "What in the world is his wife like?"

"I don't know; never met her," Rett shrugged. "But she's got to be interesting to be married to him."

"You've never met his wife? And you work at a church together?" Nathan raised an eyebrow.

"She works nights or weekends or both," Rett shrugged.

"What does she do?"

"She's a nurse? I think; I don't remember. We'll find out on Monday though. Sorry." Rett shrugged again. "I've got nothing, so I don't know anything to help with you the sister-in-law." He knew why Nathan was really asking.

"It's okay. I wish I had thought to at least ask what her name was," Nathan mused. He shook his head. "Oh, well. When do the kids get here?"

"I'll open the doors in five minutes. Pray with me?" Rett asked as he got ready to start the Wednesday night service. The friends prayed before letting the youth group into the room for the service to start. Nathan listened as Rett preached, but he couldn't quite keep his thoughts from wandering to the mystery girl he was going to meet this weekend.

* * *

"I can't believe we're actually going to Chad's house! And they have a pool?" Kate asked as they got ready to leave on Saturday morning. They had talked Chad into moving the cook out to Saturday when Rett realized he had forgotten that Kate was flying out on Monday morning. Soon, she'd be on her way to spend the summer in San Antonio with Caroline teaching ESL classes.

"Have you seen that dude's tan? Of course, they have a pool. I would bet money on him having a tanning bed in that house," Nathan grinned, grabbing towels for everyone. "Ready?" He looked at Rett.

"Let's go," Rett laughed, and they piled into the car to drive the short distance to Chad's house.

"Hi! I'm Jenna, Chad's wife," the brunette introduced herself as she answered the door. "Welcome to our home. We're so glad that you were able to come today," she added as she ushered them into the house.

"Hey Jenn, where's the—" a girl with auburn hair thrown up into a top knot wearing a blue bikini froze when she saw them. Shooting her sister a look, she regained her composure and introduced herself. "Hi, I'm Hanna."

"Hann, these are Chad's friends." Jenna was clearly suppressing laughter.

"I'm Rett. This is my girlfriend, Kate, and my best friend, Nathan,"

Rett introduced the group to the two sisters.

"It's nice to meet you," Jenna smiled.

"I would ask where Chad is, but it's almost eleven, so I'm sure he's already out by the pool," Hanna said, rolling her eyes. "Gotta get that even bake." Everyone laughed as they walked into the backyard.

"You made it!" Chad got up from the pool chair he had been occupying.

"Yep! Chad, this is Kate," Rett introduced his girlfriend.

"It's nice to finally meet you," Chad smiled, and Kate was thankful she had sunglasses on.

"You too." Kate shook his hand. "It's hot; I'm going in. You with me?" Kate's eyes sparkled with mischief as she looked at Rett and put her coverup on a chair.

"Of course," he laughed. As soon as he set his phone on the table, Kate pushed him in the pool and jumped in after him.

"Okay, they're adorable," Hanna said to Nathan as Rett and Kate got settled on a float.

"Oh, you have no idea," Nathan sighed.

"How long have they been together?"

"About a year and half, I think," Nathan shrugged.

"So, when are they getting engaged?" Jenna interjected, joining them on the lounge chairs.

"It's going to be a while. Kate's still got two years of college left."

"Dang, she's young." Hanna sighed dramatically, adding, "Oh, to be young and in love!"

"Shut up, Hann. You're still young," Jenna chided, playfully hitting her sister.

"Younger than you," she shot back.

"By eighteen months," Jenna retorted, rolling her eyes.

Stopping the spat, Chad joined the conversation and asked, "So, Nathan, how to you know Rett?"

"We grew up together. My parents work for Rett's parents. He's like my brother."

"Gotta love friends like that," Hanna said, cutting a sideways look at her sister as she joked, "Just like family, but you can give them back." She could see the light in Nathan's eyes as he nodded.

"That's cool." Chad cast a significant glance at Hanna before he stood dramatically and said, "I need to fire up the grill. I'll be back."

"I'll pull lunch out," Jenna added, jumping up to hurry after him.

"Subtle," Hanna said, rolling her eyes. "I do not understand how she married that man."

"He's—" Nathan started, but he didn't have the right words.

"A lot? Yeah," Hanna finished for him.

"How long have they been married?"

"Three years." Hanna shook her head. "They met on a mission trip in California when Jenna was in college, and they've been together ever since."

"That explains so much," Nathan laughed. "Of course, he's from Cali."

"Yep. Went to college in Seattle and even worked at a coffee shop called Goldfinch's," Hanna listed. "But enough about Mr. Sun and Surf. Tell me about you, because Jenna's going to ask me all about you when she comes back."

"What do you want to know? I'm an open book," Nathan answered, smiling winningly.

"Do you have a girlfriend?"

"Do you think I would be trying to flirt with you if I did?" Nathan put a hand to his chest, feigning shock.

"It's happened before," Hanna said offhandedly. "I just had to be sure."

"No, I don't have a girlfriend. Do you have a—"

"Look, I'm going to stop you there. This was Jenna's attempt to set me up, so no, I clearly don't have a boyfriend."

"Is that okay with you?" Nathan was trying to figure out how to read this girl.

"The setup or the singleness?" she asked. "I'm talking to you, aren't I?" she added, not giving him a chance to respond. "I don't have the best dating history, but I'm finally at a place where I'm ready to try again."

"So, if I were to ask to you out?" Nathan tried.

"My policy is to always say to yes to a first date." She stood, walked over to the diving board, and did a perfect flip into the pool.

"She's something else," Nathan whispered to no one before following Hanna to the diving board and splashing everyone with his cannonball. Jenna walked out with lunch a few minutes later, and they all dried off to enjoy the salads she had fixed.

"What, no tea for you?" Kate asked Chad as she filled the glasses.

"I don't do dark liquids. Do you see these teeth?" He pointed to his perfectly white smile.

"No one cares about your dental hygiene, Chad." Hanna rolled her eyes.

"But these are my money makers," he insisted.

"Right," Hanna muttered under her breath.

"They look great, honey," Jenna reassured him.

"Why do you stroke his ego? You're just making it worse," Hanna whined.

"I think your teeth are awesome, Chad," Nathan chimed in. "How in the world do you get them that white?" Hanna shot Nathan a death glare as Chad began to explain his oral health routine. After fifteen minutes, he was still going. "I'm sorry; I didn't know," Nathan whispered in Hanna's ear.

"Clearly," she muttered. Clearing her throat, she cut into Chad's monologue, "Sorry to cut you short, but I'm ready to float in the pool for a while. Nathan, you coming?" He nodded, and they took over the floats Rett and Kate had vacated. The group spent the afternoon hanging out by the pool, talking, laughing, and getting some sun.

"Burgers okay with everyone for dinner?" Chad asked as he got out of the pool a while later.

"Yes! Always the burger," Nathan said, high-fiving Chad.

"You want some help?" Rett offered.

"Sure," Chad said as Rett followed him up to the back porch.

"You coming?" Rett eyed his best friend, who was sitting on the pool steps next to Hanna.

"I'm sure the two of you can handle six burgers," Nathan retorted, grinning at Hanna. "But if you can't, just yell."

"You are shameless," Kate teased, rolling her eyes.

"It's fine; I like him here." Hanna smiled back at Nathan. They had been getting along perfectly all afternoon. Kate had never really seen a girl hold her own with Nathan, but Hanna was keeping him on his toes. She laughed at his jokes and didn't take his crap when he tried to pull a smooth move on her. Kate could tell that Nathan liked her, and she was pretty sure that Hanna liked him too.

"Hey, Kate, do you want to help me get some stuff done in the kitchen?" Jenna asked after a few minutes.

"Sure." They left budding love birds sitting on the steps together.

"Hanna and Nathan seem to be hitting it off?" Kate hinted as soon as they were in the kitchen.

"That was the plan," Jenna grinned. "She's been moping over her ex for too long. When Chad mentioned new guys our age at church, I knew I had to do something."

"Nathan's a great guy," Kate assured her.

"Good, because she needs a great guy." Jenna shook her head. "I'm just glad I talked her into coming this weekend. I didn't think she was actually going to leave the shop."

"Shop?" Kate asked.

"Hanna owns a bridal shop. She just hired a great manager, but she was nervous about leaving anyway. It's been fine, though."

"That's cool."

"Yeah. She's so good at it. She's got this crazy eye for fashion and the way dresses fit on people," Jenna explained as she cut up fruit and pulled chips out of the pantry. "You and Rett seem really happy," she added subtly.

"We are," Kate said, ignoring the connection to the bridal shop. "He's the best thing that's ever happened to me. I love him so much. I'm going to miss him this summer."

"Where are you going?"

"San Antonio, Texas. My roommate is from there, and she found us a job teaching ESL classes for six weeks."

"ESL?" Jenna questioned.

"English as a second language," Kate clarified.

"That's awesome!"

"Yeah, I'm excited."

"Five more minutes on the burgers," Chad called, sticking his head in the house.

"Thanks, honey," Jenna smiled.

"So, you and Chad, huh?"

"I don't know what to tell you," Jenna shrugged. "Opposites attract? He's my everything. I know he's a lot, but I wouldn't want him any other way. He helps pull me out of my shell, and I like to think I help balance him a little."

"That's sweet," Kate said as they gathered things to take outside for dinner.

Everyone crowded around and fixed a plate. "Are you coming to church tomorrow?" Nathan asked Hanna.

"I think so. Jenna?"

"Yes, we will both be there. I'm off this weekend, so I actually get to come."

"Do you work most weekends?" Kate asked.

"Yes, weekend nights. I'm in the NICU at Egleston," Jenna told them. Egleston was the Children's Hospital in Atlanta.

"Dang, girl," Kate's mouth fell open.

"Yeah, she's brilliant," Chad crowed.

"How in the world did she end up with you?" Rett laughed.

"I've been asking that for last five years, and I still don't have a satisfying answer," Hanna commented, needling her brother-in-law.

"God. Because I'm a pastor. It had to be God," Chad smiled triumphantly.

"You can't really argue with that one," Nathan shrugged, looking at Hanna.

"No, I can't. That's definitely the reason," Hanna said definitively, and everyone laughed as they helped clean up. When everything was picked up, Kate and Rett thanked Chad and Jenna for having them and got ready to leave.

"See you at church tomorrow," Kate said as she hugged Jenna. She waved to Chad as she got in the car. "Where's Nathan?" she asked, looking curiously at Rett.

"Hopefully asking Hanna out," Jenna answered, still standing by the open car window. "See you guys in the morning. And Kate, if you ever need a place to stay in Atlanta, you're always welcome here."

"Thank you, Jenna. Truly," Kate smiled.

Nathan finally made his way to the car. "So?" Jenna asked.

"We're going to the zoo on Monday," he laughed as he climbed into the back seat.

"Praise the Lord," Jenna cheered. "But listen, if you hurt my sister, I will kill you. And I'm a nurse, so I know how to do it," she added as menacingly as she could.

"Message received, loud and clear," Nathan winked. "See ya tomorrow."

They pulled out of the driveway and Kate turned to him. "If Rett got the idea for my roses from Joshua, what idea did you get for your future wife?"

"Slow down! We haven't even gone on a first date yet," Nathan said, but he couldn't stop smiling. "And I'm not Rett," he added. "I don't have everything planned out; I'm more of fly by the seat of my pants kinda guy. Yes, Joshua did teach us both about pursuing a girl's heart, but that doesn't mean our relationships will look the same."

That lesson was one thing Kate was learning—that no two relationships had to look the same. Because everyone is different. But she couldn't help imagining what Nathan and Hanna's relationship could look like.

Chapter Twenty

"You're here!" Caroline screamed. As soon as Kate's bag was in her hand from the baggage claim at the San Antonio Airport, they headed to Caroline's house. Kate was thankful the flight had been uneventful. "You're going to love your visit! We start first thing in the morning," Caroline gushed. She and Kate were volunteering as ESL teachers for six weeks. Most of their work would be with recent immigrants at a community center, but they would also serve once a week in a soup kitchen that fed many of the immigrants.

"Mom, we're home!" Caroline shouted as she busted through the door.

"Hey there, Kate," Tessa Drews greeted their guest. "Caro, dinner will be ready in ten minutes," she called after the babbling girls as they disappeared around the corner.

***

After a week working with the immigrants at the community center, Kate was enjoying her time with Caroline and all they were doing. Her first time at the soup kitchen was busier than she expected, though. She barely glanced up as she heard two of the younger guys ask for more bread. "Can we have more bread and another piece of cake?"

"You can have more bread, but we don't have enough cake for seconds," she replied as she handed them each a roll.

"Thanks."

"You're welcome." Just as they turned to walk away, Kate finally looked up and caught a glimpse of their faces. She nearly gasped. They looked just like the guys from that summer—the summer she turned fifteen. Suddenly, she couldn't be in the room anymore. Ripping off her gloves, she stepped outside to breathe, and Caroline followed her out.

"What's wrong?" Caroline asked, worried by her friend's quick exit.

"I'm so sorry. Those guys just brought up an awful memory," Kate apologized, still trying to catch her breath. She knew she had to explain herself to her best friend, so she managed to continue, "The summer before my sophomore year, we had a break-in. Two guys were trying to get into a gang, and they had to rob a house as part of initiation. My sister and I the only ones at home when it happened. I haven't thought about it in a while, but the two guys I just served looked exactly like the thieves. I mean, there is no way it could be the same guys. The ones who broke into our house are in prison in Georgia. And it was five years ago; they'd be older by now." Though what she said was true, Kate was visibly shaken.

"What in the world? Do you feel up to talking about what happened?" Caroline had no idea her friend had gone through something so extreme.

"Sure." Kate took a deep breath and began to tell Caroline what had happened. "My parents were gone, and Emmie Wren was supposed to be studying. She was on the phone, so I sat in the living room watching TV and waiting for Sky to get there to help her with school stuff." Kate let the memory come back for the first time in a while...

"Kate! Make sure you tell me as soon as Sky gets here!" Emmie Wren yelled from her room. Kate rolled her eyes. Of course, she would let her know; he was coming to see Emmie Wren, after all.

When Kate heard someone knock, she ran to let Sky in. Opening the door, she realized too late that Sky had not been the one knocking. Instead, in front of her stood two guys who were about Emmie Wren's age, and they both wore menacing-looking grins. She knew immediately they were up to no good. She tried to slam the door, but they were quicker, and the shorter one stuck his arm through the crack in the door to grab ahold of her.

They pushed her aside as she screamed, "Emmie Wren!" She saw the guys exchange a glance, and the taller one—the one who wasn't holding her arm—said, "You keep her. I'll go find the other one." He disappeared around the corner.

The shorter guy pushed her into the living room and pulled out a switchblade. "Go sit on the couch." Kate willingly sat down and then froze. What's gonna happen to me? I don't think these guys are here to just talk. Oh my gosh, what if he tries to rape me? *She was frozen at the thought. Then another horrifying thought passed through her head as she realized that Tall Guy hadn't come back yet. She had already named them "Tall Guy" and "Short Guy" in her head.* Where's

Emmie Wren? What's gonna happen to her? Oh, Jesus, help us!

Meanwhile, Emmie Wren was huddled behind the hamper in her closet. She still clutched her cell phone from her phone call. She had just hung up the phone when she heard Kate scream her name. Immediately, she knew something was very wrong, but instead of being a brave big sister, she ran and hid. She could hear the voices of two men. There was no telling what would happen to Kate. Suddenly, she remembered her cell phone. "Idiot!" she muttered to herself as she called 911.

"911, what's your emergency?"

"I think someone just broke into my house! It's just me and my sister, but I don't know where she is. I hear two men, and I think whoever broke in might have my sister. She screamed a few minutes ago, but I haven't heard her at all since. Please help us!" Emmie Wren was almost crying. "Our address is 615 Jay Bird Trail. Hurry!" She did start crying now.

"Okay, can you tell me your name?" the 911 operator asked, and Emmie Wren told her. She whispered for a few minutes while the operator tried to keep her on the phone. When she heard her bedroom door open, Emmie Wren hung up despite the operator's protests.

Tall Guy had checked all the rooms except one. He paused in the doorway of what he guessed had to be the other girl's room. Where was she? He blew out a breath. After all this, we had better get into the Hoods, *he thought.* Wait a sec. *A small sound from the closet got his attention. He opened the door and looked inside. It was a mess. Shoes and clothes were everywhere. Then he noticed the hamper at the back of the closet. Moving it aside, he finally saw the other girl. "Ha, found ya!" She whimpered as he grabbed her arm and pulled her out.*

Kate looked around the room, trying to find something to distract Short Guy or a way to get out of the house. Short Guy was pacing back and forth in between the front and back doors, both of which led outside, and simply running to another part of the house seemed pointless, especially with Tall Guy snooping around. If she could just distract him, she could at least get to the kitchen and maybe grab something to defend herself. On her third glance around the room, she finally saw the phone. It was on the end table to her right. She waited until Short Guy was facing away from her, and then she reached for it.

"Hey!" he shouted. As her fingers touched the phone, Kate felt a searing pain along her left side and back. "Don't do that!" he commanded as he yanked her arm back to her side.

"You—You cut me!" Kate gasped in pain as she shoved him away and tried to see how bad it was. She touched her left side, and her hand came away covered with blood.

Emmie Wren thought she was going to throw up when the guy grabbed her arm and pulled her out of the closet. He spotted her cell phone, snatched it away, and threw it somewhere in her room. As he did, they both heard the other man yell, "Hey!"

What's happened to Kate? Emmie Wren thought as she was dragged down the hall toward the living room.

As soon as they got to the living room, Emmie Wren saw Kate slouched on the couch, bleeding from a wound on her back. She wrenched free of the grip on her arm and hurried to her sister. "Kate, what happened?" Emmie Wren began to frantically run her hands over Kate, checking her wound, she was in nursing school, after all.

"Emmie Wren! I'm okay . . . for the most part," Kate said, trying to sound reassuring.

Then Kate saw the blood on Emmie Wren's hands and cried out. "Emmie Wren! What did they do to you?" In her confusion, she thought the blood was Emmie Wren's.

"I'm fine," her sister answered. "It's you we need to worry about. Can you calm down for me? And tell me what happened?" The shorter of the two invaders shifted uncomfortably, but surprisingly, neither of the men spoke. It was as though they didn't know what to do any more.

Kate nodded. "I didn't know if you were okay! I was trying to think of a way out when I saw the phone and thought maybe I could call for help, so reached for the phone, but he"—she nodded toward the shorter guy— "saw me before I could reach it. When he tried to stop me, he cut me with the switchblade he was holding." Kate grimaced. She felt light-headed and wondered how much blood she had lost.

The intruders had been standing by uncomfortably while the girls were talking, but now Short Guy spoke defensively, "I didn't mean to! She was trying to get the phone, and I just tried to stop her. The switchblade got her before I even remembered I was holding it."

His partner shoved him, hard. "You idiot! What are we gonna tell the gang now?"

Emmie Wren gasped and turned to face them, asking, "Are you gang members?" Seeing the fear on their faces, she closed her eyes and prayed without thinking, "Dear God, please help us."

Tall Guy—whatever his name was—looked startled. "God?" Then he sneered. "Like the 'Big Man Upstairs' is gonna help you." He threw his hands out and gestured around the room. "Don't you realize that we're in control here? You're fixin' to be just another statistic on somebody's whiteboard. I suggest you get over it. Besides, there isn't a God, anyway."

Emmie Wren sighed, this was not going like she thought it would. Where were the police? And Sky should have been there by now. She had to worry about the cut on her sister. Her hands were not helping stop the bleeding as much as she would have liked, but she was stuck on the couch without access to even paper towels. She was busy running her fingers over the wound, trying to make it wasn't too deep when a *flashbang device came rolling in through the back door. It went off, and before any of them registered what was happening, there were police streaming in.*

"Police! Everybody, freeze!" Emmie Wren and Kate couldn't have move if they wanted to. They stayed on the couch, exhausted and weak with relief as the officers arrested both guys.

"Hey, somebody get the EMTs in here!" an officer shouted as he noticed Kate's back. "This girl's got some problems."

The EMTs rushed in, put Kate on a gurney, and rolled her to the ambulance.

"Emmie Wren!" Kate heard Sky's voice and was thankful when they both climbed in the ambulance with her.

As Kate finished reliving that terrifying day, Caroline's voice brought her back to the present. "Kate, I had no idea. Are you sure you're okay? What happened next?"

"Emmie Wren and Sky stayed with me at the hospital until my parents came. It turns out he got stuck behind a tractor on the way over. I'm so glad he didn't show up in the middle of everything, but I'm also grateful he could be there for her while we waited. I lost a lot of blood and was in the hospital for about a day, but the blade didn't hit more than muscle and bone, thankfully. It took me a few weeks to recover, but I was fine overall. Now I just have nasty scar that runs from my left shoulder blade to just under my left breast, right along my bra line."

"Wow," Caroline breathed. "I wish I knew what to tell you, but I'm at a loss for words. I'm sure glad you told me, though. Have you told Rett?" she asked after a beat. "I feel like this story is probably something he should know about."

"I honestly don't think about it enough for it to have come up," Kate answered truthfully. "I'll call him later. Or maybe I'll wait until I see him. But I will tell him," she insisted after a significant look from Caroline. "Can you give me a few minutes to just pray before I come back inside?"

Caroline nodded and walked back in to keep serving. There was still a long line of people waiting for lunch. Kate prayed and forgave the thieves for the hundredth time. She thanked God for His protection and the peace that usually ruled in her heart, knowing that only He could heal her to the point that she sometimes even forgot about the entire incident. Then she took a few deep breaths before getting back to work.

Once Kate and Caroline were back at the Drews' house, they continued to speak in Spanish. They barely even realized they were doing it until Tessa pointed out that she had no idea was they were saying.

"Sorry, Mom!" Caroline laughed. "It's funny how we can just go into Spanish mode now that we're both getting so fluent. But the best is when we do it to annoy the boys," she winked.

Kate laughed. None of the boys understood Spanish, so it was easy for the girls to make them feel uncomfortable, especially because they always assumed the girls were talking about them. "The best was the night we just started saying random sentences in Spanish that made absolutely no sense," Kate agreed.

"Are Caleb and Cat coming for dinner?" Caroline asked, changing the subject to ask about her older siblings. They were both married, so they didn't all get together very often.

"All four of them should be here in about 30 minutes," her mom responded. It would be good to have her family together for the night.

As the girls were helping Tessa with dinner, the first couple showed up. "Kate, this is my brother, Caleb, and his wife, Cecily," Caroline introduced the couple that appeared in the kitchen.

"It's nice to finally meet you, Kate," Caleb said enthusiastically, hugging her. She felt like she already knew Caroline's siblings from the way her roommate talked about them.

The five of them were talking about school when the door opened again. "Hey Mom," Cat said as she walked in. Kate didn't realize how much Caroline looked like her sister until they were standing next to each other. "You must be Kate. I'm Catherine, but you can call me Cat."

"It's nice to finally meet you, Cat," Kate said.

"Where's Kyle?" Caroline asked about Cat's husband when she didn't hear the door open again.

"He's working this weekend," Cat answered, rolling her eyes.

"He's an ICU nurse who works mainly weekend nights," Tessa explained for Kate's benefit.

After a light-hearted dinner, the family worked together to clear the table and get the dishes put away. Then they all played a card game called Nertz. It was like a combination of solitaire and speed, and everyone got his or her own deck. It was Drews family tradition, but Kate held her own. She had been playing with Caroline since she introduced her to the game their first week of school.

Kate's time with Caroline passed too quickly. She learned so much about herself and about teaching during their six weeks in San Antonio, but as her time wound to a close, she knew she still had to tell Rett about the break in.

Chapter Twenty-One

"Welcome home!" Rett was waiting for her at the airport in Atlanta.

"I've missed you!" Kate kissed him, thankful she'd be able to spend a little time in the city before heading home to Albany for the rest of the summer.

"I thought we'd celebrate just the two of us and catch up before we meet your family for your birthday celebration tonight."

"I love that idea," she answered gratefully. Kate was thankful to be back with him. "Where are we?" she asked as the car stopped a short while later.

"Piedmont Park." Rett opened the door and walked around to let her out. They found a shaded spot and spread out a blanket he had brought to lounge on while they caught up on their summers.

"So, remember when I told you I needed to tell you something in person?" Kate started the conversation. Rett nodded, and Kate unfolded the story of the break-in, the two guys, and her scar. Telling it all to Caroline earlier in the summer made this re-telling easier than she expected.

"Wow, Kate. I had no idea you had gone through all that. I'm so sorry," Rett said, pulling her closer. Rett was quiet, lost in his own thoughts. She had told him about her scar, but he had his own story still to finish telling.

"Hey. Hey! What's wrong?" Kate's voice interrupted his thoughts as she looked up at him. Rett didn't even realize tears were running down his cheeks.

"Kate," he said softly. "I've only told you part of my story. You need to know the truth, but it's really hard for me to talk about. You know I was adopted by the Johnsons, but you don't know why." Rett took a shaky breath before continuing, "My mom— my birth mother—was a drug addict. I never knew my biological father. My mom was also physically abusive, especially when she was high, and she never made good choices with men. I can't remember how many apartments, houses, and dumps I lived in when I was younger. The one guy I actually remember her being with was Jack, and unfortunately, Jack didn't like kids much. He especially didn't like me—I guess because I took up some of my mother's time, which he'd prefer she spent with him?"

Questions were piling up in Kate's mind, but she could tell that Rett needed to finish the whole story at once, so she stayed silent. "Jack was a drunk and a druggie. He was always really mean when he was drunk or high, but I could usually avoid him. He did manage to send me to the hospital a few times when I got in his way, though. The last time it was really bad. That's when I ended up in foster care permanently, which is how the Johnsons ended up adopting me. But the Lord has brought me a long way, and I've forgiven my birth mother and even Jack—with God's help." There. He had finally told her all of it—well, almost all of it.

Kate clung to him tighter, she had a thousand questions running through her mind, but she knew he would tell her when he was ready. They remained silent, each lost in their own thoughts. Rett would never understand how he deserved this woman, who accepted him no matter what and seemed to take everything in stride.

They sat in an embrace for a long while until Kate broke the silence. "I love you," she said quietly. Then, after a pause, she said it again. "Hey—did you hear me?" She turned around to look him in the eye. "I love you so much," she repeated and kissed him.

"I love you too. Katie, when I'm with you, I feel like I'm home," Rett choked as he broke down. Kate didn't know what to do; she had never seen him like this. It was the first time he had truly sobbed around her. She just held him close and let the tears fall.

When I'm with you, I feel like I'm home, replayed over and over in her mind. This man she had fallen love with may have been Superman, but his kryptonite had defeated him today. She waited for his tears to stop, and when she finally felt him running his fingers through her hair, she knew everything was going to be okay.

"Sorry," his gravelly voice interrupted her thoughts.

"Don't be. I love you, Rett. *Nothing* is going to change that." Kate kissed him and wiped some of the tears off his face.

"You are too good to me," he whispered, putting his forehead to hers. "I love you more you can possibly know," he said as he kissed her. As they pulled away, he checked the time on his phone. "Time to go get your birthday gift before dinner. You ready?"

"Rett, you don't have to get me something extravagant," Kate insisted, standing up next to him.

"Your parents invited us to a fancy dinner to celebrate your birthday. I just want to get you a dress," Rett said. She crossed her arms and glared at him. "That's it, I promise!" He threw his hands up in surrender.

"Okay. You better not hand me a gift at dinner, too." Kate knew him well.

"Let's just go," Rett laughed softly, opening the car door for her. They headed to a cute little boutique where Kate settled on a simple dress made of soft pink lace. Rett paid, and they headed back to his apartment to get ready. When they got there, a bouquet of roses sat on Rett's coffee table, waiting for her. She kissed him in thanks and headed into the guest room.

Six, he thought as he went to change.

A short time later, they meet Kate's family at the Sun Dial restaurant in the Westin in downtown Atlanta. The restaurant featured a fabulous view of the sunset and the Atlanta skyline.

"Happy birthday, Katie," Charlie sang as soon as he saw his daughter, pulling her into a tight hug. "You look beautiful. How was San Antonio?"

"Thank you. It was a lot of fun! I learned so much," Kate answered.

"I'm glad! But I don't like you being that far from home." Emily hugged her daughter.

"Mom, I missed you too," Kate laughed. "This place is nice," she added, looking around at the restaurant and the incredible views of the city.

"We wanted to celebrate your birthday in style. It's not every day that my baby turns 20," Charlie said.

"Besides, if Dad was going to drive all the way to Atlanta just to come get you, he was going to make the trip a big deal," Emmie Wren added as she and Sky walked in.

"You're here!"

"Of course, I'm here. We weren't going to miss celebrating your birthday," Emmie Wren smiled.

Kate was glad to see everyone. As much as she had loved her time in San Antonio with Caroline, she had missed her family.

She only had a few more weeks until she would be heading back to Schaeffer.

She didn't want to think about the fact that this time,

It would be without Rett.

Chapter Twenty-Two

"Kate, you have to go. You're going to miss the welcome back party," Rett warned. He had been trying to get her out the door for the last hour. He was glad she had stopped by on her way to school, but he'd rather she get back before dark.

"I don't care. Schaeffer's not going to be the same without you. How am I supposed to leave you here?" Kate sighed. She didn't realize how hard starting a new year at school would be now that Rett had graduated.

"You are going to be fine. You've got Caroline, Lynne, and Mariah to keep you company," he reminded her.

"But they aren't you," she lamented.

"Katie, I know you don't like the idea of being in a long-distance relationship, and quite frankly, neither do I. But we don't really have a choice in the matter. You have to finish college so you can start teaching, and my job is here. But the good news is you only have to wait a month until you get to see me again. Remember, you're coming down for our anniversary and Kaden's birthday. A month; can you handle that?"

"You're still going to call and wake me every morning?" she asked, looking at him with her eyes wide.

"Of course." He kissed her. "Now go before Caroline starts calling me."

"Wait. Will you pray before I go?" Kate asked, and a smile spread across Rett's face. He pulled her close and prayed for a safe drive, for a good school year, and over their relationship as the long-distance began. After he finished, they put the last of her stuff in the car.

"You can do this; I will see you in a month." Rett kissed her again and sent her on her way.

* * *

"There you are! You're late," Caroline fussed when Kate walked into their apartment.

"Sorry; I didn't want to leave Rett," Kate half-smiled.

"Oh, girl, you are going to have to get over all that! We are going to have the best year," Caroline insisted. "Let's go! Lynne and Mariah are already there." They jumped in her car to head to campus for the welcome back party and concert. Once Kate was back with her friends on the college campus she loved, she was able to relax. It was going to be a great year, even if she was five hours from her boyfriend.

"Did you get to meet Nathan's girlfriend?" Mariah asked curiously when all four girls were back at their apartment.

"Yes. Honestly, she's awesome. Hanna's the perfect match for

Nathan's craziness," Kate answered carefully but truthfully.

"Good," Mariah nodded. "How'd they meet?"

"Her sister is married to one of the pastors at Rett's church," Kate said.

"Ah, okay." Mariah smiled. "I just hope she's good enough for him."

"Rye—" Lynne started.

"I don't like Nathan," Mariah interrupted, waving her hand at Lynne. "I have never liked Nathan. We are friends, and I am perfectly capable of being happy for him. Besides, I'm leaving at the end of the school year," she finished firmly. Then she got up and headed to her room before anyone else could say anything.

"I was just going to say that Nathan dating Hanna definitely wasn't a decision he made lightly," Lynne said, and the other girls both laughed.

***

"How's the school year going?" Rett asked as he finished getting dinner on the table. Kate had just arrived in Atlanta to celebrate their two-year anniversary. Thankfully, the first month had gone much faster than she expected.

"It's fine. Spanish is going to kill me, I'm pretty sure," Kate sighed.

"That rough?"

"It's my last year of it since I'll have to be in a classroom next year for student teaching. It's just advanced, like they're trying to teach us the entire language as fast as they can. I don't know how in the world Rye is majoring in it."

"You're going to be great. Just remember, it will be worth it when you're actually teaching Spanish," he assured her. Rett sat down in the seat across from her and prayed before they ate.

"Where's Nathan?" she asked. He was always around when there was food available.

"With Hanna. They are inseparable these days," Rett answered, smiling.

"It's getting pretty serious, huh?"

"She's coming with us to Texas for Thanksgiving, and they are going to see her parents in the next couple weeks," Rett said.

"Okay then!" Kate laughed. "Good for them. Do you like her?"

"She's great. She's Nathan's perfect match—which I never thought I'd say."

"Why is that?"

"Because I might be picky, but Nathan—he's a whole other story. He dated a couple girls in high school, but it was never very serious. When we got to college, I thought he'd date girls like he'd done before. But after our talk with Joshua, he decided he wasn't going to date a girl unless he could marry her. Then he was hung up on Rye for like a year, I'm not going to lie. But she was never interested in him, and they were such good friends that I think it scared other girls off. Anyway, I always knew it was going to take a special girl to get Nathan to commit, and Hanna is definitely that girl," Rett explained.

"Do you think they'll get married?"

"Yeah, I do," Rett smiled. "But don't repeat that. Ever."

"Got it," Kate promised, shaking her head. "What's the plan for tomorrow?"

"It's my day off, so feel free to sleep in. Just let me know when you're up, and then I thought we'd explore this cool city. There are some cute little downtown areas around here," Rett said as they finished up. "You up for a movie?"

"Sure," Kate said, and she helped him clean up the mess from dinner before they moved into the living room. They enjoyed a chill night in, and after the movie, Kate headed to Jenna and Chad's to spend the night.

* * *

"I surprised you're still here," Jenna said, offering Kate a cup of coffee when she walked into the kitchen the next morning. "I really didn't expect to see you."

"It's Rett's day off. I texted him when I got up." Kate sat down at the table with Jenna.

"Nice! Y'all are celebrating your anniversary, right?" her host asked.

"Yep! Two years," Kate grinned.

"That's awesome. Rett seems like a great guy," Jenna observed.

"He's the best. And Nathan is too, for the record," Kate added.

"I know; he's proven it. Hanna's head-over-heels for that boy, and he's kept up with her every step of the way," Jenna smiled.

"Good! I was always worried about someone having to keep up with Nathan," Kate laughed. "Thanks for the coffee. I really do need to go ahead and get ready. See you later," Kate excused herself as her phone lit up with a text from Rett. She got to Rett's apartment in time for them to head out for lunch. They ate at a little place before spending the day exploring the different neighborhoods around Atlanta. Dinner was a nice, quiet affair and the best way they could think of to celebrate two years of dating. They made a plan for the next morning and headed their separate ways for the night.

* * *

"Good morning, beautiful." After letting her sleep in the day before, Rett called Kate to wake her early the next morning.

"Five more minutes, handsome," Kate pleaded.

"We're going to Albany!" he reminded her. "You have to get up; Kaden's first birthday party is today. I will be there in thirty minutes."

"Bring coffee," Kate groaned, and she started to get ready. Rett pulled up at Chad and Jenna's at 7:30 am, and they got on the road.

"Happy birthday, Kaden!" Kate scooped up the birthday boy the minute they to Sky and Emmie Wren's. She gave him a big hug before asking her sister, "What do you need help with?" She set Kaden down and turned to help her sister and her mom with whatever they needed.

"Help us get all this food ready," her sister answer immediately. "Mom, will you find something keep Kaden entertained so you can help us too?" Emily laughed and got some of Kaden's toys for him to play with while they worked. Rett was helping the men in the backyard as they got everything ready for the *Cat in the Hat* themed party. They would celebrate Kaden with all things red and blue, popcorn, and Dr. Seuss. Emmie Wren, ever the master planner, had everything coordinated and looking perfect. There were pictures of Kaden from each month of his life, and soon he would be dressed in a onesie that said, "One I am." There were books for the guests to sign with prayers and words of encouragement for the years to come.

After most people had arrived, Emmie Wren stripped Kaden

178

down to his diaper and set a small cake in front of him. The one year old wasn't quite sure what to do with it at first, but as soon as some of the icing made it to his mouth, he was hooked. He was covered by the time he was finished eating. With much laughter, they got him cleaned up again. After games and great conversation, it was time to say goodbye to the guests and get things put away again. Overall, the day was a total whirlwind, but so much fun.

"Thanks for coming," Emmie Wren hugged Kate.

"We wouldn't have missed it," Kate gushed. "Bye, Kaden!" Kate kissed Kaden and hugged Sky as she and Rett headed to her parents' house for a quiet dinner before heading back to Atlanta. It was weird to think this was last time she would see her family before Christmas, since she and Rett were going to Texas for Thanksgiving.

"So, about tomorrow . . ." Rett started casually as he dropped her off at Chad and Jenna's house.

"What's tomorrow?" Kate grinned innocently. Even though they had already celebrated, the actual date of their anniversary was the next day.

"Oh nothing," Rett answered just as mischievously, keeping his hands on her hips. "I figured we'd just go to lunch so you can get on the road as soon as possible after church. I love you, you know. And I had a blast today."

"Lunch sounds perfect," she replied. "Today was a lot of fun, wasn't it? I'm so glad we were able to be there to celebrate with my family. Good night." Kate kissed him.

"Night. Oh, this is for tomorrow." Rett handed her a gift bag and got into his car before she could protest.

* * *

"Happy anniversary, beautiful," Rett said, waking her with his usual call on Sunday morning.

"Happy anniversary, handsome," Kate replied.

"I can't talk now, but I'll see you at church," he promised.

Kate spotted the gift bag on the floor and smiled. She had decided to wait to open it until this morning, on their actual anniversary. It was just like Rett to have one last anniversary surprise planned for her. She opened the bag a find another new dress. She did her makeup and curled her hair before putting it on. It was turquoise with a top that crisscrossed in the back. Where the straps met, there was a bow, and the skirt of the dress was covered in a Moroccan tile print. She managed to fix a cup of coffee and grab a bagel before Jenna came into the kitchen.

"I like that dress," she commented.

"Thanks. It's an anniversary gift from Rett. You ready?" Since the guys were already at church, the girls rode together to meet up with them.

"Have I mentioned that I love that dress on you?" Rett teased, wrapping his arms around Kate's waist when he saw her at church.

"Not yet," Kate laughed. Rett certainly liked to spoil her with gifts and time spent together. It felt good to celebrate two years together, and Kate was already dreaming about all the years to come.

But for now, she would go back to counting down the days until she got to see him again—

For Thanksgiving at Star Bright.

Chapter Twenty-Three

"I can't believe I only have few weeks left in this semester," Kate said, once again passing through Atlanta after Thanksgiving with Rett's family. "What did you think of Texas, Hanna?"

"Star Bright is special," she smiled. "I understand why y'all love it so much."

"And my parents love you," Nathan added, kissing her.

"I expected them to," Hanna teased before adding, "Especially since my parents love you."

"Your parents are just glad I'm not Chad," Nathan laughed.

"Not true! My parents think Chad hung the moon. But they think you're great too," Hanna replied.

"Nate, help me get Kate's suitcase in the car," Rett called, and the boys walked out of the apartment to load up Kate's car. She had driven to Atlanta and left her car at the boys' apartment while they were in Texas. It was just about time to start the five-hour drive back to Schaeffer.

"How have you only been dating six months?" Kate marveled at her friend as the door closed behind the boys.

"Yeah, it seems like things have moved pretty quickly, but we are at a different stage of life than you—"

"I swear, if one more person says that to me," Kate interrupted, blowing out a breath.

"Been a rough week?" Hanna asked.

"It's just—I have a year and a half of college left. All I want to is to be married to that man, but I'm stuck at Schaeffer, five hours from him."

"In the grand scheme of life, a year and a half is nothing," Hanna tried to console her. "I know it feels like forever right now, and I know it sucks. But college will be over in the blink of an eye."

"Blah, blah, blah," Kate responded, rolling her eyes. Then she changed her tone. "Sorry; I'm just so sick of hearing the same crap—from you, from Rett, from Emmie Wren. . . I just want to be able to see my boyfriend when I want." Kate pulled her knees into her chest.

Hanna knew the feeling of waiting for what you wanted, and it wasn't fun. She also knew that she was going to have to try a different approach with Kate if she was going to help her friend snap out of her funk. "Unfortunately, you don't get that luxury. So, what are you going to do about it?" she asked bluntly.

"Are you saying I need to fix my attitude?" Kate was impressed again at Hanna's ability to get right to the point.

"I'm saying you need figure out how to make the best of a bad situation. There is nothing you can do to change it," Hanna clarified.

"I know, I know."

"On the bright side, you only have two weeks before you're out for Christmas, and you get to spend the majority of the break with Rett. You can do this," Hanna added, trying to encourage Kate again after challenging her so directly. "Just take it one day at a time."

"Thanks," Kate sighed. "I'm just annoyed. But I did enjoy spending the week with you," she added, trying to pull herself out of her funk. "I'm truly glad you're dating Nathan. Y'all are great together."

"Thanks. He's something special," Hanna agreed.

"Okay, I really do need to get on the road," Kate sighed again. "I have class in the morning." Kate hugged Hanna on her way out the door.

Hanna closed the door behind Kate as she walked out. She told Rett and Nathan good-bye at the car, where they had been goofing off as they waited for her. On her way back to Schaeffer, she thought about her conversation with Hanna. She was right; Kate needed to make the most out of a bad situation. Besides, it would only be two weeks she got to see him again.

* * *

"Good morning, beautiful." Rett's phone call woke her up her first morning back in Atlanta after the semester ended. After two weeks of exams, she groaned, ready to sleep in a bit longer. "I'll see you after work," he reminded her. "I love you."

Kate smiled and rolled over. She loved being woken up by her boyfriend. When she finally managed to pull herself out of the bed, she got ready for the day.

"Sleep good?" Jenna greeted her, handing her a cup of coffee.

"I did. Thanks again for letting me stay," Kate said.

"Of course! You are always welcome here," Jenna assured her. They hung out for a little while before Jenna had to run a few errands. Kate enjoyed some time by herself after a hectic end to the semester before heading to Rett's. She got there just as he came home from work.

"Hi! I'm so glad you're here," Rett said, pulling her in for a kiss. "Oh, and this for you." He pulled out a button-up gaudy red and white sweater. It was covered with crazy decorations like a Christmas tree, a candy cane, and Santa Claus.

"That is fantastic," she grinned.

"It gets better," Rett said, holding up a matching sweater. Kate doubled over in laughter. They were going to have fun in their matching tacky Christmas sweaters at the youth Christmas party.

The party was at one of the youth kids' houses. When Kate and Rett pulled up to a house in one of the nicest areas in Atlanta, Kate was amazed. "Pick your jaw up off the floor," Rett jokingly chided her. "I told you it was nice."

The house that lay before her reminded her of an old plantation home with a wraparound porch and windows every ten feet. It was beautiful, and it was definitely big. "Oh, my word," Kate kept repeating as they walked up to a front door adorned with a cute wreath. The wreath was made of sticks with ribbon, ball ornaments, and a red and white polka-dotted G on it.

Rett knocked on the door, and they heard someone inside invite them in. "You're here!" Jane Gordon greeted them when they opened the door. "Rett, the guys are upstairs. And you must be Kate," she said approvingly. Rett laughed and shrugged at Kate before disappearing around the corner.

Kate took her coat off and found herself put to work in the kitchen. "So, tell me about yourself," Jane suggested as they prepared the food.

"I'm Kate Adams," Kate said, launching into a speech she had down to a tee thanks to all the introductions she had to make around campus. "I'm a junior Spanish education major at Schaeffer University in Tennessee, but I'm from Albany, Georgia. I have one older sister who has been married for four years. They have a precious little boy who is fifteen months old. Oh, and Rett and I have been dating for a little over two years."

"It's nice to meet you, Kate. I'm Jane. Welcome to our home," Jane said before her daughter interrupted her introduction.

"Mom, can I come downstairs now?"

"Is it clean up there?"

"Yes!"

"Okay. Kate's here," Jane replied as a girl who appeared to be about twelve rounded the corner.

"You're Kate? You're much prettier than Rett said. I'm Kayla, and I'm in sixth grade," she bubbled, and Kate felt her face turn red. Kayla was a cutie, and Jane put her to work as they started putting the food on the table. Jane gave Kate a grand tour of the house just before the kids started to arrive. After seeing the area of town and the splendor of the homes, Kate was surprised at how casual everything was in the Gordon house.

"I love the atmosphere of your home," Kate said to Jane after a while. "You have teenagers over here all the time, don't you?"

"Every day," Jane laughed. "My son, Rusty, always has friends over, and Kayla is starting to be the same way. Rusty is in Rett's discipleship group and just thinks the world of him," Jane explained.

Teenagers filled the house all evening, and Kate was truly happy to be with them. They all had a blast laughing, playing games, and eating the amazing food Jane had prepared. It was late when Kate and Rett finished helping the Gordons clean up and finally told them goodnight.

"I had a blast! Thank you for coming with me," Rett crowed, kissing her as they got out of the car at the apartment.

"I wouldn't have missed it," Kate replied. As she kissed him back, passion burned in her. They walked in the door and headed for the couch, where he kissed her deeply again. Neither one wanted to stop.

"How was tonight?" Nathan interrupted, stepping out of his room. They pulled apart so Rett could answer, and Kate caught her breath. As the boys talked, she smiled, waved, and slipped out the door.

"That was a close one. Thanks, dude," Rett breathed, sinking into the couch, thankful for his best friend.

"No problem; that's what friends are for. No need to make stupid mistakes as long as I'm around," Nathan joked, slapping him on the back. As the two talked, Rett's mind kept running through what had just happened and the desires he had for Kate—both physically and to protect their relationship from actions they might regret later.

* * *

"There is nothing wrong with what you're feeling," Emmie Wren assured her sister. Kate had called her near tears as soon as she got to her car. "It's called being sexually attracted to him, and it's part of being in a loving relationship. You just have to be careful—like you were tonight—and you'll be fine."

"Thank you, Emmie Wren. It's just never been this bad; I'm shaking." Kate was thankful she could be so honest with her sister. They talked for a few more minutes, and Emmie Wren prayed over Kate before she hung up. She gathered herself before walking into Chad and Jenna's, heading straight to the guest room.

"Good morning, beautiful," Rett said when he called the next morning.

"Good morning, handsome," Kate said groggily. "I'll be there soon." Knowing she needed to talk to Rett before she saw anyone else, Kate pulled herself out of bed, quickly got ready, and was out the door before Jenna and Chad were even out of their room.

"Sorry about last night," Rett began, hugging her when she walked in the door.

"Stop, Rett," Kate admonished. "I was part of it too. Thankfully nothing happened. But the fact that it could have is worrying me. Maybe it's time we talked about our boundaries again?" Talking about their boundaries had been her sister's idea, but she knew it was a good one. They had agreed when they first started dating that they wanted to wait to have sex until after marriage, but it had been a while, and there was so much grey area between kissing and sex.

"I'm going to pray before we have this conversation," Rett said, bowing his head. "Dear God, we want this relationship to honor you, and the biggest way we can do that is by treating each other with love and respect. May our conversation help us maintain the standards we have set for ourselves and each other in a way that glorifies you. Help us to show each other love and remember that every good thing is from you including our relationship with each other. In your son's name I pray, Amen." The couple sat on the couch and talked about their physical and emotional boundaries and their relationship in ways they had not done in a while. It was definitely a needed conversation.

They finished, and Kate kissed him gently. "Thanks," she sighed. "I love you."

"And I love you, Katherine Joy," Rett said as they walked into the kitchen. Kate grinned when she saw the bouquet of roses sitting on the table. "I bought these knowing that we needed to have that conversation. I'm glad it went well so I don't look ridiculous right now," he said.

"They are beautiful. Thank you, Superman," Kate answered, staring at bouquet number seven. It dawned on her that she was officially over halfway to getting engaged to the man of her dreams—if everything went according to plan.

For now, she couldn't think too far ahead.

Instead, she'd focus on looking forward to spending Christmas with her Superman.

Chapter Twenty-Four

"It should not be this hard to find mason jars," Lynne sighed, pushing her computer away.

"Wedding planning getting to you?" Kate giggled from the kitchen table where all her stuff was spread out for studying.

"Like you wouldn't believe. It was supposed to be a nice study break, but now I'm more frustrated than I was before," she sighed. "I wanted to use mason jars as part of the centerpieces, but I can't find enough, and the ones I do find are ridiculously expensive. It might be time to re-think things. How's the paper coming?"

"It's coming. I have no motivation, but it has to get done." Kate stood to stretch after sitting for so long.

"I understand that feeling all too well," Lynne laughed.

"I'm sure, Miss English major." Kate shook her head. "Hey, it's just us for the evening. Caroline's with Patrick and Rye's working late. Do you want to take a real break? I can help with wedding stuff."

"How far you into that paper?" Lynne, ever the mom of the group, wanted to know.

"About a page." Kate ran her hands down her face. "It's only supposed to be three pages long, and it's not due until next weekend," she reassured her roommate.

"Okay. I need an hour to finish up some work but then yes, let's take a break." The friends did just that. Once the hour of studying was up, they fixed dinner together.

"What do you need my help with?" Kate asked as they ate.

"I know it's not exciting, but I really need some help getting the guest list under control. I have a list, Houston has list, and our parents have lists, and every time I go to combine them, I just get overwhelmed. But I'm running out of time. We are going to have to actually send invitations in a few weeks," Lynne said.

"I'm here to help however I can," Kate smiled. Despite the seemingly boring task, they laughed and enjoyed the break from schoolwork in the midst of the heaviness of the semester. It was hard to believe that they only had a couple more months of living together before everything changed again.

* * *

"Sorry; I got caught in awful traffic," Kate apologized, walking into Rett's apartment Friday night. She was so glad to be on spring break. It was hard to believe how fast the semester had gone. Even though she missed Rett every day, she was trying to soak up being with Mariah and Lynne as much as possible during their last semester.

"You're fine," Jenna answered, walking out of the kitchen.

"What are you doing here?" Kate asked, confused.

190

"Nathan's proposing tonight, so we're here to celebrate when he and Hanna get back," Jenna said, grinning from ear to ear.

"What?" Kate asked excitedly. "Wait, where's Chad?"

"He just took his bleach trays out," Rett joked, coming into the room and rolling his eyes. Kate bit her lip to stifle her laugh.

"You're as bad as Nathan," Jenna chided. "No, he's almost here. He went to pick up dinner," she informed Kate.

"Oh, okay," Kate laughed. It was crazy that Nathan was already proposing when he and Hanna had not even been dating a year yet. But they had been very intentional about everything in their relationship, and they were confident they wanted to be together for the rest of their lives. Kate, Jenna, Rett, and Chad were about to put a movie in when the door opened.

"We're engaged!" Hanna screamed. Kate jumped up to hug her and see the ring. It was beautiful vintage-style ring with a round cut diamond. Then Kate stepped aside to watch as the sisters embraced and squealed in excitement.

"I'm so happy for you, Hann, really," Jenna said.

"Dang boy, you did good!" Kate said approvingly to Nathan. "You better help him pick out mine out," she added, elbowing Rett in the ribs.

"What makes you think he picked out that one?" Rett shot back, and Kate cocked an eyebrow.

"Whatever. When the time comes, tag team, okay?" Kate responded.

"What's the story? How'd you propose?" Chad asked as they all sat down in the living room.

Hanna started the story, "I have always wanted a monogrammed necklace and have brought it up to Nathan a few—"

"A few hundred times," Nathan interrupted, rolling his eyes. "After dinner, we were on a bench, and I pulled out a wrapped gift."

"I was really confused until I opened it to find a silver monogrammed necklace. I was thanking him profusely, but he was still acting really weird. That's when I noticed it." Hanna paused and pulled the necklace out her pocket. "The middle initial wasn't a B; it was a D!" Kate's hand flew over her mouth.

"Hanna got really quiet when she finally noticed. I said, 'I know you can't wear it yet, so I got you something you can and got off the bench and knelt in front of her and—"

"Said a bunch of stuff I didn't hear because I was too excited. But I was pretty sure he asked me marry him somewhere in there, so I said yes! We grabbed some dessert to spend a few more minutes together before coming back here," Hanna finished the story.

"You don't know what I said?"

"Nope," Hanna laughed. "You'll have to tell me again when I'm not so excited and can actually focus on it." She kissed him, and he laughed.

"You did good, Nathan." Jenna hugged him. "Welcome to the fam, officially."

"Are we still good for joining your Atlanta adventures tomorrow?" Chad asked.

"Yes," Rett answered. "Are y'all heading out now?"

"Yep. Kate, do you want to just ride with us?" Jenna offered, and Kate took her up on it. They said their goodbyes, and the apartment cleared out.

"You're really getting married, huh?" Rett looked at his best friend.

"Finally! I'm so excited about the things God has in store for my life. Hey, will you be my best man?" Nathan asked.

"Like I would let you ask anyone else."

* * *

"Good morning, beautiful," Rett greeted her with a kiss when she got to the apartment with Jenna, Chad, and Hanna the next morning. The group was spending the day at the aquarium and the World of Coke. It was something they had never done, and Rett was looking forward to a fun day out with his friends.

At the aquarium, they enjoyed seeing all the fish and sea creatures. Kate's favorite was the jellyfish, and Hanna's favorites were the penguins. Chad was all about the whale sharks, and he had even set up a swim with them. They all got to watch him dive with animals in the tank.

"Of course, Chad has his SCUBA license," Nathan laughed. "You didn't want to do that with him?" he asked Jenna.

"No. I don't like SCUBA diving at all. He tried to talk me into getting my SCUBA license while we were dating, but it's not my thing. He spent a couple summers in Hawaii while he was college. That's when he got certified," Jenna explained.

Once they had seen and done everything they wanted to at the aquarium, the group headed to the World of Coke, which was right next door. "You have to taste this one," Nathan insisted, handing Rett a sample of the Coke flavor he had just tried.

Rett drank it and nearly spit it out. "That is disgusting!" Everyone laughed, and they continued to try the flavors of Coke from all over the world. Rett and Nathan especially loved it.

"This has been the perfect weekend," Hanna announced as they ate dinner at their favorite restaurant downtown. She looked lovingly at her fiancé. "I can't wait to spend the rest of my life with you." They kissed, and everyone laughed.

"Y'all are too cute," Kate said as their waiter walked up. They ordered and talked about Nathan and Hanna's plans.

"How long have y'all been friends?" Hanna asked Nathan and Rett.

"Too long," Nathan said looking at Rett, who didn't know what to say. They had been friends since the day Rett came home from the hospital with Johnsons.

"Since we were six," Rett said. It was the truth, and Kate was starting to recognize the moments when Rett's answers pointed to—or rather skirted around—the story of his adoption. "We've always been pretty inseparable."

"Dang, that *is* too long," Hanna laughed. Kate smiled, pulled out of her thoughts; she was thankful Rett had Nathan in his life.

"Which is why Rett is going to be my best man," Nathan told Hanna. She was clearly happy for him, even though they had not really talked about the bridal party yet. Nathan and Rett shared some of their favorite memories, each man trying to embarrass the other just a bit more with each story. They were all in stitches by the end of dinner.

* * *

"When do y'all leave for D.C.?" Nathan asked at lunch after church on Sunday.

"Thursday morning," Kate answered him.

"D.C.?" Hanna asked, confused.

"My brother-in-law is a baseball coach, and his team has a tournament in D.C. this week. He's staying through the weekend and invited us to join him and my sister," Kate explained.

"That will be fun! Are y'all doing anything special while you're there?"

"Nope, just sightseeing and exploring," Rett grinned.

"I'm sure Emmie Wren has a whole schedule for us," Kate countered, rolling her eyes. Sometimes Emmie Wren could go a little overboard when it came to planning.

"I'm all for it. I've never been to D.C., so I want to see as much as possible," Rett assured her.

"Let's hope you don't regret that statement," Kate laughed. She knew how her sister could be. The week with Rett flew by, but she enjoyed her time with him before they headed to D.C.

"This place is nice," Kate observed as she set her bag down in the hotel room she was sharing with her sister.

"I know! I'm going to see a few of Sky's games. Do you and Rett want to come? Or you are welcome to explore the National Mall this afternoon instead."

"I think we'll see the National Mall," Kate laughed. "Have fun, though. See you for dinner?"

"I'll let you know if they win," Emmie Wren replied. As she walked out of the room, Kate texted Rett to meet her in the lobby. They had a quick lunch and spent the afternoon exploring the National Mall. They saw all the major monuments together. Rett's favorite was the Martin Luther King, Jr. Memorial, and Kate loved the view from the Lincoln Memorial. When Kate got a text from Emmie Wren, she and Rett headed back to the hotel to get changed for dinner. Sky's team didn't win, but it meant they would get to spend the rest of the weekend with her sister and brother-in-law.

Friday was spent at Museum of the Bible, which they all loved. It was an extremely put-together museum, and they each learned something new. On Saturday, they spent the morning at Arlington National Cemetery seeing the Tomb of the Unknown Soldier and finding JFK's grave before lunch. They bounced around museums for the afternoon, but their favorite was the Holocaust Museum. Even the guys were nearly moved to tears by the things they saw and learned. On Sunday morning, the group found a church to visit before their flight that afternoon.

"This weekend was so much fun! Thanks for inviting me," Rett said as they parted ways with Sky and Emmie Wren in the Atlanta airport.

"I'm just glad you were able to come. I hope this is the first of many vacations together," Sky grinned.

"Me too!" Kate chimed in. She couldn't stop smiling. After one last goodbye, Kate headed back to Schaeffer. As soon as she was out of sight, he called the florist so that bouquet number eight would be waiting on her when she got back to her apartment in Jackson for the last few weeks before Lynne and Mariah graduated.

Chapter Twenty-Five

"I can't believe y'all are really graduating," Caroline marveled, bobby pinning Mariah's cap into her hair. It had been a quick run to the end of the semester.

"Graduating is not the thing I'm worried about," Mariah smiled wryly.

"We're not talking about you leaving," Caroline insisted, finishing with Mariah's cap.

"Okay, listen." Mariah stood up and closed the door. "This is, like, my one chance to talk to you without Lynne and Kate around. There's something else we need to talk about."

"Why do you have to be so dramatic?" Caroline asked, rolling her own eyes dramatically.

"It's who I am; deal with it," Mariah answered bluntly. "We need to talk about you and Patrick," she started.

"Rye, what are you talking about?"

"Do you love him?"

"Patrick? Yeah. Or at least I think I do," Caroline smiled.

"You've been dating him for nearly three years and you can't answer that question with one hundred percent certainty?" Mariah stared hard at her friend. "That boy would marry you tomorrow; I know, because he's talked about it with the guys. So, you need to either get serious or cut him loose. You're about to be a senior in college; it's time to figure out what you want. You both only have one year left at this school. Then you're going to get jobs. You have to decide if he's going to factor into the decisions you will be making or not."

"Who are you to—" Caroline started to get defensive.

"I am the girl who is about to watch her best friend get married to a girl who is not me," Mariah answered, knowing where Caroline's sentence was going. Caroline's head snapped to face her. "For the last four years, more people than you think have told me that someday Nathan and I would end up together. I came to college with a plan: get my Spanish degree and go to the mission field. I wasn't willing to compromise that for some college romance, some boy. So, I friend-zoned Nathan, regardless of how I could have felt for him. I friend-zoned him so hard. But the more people tell you something, the more you begin to believe it. Somewhere in the back of my mind, I always thought that someday, it would be me and Nathan. But here we are, a month out from his wedding to a lovely girl. Therefore, I am the most qualified person to have this conversation with you," Mariah ended emphatically.

"Okay, okay. I hear you," Caroline said.

"I don't think you do," Mariah observed, "but I've said my piece, and that's all I can do. Now, I have to go or I'm going to late. Do you want a ride to campus?"

"Sure," Caroline answered, trying to shake off their conversation. While she waited on graduation to start, she thought about her relationship with Patrick.

"There you are! I've been texting you," Kate told her as she sat down next to her.

"Sorry." Caroline shook out the cobwebs. "Mariah said some things to me earlier, and I can't—"

"Rye doesn't always have the best timing," Kate interjected, "but normally, when she does say something, you know she spent a long time thinking through it. She's getting ready to leave, so she's trying to say everything before she does. She gave me a whole speech about senior year earlier this week," Kate laughed.

"Glad I'm not the only one," Caroline smiled.

"Do you want to talk about it?"

"Not yet. It's hard to believe it's going to be just us next year," Caroline sighed.

"I know; I'm not really sure how to handle it," Kate said as the graduation ceremony started. They watched as two of their best friends graduated, each lost in her own thoughts about the future. The four roommates celebrated together before Caroline and Kate headed to Albany to spend the few weeks before the flurry of upcoming weddings.

* * *

"Happy wedding day!" Kate chirped as she and Caroline walked into the room where Lynne was getting her hair and makeup done. "We brought you coffee."

"You're the best! I love you," Lynne said as she took the coffee cup from her friend.

"You look beautiful," Caroline gushed, squeezing Lynne's hand.

"Make yourselves at home." Lynne smiled, and it was easy to see how happy she was. Kate and Caroline settled in among the bridesmaids. With Lynne's four sisters, Houston's sister, and Mariah all serving as bridesmaids, Lynne's wedding party was pretty big. The group of girls talked and laughed, reminiscing about Houston and Lynne. The bride and groom had been together for six years and were hours away from stepping into marriage, but it was also fun for Kate and Caroline to hear stories of what each had been like before their relationship.

Throughout the morning, Caroline and Kate busied themselves with helping however they could. They set up the candy bar at the reception, finished hanging decorations in the sanctuary with Lynne's mom's friends, and made sure the boys had everything they needed. Once the bridesmaids headed out to take pictures, Kate and Caroline got ready for the wedding themselves. Once they had changed, Lynne even had them join in a couple of pictures.

Caroline and Kate found seats in the church and watched as two of their dearest friends became husband and wife. It was beautiful ceremony, full of personal touches like their own vows, Lynne's sisters singing "How Great Thou Art" while the bride and groom took communion, and a recessional dance down the aisle to the song "Signed, Sealed, Delivered."

The reception was in the fellowship hall of the church where Lynne had grown up. Caroline, Kate, and Hanna found the table they would share with the guys, who wouldn't arrive for a while since they were groomsmen. They talked to some of Lynne's high school friends while they waited for the bridal party. Once the bridal party was introduced, Houston and Lynne had their first dance, and the speeches began. Lynne's sisters had worked together on a speech that had everyone in stitches, and Houston's siblings told the story of him asking her to prom all those years ago. Lynne's grandad—who had officiated the wedding—said the blessing, and dinner was served.

"You are beautiful," Rett whispered as he finally sat down next to Kate.

"Thank you," she answered, kissing him.

As the newly married Singletarys made the rounds to say hello to their guests, Nathan asked, "So how does it feel? Any different?"

"Ask me next weekend when I see you at your own wedding; I'll have a better answer for you," Houston laughed.

* * *

"I can't believe you're really getting married," Rett helped Nathan tie his bowtie the very next weekend.

"Me neither, but I'm so glad to be. You're not going to be too far behind me, right?"

"Not planning to be," Rett smiled. "Hopefully sometime next summer."

"Seriously? I don't think I've ever heard a timeline." Nathan shrugged his tuxedo jacket on. "What you think?"

"You look good, dude."

"I'm just ready to see Hanna," Nathan said as they met up with the photographer. They took pictures of the groomsmen before Nathan headed to have a special first look at his bride before the wedding. Rett went with him because he was best man and Nathan wanted him there, but he stayed back as Hanna appeared with her auburn hair pulled up in a low bun. She wore a beautiful lace wedding gown, smiling and trying not to cry all at the same time as she made her way to Nathan.

"Nathan," she managed to get out, and he turned around.

He uttered an audible gasp, and tears formed in his eyes. "Wow! You are beautiful. I love you," he choked.

"I love you, too." Their lips touched, and he realized that she was almost his; it was only a matter of minutes before they would be husband and wife. They took a few pictures together and got ready for the ceremony. Though it seemed to fly by, their wedding was a beautiful expression of the gospel and the joyous union of two people who loved the Lord.

"Happy birthday, beautiful," Rett said when he finally got some time with Kate after the ceremony. He wrapped his arms around her and kissed her.

"Thank you. You look amazing in a tux, for the record," she noted as she smoothed out his jacket.

"Good to know," he laughed as they walked to the car for the ride to the reception. "Have you had a good day so far?"

"Yes! The girls and I managed to find a brunch spot this morning to celebrate my birthday and say goodbye to Rye," Kate told him.

"That sounds like fun. I just spent the day with Nathan," Rett shrugged.

"So, a normal day then?" Kate laughed. They pulled into the reception venue a few minutes later—a lake house with beautiful back porch. In the house, they split up one last time so that Rett could be introduced with the bridal party. Kate had a spot at the head table since Rett was the best man, so she started to head to her seat.

"Kate!" someone shouted.

She spun around to see Rachel standing there. "Hi," she answered, hugging her. "Sorry I didn't see you! I'm lost in my head, I guess. It's been a crazy day."

"You're fine," Rachel smiled. "Happy birthday, by the way. Want to join me for a bit? I know everyone will want to say hello." Rachel motioned to the rest of the Johnson family, and Kate walked over to chat until the reception formally started. When the bridal party arrived, she found her seat as they introduced the bridesmaids, groomsmen, and the new husband and wife. Then Jenna and Rett each toasted Nathan and Hanna.

"You did great, Superman," Kate whispered as he sat down. They spent the evening dancing the night away with their closest friends, all together for one last time.

"I can't wait for it to be us," Kate sighed. She and Rett kissed as they stood outside the hotel she was staying at with Caroline.

"Me neither." His eyes sparkled, but he was a little distracted. "Can we talk about something?"

"Anything," she replied.

"Today, Hanna and Nathan kissed before the ceremony, during their first look. I just don't know that I want to do that."

"What are you talking about? Do you mean that you don't want to have a first look?"

"No. I mean. . . We can decide on that later. But what if we made the decision—and this may sound a little strange—but what if we decided that we wouldn't kiss from the time we got engaged until our wedding day?" Rett asked cautiously.

"Where is this coming from?" Kate loved kissing him, and she wasn't sure she would want to give it up once a wedding was in view.

"I don't know. I just I want our wedding kiss to be special, and temptation is only going to get worse as the big day approaches. I love you, and I just don't want to mess anything up," he tried to explain. Rett's hands were shaking.

"Rett," she said gently as she took his hands, "if this something you want to commit to, I'll try. But I honestly don't think it will work."

"Katie?" He was a little taken aback by her doubt.

"What? We've been dating for close to three years already," she explained. "By the time we get engaged, it will have been even longer. It would be really hard"—she shrugged— "If you want to try, we can, but it's going to take some major accountability. I agree that our wedding kiss should be special, but I just think there are other ways to do it. For starters, I was in total agreement when I thought you didn't want to do a first look. I don't plan to see you on our wedding day until I walk down the aisle, so the first time we kiss that day will be when Joshua says, 'I now pronounce you man and wife. You may kiss the bride.'" She ended with a smile as she thought of what their wedding day could be like.

"That sounds like a much more doable plan," he agreed. "Why are you so awesome?"

"Because I have you, and I love you more than anything." Kate kissed him. "You really want to give those up—for any amount of time?" she laughed.

"Yeah, I don't know what I was thinking," he smiled.

"We could try the wedding week if you *really* want to. That's another option," Kate said as the smile continued to spread across her face.

"I can't believe you're really leaving in the morning," Rett sighed, abruptly changing the subject. "I'm so excited for you, though."

"I'm excited about all the Spanish I'll be speaking this summer. I'm going to miss you while I'm San Antonio. But first, we have to say goodbye to Rye."

Chapter Twenty-Six

"I can't believe this is it," Lynne said as the four girls stood in the lobby. She and Houston had returned from their honeymoon in time for Nathan and Hanna's wedding, but she had been most adamant about being back in time to see Mariah off to her Journeyman orientation.

"You'll see me before I leave for Mexico, I promise," Mariah assured her as they hugged.

"I better! Two years is a long time." Lynne had tears running down her cheeks.

"No; no tears. You promised. You knew this was coming. This trip to Mexico, these years as a missionary—this is what I've always wanted to do," Mariah reminded her friend.

"You're right. I just don't like that you're going to be so far away."

"I'm just going to Mexico," Mariah laughed. "I'm still going to be in the same time zone as you! Besides, you are a married woman now, so it's not like we can live together anymore," she teased.

"We're still going to miss you," Caroline chimed in.

"Schaeffer is going to so weird without both of you," Kate added.

"You survived a year without the boys; you can handle a year without us," Lynne said, smiling and drying her tears.

"But I'm just glad to know that I will be missed," Mariah laughed again. "And Kate, I expect an invite to the wedding of the century, even if I can't come."

"Of course, but you'll probably miss Caroline's too," Kate said, but Caroline seemed to find something on the ground more interesting than their conversation just then.

"Caroline, care to comment?" Mariah nudged her friend's foot, causing her look up.

"Don't worry, we won't let you miss it, even if we have to do it over the phone." Caroline wasn't ready to talk about her own potential wedding when she had not even fully figured things out with Patrick yet. "We love you, Rye. You're going to do great things. And you know that all you have to do is pick up the phone if you need us. We're always going to answer."

"Yes, and we're praying for you—always," Kate added reassuringly. "And don't forget to have fun!" Kate hugged her before Lynne, who didn't want to let her go.

"If I don't leave now, I'm going to be late. It's long drive to Richmond," Mariah said as she peeled her best friend's arms off her.

"Wait, let's pray before you leave," Kate said as Rett, Houston, and Patrick walked up. "Perfect! Y'all are just in time. We're going to pray for Rye before she leaves."

"That sounds like a great plan," Houston said as the seven of them gathered together.

"I'll start. Lynne, you want to close?" Rett asked, and she nodded. They took turns praying for Mariah and her commitment to spend the next two years of her life serving the Lord in Mexico. They prayed she would have community and serve the Lord faithfully. It was a sweet sendoff for Mariah, who was tearing up as she got in her car to head to Virginia for orientation.

"Do y'all time have for brunch before your flight?" Lynne asked Kate and Caroline.

"Yes, that would be great," Caroline answered, and they found a spot to eat together before going their separate ways for the summer.

Patrick and Rett dropped the girls off at the airport. "I'm going to miss you so much while you are in San Antonio," Rett said, hugging Kate.

"I'm going to miss you too," Kate smiled. "It's only two months. We survived last summer, and this is literally the exact same thing."

"Two months," he repeated and kissed her. "Last time you came back from teaching Spanish in San Antonio, though, you told me about the break-in. Hopefully you won't have any big news to share when you get back this year," he smiled. "I just want you to have a fun, productive, uneventful summer."

Kate noticed that things seemed a little tense between Patrick and Caroline as they said goodbye. As soon as the girls had walked through security, she started cautiously, "Can we talk about what is going with you and Patrick? Because you've been acting strange since Lynne's wedding."

"Mariah got in my head at graduation. Basically, she said that I needed to decide what I was doing in my relationship with Patrick because he was head over heels for me." Caroline rolled her eyes.

"Wow!" Kate let out a low whistle.

"Yeah, so, things with Patrick haven't been the greatest the last couple weeks." Caroline sighed dramatically as she found a seat at their gate.

"I take it that means you're still figuring things out?" Kate asked, and Caroline gave her one of her signature stares. "Got it. Well, if you need to talk things through, I'm here." Kate reached into her bag for her book, leaving Caroline to stew in her own thoughts. Kate hoped Caroline would take her up on her offer to talk, but it didn't happen in the airport or on the plane. They met up with Caroline's parents in the airport, and when they got back to the house, there were two bouquets of flowers sitting on the counter. One was a dozen red roses, which Kate knew was her ninth bouquet from Rett. The other was a beautiful arrangement for Caroline from Patrick. As Kate watched her friend breathe in the beautiful fragrance, she thought things might work out for them after all.

* * *

"Welcome home!" Emmie Wren said, hugging her sister. The two months had seemed to fly by, and Kate was already back in Albany for a quick visit before senior year began. "How was San Antonio?"

"It was really good!" Kate replied enthusiastically. "I have really enjoyed getting to spend the last two summers teaching with Caroline and improving my Spanish."

"You ready for senior year?"

"Senior year; that's insane. I'm still not sure how I got here," Kate sighed, shaking her head in wonder.

"College goes by too fast, but I'm ready for you to be back here in Albany, teaching with Sky and helping with our kids," Emmie

Wren said, smiling wryly.

"That's the dream. I just hope Rett gets a job in Albany soon, because I would like to be married to him in this dream, too." Then Kate realized what Emmie Wren was smiling about. "Wait, did you say kids? As in more than Kaden?"

"I did," Emmie Wren nodded.

"You're pregnant?" Kate was thrilled.

"Yep! You ready to be an aunt again?"

"So ready! Are you going to find out what you're having this time?"

"Nope; it's going to be a surprise again," Emmie Wren laughed before bringing the conversation back to the dream life Kate had described. "So . . . you and Rett . . . do you have any idea when you think you'll get married?"

"He's given me nine bouquets so far. Three more before he proposes, but it is senior year, and I'm hopeful we'll be engaged by graduation. So maybe next summer or the fall?"

"What about jobs?"

"That's something we'll have to figure out when the time comes. I can't think about it all at once or it stresses me out," Kate sighed.

"Fair enough," Emmie Wren laughed. "How long before you leave me again?"

"Two weeks," Kate smiled. "And I'm going to enjoy every last second of it."

Two weeks with her sister flew by as she got ready for one final year at Schaeffer—one that would very different from the rest. She and Caroline were the only two left in the apartment they had shared for two years with Mariah and Lynne. Patrick, in his final year of grad school, was the only guy left from their group.

Lynne and Houston had moved to Memphis where Houston was in dental school, and Mariah was headed to Mexico now that her orientation was over.

Since Kate and Caroline were both education majors, even their course load looked different. Senior year meant they would spend more time in actual schools than in college classes. They'd observe classrooms in the fall semester and then work as student teachers in the spring. They were excited about the possibilities in front of them, and the first few weeks passed quickly. Labor Day was there before they knew it.

Chapter Twenty-Seven

"Are you ready yet?" Rett stood impatiently in the doorway of the guest bathroom at his apartment. Kate was beautiful with her long blonde hair hanging down her back, but she was also taking forever to get ready.

"Why are you rushing me? We aren't leaving till Nathan and Hanna get here."

"Which should have been five minutes ago," he responded. He was excited about their trip to Destin, Florida, and was anxious to get on the road. Caroline and Patrick had gone to Nashville to spend the long weekend with his family, which was a major step for them. To round out their beach group, Rett had invited Rachel and a couple of her friends to join them. He was thankful his sister was finally old enough to be a fun addition to a trip like this.

Kate turned around and glared at him. "Don't make me hurt you." There was a fierceness in her ocean blue eyes, but Rett just laughed as they heard the door open.

"Are we leaving?" Nathan asked as soon as he walked in. Kate rolled her eyes and quickly finished her hair so they could head out to the car. "How's old Schaeffer treatin' ya?" Nathan asked once they were on the road.

"It's good! Hard to believe it's my last year," Kate answered.

Once they were outside Atlanta, they stopped for dinner before making the rest of the trip. They all talked until Kate and Hanna fell asleep just a few hours from Destin.

"What?" Rett felt his best friend's eyes on him.

"Does she know everything?" Nathan finally asked.

"Yes. Almost. Everything but what Jack did to me," Rett replied.

"Your shirt still hasn't come off?"

"Nathan," Rett said, rolling his eyes.

"EJ, we are going to the *beach*, and she isn't going to be the only one asking why your shirt is on. Hanna knows *nothing*, and Rachel's friends surely don't."

Nathan's insight got him thinking. "Fine. Fine; I will think about telling her. I'm just not really sure this is right time," Rett said.

"There is never going to be a right time," his best friend answered.

Rett took a deep breath; he knew Nathan was right. "Hanna really doesn't know anything?"

"I didn't know what you would want me to tell her. It's your story to tell," Nathan answered, shrugging.

"You really are the best friend a guy could ask for," Rett said as he shook his head. "God knew what he was doing when he put me with a family that lived on the same ranch as you." Nathan didn't have to say anything. Rett was the best friend he could possibly have, too, and he knew it just as strongly as Rett did.

The car pulled up to the beach house at about one in the morning, and they woke the girls up. Rachel and her friends were still awake. They had been waiting to help the travelers get settled in. Hanna and Nathan took the master bedroom. Rett got his own room, and Kate was in a room with Rachel and her two friends.

"Dang, he is even cuter in person, Rach," the girl with long, light brown hair said as she climbed into bed.

"Samantha, this is Kate—Rett's girlfriend," Rachel laughed as she introduced them.

"That means that Rett is off limits, Sam. Like Rachel's been telling you since freshman year," the other girl with mousy curls reminded her.

"I know he's off limits, Liz, but that doesn't mean that I can't admire a fine man," Samantha laughed.

"He is beautiful, but if you touch my man, I will end you," Kate clarified as she rolled over, exhausted.

"I wouldn't put it past her," Kate heard Rachel add before they all fell asleep.

Kate managed to pull herself out of bed the next morning about an hour after Nathan, Rett, and Rachel had already left for the beach. Life on Star Bright made it impossible for them to sleep in, no matter how late they stayed up. After digging through her bag to find a swimsuit, she finally found a red and white polka-dot tankini, and she stepped into the bathroom to change.

"What, do you not wear bikinis?" Samantha asked with a hint of disdain. She seemed to think Kate might be morally opposed to them for some reason.

"No; I have a nasty scar that would show in a bikini," Kate laughed. That seemed to satisfy Samantha, and Liz gave her friend a look.

"Ready?" Hanna asked when Kate had her cover up on. Kate nodded, and the two of them grabbed a cooler and headed for the water. "I'm not sure how we're going to find the Texas crew on this beach," Hanna said, looking up and down the sand.

"Well, I can pretty much guarantee Rett is going to have a shirt on, so he won't be that hard to find," Kate said offhandedly as she joined Hanna in looking for them.

"A shirt on the beach, seriously?"

"I've never seen him without a shirt on." Kate spotted Rett sitting on towel not far from them, and they met up with the group before Hanna could form the words of her next question.

"There you are!" Nathan greeted them, kissing his wife.

"Where are Samantha and Liz?" Rachel asked. Kate shrugged. "Oh well; I guess they'll be here soon." Rachel filled them in on her life as they all set up their towels and chairs. She was a junior and majoring in journalism. She was already editor of the school's newspaper, and she was involved in her sorority and a campus ministry.

"How do you have time to sleep?" Hanna asked just as Samantha and Liz walked up.

"She doesn't," Liz spread out her towel.

"I do sleep!" Rachel said defensively as she nodded significantly toward Rett to remind Liz that her brother was listening.

"What? It's the truth; you don't sleep," Samantha confirmed, pulling a book out of her bag. She winked at Rett with a flirty smile as she settled on her towel.

"Thanks, guys. Really," Rachel groaned, rolling her eyes as Rett began to lecture her on the benefits of sleep.

Around noon, Hanna and Kate headed back to the house to fix

lunch for everyone, and Hanna brought up their earlier conversation. "Back to what we were talking about this morning . . . you've really never seen Rett shirtless? Didn't Houston propose to Lynne on a beach trip y'all were a part of? And you guys spend so much time at my sister's place. Does he not swim or something?"

"Rett is complicated," Kate answered a bit defensively. "I don't know what Nathan's told you; actually, I doubt he's said anything. Nathan would never tell Rett's story—or anyone's story, for that matter—without permission. But anyway, Rett has been through a lot. I don't fully understand how, but what he went through is the reason his shirt never comes off," Kate explained as they made sandwiches for the men and pulled out chicken salad for the girls.

"I'm sorry," Hanna responded. "It's definitely a bit strange, but I can tell it's really bugging you. I wish I knew what to tell you. I mean, if he plans on marrying you—which I know he does— the shirt will have to come off eventually," Hanna noted with a sly smile as they headed back down to the beach. Kate wasn't the least bit surprised to see that Samantha had taken the spot she had vacated next to Rett. This girl was really starting to get on her nerves. Hanna looked at Kate, who blew out a breath and announced they had lunch with them. Rett made room for Kate next to him for them to enjoy lunch together. After they were done eating, Kate and Rett went for a walk on the beach, and Kate made sure to be holding his hand as Samantha watched them.

When the girls were getting ready for dinner that night, the subject of Rett's shirt came up again. "Why does your brother wear a shirt on the beach?" Samantha asked Rachel as they got ready. Kate listened from the bathroom.

"He gets burned easily, so it's just easier for him to keep a shirt on,"

Rachel shrugged, giving the answer Kate had heard Rett give many times before. It was obviously easier than whatever the truth was.

Forgetting about Rett's shirt and instead worrying about why Samantha was so worried about her boyfriend's habits, Kate finished getting ready, and the group headed to Baytowne Wharf at Sandestin. They found a parking spot and started to head in. Just next to the restaurant, however, was a jewelry store.

"Babe, can we see if they have it please?" Hanna asked when she saw the store. Hanna was in search of a certain tennis bracelet, and they had been looking for it since the wedding in June. Nathan nodded, and to Kate's amazement, she and Rett followed them in. Without thinking, Kate headed for a case full of engagement rings.

"Isn't it beautiful?" she sighed when Rett walked up behind her.

"Which one?" he asked. She pointed to a white gold, three-stone ring, and he smiled. Everything had gone according to plan, and he would have to thank Hanna and Nathan later. The store didn't have the bracelet, though, so they headed over to the restaurant to meet the girls.

Throughout dinner, the conversation centered on the two couples. Rett and Kate and Nathan and Hanna took turns telling the stories of how they met. Then Nathan told everyone how he proposed, and Hanna talked about their wedding. Kate smiled. Rett watched her, knowing she was starting to try to figure when their own engagement would come, especially now that he had some idea of what she wanted in an engagement ring. After dinner, the group played mini-golf and rode go-karts to finish off the night.

"Rett," Kate started as they waited for Rachel and her friends to finish one of the holes. Rett's eyes twinkled mischievously; he already knew what she was going to ask. "What was with the jewelry store?"

"I thought we were helping Nathan find Hanna's bracelet?" Rett answered innocently. He wasn't going to admit that he took full advantage of Nathan and Hanna's search to get Kate to point out the type of ring she wanted. Kate shook her head, and the group moved on to the next hole.

It was fun night, but Kate's mind stayed on those rings. She texted Caroline as soon as the group was in the car to tell her about the mysterious jewelry store visit. Caroline called back just as they were walking in the door of the beach house, so Kate closed herself on the porch for a few minutes of privacy to talk things through with her best friend.

"Are you serious?" Caroline asked when Kate told her she had showed Rett a ring and shared her suspicions that he had set up the entire visit in the first place.

"Why would I joke about this?" Kate exclaimed. "But he wouldn't admit to anything when I asked him."

"Of course, he wouldn't! He's not going to admit that he was looking for your engagement ring. That boy isn't going to give you any hints past what he's already told you about the dozen bouquets," Caroline laughed.

"How do you know me so well?"

"Because I'm your best friend. I take it this means the weekend is going well?"

"Other than Rachel's friend who won't quit ogling my boyfriend, it's going great," Kate sighed.

"You need to nip that in the bud," Caroline laughed.

"That's what I'm trying to do. How are things in Nashville?"

"Good. I understand so much more about Patrick now that I've met his parents," Caroline said.

"I know that feeling, I hope it's as good a visit as my first trip to Star Bright," Kate said.

"Slow down; Patrick and I are still just figuring out this whole serious dating thing," Caroline reminded her.

"It doesn't get any easier, even after almost three years," Kate cautioned her.

"He's been wearing a shirt every day, hasn't he? Still nothing about why his shirt never comes off?" Caroline knew what Kate wasn't saying; the two had talked about Rett's mystery several times.

"Rachel used the sun line on her friends, and I can't tell if she thinks that's the truth or not. I don't even know how much his own sister knows. I wish he would just tell me," Kate vented her to best friend. She was getting so tired of the secrets and the lies.

It was time to actually ask the tough questions,

No matter what the outcome might be.

Chapter Twenty-Eight

"There you are," Rett said, kissing Kate when he found her on the porch where she was reading her Bible early the next morning. "Are you okay?" He could tell something was wrong; usually it was a battle to get her out of bed.

"Are we going to get some time alone?" she asked with a half-smile.

"Tonight," Rett promised. "Just me and you." He left her to finish her quiet time.

She finished reading the chapter in Psalms and prayed that Rett would have the strength he needed to be able to tell her the rest of his story. When she finished, she changed and headed down to find everyone on the beach. As everyone laughed and joked, Kate moved down to the water and sat with her feet in the ocean.

Nathan followed her. "What is going on? What did you end up telling Hanna about Rett? She told me about your conversation yesterday."

"The truth: that life with Rett is complicated, and in the three years I've dated him, I've never seen him without a shirt on. Nate, I'm done buying the line that he gets burnt easily, because you and I both know that he doesn't." Kate turned to look at him so he couldn't avoid her questioning stare.

"Kate, this is Rett's deal," he answered, putting his hands up. "I won't say anything specific, but I do know that this is something incredibly hard for Rett to talk about. I've known him since the day he moved in with his parents. I even shared an apartment with him for five years. And in all that time, I've only seen him without a shirt on for about a minute—the day I found out about everything. The man doesn't go without a shirt around *anyone*. When he tells you why, you'll understand. And let's be real for minute—you are eventually going to be the one who sees him shirtless the most, so you have plenty of time." Nathan wiggled his eyebrows and winked at her, hoping to lighten the moment a bit. When he saw her sigh, he nudged her shoulder. "Are you gonna be okay?"

"I'll be fine. I'm just tired of all the secrets," she admitted hesitantly.

"I know, and I'm sorry. Rett can be stubborn sometimes." Nathan smiled, and Kate pulled her knees to her chest. This wasn't easy. She sat there for a long time, taking in the ocean and praying about what to say to Rett.

"What's going on with you?" Rett asked as he sat down next to her.

"Just thinking," she said as she put her head on her knees to avoid looking at him.

"About what?"

"This is not the time," she answered, lifting her head to nod to the group behind them. She knew they would have to be alone to talk about all that was in her mind and heart.

"Okay, well—can I just sit here with you?" Rett asked, and Kate nodded.

"Where's Samantha?" Kate asked after a few minutes.

"You noticed that too, huh?" Rett rolled his eyes.

"She's practically drooling over you," Kate laughed and Rett shook his head.

"I keep trying to push her away but it's like that makes it even more interesting for her," he sighed.

"Is this what the girls were like at Schaeffer before me?" she asked.

"Why do you think I got coffee with so many of them?" Rett said and Kate laughed.

"Rett! I got your sandwich and chips, ham and cheese and Doritos, just what you ordered," Samantha called from where their chairs were set up.

"I got this." Kate looked at Rett and stood. Rett turned around to watch what was about to happen. "Thanks so much, Samantha. I will take that to my boyfriend," she started, taking the food from her hands. "Look, I understand Rett is extremely handsome and is fun to look at, but he is my boyfriend who I've been dating for almost *three full years*. And you're adorable, but if you think that you can break us up in one long weekend, you are sadly mistaken. So, I suggest you take your bikini and your little flirty flirt somewhere else." Kate spun on her heel, taking the sandwiches and the bags of chips back down to where Rett was sitting.

"I did warn you not to cross her," she heard Rachel say.

"Wow! Who are you, and what have you done with my chill, laid-back girlfriend?" Rett kissed her as she sat down handing him his lunch.

"No messes with *my* relationship." Kate shrugged her shoulders and wasn't surprised when Nathan sat down on the other side of Rett and started clapping.

"That was amazing. Best thing that's happened all weekend, thank you," he laughed. Samantha steered clear of Rett for the rest of the afternoon.

Kate walked out of her room with her blonde hair curled and wearing a teal shirt that lit up her eyes that night. "Still not telling me anything?" she asked flatly. She was talking about their date that evening, which he had of course kept a surprise, but she was also thinking about the rest of his story.

"You're beautiful," Rett said, kissing her to avoid answering.

"You don't look so bad yourself," she admitted, allowing herself to admire his red-striped button down. "How are we getting to dinner?"

"Nathan and Hanna walked," he answered, pulling the car keys out of his pocket. They were quiet on the drive to the Ocean Club restaurant. It was a bit fancier than Kate was expecting, but it was a great restaurant.

"What do you think you'll do after graduation?" Rett asked, finally breaking the silence. He would ask questions all evening to figure out what was troubling her. After the Samantha drama had cleared up, she had gone back to being silent and prickly.

"I don't know," Kate answered. "A Spanish teacher position is opening at Generations Christian Academy at the end of the year. I'm considering applying for it." This was not the conversation Kate wanted to have, but she went along with it.

"Why wouldn't you? That's the job you've always wanted." Rett thought he already knew the answer, but he still couldn't quite understand why she was acting so reserved.

"Because I don't know where that leaves us," Kate said, exasperated.

"The job is in Albany, but you're still working in Atlanta. I don't want to be long distance longer than we absolutely have to."

"Kate, I want to be together too, but I don't want you to miss out on an awesome opportunity. You know that I plan to be in Albany at some point. Between you and me, Joshua actually thinks I'll be there sooner than we originally thought. So, pursue your dreams, and hopefully we'll be together soon."

"Rett—"

"Look at me," he said, and she lifted her eyes, not realizing she had been avoiding eye contact. "I am going to spend the rest of my life with you. A few more months apart—which we don't even know for sure—isn't going to hurt anything," Rett reassured her, thinking he had finally gotten to the heart of the issue.

"You still want to marry me?" Kate asked, but it came out barely a whisper. She was thankful, too, because their food arrived as soon as she said it, and she didn't want their waitress to be a part of their conversation. Rett said a blessing and looked at Kate, waiting for her to repeat whatever she had just said.

"You still want to marry me?" she repeated.

"Of course, I still want to marry you! Why do you think I walked into that jewelry store?" Kate was still trying her best not to lose it. "What's wrong?"

"Not here," Kate was fighting back tears. "Not here," she repeated. They finished the meal in silence. Kate was scared to talk for fear that she would start crying, and Rett wanted to give her space for whatever was going on. The bill finally came, and they walked out to the car.

"Do you not want to marry me?" Rett managed to get out. He didn't know what to think anymore.

"Are you an idiot? Of course, I want to marry you! I'm sorry if I've made you think anything else today. I love you, and spending the rest of my life with you is what I want more than anything. But"—she choked on her last words—"I can't marry you if you don't trust me."

"What you talking about?" His response, how oblivious he was being, just riled Kate up.

"I'm done buying the lie that you get sunburnt easy, because you don't. You're outside for five minutes and are darker than I could ever think about being. I've never seen you get slightest bit burnt! Your lie may work for Rachel's friends, but clearly, you don't trust me with whatever happened to you."

"Kate. . ." Rett faltered for a minute.

"Let's just go back," Kate fumed. She turned towards the window as hot tears rolled down her cheeks.

"I'm sorry," Rett finally said when they had parked the car at the beach house.

"For what?" Kate turned to look at him, her eyes red and puffy. But when he didn't answer quickly, she threw open the car door and slammed it behind her as she stormed to grab her Bible and towel from the room.

"Is everything okay?" Rachel asked when she noticed how hard Kate was crying.

"I don't know," Kate answered over her shoulder.

"Kate, wait," Rett called as she walked out of the house.

"I'm done waiting on you," she answered quietly, wiping tears from her eyes as she walked out to the beach. It was too dark for her to try to read when she got to the water, so she just took in the peacefulness and expansiveness of the ocean, amazed that the same God who created something so immense would care about her and her relationship with Rett. She prayed for God's peace to fill her and for understanding as she tried to figure out what to do.

"Are you okay?" Rett sat down next to her a few minutes later.

"Don't make me yell at you," she answered, still not quite full of the peace she was praying for.

"I'm sorry."

"You keep saying that, yet here we are. I'm not even sure what you're sorry for. Are you sorry for not telling me? Are you sorry you've upset me? Are you sorry that I've pushed you to tell me something because I'm tired of waiting? We're talking about getting *married*," Kate railed. "You told me we would be getting engaged after twelve bouquets of roses, and I have gotten nine. Nine, Rett! Which means we're close. And you are still lying to me about why you don't ever take your shirt off. It's not that I just want to see you shirtless, because—I mean, I do, but that's not the point. . ." Kate faltered, momentarily distracted by the thought of all that seeing Rett without a shirt on could mean.

"What *is* the point?" Rett marveled at the woman he was dating; this was a side of her he had never seen—strong, angry, upset, and yet still considerate in all of it.

"That I need you to trust me," she said plainly as her eyes met his.

"I do! It all—"

"No; don't even think about telling me right now," Kate jumped in.

"What?" Now Rett was the one to get angry. She spent the whole day mad at him for not telling her, and now she didn't want to hear?

"If you tell me right now, it will be because I dragged it out of you or because you think I am going to leave you, and that's not what I want. I want you to tell me because you trust me," Kate shook her head, looking back at the sky.

"What can I do?"

"Think long and hard about why you haven't told me," she answered, breathing more peacefully at last. "You have to decide if and when you're going to tell me. And when you do, you had better be ready to talk to me about all of it. All of it, Rett. But right now? I need some space. I love you. I love you so much, but I can't do this if you're not going to trust me." Kate stood, leaving him to think. She got ready for bed and was asleep by the time Rachel and her friends got back from their late meal.

The next morning as the group got ready to go back to Atlanta, there was tension in the air between Kate and Rett, but no one talked about it. In the Daly's car, the drive back was long and awkward. Kate sat in the back seat with Hanna, who clearly wanted to know what was going on. Thankfully, she didn't ask while they were all together. Nathan did his best to diffuse the tension by keeping them all laughing.

When they finally got back to Rett's apartment, Kate gathered her stuff. "I'm just going to head back to school," she sighed.

"You don't have to go now," Nathan insisted, looking up at her.

"I have class tomorrow." She hugged him. "Thanks for coming with us this weekend," she added, hugging Hanna, too, before walking out with Rett.

"Where does this leave us?" he asked as the door closed behind them.

"That's up to you," she answered, kissing him. "I love you, Rett."

Rett lingered in the moment as she walked out to her car. He had a lot to think through and figure out, but he knew without a doubt that he had to do something.

He couldn't lose her.

Chapter Twenty-Nine

"Are you okay?" Nathan asked when Rett walked back into the apartment.

"Not really," Rett answered truthfully, sinking down on the couch.

"I think I'm going to stay with Rett tonight, if that's okay with you," Nathan said, turning to Hanna.

"Of course." She could tell something was really wrong. "Let me know if y'all need anything," she added as she grabbed her keys and walked out.

"You didn't have to do that," Rett sighed as the door closed.

"I'm not leaving you here by yourself," Nathan scoffed. "But now you're going to tell me what's going on." Rett explained in more detail what had happened over the weekend, and Nathan could see how defeated he was. They ordered pizza and watched a movie together so that Rett could just keep his mind empty. Nathan knew his best friend had a lot to think about, but Rett was too emotionally spent for thinking to do him any good tonight.

"Thanks for staying. I'm going to try and get some sleep," Rett said when the movie ended.

* * *

"No, Mom. No, don't!" Rett cringed against the wall, waiting for the blow he knew would come and wishing he could shrink, like Alice in <u>Alice in Wonderland</u>. He just wanted to run away.

His mom swatted at his head. "I told you to clean the kitchen while I was gone, and you just sat around and watched TV, didn't you?"

"No! I was doing my homework! I was going to start cleaning after I finished, but I had a lot to do today. Mrs. Avery gave us more than usual 'cuz we're gonna have spring break next week," Rett cried, trying to explain.

"I don't want excuses. Go get the switch. Now!" Rett hated hearing those words, but he knew that if he didn't do what he was told, his mother would hit him that much harder. So, he got the switch and brought it to his mother. "Mom, I promise I was going to do it! Give me another chance!"

"Another chance?" She laughed a cold, humorless laugh that said more than her words. "Like that second chance your sorry father was gonna give me? Oh no! He got away with everything, but you won't!" She raised the switch and started to bring it down on him.

The switch was almost on him when Rett suddenly jerked awake, breathing like he had run a marathon. He sat up, put his head in his hands, and shuddered. Glancing at the clock, he saw that it was 3:30 am. Like clockwork, Rett thought as he headed to the shower.

He turned it on as hot as he could stand and let the memories come in slowly. He saw his mother, her face twisted in rage, raising the hickory switch and bringing it down harder than Rett thought she could in her emaciated state. Drugs did that to a person.

After he got out of the shower, Rett climbed back into bed to pray and thank his great comforter, his heavenly Father. "Lord, help me, please. I still remember everything. I really don't want to remember as much as I do. It would be so much easier to forgive if I could just forget. Help me to forgive as you do. Thank you for all you've done for me. I love you, Lord," Rett rolled onto his stomach and let the awful scenes—the ones that scrolled through his mind like a movie—come.

"I didn't do it, Jack! It wasn't me! Tommy across the street was hanging around here yesterday; maybe he did it. But it wasn't me, I promise!" Rett ran around the table, trying to stay away from his mother's boyfriend.

"Come here, boy, before I get real riled. I know you done messed up my hothouse." Jack followed Rett's movements. He tried to grab him, but in his drunken state, he missed. "Now I said, boy!" But Rett stayed away, afraid of what Jack would do to him if he were caught.

"No. You're gonna hurt me again!" Jack's eyes looked really scary. They were black and hard, and it looked like Jack would kill him if he got close enough.

"Rett, come here right now, boy."

Rett ran out of the room and then snuck into the backyard to find a hiding place. He looked around frantically, trying to find a solution before Jack figured out where he was. He finally spotted a rough, jagged hole in the fence. He was sure he could squeeze through it if he just had enough time. Dashing over to the hole, Rett moved the clutter away from the fence, praying Jack wouldn't guess he was outside. After several agonizing moments of shoving stuff aside as quietly as possible, peeking over his shoulder all the time, Rett had moved enough of the junk to slip through the hole. He stuck his head through the hole, scanned the alley, and began wiggling out of the yard. Rett had just gotten his stomach over the jagged edge of the alley's concrete when a hand grabbed his legs and jerked him back inside.

He yelled, his stomach burning where a scrap of metal cut him. Jack's angry face appeared in his line of vision. "Boy, I told you not to mess with my stuff or you were gonna get it. Now you done messed with it, and yer really gonna get it." Jack held a brown unmarked bottle in one hand. He raised it, almost bringing it down on Rett's head, but moving it at the very last second so it smashed on the ground next to Rett.

"What are you going to do?" Rett hated how his voice quivered, betraying his fear.

"Do? Hmm . . . What am I gonna do with a little rat like you?" Jack snarled. "I tell ya what I'm gonna do. I'm gonna make you wish you were never born!"

Rett stared. Even in a moment like this, he realized how ridiculous Jack's threat sounded. I wish that every day, Rett thought. But he knew that Jack could make it worse.

Jack grabbed Rett's arm and dragged him over to the little shed that sat in the very corner of the property—the same hothouse Jack was accusing Rett of trashing. "You holler, and I'll make you wish you hadn't," Jack said as they entered the dirty shed. An evil smile spread across Jack's face as he spoke. "Take off that shirt, boy, and lean over that barrel." Rett's stomach began churning as he saw what Jack held in his hand: a big, thick leather strap.

"No, Jack. You're gonna hurt me. No, no, no! I don't want another broken bone." To Rett's shame, he began to cry, and it made Jack madder than before.

"I don't care about what you want. Take off that shirt and lean over."

Rett did as he was told and leaned over the barrel. The damp wood and cold metal felt surprisingly good against the cut in his stomach, but he knew the relief would be short lived. Jack raised the strap and brought it down with all the force he could muster in his inebriated state. Rett gasped and flinched as the strap came down again and again.

He tried to slide off the barrel as though he had passed out, but Jack only hit him harder. The first blows raised welts; then the welts broke and began to bleed. The bleeding from the cut on Rett's stomach was nothing compared to what Jack was doing to his back. He heard himself beg Jack to stop and let him go.

Jack kept on and on, but finally he quit as Rett went silent, unable to do much more than whimper. Jack glared at Rett, and growled, "Don't cross me again, boy. You won't live to regret it." He walked out and slammed the door behind him.

Rett slumped down on the floor and felt a warm stickiness running down his back. He knew it was blood and that he would get an infection if he got dirt in the cuts and welts. An infection might land him in the hospital, which scared him nearly as much as facing Jack, so he shakily stood and spread his shirt on the ground. He lay down on his stomach on top of his shirt, lost in the fog of pain and hurt. *What did I do this time? Rett wondered.* At least he didn't break my arm—or my leg, like last time.

When he started having trouble thinking clearly, Rett knew he needed to move. He tried to convince himself that he needed to get up and go inside, but he instinctively knew that would anger Jack more than ever... So Rett got up very slowly, put on his bloodied shirt, and stepped out of the shed. He had more trouble walking than he expected, but he managed to make it through the house and over a few streets to his friend's house. Knocking on the door, he stepped back and waited. "Mrs. Matthews, I'm sorry to bother you. I know it's late, but I . . ." Rett suddenly couldn't remember what he was going to say.

"Oh, are you—" Mrs. Matthews stopped mid-sentence and caught Rett as he passed out.

* * *

Feeling like he was swimming in a dark, thick liquid, Rett heard people talking about him, but he couldn't understand them. He guessed he was in a hospital because of the smell; this wasn't his first time. He kept falling back asleep for long stretches of time. Each time he woke up again, it was disorienting. Soon, though, he could make out some of the words floating around him ". . .possible internal hemorrhaging . . . might make it . . . mom . . . when he wakes up . . ." Rett couldn't make out everything they were saying, but he got the idea. Then he thought he felt his heart stop. What if Jack finds me the hospital? Will he hurt me again if he finds me? What is going to happen to me? Lying on his stomach, Rett began to open his eyes, determined to be strong.

"He's waking up." Two nurses rushed over to check on him before an older man with white hair and a kind smile walked into the room.

"Rett, are you feeling better?"

Rett looked up fearfully. "Yes, sir. I could go if you need the bed, but I really don't want to be put into jars, please." Rett began tearing up at the idea of dying before he got to play football.

The older man, whom Rett assumed was his doctor, looked at him with a puzzled expression. *"Jars? Why would we put you in a jar?"* Rett really was crying by this time. His sobs hurt his back and stomach, but he tried not to let it show. *"That's what Jack said hospitals do to you if you take up a bed for too long. They kill you so they can cut you up and put you in jars. Then the bed is free for the next person. Please, please don't put me in a jar. I can go now."* He tried to stand, but he could barely raise his head off the pillow.

Rett saw the doctor tighten his jaw before he leaned close and asked in a kind but stern voice, *"Rett, is Jack the man who hurt your back?"*

Rett froze. *"How do you know Jack?"*

The doctor looked away for a moment, as if to gather his composure. *"I don't know him, son. I just need to know if he hurt you."* Rett nodded. *"He won't hurt you again. Rett, there is someone here to talk to you."*

"Hey Rett," a middle-aged woman said, appearing in his line of vision. *"My name is Ellen, and I'm a social worker."* Rett knew what that meant. He had been with social workers before, and it usually meant they took him away from his mom for a few weeks and sent him to live with someone else until she got better.

"When am I going to see my mom again?" Rett asked immediately.

"Oh, sweetheart." Tears pooled in Ellen's eyes. *"She's getting some help, and I don't know when you might see her. But she and Jack are never going to hurt you again."* Rett started to cry. *"Rett, there's more. Do you want to hear it or wait?"*

"Is it good news?" Rett asked hesitantly.

"Yes," Ellen answered, and Rett nodded. *"Jack is jail, Rett. You're in no danger now."* Tears flowed from Rett's eyes before he could stop them. *"You're in one of the best hospitals in Dallas, and there is family here who wants to meet you."*

"Am I going to live with them?" Rett had been placed in foster care a few times before, so he knew the drill. He was terrified and in a lot of pain, but he was starting to understand the good news that Jack was in jail.

"Yes," Ellen answered.

"When can I see my mom?" the six-year-old asked again.

"I'm not sure," Ellen answered honestly.

"Please, I want to see her," Rett cried.

"I know you do, but she's getting some help, and you can't see her right now," Ellen repeated softly but firmly.

"When?" It was soft sob. For all that she put him through, she was still the only mom he had ever known, and he loved her as any child loves his mother.

"I really don't know. I'm so sorry, Rett," Ellen told him gently. "Do you want to meet the family?" Rett nodded, knowing it was going to happen whether he wanted it to or not.

A few minutes later Ellen walked into the room with a woman who had obviously been crying and a man in a cowboy hat. "Hey Rett," the woman whispered, smiling. "I'm Esther Johnson. We're so glad you're okay. We've been praying for you from the minute Ellen called us."

"Hey there," the man echoed. He spoke with a deep Texas draw. "I'm Dale. I'm glad to see you awake." Rett didn't know what to say. How long had they known about him?

"Thank you for being here," he said politely, "but I'm kinda tired." The Johnsons exchanged a look with Ellen as they walked out.

"Rett, you're doing great," Ellen tried to assure him. "I'm proud of you. Get some rest."

Rett sat up and held his head in his hands. It was late enough to actually start getting ready for the day, but he sat for just a few more minutes to thank God for his parents, who were able to get him out of the horrible situation his mother got him into.

"Are you okay?" Nathan asked. He opened the door when he heard Rett get out of bed, but he stayed in the doorway.

"I don't know how to answer that question," Rett answered, sitting down again. "No, I'm not. I don't know how in the world I'm supposed to tell Kate about these PTSD nightmares. But if I don't, our relationship is going to end with me letting my past get the best of me. You were right."

"I didn't want to be right; I just want the best for you," Nathan sighed. "I've known you a long time, Rett. I can still remember the day my dad told me that Mr. Dale and Mrs. Esther had brought home a little boy my age. I was so excited, but I didn't understand everything that had happened to you. I didn't understand why you didn't want to come to my house to play with my toys, why you flinched any time someone scolded you, or why you spent so much time in the barn with the horse. Then the first time I spent the night at your house, you woke up screaming. Mr. Dale walked in your room and asked me to go wait in the living room but—"

"I asked you to stay. If we were going to be friends, you needed to know the truth," Rett interjected. "And I want Kate to know the truth, too. I just don't know if I can take my shirt off in front of her. Just the movement can sometimes bring back flashes of that day with Jack."

"I don't think Kate's really asking you to take off your shirt. She just wants to know the truth, and that's her way of asking for your story. For both of your sakes, you have to figure out why you haven't told her. Fair warning from a newlywed, though: since you plan on marrying the girl, she is going to see the scars at some point—along with the rest of you." Nathan winked.

"You're ridiculous," Rett sighed. He knew Nathan was trying to get him out of his head.

"Just reminding you that marriage comes with certain perks," Nathan smiled as he played with his wedding ring. "I'm going to fix some coffee; do you want me to bring you some?"

"Thanks, I'll come get some in a minute." Nathan shut the door behind him, leaving Rett to think everything through. And he would think about it—after he sent her the next bouquet of roses. The beach trip might not have been the happiest memory, but it certainly was an important one.

Ten down, two to go, Rett thought as he reached for his Bible. *I just have to figure out how to tell her what happened to me.*

Chapter Thirty

"Are we still mad at Rett?" Caroline asked two weeks later as she and Kate sat in the living room of their apartment working on lesson plans. Kate glanced at the wilted roses across the room.

"I'll let you know how this weekend goes," Kate replied and rolled her eyes.

"Oh, okay." Caroline hesitated before asking, "But is this still about the fact that you haven't seen Rett without a shirt on?"

"Yes," Kate snipped, still not looking up.

Caroline bit her lip, trying to decide whether to push the issue or not. She swallowed, took a deep breath and opened her mouth, "Why now?" Kate's head turned sharply as she looked at her best friend. "I mean, you've been dating for three years, and you have been extremely patient with him," Caroline clarified. "Seeing him shirtless seems like such a small thing, especially when you may have a whole lifetime to spend together. Why are you picking now to dig your heels in? Why are you staking your whole relationship on this?"

"He told me that he's planning on marrying me. We kinda went to look at rings together. But he can't even tell me the real reason his shirt never comes off? It's not that I just want to see him shirtless; I don't want to plan a wedding and marry him if he doesn't trust me enough to tell me the whole truth," Kate explained all at once.

"How do you know he doesn't trust you?" This was the conversation Caroline had been trying to have since Kate got back from beach, and it wasn't an easy one.

"Because if he did, he would tell me," Kate said, getting defensive.

"What exactly is it that don't you know?" Caroline pushed.

"The reason he never takes his shirt off."

"But you know everything else? His past, his story, his present and future plans?" Caroline wanted Kate to think about this from his perspective.

"Well, yeah," Kate paused slightly, thinking.

"Then did you ever stop to think that maybe this one detail is the hardest for him to talk about?" Caroline's eyes were earnest as she leaned towards her best friend. "Rett is a very private person, but he's let you in." Kate started to protest, but Caroline waved her hand to silence her. "I'm not saying you're wrong for wanting to know it all before you are married. In fact, I think you're right that you will need to know before your wedding night. I'm just saying that you have to think about this from every side, including his. You want to him to tell you when he's ready, not because you give him an ultimatum." Caroline looked back down at her lesson plans and chewed on her pen as she waited for Kate to process all she had said.

"I didn't give him an ultimatum; I just left the ball in his court.

I'm not going to make him tell me this weekend. But I'm hoping that we can at least have a conversation about why he hasn't told me." Kate threw her head back and blew out a breath. She knew she was being stubborn, but she also knew that trust was an important issue. "Why are relationships so hard?"

"Because it's two sinners trying to do life together," Caroline laughed. Just then, Kate's phone dinged with a text message. "Rett?"

"Yeah. He's on his way." Kate took a deep breath. "Am I crazy? I've been dating this guy for three years. I know I want to marry him, but I'm terrified this might be the end of our relationship."

"Oh, Kate, I think that's what they call love," Caroline said as she patted her friend's hand. "But let's pray; it will probably help." Kate nodded, and Caroline pulled her close. "Dear God, you have great and mighty plans for Kate. If they include, Rett, even better. But if they don't, make it clear to both of them. Give Kate peace about what is going to happen, and allow her to get some clarity. You are our peace and comfort; continue to prove that to Kate. In your name we pray, amen. You okay?"

"I will be," Kate sighed. "Thank you, Caro, for everything. While we're on the subject . . . what's going on with you and Patrick?"

"I don't know," Caroline sighed. "Now that I've met his parents, he wants to meet mine. We've been talking about going to San Antonio for Thanksgiving."

"Really? Good for you," Kate was surprised to hear that. Caroline seemed to take every step of her relationship with Patrick at a glacial pace.

"Stop judging me," Caroline rolled her eyes.

"I'm not, I'm just glad to know that things are finally going somewhere with Patrick," Kate said, stifling a laugh.

"Whatever. Fix your love life before you worry about mine," Caroline laughed, throwing a pillow at Kate playfully as she walked back to her bedroom, leaving Kate to sit and think about her relationship with Rett.

* * *

"Hey, beautiful," Rett greeted her with a smile when she opened the door.

"Hey, handsome," she laughed. Her laughter surprised her. She had missed him, that much she knew was true. But in spite of those feelings, they had barely been together for thirty seconds, and there was already tension between them. "I'm glad you're here," she added truthfully.

"I've missed you," he replied, kissing her.

"I missed you too."

"Dinner at Bistro?" Rett asked.

"Sure. Let me grab my purse." Kate walked back to her room and told Caroline they were leaving. It was quiet ride as they made their way to the restaurant and got settled in a booth.

"I think we just need to go ahead and talk about this so that my whole visit isn't awkward," Rett said as he reached for her hand. Kate was relieved that she wouldn't have to pretend nothing was going on for an entire meal. "I need a little more time, but it's not because I don't trust you. The reason I never take my shirt off is not an easy story for me to tell. I promise you this: before I propose, I will tell you."

"It's not because you don't trust me?" Kate smiled as tears of relief filled her eyes.

"I trust you, Katie. You're the first person I've told my story to who didn't live through at least some of it with me. My life before the Johnsons—life with my birth mother and Jack—was horrible. I'm thankful every day that the Lord placed me with my parents. But I don't talk about life before them because I don't even like to think about it," Rett explained.

"I'm sorry that you had to experience such awfulness at the hands of someone who was supposed to love you," Kate said as she squeezed his hand.

"Me too," Rett sighed. "Thank you for being patient as possible with me." Kate just smiled a small smile. She didn't know how much longer she could wait, but she didn't have much of a choice. Rett leaned across the table for quick kiss just as the waitress came with their food.

"Three years," Kate exclaimed, putting all the stress of their conversation behind her and focusing on their anniversary. "It's been three years. How is that possible?"

"I don't know; it's amazing how fast the time as gone. I can't believe you're a senior!" Rett shook his head.

"I can't believe we're talking about getting married," Kate exhaled. Thankfully, they were able to truly enjoy dinner together at their favorite restaurant in Jackson before heading back to Kate's apartment to spend some time with Caroline and Patrick.

"Rett! Welcome back to Schaeffer. It's been too long!" Patrick hugged Rett as soon as they walked in the door.

"I know. I love the church and my job in Atlanta, but working on Sundays means I can't come up on weekends." Rett rolled his eyes. "How's grad school?"

"It's good. A lot of work, but it's going to be worth it. Teaching is harder than I thought, but I'm still loving it."

"I wish I could take your class. Stupid education schedule," Caroline griped, putting her head on Patrick's shoulder.

"It's fine, Caro. I would be more stressed with you in there," Patrick laughed as he assured her. "What would you ladies think of going to see Houston and Lynne tomorrow?" he asked, changing the subject.

Kate and Caroline exchanged glances. "I'm in," Kate laughed.

"What is it?" Rett had seen the look the roommates shared, but he was confused.

"Kate was just there last weekend," Caroline said, joining in Kate's laughter. "But yeah, let's go."

"I totally forgot about that. We don't have to go," Rett sighed.

"No, I want to," Kate reiterated. "What are we going to do if stay here—go to Cypress Grove? I'd much rather spend time with Houston and Lynne."

"Alright then. Houston wants us to meet them for brunch, so we're going to have to get on the road early in the morning," Patrick explained.

"Fine by me; movie?" Caroline looked from person to person.

Patrick got settled on the couch as Caroline put in a movie they had been talking about watching for a while. The movie went late, and the boys left as soon as it was over.

"Did you fix things with Kate?" Patrick asked as they picked up coffee for the girls the next morning.

"I did the best I could," Rett answered truthfully. "What's new with you and Caroline?"

"She's still skittish, but things are starting to look up. I might actually be engaged by graduation, after all," Patrick sighed.

"Give her time. She's crazy about you, even if she is terrified of commitment," Rett reminded him with a smile. It was 8:30 am when they arrived at the girls' apartment, armed with caffeine.

"Please tell me you have coffee," Caroline begged as they climbed in the car.

"Yes." Rett handed them each a cup.

"You're the best," Kate smiled, clutching her drink. The drive to Memphis did not seem like an hour and half with four friends talking non-stop.

"Welcome to Memphis," Lynne greeted them in the parking lot of the restaurant the Singletarys had suggested.

"Thanks guys," Rett said as they got settled at a table.

"Feels surprisingly familiar," Kate joked.

"How's school going, Houston?" Patrick asked. Kate may have been there just a week before, but it had been a while since everyone else had seen the couple.

"It's good. Kicking my butt, but it's good. What about you?" Houston laughed. They caught up on life over brunch before going to the Peabody to see the ducks that famously grace the lobby. Then they spent time milling around downtown, exploring.

Kate and Lynne talked as they looked through some Memphis t-shirts. "I take it you straightened things out with Rett?" Lynne asked. "Things don't seem as tense as I thought they'd be based on our conversations last weekend."

"For the most part. I guess I'm back to being patient," Kate sighed. "I don't know how much more of this I can take, but he did tell me that the whole story is just hard for him to talk about. At least I have a bit more peace knowing that it doesn't have to do with a lack of trust."

"Well, that's good. You can at least breathe a little easier about it," Lynne smiled.

"Thanks again for letting me crash last weekend. I needed that," Kate hugged her. She was thankful for her friends and their willingness to talk honestly with her. After the disastrous beach trip, she had realized she wasn't focusing on classes at all. She had escaped to Lynne and Houston's house, where Lynne had let her cry and get her mind and heart back together before another week of school.

"Anytime! That's what friends are for," Lynne smiled brightly. The group enjoyed their time in downtown Memphis and went to a nice restaurant for dinner. Kate was thankful for a fun anniversary with their friends after the tense weekend she had anticipated. When Rett left, things were a lot better between him and Kate. They weren't totally back to normal, but they were better. Hopefully Thanksgiving would provide an opportunity for Rett to tell her.

After all, Star Bright was where he had told her about being adopted.

Chapter Thirty-One

"How is it already Thanksgiving?" Caroline asked as she and Kate packed to leave.

"I don't know," Kate replied, shaking her head. "Senior year is going too fast! I can't believe it's almost time for us to be student teaching." She zipped her suitcase. "Have a fabulous week with Patrick; I will see you when I get back. And I'll be praying for you two while you're in Texas." Kate hugged her friend and got in the car for her drive to Atlanta.

"Do you have Nathan and Hanna's address?" Rett asked when she called to tell him she was getting on the road.

"No; I've gotten so used to staying with Chad and Jenna," Kate laughed. Since Nathan and Hanna were going to Texas with Rett and Kate, they had all decided it was best for her to stay with them during her short stop in Atlanta. She pulled up at the Daly's house in time for dinner. They had an early flight and were going to have to be at the airport before 7:00 am.

"Whose brilliant idea was it to fly out at the crack of dawn?" Nathan asked as they all waited in the security line the next morning.

"Yours, babe," Hanna laughed.

"That's right. I'm sorry," he said, hanging his head.

"It's just going to get us to Texas earlier," Rett reassured him.

"But it's too early," Kate reiterated, and Hanna high-fived her.

Once the group made it to Star Bright, the boys headed out to help their dads, Hanna went with Nathan's mom, and Kate settled in the guest room at the Johnsons.

"You're here!" Rachel burst in to hug her.

"Where's Rett?" Abbie asked, following on her sister's heels.

"He went straight to the barn. How's college?"

"Hard, but soccer's fun," Abbie shrugged as she walked off to find Rett.

"She's in a good mood," Kate laughed.

"Rett's home," Rachel smiled, shrugging her own shoulders. "So, um . . ." she hesitated and bit her lip. "You and Rett are better now? I haven't seen either of you since the crazy beach trip, and I know things were hairy for a while there."

"Rett and I are fine," Kate said, and Rachel cocked her head. "I promise," Kate assured her.

"Okay. So, one of the cows is having her calf today," Rachel said, changing the subject. "You interested in watching? I'm sure that's where the boys are."

"Are you serious?" Kate blinked a few times.

"Yep." Rachel ran the toe of her boot on the carpet as she waited for Kate's answer.

"I think I'm going to pass on that one. Not my thing. I'll just hang out in the house." Rachel nodded as she left, and Kate pulled out the book she brought with her. Walking into the living room, she settled into the couch to read.

"No calf for you?" Esther asked when she saw Kate laid out on the couch.

"No thanks; I don't think it's for me," Kate replied, shaking her head.

"That's okay. I've seen too many," Esther laughed. "But just so you know, they will probably be out there all day." Kate nodded and went back to reading her book. Esther spent the day cleaning up around the house, bringing Kate lunch as she headed out to work in the garden. It was late in the afternoon when Dale and Rett finally made it back to the house.

"Esther, honey, I'm going to shower and take a nap. Wake me up for dinner," Dale called out to her as the boys walked into the house. Rett disappeared up the stairs to shower and change himself. Once he had freshened up, he joined Kate on the couch.

"How's that book?" he asked, kissing her as he sat down next to her.

"Pretty good. It's nice to be able to read for pleasure after such a crazy semester. How was helping with the calf birth?"

"Tiring. There are definitely some things I don't miss about working on the ranch," he laughed. Within about five minutes, he was asleep.

"I knew he was tired," Kate said to no one in particular as she stood up. "Can I help with dinner?" she asked Esther, who had just come in with a basket of carrots, the last of the harvest for the year. Esther nodded, and Kate followed her into the kitchen. Once dinner was basically on the table, the women woke up Rett and Dale and called the girls to the table. Dinner was a quiet affair after the day they had, but it was wonderful to be with the Johnsons again.

"Mom, Kate and I are going out to the field. Is that okay, or do you need her to help you get things ready for Thanksgiving tomorrow?" Rett asked as they cleaned up.

"Go; I'll be fine. I've got your sisters, but I will need her in the morning," Esther replied, shooing them out the door.

Kate and Rett sat in the field, stargazing and talking until things actually felt normal between them for the first time in months.

"I love you," Rett said, kissing her as they walked back up to the house.

"I love you too," Kate smiled as they parted. "Thank you for tonight; I needed it."

"We needed it," he said, his finger tracing her jawline.

"Well, I guess I'll see you in the morning for Thanksgiving," she said lightly, shivering and stepping out of his embrace. He nodded, and they walked in the house, hand-in-hand.

"Good night, Katie." Rett kissed her once more outside her door.

The next morning, Esther woke Kate up to help with Thanksgiving prep. It was mid-morning when Rett appeared in the doorway, looking dashing as the sun reflected off the sweat beads that gathered around his hairline. He'd been checking on the calf and taking care of chores with his dad and Nathan.

"Well, hey there, Superman," Kate greeted him. She made her way to him and kissed him as a fire sparked inside her. She pulled away with a slight shiver. "I love you," she whispered before walking away to stir something on the stove.

Rett watched her at the stove and breathed deep. *God, help me*, he prayed, thinking about changing his proposal timeline—like he did every time they were together. His mom and sisters watched as he turned around and walked back to the barn, completely forgetting why he had gone to the house in the first place.

"Did you get them?" Dale asked, looking at Rett's empty hands.

"Get what?" Rett asked, confused. His interaction with Kate had erased Rett's memory for a second. "Oh, sorry. I got distracted." Rett turned to go back to the house again.

"When are you proposing to that girl?" Dale asked after him, laughing.

"I still have one bouquet to give her. But March-ish, I think. I have a plan."

"EJ always has a plan," Nathan reminded Dale as they got back to work. Rett ran back to the house again for the towels they needed, avoiding the kitchen this time. The men finished cleaning things up from the day before and headed in to get ready for the Thanksgiving meal.

"Thirty minutes!" Esther called when she heard the door open, not even turning from her gravy to greet the dusty men.

The girls were putting the finishing touches on dinner when Nathan's family arrived. "It smells amazing in here," Nathan said, offering hugs to the Johnsons.

The two families got settled around the table and took turns saying what they were thankful for. Abbie talked all about her first soccer season at the University of Texas and how much she was enjoying being off at school. Nathan's sister, Kasey, filled them in on all she was doing to prepare for her first baby; it was easy to see how excited she was. Rett filled the group in on how things were going at the church, and Hanna talked about the latest shipment of wedding dresses she had gotten for the store. It was a fun time of catching up, and once everything was cleaned up, they settled in the living room to watch football for the evening.

"You're going shopping, right?" Rachel asked Kate during a commercial break.

"Of course," Kate laughed. She had never been a Black Friday shopper until she met Rett's mom.

"Good! When are we leaving?" Rachel asked her mom.

"About 4:00 am," Esther said. "Abbie, are you coming?"

"Are you insane? No way. That is way too many people." Abbie looked at them like they were crazy, and they all laughed.

The next morning, the girls were up early to get ready. When they left, it was with coffee in hand. They hit a few stores before stopping for some food.

"How are things with Rett, really?" Esther asked Kate as they walked around Target. The group had split up to cover more ground, so Rachel was away with her aunts, leaving Esther and Kate some real time to talk.

"I take it you heard about the beach?" Kate bit her lip.

"About time you stood up for yourself," Esther nodded. Then she paused, gathering herself. "Rett is my son. He's been always been my son, and the fact that he went through so much as a child breaks my heart. You have only seen grown-up Rett, made whole after years of therapy and Jesus getting ahold of his heart. But when I met that broken little boy in the hospital, he was scared to death. He would never admit it, but I think he's still scared—scared that if you knew it all, you would run so fast. He's so terrified to lose you that he's doing crazy things to try and keep you, without realizing that it's pushing you farther away. I know you have been patient with him. I know you are having to continue to be patient. I just wanted to remind you that he's worth it. I had to learn that the hard way, and my prayer is that all we went through saved you from having to learn it the same way." Esther wiped at her eyes and blew out a breath. "Sorry; I didn't mean to unload on you, but you mean the world to him."

"He means the world to me. I can't imagine my life without him in it. Yes, I got frustrated. I was—and still am, to some degree—so tired of the secrets and the lies and him not trusting me. But we were able have an actual conversation about it. He told me that I'm the only person he's had to tell, the first person not to know at least part of his story before meeting him. And he said he doesn't even like to think about life before y'all." Kate never dreamed Esther would be the one she would have this conversation with—a conversation she had been longing to have—but she couldn't have asked for a better person.

"He's right. The Daly's were with us when we got the call. Rachel was three, and Abbie had just turned one. We even had to fill Joshua in before he started spending time with Rett. His life before us was not a good one; I don't like thinking about it, either. And I didn't live through it like he did," Esther said thoughtfully.

"Do you . . . does he . . ." Kate faltered, unable to form the question she already knew the answer to.

"I honestly don't think this has anything to do with trust," Esther answered, knowing Kate's fear. "I think he trusts you because he loves you. You know basically everything, and that's more than he's ever had to tell. I just think he doesn't really know how to tell you because he's never had to do it before." Esther pulled her into a tight embrace. "Love is a choice, and every day you have to choose to love those around you, especially when it's not easy."

"Thank you," Kate said, wiping the tears from her eyes. As she and Esther met back up with Rachel, Aunt Ruth, and Aunt Sophie, Kate realized that a weight had been lifted. She had been able to have real conversation with someone who knew Rett and his heart, and Esther had spoken straight into the hurting and longing places in Kate's heart.

"Did you have a good time?" Rett asked when they got back.

"Yes. It was great, but I'm exhausted. I'm going to take a nap," Kate answered, kissing him before she crawled into bed.

Since they were leaving the next day, Abbie woke her up for dinner and to decorate the tree. It was fun night of laughter and getting ready for Christmas. Kate relaxed and allowed herself to dream about life with Rett, which could include being at Star Bright every year. It was special place, and every trip continued to prove it. This trip had not held the answers she was hoping for, but waiting did not seem so daunting now—now that she knew it wasn't about trust.

And Christmas was just around the corner.

Chapter Thirty-Two

"Fill me in! How was Thanksgiving with Patrick?" Kate asked as she and Caroline got ready for their last few weeks before Christmas break.

"It was really good and needed. He fits so well with my family," Caroline answered, putting her head in her hands.

"Why do you seem so conflicted about it?" Kate was confused.

"Because now I don't have a reason for keeping things casual with Patrick. Stupid Mariah, why does she have to be right about everything?" Caroline groaned and sank into the couch.

"Rye is extremely good at reading people and isn't afraid to speak the truth," Kate smiled. She missed her friend.

"Patrick told me loves me." Caroline blew out a breath.

"Do you love him?" Kate bit her lip, hoping it wasn't too personal of a question.

"That's exactly what Mariah asked me right before graduation, and I couldn't answer her. But after the summer of soul-searching, I decided that I was going to stay with him. And then, after this semester of being more serious, I knew my answer. But when he said it, I froze. I wasn't ready." She leaned her head back, fighting tears. Kate waited; this felt like too big of moment to push her friend.

"After this week, I knew I loved him. I've been in love with him for a long time. I never wanted to be the girl who was caught up with a guy, so I kept Patrick at arm's length. I think honestly, I was a bit afraid of commitment. He wanted things to be serious a long time ago, but I wasn't there. And he waited until I was. He's been so patient with me, but I can't even get up the nerve to tell him that I love him." Tears spilled down Caroline's cheeks.

"Taking that step is a big deal, and it is scary. But you'll find the right time," Kate comforted her.

"I really hope so. Timing has never been my strong suit," Caroline sighed. "I'm exhausted; I'm going to bed." Kate watched as she disappeared into her room and whispered a prayer that Caroline would have the perfect opportunity to talk to Patrick.

The next couple of days passed quickly as they settled back into their normal school rhythms. Kate and Caroline were finishing up their classes for the semester and getting ready to be in the classroom fulltime in the spring. The girls barely even saw each other, but the weekend before finals, Caroline and Patrick finally got to spend some time together.

After walking around campus and enjoying each other's company, Patrick finally admitted that he had work to do. "Well, unfortunately, I have to get back to the library. Those papers aren't going to grade themselves," he laughed. "Thank you for the perfect study break."

"No one I'd rather spend this time with," Caroline answered, kissing him.

"Me neither, but I think I'm going have to hole myself up until I get things done, so I'm not sure when I'm going to see you again." Patrick blew out a breath.

"You can do it! Work hard, and I'll see you on the other side," Caroline smiled. "I love you," she added.

Patrick's wide grin spread across his face. "I love you too. Good luck on finals." Caroline practically skipped to her car. Even though the timing seemed random, it was also perfect. Patrick finally knew how she really felt, even if her own feelings still scared her from time to time.

* * *

"The next time I see you, we will be student teachers!" Kate squealed as she told Caroline good-bye and headed to Atlanta for a quick weekend with Rett. Kate loved that she and Rett would have a few days together in the city before they both headed to Albany to spend Christmas with her family. Once again, she got to be part of The Well youth group's annual tacky sweater Christmas party. Just like the year before, she had a blast. It was always great to see the kids in the youth group and to see how much they loved Rett.

On Monday, Kate and Rett headed to Albany. They pulled up to her parents' house around noon. Emmie Wren and Sky were already there, and Kaden was so happy to see his Aunt Kate. She spent the afternoon playing with her nephew as the family put the finishing touches on Christmas preparations.

On Christmas morning, the whole family gathered at the Adams' house for breakfast and to exchange gifts. "You all have to open your presents at the same time," Emily announced as she handed similar boxes to Kate, Emmie Wren, Sky, and Rett. She laughed at their confusion. She and Charlie had been planning this surprise for their family for a while.

When the four young adults opened their presents, they realized the whole family was going on a trip to mountains of Tennessee for New Year's Eve. As they gushed their thank yous to Emily and Charlie, Kate smiled to herself. She was excited about the trip, but she was also hopeful she and Rett might be able to have a private conversation while they were in the mountains.

"Merry Christmas, beautiful," Rett interrupted her thoughts as he slipped his arm around her. "I have a little something else for you." He pulled out a gift bag, and she eyed him. When she dug in, she pulled out the exact scarf she had been eying for weeks.

"How in the world?" she asked, smiling. She was pretty sure she hadn't even mentioned wanting the scarf. "Thank you so much," she said, kissing him. He knew her so well.

When all the wrapping paper had been cleaned up, Emmie Wren and Sky started to make dinner while Emily and Charlie played with Kaden. "Emmie Wren, when are you due?" Rett asked, moving from the couch to add his help to the dinner preparations.

"March 15," came her answer from inside the fridge. Dinner was wonderful, and as they ate, Kate looked around the table. She was thankful for another great Christmas, and she realized with hope that it would most likely be her last one as a single woman.

* * *

A few days before the new year, the whole family pulled into Pigeon Forge. They were just in time to eat dinner at one of their favorite restaurants before going to the grocery store. They'd be cooking most of their meals at the cabin the Adams had rented. Grocery shopping for such a large group took more time than they anticipated, however, and it was late that evening when they finally got settled in the cabin for the night. As things settled down, Kate walked outside to breathe in the mountain air.

"What are you doing?" Rett asked, following her.

"I just wanted to be outside for a minute," Kate answered as she sat down on the steps of the front porch. "It's so beautiful and peaceful out here." Rett sat down beside her, and she leaned in to rest her head on his shoulder. "I'm glad you're here." Rett didn't say anything but slung an arm around her back, pulling her closer to him.

They enjoyed being alone for a few minutes before Rett finally interrupted the silence. "Hey, Katie . . . I love you. I can't wait for more nights like this."

"I love you too," she whispered. After a moment more, she walked back into the house and away from the temptation that being alone with him brought. Rett stayed on the porch for a few minutes longer and prayed for a real opportunity to talk to Kate alone. He pulled out his phone and texted Nathan, "I'm going to tell her."

There was an instantaneous response. "Keep me posted. Praying, like always." Rett thanked God for Nathan and headed back inside.

* * *

"Good morning, beautiful." Rett kissed Kate.

Her eyelids fluttered open. "Good morning, handsome."

"Breakfast in fifteen." He kissed her once more before walking out of the room. *She is beautiful,* he thought for the millionth time. Kate got dressed and headed to the kitchen for a breakfast of biscuits, bacon, eggs, and grits. The whole family spent the day at Dollywood, riding the rides and enjoying the Christmas shows. That evening, Charlie fried chicken while Emily prepared the rest of dinner.

"Can we talk for a minute?" Rett asked, taking advantage of a lull in their activities to lead her out to the porch.

"Of course." Kate's breath hitched in her throat; this was it.

Before Rett could say anything, though, the door flew open, and a naked two-year-old ran out with Emmie Wren screaming behind him. Kate caught Kaden and carried him back inside to hand him to Emmie Wren.

"Almost time for dinner," Emily said as Kate moved to step back onto the porch.

"Rett and I are going to need a minute. Start without us if you have to," Kate informed her mom before walking back outside and shutting the door behind her. "Where were we?" she asked Rett as she breathed a sigh of relief and sat down opposite him.

"I was going to tell you why I don't take my shirt off," Rett said mater-of-factly, and Kate instinctively reached for his hand.

He jumped right into the conversation, not trusting himself with small talk. "Do you remember me telling you that Jack sent me to the hospital a couple times?" Kate nodded, not wanting to interrupt him. "Well, I generally tried to use school as a sort of escape from him. There was an after-school program I could go to, even in first grade. My teachers really liked me; they thought I was just working hard. They had no idea I was trying to stay away from a bad home situation. It worked until I happened to come home at the same time as Jack one day. Even though it was only about 3:00 pm, he was drunk. When he realized he wouldn't have the house to himself, he threw a chair at me and broke my arm. The second time, I was in the wrong place at the wrong time, and I overheard a conversation I wasn't supposed to. He broke my leg that time when he sent me tumbling down the stairs to the backyard. Each time, I blamed sports or an accident while I was playing in the yard.

"The last time he got me, though, was the worst. Jack came home from a friend's house that day to find the hothouse where he grew marijuana completely destroyed. I told him the truth—that the boy across the street did it—but Jack didn't believe me. He was livid. I could tell he would really hurt me if he got ahold of me, so I ran away from him. I was almost out into the alley behind our house when he caught me and dragged me back into our yard. After Jack caught me, he took me to the shed on the edge of our property. He told me to take off my shirt. Once I did, he made me lean over a barrel, and then he beat my back with a really big, thick strip of leather." Rett faltered. "It was bad. I was in the hospital for a really long time. To this day, just taking off my shirt can trigger memories of that shed. It doesn't happen often, but I don't want to risk having a flashback in front of people."

Kate was crying by the time he finished. She took deep, ragged breath before responding, "I don't know what to say, Rett. Thank you for telling me." She squeezed his hand.

"I'm sorry it took me so long. I—"

"I think I understand now," Kate interrupted him. "I can't imagine the things you have gone through. I love you, Rett Johnson, and I can't wait to be your wife." She leaned over and kissed him.

"And I can't wait to be your husband," he responded, wiping his eyes. Kate moved to sit next to him, and he wrapped his arm around her. There were finally no more secrets between them. The tension that had been there for the last few months was finally gone—for good.

"Everything okay out here?" Charlie asked from the doorway.

"Yes, Daddy, it is," Kate answered.

"Well, then . . . can we eat, please? I'm hungry."

"Yes, we're coming." Rett and Kate walked inside. It was clear that they had both been crying, but thankfully, no one asked them about it. It was also obvious that whatever they talked about had lifted the tension everyone had felt between them. Dinner was peaceful, and the adults all watched a movie before heading to bed.

* * *

The next morning started with a trip to Pancake Pantry. Taking advantage of a short wait at the popular breakfast stop, they took some family pictures in front of the store's scenic windows. Once they were seated, Kate ordered the Hayley Special, which meant she got old-fashioned pancakes with bananas, bacon, and peanut butter syrup. Emmie Wren got peanut butter and jelly with her pancakes, but the sisters were the only ones to order something unusual from the fun restaurant.

After breakfast, everyone spent the day exploring Gatlinburg together. They even went to the aquarium and managed to eat dinner before riding on the trolley, that was part of Gatlinburg's Christmas experience. It was a long day, and Kate and Rett didn't get a minute alone, but they were thankful for time together with Kate's family.

The next morning, Rett followed tradition by waking Kate up. "Good morning, beautiful," Rett said as he kissed her.

She groaned and rolled over. "Five more minutes."

Rett rolled his eyes and sat down next to her bed, taking advantage of the rare chance to watch her sleep. He couldn't wait to wake up next to her every morning. After a few minutes, Kate rolled back over with her eyes open. "Hey," she said sleepily, surprised that he was still there.

"Good morning, beautiful," he repeated as he kissed her again.

"Good morning, handsome," Kate replied, sitting up. "I guess I should get up now."

Rett stole another kiss before walking out of the room. As he sat down on the couch, Kaden climbed up next to him. "Mornin', Wett."

"Hey, buddy," Rett smiled, and Kaden hugged him.

"I love you, Wett."

"I love you too, Kaden."

Kate had followed Rett out of her room, and she watched the two boys from the kitchen. Rett was going to be great dad one day. Before Kate could say anything, though, Emily and Charlie shooed her back to her room to get ready for the day. The family had another long day ahead, and her parents were anxious to get started. The day was full of fun activities that included sledding and shopping. By the time they got back to the house, everyone was exhausted and went straight to bed.

Rett let Kate sleep late on New Year's Eve Day, but he woke her up at 9:30 am as Emmie Wren and Sky were starting breakfast. They made sausage, egg, and cheese biscuits. Kate got to the kitchen just as Emmie Wren was putting the plate of biscuits on the table.

"It smells awesome. You're the best, Emmie Wren." Kate hugged her sister and put a biscuit on her plate. Over breakfast, the group talked about their plans for that night. There was a New Year's Eve ball drop and fireworks show they could attend downtown, but after the two busy days they had had, they decided to spend a quiet night in the cabin. The day was spent simply, just playing games and hanging out.

Kate and Rett were in charge of dinner, and they fell into step together. Soon, they had a chicken dish ready to serve. Emmie Wren and Kate exchanged a glance as Kate plated the chicken and Rett set out the sides. Kate knew her sister was thinking about what life would be like for her and Rett after they got married. Everyone was impressed with Kate and Rett's dinner and kept commenting on how much they loved the chicken, broccoli, and rice—even Kaden.

After Kaden went to bed, the adults settled in to watch the New Year's Special and the ball drop in New York City. Kate and Rett were snuggled up on the couch. Looking around, Kate realized that this was how she wanted to spend the rest of her life.

Rett kissed the top of her head. *I can't wait for you to be my wife*, he thought. He went to bed thinking about the changes the new year would bring—especially his engagement and marriage to the girl he loved. And if things went the way he was praying they would, they would also be able to move to Albany for him to start a job at Generations.

The next morning, he spent time reading his Bible and praying for the big year ahead of him and Kate. When he finished, he headed to Kate's room, opened her door, and sat down next to the bed. Her beautiful blonde hair was laid out on the pillow as Rett began to pray for her like he did so many mornings. This morning, with her beside him, he prayed a special prayer for her semester student teaching, her job search, and the changes that were coming in their relationship. He thanked God for the opportunity he had had to talk to her and how she handled everything. When he was done, he kissed her, and she woke up.

"Good morning, beautiful. Happy new year."

"Happy new year, handsome," she replied, her hand touching his face as she kissed him once more. "I love you."

"I love you, too." Rett smiled and walked out. *If she only knew all this year holds.* Rett knew she had an idea of his plans; he had explained the roses to her, after all. But she couldn't be positive about anything, because the proposal was up to Rett—the proposal that would set their future in motion.

When Rett got to the kitchen, he was ready to see what he could do to help with Emily's traditional New Year's lunch of black-eyed peas, greens, pork, and cornbread. After they finished eating, Rett volunteered to clean up the kitchen with Emily and Charlie while Kate soaked in as much time with Kaden as possible.

"I have something I need to talk to you about," Rett said when Kate was out of earshot.

"I was wondering when this was coming," Charlie laughed, setting down the bowl he was washing.

"I would like your blessing to marry Kate," Rett exhaled.

"And why should we give it to you?" Charlie asked him the same thing he had asked Sky years earlier.

"Because," Rett answered confidently, "Kate is my next breath and my song. More importantly, I feel at home when I'm with her. I love her so very much. And I know that she loves me." Rett could not help but smile, and his love for Kate lit up his eyes.

"Promise me that you'll always choose to love and cherish her, and I will gladly give you my permission," answered Charlie. "There is no other man for her."

"I wholeheartedly agree." Unshed tears shone in Emily's eyes as she stood beside her husband.

Rett gave them his word and hugged them both. It was exactly how he hoped the conversation would go.

When the week ended and everyone parted ways, Rett headed back to Atlanta and sent the eleventh bouquet to Kate's apartment in Jackson. He only had twelve roses left to give her before she had her engagement ring.

It was finally time to set the last stage of his plan in motion.

Chapter Thirty-Three

Hey, Rye! I hope things are going well down in Mexico. Kate keeps me informed, and I've got my youth group praying for you. But to be honest, I'm really writing because I need a favor. I'm getting ready to propose to Kate! For the proposal, I have been collecting things that symbolize what I love about her. One of the things I love about her is her passion for the Spanish language. Since you are living in a Hispanic country, I was hoping you could help me out by sending something for her from Mexico. I'll leave the specifics up to you since you know what she likes. Don't worry too much about the price; I can pay you for it.

Thanks! You're the best.

Praying for you, Rett

Mariah read the email for the third time. It was finally happening! Kate and Rett were getting engaged, and she was so excited that she would get to be a part of it in some small way. She emailed him back saying she'd be glad to help and that he didn't have to pay her for anything; it would be her engagement gift.

"Ready, Mariah?" Kinsley stuck her head in the door.

"One second." Mariah hit send and closed the computer as they headed to teach. "Next time we go the Mercado, I have to get something for my friend Kate. Just help me keep that in mind." Her head was spinning with thoughts and ideas, and she barely heard what Kinsley was saying.

"Are you okay?" Kinsley asked as they walked to the church where they taught English class.

"Sorry to be so distracted. I'm just missing out on a lot," Mariah responded. "That email I was responding to came from one of my best friends' boyfriends. She's going to be getting engaged any day now, and I won't get to be there to celebrate with her. I knew it was going to be like this; it's just harder than I thought. I'm fine, but I miss my friends."

The two girls walked into the church together and got things ready for class that night. Mariah had to focus, so she mercifully got a break from her swirling thoughts. Their students were working on verbs and sentence structure—something that was not easy to explain to Americans, much less non-native speakers.

"Are you going to go the wedding?" Kinsley asked over dinner.

"As much as I would like to, I don't think I will. It's just lot for a weekend, and it will be so close to the end of term that I'm not sure it will be worth taking the time off."

"I get that. It's hard to have to miss out on things happening at home. But the friend we have to get a gift for—Kate? She's already engaged?"

"Not yet; soon. Her boyfriend is getting ready to propose and wants me to send him something from Mexico."

"What?"

"Her boyfriend is a super planner and very romantic. Kate's going to be a Spanish teacher, so he thought it would be fitting. I know he has everything laid out perfectly for how he wants it all to go down. They've been dating for three and a half years, so it's been a long time coming." Mariah sighed. "He's a great guy, and I'm actually really thankful he thought to include me in his plans. It does make missing out on their engagement celebrations a bit easier."

The next morning, Mariah and Kinsley headed to the local school to help with the kids. It was the highlight of Mariah's week. She loved getting to teach them and love on them while sharing God's Word with them. Mariah helped with the oldest kids at the school while Kinsley dealt with the little ones.

The teacher smiled when Mariah walked in the door. They were becoming friends. Mariah would be teaching a history lesson and helping with reading. When it was time to play, everyone gathered around as Mariah told Bible stories for them to act out. She couldn't help but laugh when the boys pretended to be the lions in the den Daniel was thrown into. Meanwhile, the girls flitted around as angels, shutting the boys' mouths. Kinsley walked in to hear Mariah finish explaining the story just before it was time for them to go.

"I'm so jealous of your Spanish skills," Kinsley said for the hundredth time as they walked toward the city center.

"I've been working on them a bit longer than you," Mariah

reminded her. "You just have to practice. I can speak fluently around you all the time, if you want." They both laughed, knowing that would probably not be the best decision for their friendship. At the market, they searched together for the perfect gift for Kate. "I want something that screams Mexico, but that Kate would be able to use or display in her new house," Mariah told her friend. They walked past people selling pottery, skirts that she liked but couldn't see Kate actually wearing, and jewelry that didn't quite grab her attention. Then they rounded a corner to see a man standing at a loom weaving beautiful tapetes. Immediately, Mariah realized Kate could use one of the colorful pieces of fabric as a rug.

"This it is," Mariah exclaimed. She looked at Kinsley, who nodded. There were so many to choose from, but they finally decided on one about two feet wide and three feet long. It was brown, blue, and pink with a Mayan pattern in the center. Mariah knew it would go nicely with Kate's style, and she could already imagine her friend planning a bathroom around the colors in the rug. They finished their trip to the Mercado by picking up the groceries they needed before walking back to the house. As Mariah got the tapete ready to mail, she prayed for Kate and Rett's relationship as they prepared for marriage.

***

"Well, well. What do we have here?" Rett noticed the package sitting outside his door as soon as he got home. He had spent Valentine's Day with Kate in Jackson, but it was the last time he would see her before she stopped in Atlanta on her way home for spring break. As he unlocked the door and brought the package inside, he noticed that the return address was Mexico, which meant it was from Mariah. It was the gift he had asked her to find for Kate; the last piece of the puzzle for his engagement plan had fallen into place.

Rett's excitement kicked into high gear as he pulled out a beautiful piece of fabric he assumed would be a rug. Then he found the note from Mariah explaining that it was a hand-woven art form known in Mexico as a "tapete." It was perfect. He put the rug in the room that had been Nathan's along with everything else he had been collecting as part of his engagement plan. As he looked it all over, he knew Kate would love it, but he was still somehow nervous.

"What are you doing for lunch tomorrow?" Rett asked Nathan after church the next day.

"I don't think I have anything planned. Why?"

"I'm going to buy Kate's engagement ring, and I was hoping you'd come with me," Rett answered nonchalantly.

"You're buying what?" Hanna coughed as she nearly choked on the piece of bread in her mouth.

Rett grinned. "She's graduating in a couple of months, and I want her to have a ring on her finger."

"No! I mean—"

"*About dang time* is what I think she's trying to say," Nathan said as he laughed at his wife's speechlessness. "I'd be honored to go with you. Plus, she might have told me what she wanted."

"Has it changed since the beach?" Rett asked in surprise.

"No, but I know details—like her ring size, for example. Because she was smart enough to know that you were going to take me with you," Nathan gloated. Rett rolled his eyes, but he knew Nathan was right.

Rett and Nathan met at the jewelry store on Monday and were greeted by one of the salesmen. "I'm here to buy an engagement ring," Rett declared. The man smiled and led them over to the case holding all the rings.

"Do you know what you want?"

"I know she wants a three-stone ring."

The man nodded, pulling out a tray of three-stone rings, and began to explain the differences. With Nathan's input, Rett settled on one with three princess-cut stones.

Nathan had to get back to work, so Rett finished up the details on his own. He picked out a matching wedding band and paid for the rings. Kate was going to love it, but it was a good thing he wasn't seeing her again until spring break. If he saw her before he planned to propose, he didn't know how he'd be able to stop himself from giving it to her and spoiling his entire plan.

About week later, Rett picked up the rings after work before heading to Nathan and Hanna's for dinner. "Oh, my word," Hanna gasped when she saw what the boys had chosen. "She's going to love it!"

"I just can't believe you're really about to propose to this girl. I remember when you walked into our apartment after that first day. You had just met her, and you told me that you thought you might like her," Nathan laughed. "Although I'm pretty sure you knew you'd be marrying her from the first time you talked—if she'd have you, that is."

"Wait, I don't think I've heard this story," Hanna realized.

"Oh!" Nathan exclaimed. "Well, Rett, I think you need to tell her about how y'all met."

Rett blushed. "Well, when you start at Schaeffer, you are put into a group with other freshman to help you get to know the campus and other students. They're called 'Welcome Groups,' and I was a Welcome Leader for three years. Junior year, one of the girls on my list was from Albany, Georgia. Joshua gave me a heads-up that he knew someone in the incoming class, but I never dreamed that someone would end up being a beautiful girl. And then to have her end up in my group. . . it just seemed like a bit of a God thing. I didn't get to talk to her during the first orientation meeting, but I managed to end up sitting next to her during the worship service, and we talked afterward. It did my heart good to know that she knew Joshua and went to Generations. Over the course of that weekend, I developed a major crush on her. My chance came at the welcome back dinner when I spotted her with Caroline. They had all just eaten, and as I was casually trying to catch up to them, she tripped and literally fell right into my arms," Rett laughed. "I caught her and asked her to get coffee. My heart was pounding, but she said yes." Hanna just stared as Rett finished telling the story.

"It's one of those stories will be Schaeffer legend in a few years," Nathan said between bites of food. "Most people already know about a couple who met because the guy was the girl's welcome leader. It's not supposed to happen quite like that," he added, laughing. "Alright, man-with-the-plan, how's this proposal going to go down?"

"I'm glad you asked." A mischievous grin spread across Rett's face.

***

"Hey, Kate," a friendly voice said as Kate checked her voicemail after her last class. "This is Mrs. Francis at Generations Christian Academy. Give me a call when you get a chance. I hope you're having a fabulous day." Kate checked her phone; it was only three thirty. Hopefully Mrs. Francis would still be at the school. She sent Rett a quick text to let him know she was getting on the road.

"Generations Christian Academy. How can I help you?" a flowery voice answered.

"Mrs. Francis, please," Kate said, and she was transferred.

"This is Francis," answered the friendly voice Kate had heard on her voicemail.

"Hey, Mrs. Francis. This is Kate Adams. I'm returning your call."

"Hello, dear. Are you still interested in the Spanish position here at GCA?" Mrs. Francis wasted no time in getting to the reason for her call.

Kate couldn't breathe. "Yes, ma'am."

"Good! We would like to set up an interview. I know you're away at school, but will you be in Albany anytime soon?"

"Actually," Kate answered, thrilled, "We're just starting our spring break, so I will be home Monday and Tuesday. Would that work?"

"Tuesday at 10:00 am sound good?"

"That would be great! See you then. And thank you so very much!" Kate hung up the phone and called her sister, deciding to wait until she got to Atlanta to tell Rett. "I have an interview at GCA," she squealed as soon as Emmie Wren answered.

"What? Oh, my goodness; I'm so happy for you! That's awesome!" Emmie Wren matched her excitement. "I was kinda hoping you were calling to me that you were coming directly here instead of stopping in Atlanta, though," she admitted, laughing.

"Me too," Kate laughed in reply. "I promised Rett, though. I will be home on Sunday, and then I'm coming straight to your house to meet that little nugget," Kate assured her sister.

"You'd better! This precious little girl is very ready to meet her Aunt Kate," Emmie Wren said.

"I know; I'm ready to meet her, too. You're still not going to tell me her name?"

"Nope. You're going to have to wait until you see her in person."

"She's named after me, isn't she?" Kate asked slyly.

"I'm not answering that question," Emmie Wren insisted. She had been avoiding tell Kate her niece's name ever since the little girl was born a few days earlier.

"Fine. Are you home now?" Kate asked.

"Yep; got home this morning. Kaden is in love with his little sister. Listen, I gotta go, but I will see you so very soon," Emmie Wren said before hanging up, leaving Kate to finish the rest of her drive jamming to music and thanking God for the opportunity that lay before her.

"I'm so glad you're finally here," Rett greeted her as he opened the door of Nathan and Hanna's house and hugged her. Kate greeted their friends as they moved into the living room.

"You're lucky I came here first," Kate teased. "I have precious niece I haven't met yet."

"I know." Rett kissed her. "Sunday. . . it's only two more days."

"You're right. I just wish Emmie Wren would at least tell me her name," Kate groaned.

"Okay, enough about that. I have news for you," Rett said, grinning mischievously.

"You do?" Hanna asked, curious. Kate felt her breath catch her throat but she calmed herself because even though she was expecting a proposal any day, she knew him well enough to know it wasn't going to be at the dinner table with Nathan and Hanna.

"I have an interview at Generations this week," Rett announced. He had waited to tell her in person. Kate felt herself relax as she waited for more information. It was not proposal, but it was still news they had been waiting on. "Andrew—the current youth pastor at Generations—accepted a job as a lead pastor in Florida, but the information doesn't go public till Sunday. My interview for his position is Tuesday, but Joshua assures me that the interview is just a formality; they already want to hire me. I'm looking to start about the time you graduate."

"Well, Tuesday is going to be a big day for us," Kate said eagerly, "Because I have an interview at GCA."

"What's GCA?" Nathan asked.

"Generations Christian Academy," she explained, and everyone began to nod and smile with understanding. "It's where I went to school. They want to interview me for the Spanish position."

"That's a total God thing," Nathan declared.

"Right?" Kate couldn't stop smiling, but she also couldn't stop yawning. "Unfortunately, its past this schoolteacher's bedtime. Even student teachers have to be at school early," she grinned apologetically. "I know I just got here, but it's been a long day."

"It's all good," Rett assured her. "We have all day tomorrow together. Sleep well." Rett hugged her and carried her bag to the guest room. Once she was settled, he thanked Nathan and Hanna for letting her stay and headed home to get things ready for the next day. When he finally climbed into bed around midnight, he prayed that everything would go according to plan.

Then he slept peacefully,

Dreaming about the future with Kate that was about to begin.

Chapter Thirty-Four

"Hmm," Kate groaned as she looked at her phone. The numbers on the screen told her it was only 5:30 am. *Typical,* she thought before rolling over and falling back asleep for another hour. At 6:30 am, she realized her body was finally used to her school schedule, so she got up, knowing she wouldn't get any more sleep anyway. She got a shower, got ready, and sat down to have her quiet time about 7:30 am. She texted Rett to let him know she was up, and he called her.

"Good morning, beautiful," he greeted her. "I'm sorry you're up so early."

"The life of a teacher. Can I come over now?"

"Can you give me until about nine? I'm not quite ready for you yet." Until this semester, she had always slept late, and he was still trying to get used to her earlier schedule.

"Sure. See you soon," Kate answered before going in search of coffee, which she found easily. She spent some time talking to Nathan and Hanna before heading to Rett's.

When Kate walked into Rett's apartment, the table was covered with a full breakfast, and in the center of it all was a vase with a single rose in it. Kate's heart jumped. This was it! This had to be it.

"What is all this?" she asked, trying to sound casual.

"I can't make you breakfast?" he asked innocently.

"You can. I just know you," she said, kissing him playfully, "So I know and there is more to it than just breakfast."

"Maybe there is," Rett winked. "But let's eat first." He wanted everything about this day to be perfect. They ate the biscuits, bacon, and eggs he had made, letting contented silence fall between them.

When Kate had finished eating, Rett finally spoke. "Do you remember the conversation we had in the field your first time at Star Bright?"

"Which one?" Kate giggled. "But yes, I remember. It's hard to forget when your boyfriend tells you that he's been giving you roses in order to lead up to a proposal. Or that it will take twelve bouquets to get to that proposal. Or that he was adopted."

"I guess that's fair," Rett conceded. "How many have you gotten so far?"

"Eleven," Kate answered without hesitation.

"Right. And normally, you get all twelve roses at one time, but your last bouquet is going to be different. You're going to get one rose at time."

"This is really happening?" Kate's heart was in her throat; the day she had been waiting so long for was finally here.

"You okay?" Rett grinned.

"I think so." Kate took a deep, steadying breath. "Let's get engaged!" She declared happily. "One down, eleven to go." Her blue eyes were sparkling.

"Not so fast," Rett laughed. "This is going to be an all-day affair, so don't get too far ahead of yourself." He kissed her reassuringly.

"I would expect nothing less from the master planner. What's first?"

"We're going to walk through our relationship up to this point, remembering the important moments that were marked by each of the bouquets. You'll get a little gift in honor of each one." Kate looked him with her eyebrows raised in anticipation. "Do you remember when you got the first one?"

"Of course! About an hour before we were supposed to go on our first date." Kate's heart was beginning to settle back to a normal rate.

"Yes, and what had we spent the month before that doing?"

"Getting coffee. So, does my first gift have something to do with coffee?" Rett nodded, and they gathered their plates to walk into the kitchen together. Sitting next to the coffee maker were coordinating coffee mugs with "Mr." on one and "Mrs." on the other. "Are you going to make some?" She kissed him before he brewed the coffee.

"I liked you from the second you opened your mouth and said you were Kate Adams from Albany, Georgia. I spent that whole weekend trying to get close to you, but I didn't want to scare you away."

"I thought you were gorgeous from the second you walked in that classroom, and I didn't understand why you were paying attention to me. Caroline and Claire at least figured out that you had a crush on me by the end of the weekend, but I wasn't sure if I believed it. By then, I had developed a crush of my own," Kate confessed.

"I was kind of obvious, wasn't I?" Rett laughed.

"Yeah, but that's what made it so wonderful." She kissed him again.

"Then we spent a month getting to know each other over coffee—at least, I drank coffee the whole time. If I remember correctly, it took about two weeks for me to talk you into trying mine? Then you were hooked," he grinned. "During that time, I fell in love with your laugh and your ocean-blue eyes."

"And I fell in love with your gentlemanly nature and slight Texas accent. But I thought you were never going to ask me out on a real date," she laughed.

"I was terrified and definitely waited longer than I should have," Rett admitted. "When I finally did, though, I was confident enough to set this plan into motion and send you the first bouquet of roses," he added. "But it was a rollercoaster of confidence and nerves, for sure. I was so worried walking up to your dorm that night."

"Then when everything came crashing down, it probably didn't help." Kate took Rett's hand.

"You would be correct. I never dreamed that your sister would be in a car accident or that I'd be in the car on the way to Albany mere hours after starting our first date. I hate that Emmie Wren's accident is the reason I came to Albany for the first time. And I hate that her accident is how I met your family, but it happened that way for a reason. Do you remember when you got the second bouquet?"

"After our week in Albany," Kate smiled. "But where's the second gift?" she asked, looking around.

"In the living room," Rett laughed.

"Pecans?" Kate picked up the bag of Cromartie Pecans sitting on the coffee table.

"I wasn't really sure what get to you that could represent that week," Rett admitted. "But since it was my first time in Albany, those are local Albany pecans—to represent our first week together in the city we will hopefully both call home soon."

"It's perfect," Kate smiled, turning back to the coffee table. Under the table, a pair of pink sling-back heels covered in multicolored glitter had caught her eye. There was another rose laying across them.

"Rett?" Kate moved the rose and picked up one of the heels. "These are Kate Spade!" She let out a shocked laugh. They were beautiful and not something she would have splurged on for herself. "The third bouquet came during our summer in Albany. What made our summer so special? I mean—something must have, because these heels and a rose?"

"Our summer together was a special one. It started with our first kiss in the airport when you and Nathan surprised me after my semester in Israel. I felt like we grew closer together, but I also think we each grew so much spiritually that summer. The shoes are because I loved ballroom dancing with you—even if I was horrible." Rett's heart was beating fast. Kate set the shoe back under the coffee table and moved closer to him. "Wanna dance?" Rett asked, hitting play on his phone so that Russell Dickerson's Yours filled the apartment.

"Of course." Kate took his hand, and they danced around the living room. "I love you, Rett Johnson," she whispered again as she kissed him.

"I love you too," he added as the song ended. "The first bouquet was the night I asked you out. The second came after the week in Albany. And the third was on your nineteenth birthday, in the middle of the summer we spent together. Do you know when you got the fourth one?"

"After our first anniversary—when you finally told me that you loved me. That's one I'll never forget."

"What did we do for our anniversary?"

"We went to that book auction in Thomasville." Kate walked over to the bookshelf and noticed a copy of *Mere Christianity* sticking out farther than the rest of the books. "Is this for me?" She turned around grinning with the book in her hands.

"Good eye," Rett smiled. "That weekend was crazy. Once again, I had everything planned, but when Emmie Wren went into labor, my plans were ruined. I somehow had fully expected it, though, I guess. I don't why I was so nervous about saying I love you; I knew you loved me and were going to say it back. I was actually going to tell you over the summer," he confessed, "But it never happened, and I was so mad at myself."

"I didn't understand why you weren't saying it, either, and I was so frustrated. But both Caroline and Emmie Wren insisted that I let you say it first. I'm so glad I listened to them. Okay, so I got the next one—" Kate started laughing— "I got the next one after our first trip to Texas."

"Correct. That's one trip neither of us will forget." Rett shook his head. "That Thanksgiving was important because it was the first time you met my family. Even though you were nervous, they loved you." Rett kissed her and led her toward the door. "Notice anything different?"

Kate stared at the horseshoe hooks on the wall and tried to remember if she had seen them before today. "The hooks—they're from your parents," she said, finally remembering where she had seen them.

"You're good at this." Rett stole another kiss.

281

"Maybe you just made it too easy," she joked.

"Doubtful," Rett laughed. "When did you get bouquet number six?"

"The night we celebrated my twentieth birthday. I told you about my scar, and you opened up about your adoption."

"Exactly," he smiled ruefully. "You continue to surprise me with how you take my past in stride."

"I love you, Rett—every part of you. Nothing is going to change that." She wiped the tears that had started sliding down his cheeks and hugged him tighter. As Rett felt her arms tighten around him, he was thankful she never pushed him to say anything.

"Hey! I love you," Kate said after a few minutes of silence.

"I know. I love you too—more than you'll ever know." He kissed her with a long, slow kiss.

"You wanna just propose now?" Kate asked mischievously, and Rett laughed.

"No; I have worked too hard on this day. What are you on?"

"Number six," Kate smiled.

"Right. It's back in the kitchen," Rett said. Kate gave him the side-eye as she headed to the kitchen. Almost immediately, her eyes fell on something in a chair at the table. She walked over and found a picnic blanket with KJJ—her soon-to-be initials—monogrammed on it. On top of the blanket was her third rose.

"I can't wait to use it," she said as she re-appeared in the living room. She placed the rose in the vase with the two she had collected so far. "Number seven." Kate was doing some calculating in her head as she figured which bouquet she was on. "Oh, I know. Your first Christmas party at The Well—when we had to talk about boundaries again."

"Wow, I'm impressed."

"You didn't think you were the only keeping up with the bouquets, did you?"

"I mean, I figured you were, but we never really talked about it," Rett shrugged sheepishly.

"Well, I was. And I'm sure I'll tell you about it sometime," Kate winked.

"What are you talking about?"

"Don't worry about it; it will probably be part of your wedding present. Okay, what am I supposed to be looking for?" she asked, getting back to business.

"What are you on again?"

"Christmas Party," Kate answered. She laughed as Rett handed her a box wrapped in crazy Christmas paper.

"I was told we had to open it together, so I'm not entirely sure what it is." Rett and Kate sat down on the couch and opened the gift to find a photo album with pictures of the families at The Well. Throughout the album were encouraging notes, prayers, and advice from the students and their parents.

"This is incredible!" Kate sat down on the couch with Rett to read through it together. They were amazed at what people said and the things they were praying for them.

"Wow; I had no idea they were putting this together," Rett said with deep gratitude.

"We need to make sure we tell them thank you. This took a lot of work," Kate said.

"For sure," Rett said as they closed the book. "I will forever be thankful for this church."

"Me too." Kate kissed him. "Back to the roses?"

"Sure," Rett chuckled. "Do you remember where we were?"

"Youth Group Christmas party, number seven. Which would mean that we're on number eight, which came after our trip to D.C. with Emmie Wren and Sky."

"Nicely done," Rett applauded her. "That trip really showed me what it would be like to be a part of your family. Plus, Sky and I really bonded." Rett's eyes twinkled as he pointed toward the window. Kate walked over and found a D.C. ornament tucked into the blinds.

"It's perfect. I love it," she said as Rett came up behind her, wrapped his arms around her waist, and kissed the top of her head. "That trip was a lot of fun. It was really the first time we got to go somewhere with Sky and Emmie Wren but without my parents," Kate remembered.

"The first of many trips, I hope. I mean, I love your parents—don't get me wrong," Rett stammered.

Kate just laughed. "I know what you mean." Relief spread across Rett's face, and Kate kissed him, "Breathe, Superman. I know you love my parents."

"I'm sorry; today just has me on edge," Rett sighed. Kate looked at him innocently and batted her eyelashes as if to tell him he could end the edginess if he'd just propose now. "Just so you know, your engagement ring isn't here. So even if I decided to change my mind—which I won't—tempting me wouldn't do you any good."

"What do you mean my ring's not here?" Kate asked in surprise. "Where is it?"

"Somewhere safe."

"So, it's with Nathan?" Kate retorted.

"Maybe," Rett laughed. "Yeah, it is."

"I would expect nothing less," Kate smiled.

"Number nine?" Rett reminded her.

"My full summer in San Antonio teaching ESL classes."

"Yep. You were doing what you love, and I was so incredibly proud of you," Rett said. "Go in the bathroom and see if you can find your next gift."

Kate did as he instructed, but she was unsure of what she could possibly find in the bathroom to remind her of that summer. She opened the door and looked around, but she didn't see anything out of place. Just as she was about to give up, Kate looked down at the rug she was standing on; it was Hispanic looking, both in color and design. "Where did you get this? It's beautiful."

"It's a tapete from Mexico," Rett said. Kate's hand flew over her mouth; she knew what that meant.

"Did Mariah send anything else?" she asked excitedly. Even in the midst of Rett's proposal, she was delighted to hear news from her friend.

Rett nodded and started to read, "Hey, Kate. I picked this tapete out because I thought it looked like you, and I hoped you could use it as a rug in your house when you and Rett get married. I can't believe you're *finally* getting engaged. I expect a video call with all the details. I know your man has something incredibly special planned for you, especially if he's getting me in on it. I'm so happy for you and Rett. I love you, Mariah."

Tears filled Kate's eyes. "Thank you," she managed as her lips touched his. Rett handed her the note, and Kate read it a few more times. Then they prayed together for Mariah and the ministry she was doing in Mexico. "I miss her," Kate said.

"I know. Me, too," Rett smiled. Then he brought her back to the joy of the day. "Number ten?"

"The beach trip," Kate sighed.

"I know there are some not-so-great memories attached to that trip, but I'm so thankful for the friendships the Lord has blessed us with. I can't wait to see who else He brings into our lives, but I know that Nathan and Hanna, Lynne and Houston, and Patrick and Caroline will be around for the long haul," Rett grinned.

"You printed it, didn't you? Is in your room? Because I would have noticed already if it out here," Kate said excitedly as Rett opened the door to his room. On the bed lay a canvas print of a picture from Nathan and Hanna's wedding. The picture was one of Kate's absolute favorites, and she had often talked about wanting a copy of it. It so perfectly captured each of their friends' personalities. Hanna was kissing Nathan's cheek while Nathan made a stupid face and put bunny ears on his bride. Rett's eyes were wide with excitement, and he had an elbow in Nathan's side. Kate was rolling her eyes with her hands in the air, as if to say she didn't even know how to handle those boys. Patrick's arms were stretched out toward the camera in an attempt to steal some of the spotlight. On the other side of Hanna, Caroline was laughing with her hand on her forehead, like she was asking, "Who are you people?" Lynne stood next to Caroline with a book in her hand that Houston was pushing down in an attempt to high-five Patrick.

"It's going above the TV. Wanna help me hang it?" Rett asked, and Kate agreed. They continued to talk about their friends until it was hung.

"Perfect," Kate said, standing next to him. "I can't wait for it to hang in our house someday soon."

Rett pulled her into closer to his side and kissed the top of her head. "Me neither. Okay, last one?"

"Our trip to the mountains for New Year's, when you finally told me about the scars."

"Yes. New Year's Day before I woke you up, I spent a lot of time praying for you and praying for the year we had a head of us. You are going to graduate and look for a job. I asked your parents for their blessing to marry you while we were in the mountains. And honestly, I hope we will be married before the year is over." Rett held both of her hands. "This is a big year for us, and all our dreams are coming true. I want you to have something to help you transition through everything that is coming, so—" Rett walked over to the entertainment unit and opened one of the drawers. He pulled out a rose and a wrapped gift. He set the rose in the vase with the other three and handed Kate the gift. She unwrapped it to find a Bible with "Katherine Joy Johnson" embossed in silver letters on the front.

"It's perfect. I can't wait to start using it," she breathed as she kissed him.

"And I can't wait to spend my life with you," he responded.

Phase One of his proposal was complete.

Now it was time for Phase Two.

Chapter Thirty-Five

"I thought we'd go ahead and eat lunch," Rett said, "Since I know you're used to eating early at school."

"Okay, that sounds wonderful." Kate and Rett fell into step together in the kitchen, then settled at the table. "I know we're not technically engaged yet, but can we talk dates? Because you know that's the first thing we're going to get asked," Kate pleaded.

"Fine," Rett acquiesced. "If I get this job at Generations, I'll start around the time you graduate. I know that summer would be best for you with your teaching schedule, but summer is the craziest time for youth ministry."

"Fair enough. Not August because that will be right when school is starting. What about Labor Day? Or even later in September? I don't really want to wait much longer than six months."

"Why don't we just say sometime in September for now? That way it's a ballpark date, but it leaves us some options," Rett suggested.

Kate was fine with that, but before she could say anything, Rett's phone starting ringing. "Hey. What? You're serious? Okay, I'll leave in second."

"You're—you're—you're leaving?" Kate stammered. "What happened?"

"Emergency. I'm really sorry, but I'll be back in a little bit," he kissed her. "Why don't you call Hanna?" Rett added on his way out.

As the door shut, Kate smiled. Mentioning Hanna gave him away; there was no emergency—thankfully. He just needed an excuse to head out and finish whatever he was planning for the rest of the day.

"What are you doing?" Kate asked when Hanna answered.

"Just cleaning the house. What about you?" Hanna asked with a grin in her voice.

"Oh, I just got ditched by my boyfriend in the middle of our engagement day. But on his way out the door, he told me to call you."

"I'm on my way," Hanna said, her laughter bubbling over as she hung up the phone.

Kate picked up the Bible and ran her fingers over the silver letters. She was getting engaged later that day, and she would be Kate Johnson sometime in September. She opened the Bible and turned to the dedication page, which read, "To Kate Adams. Presented by Rett Johnson on March 12, the day of our engagement." Under that, he had written, "I want our marriage to start and end with God's Word. I've marked some verses for you to read that I know you will find encouraging in the crazy times ahead." Kate was about to start looking for some of the marked passages when the door opened.

"Hey, girl!" called Hanna.

"There is no emergency, is there? Rett left so you could come?" Kate asked pointedly.

"I don't know," Hanna answered distractedly. "But if you come to the car with me, you might find something of interest." She was clearly avoiding Kate's question.

"Hanna—"

"That's all I can say." Hanna zipped her lips as Kate stood up. "I'll be right behind you," Hanna added. "I just need to go to the bathroom, but I'll lock up on my way out."

Kate walked outside, and Hanna pulled out her phone to help her remember what she needed to bring with her. She opened her purse and threw in the sparkly heels and the Bible before locking the door and meeting Kate at the car.

"There's a rose in your car. I knew I was right," Kate beamed with her accomplishment. "So where are we going?"

"I can't tell you that. Rett would kill me, and Nathan—well, I don't want to cross my husband on this one. I love you, but you're not worth it," Hanna laughed as Kate's jaw dropped. "What number rose is this one?"

"Five. Only seven more to go before he proposes." Kate told her all about the morning, and they drove until Hanna stopped in front of a boutique. "What are we doing here?"

"You're supposed to pick something up." Hanna picked up her phone and read, "It will be obvious what it is."

Kate repeated Rett's words in her head as she walked into the store and started looking. Finally, it dawned on her. *Look for a rose,* she told herself.

"Can I help you?" one of the girls working asked.

"I don't think I'm supposed to ask for help. My boyfriend has me on a hunt for something specific," Kate admitted.

"Have you looked in the back of the store yet? I think you might find something there," the helpful attendant said.

Kate followed her suggestion, and at the center of the back of the store was a dress form with a solid pink dress on it. The dress matched the pink on her Kate Spade sling-backs, and there was a rose stuck in the middle of the V-neck. She checked the size; it was medium—her size.

"I think this is my dress," Kate laughed. "My name is Kate Adams," she told the girl, who nodded and pulled it off the dress form. She handed Kate the rose and bagged the dress for her. Kate thanked her and walked out the door, holding the rose and the bag. "Where to next?"

"Wouldn't you like to know? In other news, you're halfway to the ring," Hanna offered as she pulled out of the parking lot and headed to the next location. "I get to join you for this one," Hanna said as they pulled into the parking lot of a nail salon.

"I love that man! He thought of everything." Kate and Hanna each picked a color and were led to a couple of pedicure stations. Once Kate sat down, she saw a rose in another chair. "That's mine," she said, pointing to the rose.

"Kate?" the lady doing her nails asked. Kate nodded and the nail artist handed her the rose and started her nails. She had chosen a soft, light pink color for her nails so that she would be ready for the pictures she was sure would come later that night. As they were pampered, the girls talked about things to come.

The next stop was the makeup counter, where Kate got her makeup done and another rose. Afterward, they headed to Nathan and Hanna's house, where Hanna curled her hair and gave her the ninth rose. Kate shot Hanna a look, then laughed out loud as Hanna pulled the heels Rett had given her earlier out of her purse. She changed into her new dress and was finally ready for whatever Rett had in store.

"Dang, girl, you clean up good," Nathan said when she walked into the living room.

"Thanks! I can't believe I'm about to get engaged," Kate laughed.

"Me neither. He's only been planning this forever. Ready?" he asked as he led her out the door.

"That's a limo." Kate froze as soon as she saw it; it was like her feet wouldn't let her go any farther.

"Nice observation skills. You should be detective," Nathan joked as he nudged her to get her moving again. He pulled her along and opened the door for her. Sitting on the seat was a single rose. Nathan shut the door, and the limo lurched into motion. Kate's heart was in her stomach. She only had two roses left, and it was time to meet Rett. When the limo came to stop, the door opened, and Rett was standing there with another rose. It took her a minute to figure where they were, but then she realized it was Piedmont Park.

"Hi." Kate's eyes filled with tears; she had never been so happy to see him.

"Hi. You look stunning," he said as he helped her out of the limo. "Walk with me?" He extended his arm, and Kate took it. "Well, this is rose number eleven, so I know you know what's coming. But I also want you know that I love you more than anything, and I can't wait to spend the rest of my life with you." Kate kissed him, and they walked to a bench surrounded by candles. On the bench was the final rose laid over her new Bible. How he got it to the park, she would never figure out.

They sat down, and Rett took both her hands. "I want our marriage to be centered on God and His Word, which is why I gave you the Bible and marked verses in it for you. I know God's Word is the only thing that will get us through marriage. I want to lead you as Christ leads the church. I feel at home when I'm with you, and I can't wait to spend the rest of my life with you." Rett got off the bench and got down on one knee. "Katherine Joy Adams, will you do me the honor of becoming my wife?"

"Yes! Yes—a thousand times yes," Kate squealed excitedly before her lips met his. Rett slipped the ring on her finger, and Kate just stared at it. "It's beautiful. It's perfect. Thank you."

"I'm glad you like it. I love you so very much." He kissed her again. "I thought we'd get some dinner alone before we tell the world?"

"I like that like plan," Kate said as they walked back to the parking lot.

They enjoyed a meal alone and uninterrupted, and it was wonderful. "This was perfect. I have loved everything about this day. Thank you," she repeated as she kissed him before they got in his car. As they started to drive, Kate pulled out her phone. "Who do we tell first?"

"Let's wait until we get back, okay? Just a few more minutes, so we can tell everyone together." Rett reached for her hand, squeezed it, and brought it to his lips as Kate nodded.

"Congratulations!" Hanna and Nathan cheered as Rett and Kate walked into their house. Across the mantle, there was a banner that read, "Just Engaged."

"Thank you!" Kate hugged them both, and then she and Rett sat down to make phone calls and celebrate with the people closest to them. It was late when Rett left to head to his apartment.

Kate walked back to the guest room to find a bridal basket on the bed from Hanna that included a hat, some magazines, a wedding planning book, and a journal. "Congratulations, Kate," Hanna said, leaning against the doorframe.

"Thank you for everything," Kate smiled.

"Of course. I'm so excited for you and Rett."

"I'm excited, too," Kate admitted. "I've been waiting for this for a long time. I love him, so very much." It had truly been the most perfect day.

She was going to be Rett's wife in just a few short months.

She just had to get home to start wedding planning with Emmie Wren and meet her niece.

Chapter Thirty-Six

"Congratulations!" Emmie Wren squealed when Kate and Rett walked in the door Sunday afternoon.

"Thank you! Now let me see that little girl," Kate insisted, reaching immediately for the bundle in her sister's arms.

"Kate," smiled Emmie Wren, "This is your niece, Mily Kate Thomas. We are calling her Mily Kate." Emmie Wren handed over her five-day old daughter as Rett looked on with awe.

"Mily Kate. . . It's perfect," Kate whispered, looking up at her sister with eyes full of unshed tears. "She's perfect."

"Where did Mily come from?" Rett asked.

"We wanted something that was a derivative of Emily, since Mom and I share that first name, and we just fell in love with Mily."

"That's sweet," Rett said, letting the little girl wrap her fingers around one of his.

"Now that you're holding Mily Kate, I want to hear all about yesterday," Emmie Wren demanded. She smiled at Sky, who had just finished putting Kaden down for a nap.

Kate and Rett filled them in on the details of the engagement. Right away, Emmie Wren moved into wedding-planning mode. "Sorry," Kate shook her head as Emmie Wren asked a question about colors, "I can't think about it until after my interview is over. But I do know that I want you to be my matron of honor." Kate looked at her sister hopefully.

"Yes, of course!" Emmie Wren sat back; she had known it was coming, but it was still nice to be asked. The sisters grinned at each other, both thrilled with where God had brought them. For the rest of the day and all of Monday, Kate spent as much time helping her sister as she could while she prepped for her interview.

***

"I got this," Kate said to herself as she pulled up to Generations Christian Academy at 9:45 am on Tuesday morning. She was nervous but excited. Rett texted her to wish her good luck and remind her he was praying for her. She responded that she was proud of him and couldn't wait to hear about his interview, which was really just a chance for him to meet the rest of the staff. Rett's job was pretty much guaranteed, but she still had to nail her interview. *Dear God, this is my dream. Now that we know Rett will be here, I can actually be excited about it. Please give me the words to say,* Kate prayed as she walked into her alma mater.

"Kate Adams," she introduced herself as she walked to the school's reception window. The secretary had to call someone to escort her into the building, but when she hung up, she let Kate know that

Francis was coming to get her.

"Welcome back! We're glad you're here," the petite older woman said as soon as she walked in. Mrs. Francis was the headmaster's secretary. She had been around the school for a while, and Kate recognized her from her high school years.

"I'm glad to be back," Kate hugged her.

"And I'm told some congratulations are in order," Francis laughed.

"Yes; thank you! I got engaged this weekend," Kate exclaimed, extending her left hand. The two moved toward the conference room where her interview would be held, and Kate was amazed at just how little everything had changed in the last four years. If she closed her eyes, she felt like she would be a senior in high school again, counting down days until graduation. "This place hasn't changed at all," Kate smiled before stopping in front of the room where the headmaster, high school principal, and one of the Spanish teachers were waiting. She stepped through the doorway and took a deep breath; this was really happening.

For the next hour, she answered all the questions the interview board threw at her, even carrying on a brief conversation entirely in Spanish with the other teacher. She felt she proved that she knew her stuff; her professors and cooperating teacher would have been proud. She was confident the interview went well, and the board promised to let her know something by the end of the week. She left feeling good about the job and texted Rett to see how things were going for him. He was still in his interview, though, so while he finished up at the church, she headed home to get some lunch.

She had just pulled into her parents' driveway when her phone rang. "How was the interview?" Rett asked immediately.

"I feel really good about it! What about yours?"

"It's still going, but it's been great. It helps that they already know me," he laughed.

"I feel the same way," Kate smiled. "We got this. See you later?"

"Yes. We are going to celebrate these interviews being over tonight," Rett added before hanging up. They were so close to calling this city home, officially.

* * *

"I'm engaged! Can you believe it?" Kate squealed when Mariah's face filled her computer screen Friday morning. She was back in Atlanta with Rett waiting on news about her job.

"Show me that ring!" Kate held her left hand up to the camera on her laptop for Mariah to ogle. "Dang; he did good."

"Thanks! And thanks for helping out," Kate added. "I love the tapete, and your letter made me cry."

"I'm glad I was able to be a part of it since I couldn't be there," Mariah answered. Then she quickly changed the subject, not eager to think about how much she was missing during her time in Mexico. "How'd the job interview go?"

"Great. I'm supposed to find out something today," Kate shared. "Rett got the job at Generations, though, so we're moving to Albany no matter what. I can't believe everything is falling into place. I just really hope I get this job!"

Mariah assured her that everything would work out and prayed for her. Then Kate filled Mariah in on the details of Rett's proposal. They talked about the wedding and what Kate was going to do about bridesmaids. For Mariah, all of the wedding talk was hard, since she was sure she wouldn't get to be there. But it was also a breath of fresh air to be able to talk to her friend as though mere inches, rather than hundreds of miles, separated them.

Mariah shared a bit of what her ministry in Mexico looked like, too. Kate especially loved the stories of the kids at the school where Mariah worked. The two friends were just wrapping up their conversation when Kate's phone started ringing.

"It's GCA!" Kate exclaimed.

"Answer it!" Mariah muted the microphone on her computer as Kate answered so she could listen without interrupting.

"Kate, this is Francis. On behalf of Generations Christian Academy and Dr. Joiner, we would like to offer you the position of Spanish teacher to start in August." Kate couldn't breathe. This was real; she was being offered the position she had been dreaming about. "Kate?" Mrs. Francis asked after receiving no response.

"Yes! Sorry, I was too thrilled by the news to remember to respond," Kate laughed. "I will gladly accept the position," she managed. Mariah squealed silently as Kate gave Francis the information the school needed to complete her hiring process. "Is this real life?" Kate asked in a daze as she hung up.

Mariah unmuted her microphone, and the two squealed together. "Good grief," Mariah grinned. "You're engaged to the man of your dreams, and you just got your dream job; it's about as real as it gets. I have to go," she said, motioning to someone behind the computer, "But I'm glad I got to experience that moment with you! I'm so happy for you and Rett. I love you. I'll talk to you later," Mariah said before ending the video call.

Kate was in shock; she was still sitting on the living room floor staring at the computer when Rett and Nathan walked in about ten minutes later.

"Katie," Rett greeted her, pulling her back to reality.

"I got the job at GCA," she said without fanfare.

"Katie," Rett repeated as he closed her computer, pushed it out of the way, and sat down in front of her. His eyes met hers, and she finally began to take in all that was happening. "Kate," he smiled, "I'm so proud of you. I can't wait to start this journey with you."

"I love you," she sighed. "I just can't believe all our dreams are coming true." She turned and leaned her back against Rett's chest so his arms would wrap around her.

"They are. God is so good. I love you too." He kissed the top of her head before clearing his throat. "Well, we have some celebrating to do. I'm going to go change and throw some burgers on the grill."

"Oh!" Kate exclaimed, suddenly remembering to tell Rett about her video call. "I got to talk to Rye!"

"Good! Did you tell her thank you for me?"

"Of course," Kate said. Then her brow furrowed. "I wish she could make it to the wedding," she sighed. "But I know she's doing what God called her to do. And at least she got to be a part of everything, even from a distance. Hopefully she won't miss too much more. Only one more year until she can come home!"

Things were changing fast, but Kate was looking forward to all the things the future would hold for both her and her friends.

Chapter Thirty-Seven

"Promise you won't say anything," Patrick insisted as he pulled a beautiful sapphire ring out of his pocket.

"Dang boy, you didn't waste any time, did you?" Kate laughed. "She's gonna freak." She and Patrick had found a spot on campus to meet away from Caroline's prying eyes just a few days before graduation.

"I just hope she says yes," Patrick said, blowing out a breath.

"Surely you didn't buy an engagement ring if you thought she was going to say no." Kate stared at him. Patrick normally exuded confidence, so it was a rare occasion to see him doubting anything, especially himself.

"Oh, come on, that is not fair!" Patrick rolled his eyes. "You know as well as anyone what Caroline and I have been through this year. I have the right to be a little worried."

"You're right, I'm sorry. That was rude. Caroline is crazy about you, and I don't have any doubts that she will say yes whenever you decide to ask her," Kate smiled.

"That's actually why I wanted to talk to you." Patrick's signature grin appeared. "I need your help."

"I'm in," Kate laughed as Patrick went over his plan.

* * *

"I will never understand that man." Caroline walked out of her room all dressed up and ready for her date with Patrick on the Thursday night before graduation.

"You look beautiful," Kate told her friend.

"This is stupid. My family is supposed to be here any minute, but Patrick is insisting that we squeeze one last date in before the craziness of graduation weekend." Caroline rolled her eyes.

"Go; have fun. Enjoy yourself. College is over. Celebrate with your boyfriend!" Kate exhorted her. "All I have to do is sit around counting the minutes until Rett gets here tomorrow. If your family gets here before you get back, I will entertain them. They love me," Kate assured her, nearly pushing Caroline out the door.

"You have good timing," Patrick laughed as Caroline met him at the door. "You ready?"

"Sure, let's go," Caroline smiled. Kate was right—she deserved a fun night with her boyfriend after the crazy semester they both had. Plus, they were graduating.

"I can't believe this is it," Patrick sighed as they got in the car.

"I don't know how graduation got here so quickly," Caroline smiled. "So, where are we going?"

"You'll see," he smiled. But within minutes, Caroline had figured out where they were headed.

"We haven't been here in forever," she laughed as they pulled into the parking lot of the restaurant where they had their first date.

"I figured it was our last chance," Patrick told her. They enjoyed a quiet dinner together before heading to campus.

"How is college over? I feel like I blinked and it was gone," Caroline said as they started their normal route. They had gotten into a habit of wandering campus together for study breaks throughout the semester.

"I know. It's hard to believe it's almost time for me to move to North Carolina to start working on my PhD. And teaching, of course," he sighed contentedly. He had gotten into his dream PhD program.

"You are going to be the best professor," Caroline assured him.

"And you are going to be an amazing teacher. But the question remains: where are you going to teach?" Patrick laughed.

"Patrick, I—" Caroline turned to look at her boyfriend, but he wasn't walking next to her anymore. She turned around to find him down on one knee, and she gasped. She hadn't been expecting him to propose, but it didn't surprise her. "Patrick?" she walked the couple steps back to where he was.

"I know this was the last thing you expected, but I love you and I want to spend my life loving you. Caroline Elyse, will you marry me?" Patrick popped open the ring box he'd been carrying in his pocket all night. Caroline had tears in her eyes as she nodded enthusiastically, bending down to kiss him.

"I love you," she finally managed as he stood up and slipped the sapphire ring on her finger. They found a nearby bench to sit on for a minute as Caroline got used to their new relationship status. "I guess I need to move North Carolina up to the top of the list for my job search, huh?"

"I mean, it would be nice," Patrick laughed and kissed her. "We should probably go; your family is waiting on us."

"Nicely done," she smiled as they headed back to Caroline's apartment to celebrate with her family. It was the perfect way to start graduation weekend.

* * *

"There's our graduate!" Charlie hugged his youngest daughter in the parking lot of her apartment complex the next afternoon. Kate greeted everyone and helped them unload the car.

"When is Rett getting here?" Emily asked.

"He left at noon, so he should be here in about an hour," Kate informed them.

As soon as they got into the apartment, Kate took Mily Kate out of her car seat. She told her family all about Caroline's engagement and updated them on her own wedding plans. They were talking about their itinerary for the weekend when Rett walked in.

"Emmie Wren, she looks just like you," Rett said after greeting everyone. He gently took the cooing baby from Kate's arms, but not before stealing a kiss from his fiancé.

"I know; it's kinda scary," Emmie Wren admitted as she and Kate exchanged a glance. They were both thinking about what a great dad Rett would be one day.

Rett bounced and played with Mily Kate until she started crying. "I'll take over; she's hungry," Emmie Wren said. "I'll feed her, and then we can go to dinner."

"You're really not going to make it to Albany until Sunday night?"

Rett asked after Emmie Wren left the room.

"We've gone over this; there is just no way," Kate replied.

"No way for what?" Emily butted into the conversation.

Rett watched Kate out of the side of his eye as he answered, "My first day at Generations is Sunday, but Kate doesn't want to ask if she can come back with me after graduation tomorrow. She wants to do her part to help move out of the apartment." Kate glared at him.

"That's ridiculous," Emily declared. "Rett is starting at the church you grew up in and will soon be getting married in. You're going with Rett; we will move you out. Everyone understands." The others nodded as Emily put her arm around her daughter.

"Thank you," Kate said, her resentment toward Rett lessening.

"Ride with Rett and leave your car with us so we can fill it up," Charlie added, and Kate nodded. The group talked about Rett's job until Emmie Wren and Mily Kate emerged from the bedroom.

As they headed to dinner, Kate got in the car with Rett. "Thank you," she said, kissing him. "Seven hours in car, just me and you— that sounds like heaven. It's been too long since we've spent that kind of time together. I've missed you."

"I've missed you too. I'm glad your family stepped in so that you can be there for my first day."

"I'm not sure if my family stepped in or if you did," she teased, "But I'm thankful either way. You've officially moved out of the apartment in Atlanta?" she asked, changing the subject.

"Yep; it's all in storage in Albany until we find a house, which I hope will be soon. In the meantime, I'm staying with Joshua and Hope. But I'd rather not live with them once we're married," he joked.

"As soon I get home from the beach, we can start looking for a house."

"Sounds like a plan. I will let you enjoy your bachelorette trip."

"Thanks. But before I can even think about that, there's graduation tomorrow and your ordination on Sunday—a lot of celebrating for one weekend."

"I'm so proud of you," he told her for the hundredth time. "I got you a graduation gift, but I want to wait until your family clears out tonight to give it to you," Rett said as they pulled up at the restaurant.

"Fair enough," she agreed, and they walked in. Kaden kept everyone entertained all through dinner, and Kate was reminded again how thankful she was for her family.

After dinner, Emmie Wren and Sky decided it was bedtime for the kids, so they headed to the hotel while Kate and Rett headed back to her apartment. Caroline and Patrick were sitting on the couch looking through possible wedding venues when Kate and Rett walked in.

"Well, well, look who's finally engaged," Rett said as Caroline stuck her ring finger in his face. "Dang, Paddy—you did good."

"He sure did," Caroline gushed over her sapphire ring. "It's perfect." She kissed her fiancé.

"We have graduation gifts for you both," Patrick announced. "Part of it you get now, and the other part later." He and Rett handed gift bags to their fiancés, who each reached in to pull out a bikini.

"To start working on your tans at the beach next week," Rett explained. "There's something else in there." Kate felt around and pulled out an envelope. Inside was information about a resort in Mexico.

"Mexico? I didn't expect you to tell me where we are going for our—" She looked over to see that Caroline was holding the same brochure. "Wait, a joint honeymoon? Wouldn't that be a little weird?"

"Yeah, it would," laughed Rett. "No, we're each going to have our own honeymoons. But we also wanted to be able to take a trip together. Maybe next summer or fall," Rett clarified. "And for the record, you will also be able to wear the bikini on our honeymoon," he added for Kate's benefit.

"Good to know." Kate kissed him, glad to at least know they'd be going somewhere tropical. "Thank you guys so much! This will be a fun trip, whenever we decide to go," Kate said. Caroline agreed, and they packed up more of the apartment before the guys headed to Patrick's for the night.

"We're graduating, getting married, and planning trips with our husbands," Caroline laughed. "Is this real life?" Kate laughed but understood what Caroline meant.

Real life was happening faster than she thought possible—

And it all started with graduation the next day.

Chapter Thirty-Eight

"Katherine Joy Adams, Summa Cum Laude." Kate walked across the stage and shook hands with the president of the university. She received her diploma cover and snapped a picture before returning to her seat. Caroline wasn't far behind her, and then Patrick was hooded with his master's degree. When the ceremony ended, they headed back to the apartment to take pictures.

"Thanks again," Kate said, hugging everyone. "I love you guys! I'll see you at home. Bye, Caro; I'll see you at Rett's ordination." Turning to Rett as she got into the car, she exhaled, "I can't believe I'm done with college; this is so weird."

"It will get less weird," Rett assured her as he kissed her. "Ready for the next season of life?"

"So ready." She took his hand, and they pulled out of the parking lot of the apartment complex that had been their home all through college.

The ride to Albany was long without a stop in Atlanta, but it gave them time to talk about the wedding and finalize some of their summer plans. "You're going to youth camp with me, right?" Rett asked again.

"Of course," Kate assured him. "What's the plan for tomorrow?"

"Church followed by lunch with Joshua, Hope, Nathan, Hanna, and most likely Pastor Eddie and Mrs. Carol. Chill afternoon, and then my ordination ceremony Sunday night with a reception afterward. When are you leaving for the beach?"

"First thing Monday morning," Kate said, exhausted just thinking about all they would accomplish before she left for her bachelorette trip. "How are you feeling about starting at Generations?"

"I could not be more thrilled." Rett kissed her hand. "Especially with you by my side."

Kate shook her head; she loved him so much. "Next question: I don't have a car, so how I am getting to church tomorrow?"

"Um, not sure," Rett admitted. He had forgotten that detail. "But I promise, we'll get it settled before I drop you off."

They finally pulled into Joshua and Hope's driveway at about ten. After a quick hello, Hope agreed to pick Kate up in the morning. They unloaded Rett's things and then hopped back in the car for the short drive to the Adams' house. "I love you," Rett said as he walked her to the door. "Thank you for being here with me."

"I love you, too," Kate responded, and Rett kissed her the way he had wanted to since he got to Schaeffer. Kate let herself melt into him, but she pulled back when she felt the desperation in his kisses. "We can't," she insisted. "We're too close, and I love you too much. I'll see you in the morning," she added before walking into her empty house and closing the door definitively behind her.

Her parents had stayed behind to get her apartment packed up, but none of them had realized what a temptation the empty house could pose.

* * *

The next morning, Kate was greeted by Rett's usual call and perky, "Good morning, beautiful."

"Good morning, handsome," she responded. "I'm so proud of you. See you soon." Kate got up and got ready for Rett's first day at Generations. When Hope got to Kate's house at 9:00 am, Kate was ready to hop right into the car. She helped Hope drop the girls off in their classrooms before taking her seat next to Rett in the sanctuary. Just before the service ended, Pastor Eddie called Rett onto the stage.

"This is Rett Johnson, and he will officially join the staff as the youth minister tomorrow morning. Tonight, we will host his ordination service here at the church followed by a reception. We look forward to all the things the Lord is going to do in and through his young man's ministry in the years to come," Pastor Eddie said. Rett met Kate's eyes, and she was beaming. Rett knew how proud of him she was.

Nathan and Hanna tagged along as Kate joined Rett for the youth Sunday school classes. Rett spent a large part of the class time introducing himself to many of the students. "Do you see that?" Kate whispered to Hanna.

"All the girls? Of course," she laughed.

"It doesn't help that Pastor Eddie mentioned nothing about the fact that we're engaged this morning," Kate fussed, rolling her eyes.

"What do you think our ladies are talking about?" Rett asked Nathan as the kids headed to their Sunday classes.

"The fact that you're being flocked by girls as usual."

"But they are teenagers. And she's my fiancé."

"That may be true, but Pastor Eddie didn't mention your upcoming wedding when he introduced you this morning. And you are a chick magnet—always have been, always will be. I know she's ready for you to have a wedding band on," Nathan said, nodding to Kate. Rett was the one who rolled his eyes this time. Kate was the only girl he had ever cared about and the only woman he would ever love. He knew she didn't need to worry, but he saw that there could be issues if things were not made clear from the beginning.

After Rett introduced himself to a few other Sunday school classes, the four friends went to meet Joshua and Pastor Eddie. "Pastor Eddie, you do know that Kate and I are engaged and will be getting married in September, don't you?" Rett said as soon as the greetings were out of the way.

"Yes," the pastor answered in confusion.

"Well, you just didn't mention her this morning. I know she's not my wife yet, but she will be soon, so it's important to me that she be included today." Rett's determination to have her included made Kate's heart swell.

"I'm sorry; it was not intentional," Pastor Eddie apologized, smiling. "Tonight, Joshua is in charge of the ceremony, so you can rest assured that everyone will know all about Kate by the time you are ordained."

"Don't worry, Kate will be included," Joshua reassured him. "I know that your relationship with her is the most important in your life." Rett squeezed Kate's hand, and the group decided on a spot for lunch.

"When is the wedding?" Carol, Pastor Eddie's southern wife, asked. He was the typical Southern pastor who loved college football and was at home on the golf course. The two of them just made sense.

"September seventeenth," Kate answered.

"That will be here before you know it. How are the wedding plans coming?"

"They're good. We're getting married at Generations, and the reception is at Doublegate Country Club. Kim Mallory is taking our pictures, I'm excited to be working with her and Jacob. We'll even have an engagement shoot when I get back from the beach. The bridal party is set, and Rett has our honeymoon planned, so everything is coming together. Just the details that need organized now."

"Sounds like it," Hope said. "Who are your bridesmaids?"

"Emmie Wren is my matron of honor. My bridesmaids will be Caroline, Rachel, Abbie, and this girl," she said, pointing to Hanna with a smile.

"Now Hanna—how long have you and Nathan been married?" Carol asked, turning the conversation to the newlyweds.

"June eighth will be a year," she smiled.

"That's awesome. And y'all live in Atlanta, right?"

Hanna nodded, and the ladies continued to talk about the wedding and their relationships all through lunch. In the meantime, the guys were talking about Rett's plans and where Rett and Kate should buy a house. Soon, it was time to pick Rett's family up at the airport. They were excited to celebrate this milestone in his life.

To round out the party, Chad, Jenna, Houston, Lynne, Caroline, and Patrick all arrived just in time for the service that night.

Rett and Kate sat on the front row as the congregation sang. Then Joshua got up on stage and started to speak. "I met Rett when he was nine years old and a bundle of energy. I had the privilege of leading him to the Lord two years later. Throughout Rett's youth, I was able to see him grow in the Lord, and God gave me the privilege of discipling him until I came here. Thankfully, our relationship continued even after Hope and I moved. Rett is one of my closest friends, and we know each other very well.

"Being a part of this church is something Rett has been looking forward to for a long time. For the last two years, he has served as the youth minister at The Well Church in Atlanta. The ministry there thrived under his leadership, and many students came to know the Lord."

Joshua continued to talk about Rett and how the Lord had used him and worked in his life. As Rett and Kate listened, she would occasionally squeeze his hand to let him know how proud she was of him. "Almost four years ago, Rett called to ask me what I knew about Kate Adams. Some of you may even know Kate and the Adams family, as she grew up here and attended Generations Christian Academy. The day Rett called me, I knew something was brewing. For the last four years, Rett has pursued Kate with the godliest of intentions, and I was thrilled when he called me in March to tell me that he had proposed to Kate. Rett and Kate have modeled what a godly relationship should look like, and I'm excited to be officiating their wedding in September." Joshua said a few more things before inviting the couple to kneel at the altar so that the staff and deacons could pray over them.

As service ended, Rett headed to the fellowship hall, but Kate got caught up talking to some childhood friends. When she finally walked into the room, she could not spot Rett. Then she noticed a big group of girls; it took her a minute to realize he was in the middle of the huddle. Kate sighed and rolled her eyes. He was too good-looking, and girls always tended to flock around him. Rett, to his credit, handled it with tact. He only had eyes for her, but that didn't stop Kate from getting jealous or anxious from time to time. Mostly, she worried that someday, an unscrupulous girl would try to put him in a compromising situation.

Kate sized up the situation and decided to do something. These girls needed to know for sure that he was taken, since Joshua's mention of his engagement seemed to have no effect on them. She was devising a plan when Nathan walked up.

"Are you going to claim your man?" he asked, rightly assessing her thoughts. Kate turned and gave him a what-do-you-think look before walking straight into the middle of the group. She dramatically placed her left hand on Rett's shoulder so everyone could see her engagement ring and kissed him fully on the mouth. When she pulled away, Rett was laughing. After she introduced herself as Rett's fiancé, the group started to defuse.

"I knew you were going to do something dramatic," he whispered in her ear. "Thanks for that." Kate smiled. She hoped to build a relationship with a lot of the girls, but she knew that right now, her relationship with Rett had to take priority.

Joshua walked up a couple minutes later shaking his head and smiling. He had seen the whole production. "Sorry," Kate said bashfully. "I just had to do something so they would know he was taken and stop drooling over him."

"Why are you apologizing? I loved it! I've heard tales of jealous Kate staking her claim. Now I've seen it in person, and it was awesome." Joshua hugged her. "He's yours, and everyone should know that. But then, they will soon enough."

Chapter Thirty-Nine

"Is that everything?" Emmie Wren asked as they loaded up the last of the luggage.

"I think so." Kate was grinning; they were moments away from heading to the beach for her bachelorette party.

"Good! I don't know how much more the cars could hold," Emmie Wren laughed. "Okay, everyone! Pile in." Emmie Wren snapped Mily Kate's car seat into the back, and Hanna and Jenna climbed in with her. Caroline got in the car with Lynne, which left Rachel and Abbie to ride with Kate.

"Where are we going exactly?" Rachel asked.

"Emmie Wren's husband, Sky? His parents have a beach house on St. George Island, and they were willing to let us use for the week, so that's where we're headed," Kate explained.

"That's awesome! So, is this close to where we went to beach with Rett and Nathan?" Rachel asked.

"It's about three hours from Destin, so not really. There's not a whole lot to do on the Island except be at the beach, though, so be prepared for that," Kate laughed.

"Tell us about the other girls going," Abbie wanted to know.

"You know Emmie Wren and Hanna from family stuff, right? Jenna is Hanna's sister. She's married to Chad, a super California guy who worked with Rett in Atlanta. I stayed with them when I visited Rett, so Jenna and I got to be friends. Caroline and Lynne are some of my best friends from college. But Lynne and Jenna aren't in the wedding; they're just coming to the bachelorette party. Lynne's only staying until Tuesday because she has to go back to work."

"Lame," Abbie laughed. "I'm excited about a week at the beach. I thought freshman year was going to kill me."

"How's it going? And soccer?" Kate asked.

"Soccer is great. College, however, is kicking my butt," Abbie answered truthfully.

"You'll get there. Freshman year is a lot about learning your way around and getting adjusted. Sophomore year is better all the way around," Kate said.

"I hope so. Next year I'll also get to play more, which I'm excited about," Abbie smiled. "Do you think you and Rett will be able to make it out to a game?"

"Maybe. Send us your schedule, and we will do our best," Kate told her. "But things are a little crazy with the wedding this fall, so it might have to be next year. I'm just glad you were able to get things cleared to come."

"Me too!" Abbie agreed. "I'll have to leave early Sunday morning to get back for my game that night, but thankfully, that's only game the whole week of your wedding."

"What about you, Rach? You ready for senior year?" Kate asked.

"I can't believe I only have one more year left. I'm so not ready for the real world," Rachel laughed.

"You'll figure it out. There is something about senior year that just clarifies things," Kate assured her. The three girls fell into easy conversation as they drove the rest of the way to the beach. They pulled onto Sky's family's property, a beach house dubbed "Seas the Day," that was on the Plantation at St. George Island a few hours later.

"This place is incredible," Caroline whispered to Kate as Emmie Wren showed them around the house.

"Sky's dad is a doctor," Kate whispered back, and Caroline nodded. Once everyone had brought their stuff in, Kate helped Emmie Wren get the kitchen put together with all the groceries they brought.

"You really shouldn't be helping me with your own bachelorette groceries," Emmie Wren told her sister.

"I'm the only one here who knows how you like things organized and how this house works. It would take you ten minutes to explain to someone what you wanted. Or you would just spend an hour re-doing it. So, I'm helping," Kate insisted, tackling the pantry while Emmie Wren organized the fridge.

"Can I help?" Lynne asked, standing in the kitchen in her swimsuit.

"Thanks, we got it," Kate told her. "Go on; we'll be down in just a few minutes."

Once they finished, Kate donned her new suit to join the rest of the girls on the beach. She hesitated when she realized Emmie Wren would be staying behind with Mily Kate. "Go, have fun. This is your bachelorette party," Emmie Wren insisted.

"Is Mily Kate okay?" Kate asked.

"Yeah, she's napping in our room," Emmie Wren smiled. "I'll bring her out later." She shooed Kate out the door to join her friends on the beach.

"Where's Caroline?" Kate asked, spreading her towel on the sand.

"She said something about helping Emmie Wren decorate," Lynne answered with a shrug.

"Ah, that's why Emmie Wren was pushing me out the door," Kate said, and they all laughed.

"Sky's parents are just letting us stay here? Because this place is awesome," Hanna marveled.

"Yep. Dr. and Mrs. Thomas are wonderful. I've known them forever, and I think they love me even more than Emmie Wren. Which is saying a lot, because she's married to their only child," Kate laughed.

"How long have Emmie Wren and Sky been married?" Jenna asked.

"Five years, but they have been together since Emmie Wren was 15," Kate answered.

"Dang! And I thought Houston and I had been together forever," Lynne laughed.

"Yeah, Emmie Wren and Sky have y'all beat. But not by much," Kate said, closing her eyes to rest.

"I know you're the guest of honor and all, but the least you could do is stay awake after all the work we've put into this week," Caroline teased as she blocked Kate's sun.

"Sorry, I didn't mean to," she said groggily. "How long was I asleep?"

"Well, Lynne and Hanna are inside getting a break from all the sun, if that tells you anything," Jenna laughed.

"Red-heads and their fair skin." Caroline rolled her eyes, and the rest of the group laughed. Kate managed to stay awake for the rest of the afternoon, and she was pleasantly surprised with Emmie Wren and Caroline's decorating. They put up banners, and there were pictures of Kate and Rett in various places. She was thankful her sister had shot down Caroline's threats to cover the place in pictures of scantily dressed men.

"It's perfect!" Kate said, taking it all in. "Thank you."

"You're so welcome," Emmie Wren said with a hug. Then she addressed the whole group. "Your places at the table are marked by a bag with your name on it that is full of goodies for this week. Don't expect anything extravagant, though. We will mostly be eating and hanging out here. We're going to two restaurants: one tomorrow with Lynne, and one later this week. It's going to be pretty chill, but make yourself at home. Dr. Daniel and Mrs. Nancy would want nothing less. They always say they want this place to feel like home to everyone who comes," Emmie Wren explained before getting dinner ready. The girls each received fake tattoos that said, "Bride Squad," a tank top, a cup with her personal monogram, and some hair ties.

"This is too much," Lynne said pulling out her tank top, which said, "Team Bride."

"This is Emmie Wren," Kate laughed as her sister handed her a bag with a bride tank, a "Future Mrs. Johnson" sash, bride tattoos, and some hair ties. They enjoyed dinner before Emmie Wren announced that it was time to play a game.

"We're starting with game to see how well you know Kate,"

Emmie Wren explained once they had cleaned up the kitchen and were gathered in the living room.

"This is going to be fun," Kate giggled as Emmie Wren passed out pens and paper. Emmie Wren asked the fifteen questions on her list and waited as the girls answered. Once everyone was ready, Emmie Wren went over the answers, and they all laughed together.

"I got them all right!" Caroline cheered.

"I got thirteen. I just missed her first job and where she wants to go on her honeymoon," Hanna added.

"Anyone else get that close?" Emmie Wren asked. When no one said anything, she handed prizes to Caroline and Hanna.

The next morning, the girls enjoyed a morning on the beach before heading to a restaurant on the island for lunch—one of Kate's favorites. Unfortunately, after the good food and good company, they all had to say good-bye to Lynne, since she had to get back to work in Memphis.

"Thank you for coming. It means the world to me," Kate said as she hugged Lynne.

"I'm sorry I couldn't stay longer," Lynne said.

"I'm just glad you got to come at all," Kate assured her.

"Me too. It's crazy to think that the next time I see you, you'll be getting married," Lynne sing-songed.

"I finally get to join the ranks of married life." Kate swooned dramatically, and Lynne laughed.

"You're going to love it." The two friends hugged as the group walked out of the restaurant. They all said good-bye to Lynne and headed back to the beach house.

The rest of the week passed uneventfully. It was fun and relaxing to just hang out at the beach together. The girls got know each other better, and whether they were lying out on the beach, getting in the water, playing games, or taking care of Mily Kate, everyone had a blast.

"This week has been amazing," Kate gushed on their last night. "Thank you, Emmie Wren."

"I'm glad. It's been so fun getting know your friends and actually spending some time together," Emmie Wren admitted as she sat on the bed feeding the baby. "You're going to be great wife. You know that, right?"

"I do. I'm so ready to be that man's wife."

"Not much longer now," Emmie Wren smiled.

"Not at all," Kate responded.

Chapter Forty

A few weeks later, Kate appeared in Rett's office doorway just after five. "Are you ready? We're supposed to be meeting Kim in twenty minutes for our engagement pictures."

"Can I have two minutes to finish this up?" Rett asked as Kate sat down on the couch in his office. When he was done, they headed to meet Kim downtown.

"Hey girl!" Kim hugged Kate. "I'm super pumped about this."

"Me too," Kate smiled. "This is Rett. I don't know if y'all have met or not, but—"

"Not officially," Kim said. "I have son in the youth group who won't shut up about you, though."

"Oh goodness," Rett laughed. "I hope that he's saying good things."

"Of course! Though my best friend's daughter is in the youth group, too, and we think she's got a crush on you," Kim winked.

"Well, this girl right here is the only girl I have eyes for, and

I will treat her with the respect she deserves." Rett put his arms protectively around Kate.

"Okay, I like you," Kim said. "You're going to be very good for my boys."

"That he is," Kate affirmed, kissing his cheek.

"What all did you bring today?"

"We brought our Bibles, a picnic blanket and basket, and some red roses. We have two outfits and then a fun one where we're both wearing Superman shirts and Rett wears a cape." Kate opened the back end of her car. "A superman cape, roses, and picnic gear. This is going to be a fun evening," Kim said, snapping some shots of everything in the car. "Why don't we go with fun first, since it doesn't seem like you want a ton of those." They agreed, and they took turns changing in the car.

"There's a story behind the superman shirts and cape, isn't there?" Kim asked Rett while Kate changed.

"Of course, there is. Otherwise I wouldn't be standing here in a cape, would I?" Rett shot her a side eye.

"No, you probably wouldn't."

"I'll let her tell the story, but the cape was an engagement gift from my best friend. He also gave me superman cufflinks that I'm wearing for the wedding," he added slyly.

"I take she doesn't know about the cuff links?"

"No, she—ready?" he asked as Kate climbed out of the car. She nodded, and the three of them walked to find a spot for the pictures. Rett put his arm around her back as they walked, and Kate slid her hand under his cape. "I feel ridiculous in this thing," Rett admitted.

"Blame Nathan; he's the one who got it for you." She kissed him just as they stopped to take their first engagement pictures.

"What's the Superman story?" Kim asked as they worked.

Kate jumped into an explanation. "We met when Rett was the leader of my group my first weekend at Schaeffer. He had a crush on me, but I didn't think that was possible, since every girl who saw him liked him. When the weekend was over—at the big welcome back gathering that Schaeffer hosts—I tripped, and he caught me and asked me to coffee. When I told my other leader about it, she explained that Rett was harder to get a date with than Superman, and it just kinda stuck. Right, Superman?" Rett laughed and kissed her.

Kim kept giving Rett and Kate directions as they finished up the first round of pictures. Then they were ready to change into the next outfits. "Let's do the dressiest outfit last," Kim said as Kate moved some clothes out of the way. "Woah! Those shoes are awesome," she exclaimed, noticing Kate's sparkling pink heels.

"Thanks," Rett said, leaving Kim confused.

"He bought them and the dress," Kate explained. "It's what I was wearing when we got engaged." Kate grabbed her black sundress and climbed into the car to change again. Rett changed when she was done, and they carried the picnic stuff and the roses down to Turtle Park. Once the blanket was spread out, they sat down, laughing and talking while Kim took the second round of pictures.

For the final pictures, Kate changed into her engagement dress and Rett put on his suit. "You really aren't going to do a first look?" Kim asked, looking over her notes for the wedding as they both changed.

"We're really not," Kate said.

"We want our wedding kiss to be special, and one of the ways we can make that happen is to have it be our first kiss of the day."

"Fair enough," Kim shrugged. This time, Kate and Rett told her the proposal story and answered questions about the wedding as Kim worked.

"Please tell me these are your wedding shoes," Kim commented as she squatted to get a shot of them.

"Of course!"

"Good, because I'm kinda obsessed with them," Kim laughed.

Suddenly, Rett pulled Kate to him, and her foot popped into the air. "Rett," Kate squealed as she wrapped her arms around his neck.

"Kiss him!" Kim said, and as their lips locked, the camera clicked like crazy. "Okay, we have time for a couple more shots, and the sun is perfect. Is there anything else you know you want?" Kate thought for a minute and looked at Rett, who shrugged.

"This is your area of expertise," Kate laughed.

Kim positioned them in a few more formal poses, then asked, "One last question—I know you said roses were a mark of your relationship, so does that mean your bouquet is going to be made of roses?"

"Yes," Rett said as he kissed her.

"Y'all are precious," Kim said as Kate looked up at Rett. His hands were around her waist, and hers were around his neck. "Perfect; don't move," Kim got closer and took a few last photos. "And we're done."

Kate grinned, the last big thing before the wedding was complete. September would be here before they knew it.

Chapter Forty-One

"Well, if it isn't the youth minister who's getting married on Saturday. Tell me, who is this lucky girl, since the teenagers all seem to think you're so cute?" Kate leaned against the doorframe of Rett's office the Wednesday before their wedding. The summer had passed quickly, and it was hard to believe the day they had waited on for so long was so close.

"She's the most amazing girl I've ever met. And she's pretty cute, too. Her name is Kate Adams, but not for much longer. In three days, she'll be Kate Johnson, and she'll be all mine." Rett walked over to her and put his hands around her waist. "I love you, Katie. I always will," he added, kissing her.

"I love you too," Kate grinned. "I can't believe it's finally time for us to get married."

"Saturday can't get here fast enough," he agreed, kissing her again.

"Any chance I'll get out of you where we're going on our

honeymoon?" Kate batted her eyelashes.

"Really? You're still trying that one?" Rett questioned. She laughed and fell against his chest. "You'll find out when you find out," he told her again. He kissed the top of her head before breaking the embrace. "Can you do me a favor? After we eat, you might want to check Mabel's office for gifts," Rett said and Kate agreed.

They had fallen into a habit of sharing dinner before youth group every Wednesday. This week, Kate brought simple sandwiches and chips, and they enjoyed an easy meal before Rett headed upstairs. Kate stopped by the receptionist's office and grabbed a few wedding gifts from behind her desk. Throughout the week, church members who wouldn't be able to attend the wedding had been sweetly dropping gifts off for them at the church, and Mabel's desk had become the gathering place for them. She dropped off everything in Rett's office before heading upstairs to mingle with the students.

"Kate!" Megan, the girl calling her, was one of her Spanish students at Generations Christian Academy. "It's okay that I call you that here, right?"

"Yes! In fact, I like that you can call me Kate outside of school. Here, I'm just Rett's fiancé—soon to be wife! Did you need something?"

"We were talking about the wedding and wondered if you could answer some questions," Megan said, gesturing to a group of girls standing a few feet away. Kate smiled and sat down in the middle of the group, answering all the questions they fired at her—from wedding details to hers and Rett's story.

Then one of the girls asked, "Is Rett a good kisser?"

"You don't need to know that answer," Kate responded, concerned. "The only person he's going to be kissing is me. Look, I'm willing to be open with you about my relationship with Rett, but that doesn't mean you can take advantage of it. You can learn a lot from other people, us included, but I'm not going to discuss things that should private between a married couple. Deal?" They all nodded in agreement and continued talking about more appropriate topics until it was time for the youth service.

"There you are," Rett said when she and the girls walked into the youth room.

"Sorry; swooning high school girls wanting every detail of our lives," she said, smiling.

"Sounds about right," he laughed. "You'll be managing high school girls for a long time."

Kate rolled her eyes. "It's a good thing I love you," she laughed.

"Why? Because otherwise you wouldn't be putting up with high school girls? You're a high school teacher," he reminded her.

"I meant because I have to put up with you," Kate laughed.

"Watch it," Rett grinned. He loved her laugh; it was first thing about her he had fallen in love with.

"What? If I'm not careful, you're going to call off our wedding? That's never going to happen, and you know it. You love me too much."

"Isn't that the truth." Rett kissed her forehead as the service got started. He was wrapping up a series on family, and that night, he taught a lesson on honoring one's parents. After he finished, he prayed and started with announcements.

"Who's coming to our wedding on Saturday?" Rett asked as he wrapped up the night. Kate was surprised at the number of hands that went up, but she was thankful they were so well loved. Rett dismissed the students but stopped to talk to several of them before he made it to the back of the room. "Looks like most of them are coming to the wedding," he noted.

"It's because they have a wonderful youth minister they want to support. Not to mention there were will food and gorgeous dresses," Kate laughed, and Rett shook his head as they walked back to his office.

"All this wedding stuff has gone to your head," Rett said.

"No; I think it's the fact that I'm finally going to be your wife. It's just now hitting me that I will have to live with a boy," Kate teased, turning up her nose.

"Gosh, I love you." He pulled her close and kissed her.

"Knock, knock." Joshua appeared in the doorway. "I hate to interrupt."

"Since when?" Rett said, Kate still in his embrace.

"Okay fine; interrupting is my specialty," Joshua grinned.

"Joshua and I have to talk, but we're still on for lunch tomorrow," he assured Kate. "I love you." He kissed her once more before she headed home to her parents for the night.

The wedding weekend was about to begin;

She just had to make it through her final day of work.

Chapter Forty-Two

"Last day of work before the big day!" Jackie London, the English teacher across the hall, stuck her head in Kate's room Thursday morning. Kate had taken Friday off, since the day would be filled with a bridal luncheon, decorating, last-minute details, and rehearsal for her wedding.

"Crazy, isn't it?" Kate looked up from her lesson plans. "Sorry; trying to make sure things are ready for my sub—especially since my phone will be turned off all week."

"Don't worry; I'll check in on your classes while you're gone. Put the fear of God in them," Jackie said, winking.

"Thanks! I'm sure they'll need it," Kate smiled.

"Where are you going, anyway?"

"I have no idea; it's a surprise. All I know is that it's somewhere tropical," Kate said. "You're coming to the wedding, right?"

"Wouldn't miss it," Jackie grinned as she walked out. Kate was thankful for friends at work, and with all she had to do to wrap up before the wedding, her day passed quickly.

"Hungry?" Rett asked, walking in just after the students left for lunch. He closed her door so they could eat in privacy.

"Starving." He handed Kate her sandwich he had picked up on his way to the school and they turned two desks to face each other. "I feel like we should be in the cafeteria with all the kids," she admitted.

"We will—after we get home from our honeymoon," he reassured her. "Right now, I just want to be with my bride and enjoy a moment's peace before the craziness that is our wedding begins." He kissed her. Lunch went by too quickly, and Rett ducked out before her classroom was invaded by high schoolers again.

"We thought we'd celebrate, since you're getting married this weekend," the students announced as they returned from lunch. Melissa, the yearbook editor, walked in with cookies and other treats.

"Y'all are too sweet," Kate thanked them. When she left the school about 4:00 pm, everything was ready for her substitute, and she was more than ready to get married.

* * *

"Is that the last of it?" Emily shut Kate's car door, careful not to crush anything in the full back seat.

"I think so. I have my bag packed for the honeymoon and the stuff I need for this weekend, but that needs to stay here," Kate answered.

"I can't believe you're really moving out and into your own house with your husband," her mom sighed.

"I know, but I'm so ready to be married to that man."

"And you are going to be a great wife. Dinner's at 7," Emily reminded her daughter as Kate headed to her new house, which Rett had been living in since they closed on it earlier that summer. She had just finished unpacking a box when Rett walked in.

"I could get used to coming home to you," Rett greeted her with a kiss.

"You'd better! After Saturday, this is officially my house too. Help me clean; you know your parents are going to want to see the house when they get here." She kissed him and handed him a broom.

"You are evil," he said, but he smiled as he kissed her. "Pure evil."

"You want this," she said pointing to herself and then to the house, "Then you've got to work for it. Saturday is still two days away, you know." Kate danced around and made Rett laugh.

"That's so not sexy." Rett pulled her into him. "But I do love you so very much."

Even with all of their joking around, Kate and Rett managed to get the house clean before his parents and Abbie arrived at six.

"Welcome to our home," he announced.

"I'm so glad you're here!" Kate greeted them, and the soon-to-be-married couple gave them the tour of the house.

"You've got it looking good in here," Esther said.

"Thanks," Rett answered and they all looked at him. "What?"

"Thank you, Esther," Kate replied as she rolled her eyes with a smile. "It's almost done. I'm hoping we get some sheets and towels as wedding gifts. A few other things and some gift cards will let us finish this place up perfectly. It's definitely home," Kate said as Rett put his arm across her back. She asked about Rachel and was told that she would be coming from school and getting there the next morning. "Now, if y'all are ready, my parents are expecting us."

"Yes, we're excited to see them again," Dale's thick Texas accent penetrated the room, and the family got in the cars to drive across town.

"Welcome! It's so nice to see you again. Even through Rett's ordination wasn't that long ago, it's always more fun to celebrate together," Emily greeted them. "Charlie's outside on the porch. Dinner's almost ready." She buzzed around the kitchen, and Esther quickly fell into step with her while Dale joined Charlie on the back porch.

"Who is this?" Dale asked Charlie about the bundle in his arms.

"My beautiful granddaughter, Mily Kate," Charlie answered. "We watched her today so Emmie Wren could get some last-minute things together for the wedding." The men got to know each other better, and Joshua and Hope arrived a few minutes later with Sky and Emmie Wren walking in just behind them.

"Where are my babies?" Emmie Wren asked.

"Kaden is with Kate in playroom, and your dad has Mily Kate on the back porch with Dale." Emily didn't look up from the potatoes she was chopping. Emmie Wren and Hope walked to playroom with Hope's girls so Jessie and Helen could play with Kaden, Kate, and Abbie while they all waited for dinner to be ready.

"Kate!" Jessie jumped into Kate's lap. Kate wrestled Jessie to ground while the 6-year-old howled with laughter.

"Hey Emmie Wren! Hey Hope!" Kate got to her feet and hugged them both. "Is dinner ready?"

"No; I just came to see my boy, but he's clearly too busy playing." Emmie Wren laughed at Kaden, who was now playing with Helen and had yet to acknowledge that his mom was even in the room. The ladies talked for a few minutes as the kids played.

"Dinner's ready," Sky announced.

"Daddy!" Kaden went running to Sky. Emmie Wren just shrugged and laughed; she was thankful for the bond Sky had with Kaden.

The little group all walked into the kitchen and gathered around the table. Emily had made a chicken dish, mashed potatoes, green beans, and biscuits.

"This looks wonderful. Thank you, Emily," Dale said when everyone was seated.

"Thank you, Dale. We're glad y'all could be here. Charlie, will you pray?"

"Of course," Charlie answered. "Dear God, thank you for this food and for family. We pray for Kate and Rett as they honor you this weekend and as the two families represented at this table become one. We pray your blessings on them for years to come. Thank you for this wonderful food and the hands that prepared it. We love you. In your son's holy name we pray, amen."

They passed the food and enjoyed dinner together before the craziness of the weekend began. Joshua and Hope left first with their girls, and the four Thomases were not far behind them. Esther and Dale gave Kate and Rett a minute to be alone before they left.

"I can't wait to be your wife." She kissed him and brushed the hair off his forehead.

"I love you," he responded. "I'll see you tomorrow." Rett kissed her, and Kate watched as he walked to the car, thankful their days of being separated were almost over.

The wedding festivities were about begin.

Chapter Forty-Three

"You're getting married tomorrow!" Caroline said a sing-song voice, her expressive brown eyes wide with excitement. Kate hugged her best friend, who was the first to arrive at the Williams' house. Sharon and Heather, two of her mom's friends, had graciously asked to host the bridal luncheon for her, and Sharon's home was the perfect place. "Who is getting their nails done with us this afternoon?"

"Bridesmaids plus Lynne and Jenna," Kate answered. She was thankful to have more time with her favorite group of girls.

"Tomorrow I can officially call you my sister," Rachel exclaimed as she rushed from the front door to hug Kate.

"I know! I'm so glad you finally made it. The trip wasn't too bad?"

"Not at all; it was nothing compared to what I have to drive to get home from school," Rachel reminded her. Kate laughed as Esther and Abbie followed Rachel in.

"You look beautiful, Kate," Esther said.

"Last night was crazy, so I didn't get to tell you that I really am excited about this weekend," Abbie said, hugging her soon-to-be sister-in-law.

"Me too," Kate winked. "I'm glad you're here."

Kate busied herself with introducing everyone: her bridesmaids, her closest friends, and her mom's friends, who were throwing the luncheon. They were just waiting for Hanna and Jenna.

"I would apologize but Chad is the one who made us late," Hanna announced, glaring at her sister as the two bustled into the room.

"Yeah, well, he is being extra Chad with the wedding this weekend," Jenna shrugged.

"It's fine," Kate laughed, hugging them both. With everyone there, Kate handed out bridesmaid's gifts. Each girl received a monogrammed button-down to get ready in; a necklace with a single pearl next to a silver disk with her first initial; and a wooden hanger for her bridesmaid's dress with her name, the wedding date, and "bridesmaid" engraved on it. She gave Lynne and Jenna each a necklace and robe, along with an invitation to join them in the morning to get ready.

Then Sharon and Heather served the girls lunch. Kate and her bridesmaids sat in the dining room while the rest of guests sat in the kitchen. They had chicken salad and pimento cheese with a salad and crackers. For dessert, they all exclaimed over Sharon's famous banana pudding.

"Thank you so much for hosting," Kate said as everyone began to leave. "I really appreciate it." Kate hugged Heather and Sharon. "Are you coming to help decorate?"

"Yes, we'll be there as soon as we get this place cleaned up,"

Heather answered with a smile. The few remaining guests said good-bye and headed to the church to get everything ready.

* * *

"Where are you and Rett going on your honeymoon?" Laura, another of Emily's friends, asked as the group got things ready at the church.

"That's a great question. Rett's surprising me. It's his thing; that man is all about some surprises," Kate laughed. "It's somewhere tropical, though. I know that much."

"A surprise is always fun. Do you have any guesses?" Laura put some greenery where she thought it would look good.

"I stopped trying to figure out his surprises a long time ago," Kate admitted. "I know that it will be beautiful and that we will enjoy ourselves. I trust Rett's judgments; he knows me very well."

"I'm sure he does. Rett's a wonderful man," Laura agreed, arranging some flowers on the altar. In short order, Laura and Kate had the stage looking good.

"Kate, time to go," Hanna called, and the girls headed out to get nails done.

"I'm getting married tomorrow," Kate laughed for the hundredth time as she got settled into a chair for her pedicure. The girls all talked as they got their nails done, thankful for a reprieve before the busy weekend kicked into full gear. Kate got a turquoise color on her toes and had French tips put on her nails, but all the bridesmaids had some shade of turquoise or grey to coordinate with the wedding colors.

"I'm going to change," Kate announced when everyone's nails

and toes were finished. "I'll see y'all back the church very soon. Ready, Caroline?" Kate and Caroline rode together to the Adams' house to change for the rehearsal. There, Kate freshened up her make-up, pulled her hair into a ponytail, and curled it. She pulled a white dress from her closet and stepped into it.

"That dress is super cute," Caroline said, walking into the room. Kate thanked her and turned so Caroline could zip her up. The dress was knee length with a full skirt that was belted by a pink band. It had pockets, a scoop neck, and cap sleeves. "Now, let's go," Caroline insisted after one final glance in the mirror. "The bride can't be late to her own rehearsal!"

"Ow ow! My bride is gorgeous," Rett crowed when they got to the church. He slipped his arms around her waist, tipped her head back, and kissed her.

"You don't look too shabby yourself," she replied. She ran her hands down the front of his white and pink striped button down and grinned at him. "I get to be your wife tomorrow," she added with a wink. Rett laughed, and Joshua called everyone together to start the rehearsal ceremony.

Linda, the church's wedding coordinator, paired up the bridesmaids and groomsmen, and they walked through the ceremony. Even from the rehearsal, it was evident that the wedding was going to be a beautiful, Christ-centered ceremony.

As Rett and Kate drove to the rehearsal dinner about an hour later, Kate took his hand. "You ready for this?" she asked. They pulled into the parking lot of the visitor's center at Chehaw Park.

"So ready," he answered definitively. "Mom planned a fun night. Let's go." Rett opened Kate's car door.

"Well. . . dinner can't start without us," she grinned. "And this is the last time we're going to be alone together until after the reception tomorrow," she finished as she put her hand on his cheek. Rett kissed her fully on her lips. For a few minutes, they stood in the parking lot making out until he pulled back, his breathing heavy.

"If we don't go in, people are going to wonder where we are. And you might just end up in the back seat. We're only one day away," he reminded them both as he rested his forehead on hers. After almost four years, tomorrow the desires she was feeling could be met without being sinful, because he would finally be her husband.

They walked into the visitor's center for a wonderful dinner catered by Austin's Firegrill. Everyone enjoyed the meal, and when it was over, Esther and Dale invited Rett and Kate to the front of the room. "We are thrilled to be celebrating Rett and Kate this weekend," Dale began. "It's easy to see how much these two love each other. It is our hope and prayer that they will chose to love each other every day, no matter how they might feel. Weddings are a time of new beginnings, and we are honored to be joining two families as one tomorrow. Kate, welcome to this family. We hope you know just how loved you truly are, not just by your groom, but by each of us." Dale raised his glass, and everyone else followed suit. Charlie and Emily said a few words about how happy they were for Rett and Kate. Then Rachel took the microphone to lighten the mood again.

"Kate and Rett, have a seat. Abbie, your assistance please," Rachel ordered. Kate and Rett sat back-to-back in chairs and were instructed to take their shoes off. They each kept one shoe and traded the second.

"We are going to see how well you really know each other," Rachel said. "I'm going to ask you a question, and you are going to raise a shoe in the air to represent who you think best fits each answer. Understand?" She waited for both of them to answer before starting with the questions. The whole crowd had a good laugh as Kate and Rett revealed who was a better cook, a better kisser, or most likely to lose the house keys.

The couple disagreed a few times,
But they were mostly in sync,
Just as they hoped to be for the rest of their lives.

Chapter Forty-Four

"Good morning, my beautiful bride," Rett's voice came through the phone.

"Good morning, my handsome groom." Kate was more perky than she normally would be at this hour.

"You were already up," Rett pouted.

"It's our wedding day; of course, I'm up! But if it makes you feel better, I've only been up for about ten minutes. I just fixed my first cup of coffee, and I'm about to read my Bible," Kate tried to cheer him up.

"What are you reading?"

"Psalm 45. What did you read this morning?" she countered.

"First John 4—the chapter that talks about perfect love driving out fear." Kate smiled; that was the perfect passage for him. "I love you. I'll see you in a few hours."

"I love you too. When you do see me, I'll be walking down the aisle," Kate giggled. They talked for a few more minutes before hanging up.

Kate sat on her bed and read Psalm 45. Then she looked around her room. This was it; she was getting married and moving in to her house—their house—with Rett tonight. *Dear God, calm my nerves. Walk with me through this day. Be glorified through our ceremony. May it be honoring and pleasing to you. Thank you for bringing Rett into my life. I want our marriage to reflect you to this crazy world, and I know that starts with how I love him as my husband. Thank you for today. I love you. In your precious son's name, I pray, amen.*

Just as she finished her prayer, Caroline knocked and came directly in. "You're getting married today," she said dreamily as she laid across Kate's bed.

"I know! It's crazy. I need food first, though; I don't want to pass out later. Let's go find my mom and eat some breakfast so we can get this show on the road."

Kate and Caroline walked into the kitchen. "There's the beautiful bride," Emily announced as they entered. She handed Kate and Caroline each an already prepared plate with an omelet and fruit.

"This looks awesome. Thanks, Mama." Kate ate her breakfast and looked around the kitchen she had grown up in. "Where's Emmie Wren?"

"On her way. Kaden did not want her to leave this morning," Emily laughed.

"Happy wedding day, Katie," Charlie said as he walked into the kitchen and hugged his youngest daughter. "I couldn't be happier for you."

"Thanks, Daddy. I love you."

"I love you too." He kissed her on the cheek before heading out to take care of some of the last-minute errands for the wedding.

"Katie!" Emmie Wren called when she walked into the house. "I can't believe you're getting married today," she squealed as she hugged her.

"Caroline, would you mind giving us a few minutes with Kate?" Emily asked. Caroline immediately agreed and headed back to the guest room.

"Do you have your something new?" her mom wanted to know.

"My dress."

"Something old?" Emmie Wren asked, and Kate thought for a minute before shaking her head. How could she have forgotten?

"That's what we hoped. Here." Emily handed Kate a ring box. "It's your Granny's. She wore it on her wedding day, I wore it on mine, and Emmie Wren wore it on hers." Kate admired the beautiful pearl ring.

"Thank you! It's perfect."

"Something borrowed?" Kate shook her head in response to her sister's question. "Okay, then it's my turn." Emmie Wren handed her another box, and Kate opened it to find a silver bracelet with an infinity symbol on it that Sky had given Emmie Wren when they found out they were expecting Kaden.

"Thank you. I promise I'll take good care of it," Kate smiled.

"And something blue?"

"Rett's wedding gift is supposed to be a set of turquoise teardrop jewelry I've been eyeing for months," Kate admitted.

"Let's hope he comes through," Emmie Wren laughed, but Emily had faith in Rett. They talked for a few more minutes and prayed together before Kate headed back to her room to make sure she had everything she needed for the ceremony and that her bag was packed for the honeymoon.

Caroline caught her in the hallway. "I wanted to give you Mariah's gift before your day got too crazy." She handed her best friend the small box and envelope. Kate read the letter first.

Dearest Kate,

It's hard to believe that you're getting married and I'm not there. I know you are ready to have a wedding band on your man's finger. You will stop at nothing to let the world know that his heart belongs to you. Your fierce protection is one of the many things I love about you, and I know the same is true for that wonderful man of yours. He loves you more than he probably should, but thankfully, your relationship is so centered on the Lord. God's love and protection will take you far if you keep it that way. The Lord at the center is the only thing that has gotten you this far with the secrets Rett holds so dear and the ones that he has still yet to share (assuming that he hasn't already told you). Remember we're all human—even Superman is defeated by Kryptonite—but with God, all things are possible. I hope you feel my hug through this letter. I wish with all my heart I could be there with you, but I'm sending love, prayers, and well wishes your way.

I love you,

Rye

"I miss her," Kate smiled with tears in her eyes. "I wish she was here." Kate opened the box that had come with the letter to find a dainty bracelet with blue beads. "Something blue! That girl." Kate shook her head as she put on the bracelet.

"She's good," Caroline laughed. "She would be here if she could."

"I know," Kate replied, laughing and wiping her tears away. "Okay, let's go. Everyone's going to be waiting on us." Kate gathered her stuff, and they left for the church.

* * *

"Maybe this was a bad idea," Nathan laughed as Rett's ball sailed into the cup on the seventh hole.

"I could have told you that," Chad said gruffly. He hated golf.

"This is the best I've ever done! I don't what you're complaining about," Rett laughed as Nathan's ball landed on the green just outside the hole.

"He's just mad because he's losing," Patrick commented. "Glad to see you're so relaxed, though, Rett. I thought if one of us would be uptight on his wedding day, it would be you, but you just keep proving me wrong."

"That means you're the one who's going to be uptight," Houston laughed. "I was as cool as a cucumber, Nathan doesn't have a serious bone in his body, and clearly, Rett here is relaxed enough to kick our butts in this golf game."

"I hate you. Maybe no one will be uptight," Patrick grumbled.

"Just hit the ball," Nathan said. The guys continued to play and enjoy their time together. The photographer, Kim's husband, Jacob, met up with them on the course and got some shots of them finishing up the game.

* * *

Kate walked into the bridal suite at about 1:00 pm. Sitting on one of the tables was a beautiful bouquet of white roses. The florist had added baby's breath to match the bridesmaids' bouquets, which would be just baby's breath. Then Kate noticed a wrapped gift and a letter, and she knew they were from Rett. She sat down on the couch and decided to read the letter first.

Dear Katie,

I can't believe this day is finally here. You are going to be my wife, and our next adventure is beginning. The past four years have been the best of my life, but they have nothing on the ones to come. You are the love of my life, and I love learning new things about you. I know that our marriage will bring all kinds of opportunities to do just that. I love you so very much, and I can't thank you enough for loving me unconditionally. You have helped me love you by the way you love me and accept everything about my past and about me. I'm so excited about this adventure we're embarking on — you teaching and me being the youth minister at Generations. God has such big plans for us, and I'm so excited to have you my side as they unfold. Today is just the beginning.

I love you more than you will ever know,

Rett

She wiped the tears from her eyes and opened the gift. Thankfully, it was the teardrop jewelry she had mentioned to her mom and Emmie Wren. "Isn't it pretty?" Kate grinned, showing her friends as they started filtering into the room.

"I love it," Hanna said. "I'd totally be stealing it we lived close enough to share."

"There's my bride," Kim said, snapping a picture the minute she walked in. "Don't you know you're supposed to wait on me?" She laughed as she saw the opened gift. Kate reenacted opening Rett's gift for the pictures as Kathleen arrived to do her hair and makeup. The girls talked and laughed as Kathleen gave Kate a crown braid and curled the rest of her blonde hair.

"Emmie Wren!" Kate suddenly gasped in a panic. "Rett's letter and watch are in my bag still! Can you put them in the boys' room, please? I completely forgot!"

Emmie Wren laughed and took the gift to the boys' room, but they weren't there. "Done," she said as she walked back in. "And no need to worry; they're not even here yet."

"Thank you," Kate breathed a sigh of relief as Kathleen put on her blush. "Have you heard from the boys?" she asked Hanna, mildly concerned.

"They are finishing up their golf game. Rett apparently played the best game of his life," Hanna answered.

"At least he's not nervous," Kate laughed. "I'm sure Nathan's ticked."

"Probably, but he's been keeping his texts and calls short today, so I couldn't get a great feel for his mood," Hanna admitted.

* * *

After a quick shower stop, Rett and his groomsmen arrived at the church. He was excited to see a letter and gift from Kate. The watch was perfect, and the letter was so beautifully written.

Dear Rett,

It's our wedding day! In just a few hours, I will walk down the aisle in a beautiful white dress and become your wife. I'm still amazed that you chose me, but I'm sure glad you did. Thank you for pursuing me in the godliest way. Through you, the Lord has taught me how to love, how to forgive, and so much more. You pull me closer to the Lord and encourage me in my walk on a daily basis. I know that life with you will always be an adventure. I can't wait for all the surprises you will bring along the way. Those surprises may have gotten on my nerves in the beginning, but I know they are part of who you are. Thank you for always keeping things interesting. I can't wait to be your wife and for us to live together.

You are an incredible man. I know you will be an awesome husband and one day, the best dad around.

I love you so very much.

Your Bride,

Kate

"EJ, no crying; not yet," Nathan joked as Rett finished his letter. "You didn't forget the cufflinks, did you?" Rett held up the box.

"Are those the Superman cufflinks you told Kim about?" Jacob asked, and Rett nodded. He took them and Rett's ring and met up with Kim to get some pictures of a few wedding details.

* * *

"Are you ready to put the dress on?" Kim asked when she got back to the girls' room.

"Yes," Kate said, shaking her hands with excitement.

Emily got the dress off the hanger and helped her daughter into it. As Kate slipped into her gown, Emmie Wren zipped her up and buttoned the lace at the top. Hanna was there to make sure it all secured properly, but she mostly stayed out the way. The dress had come from her store, and it was magnificent. When the bride spun around, the whole room gasped. Kate's dress was an A-line, lace-covered princess gown with beaded embellishments woven throughout the lace. It was a sleeveless V-neck with a satin sash to emphasize the empire waist. Above the sash in the back, the dress was unlined lace that connected with three simple buttons.

"You look stunning," Caroline gushed.

"He's going to cry, you know," Rachel added.

"That's kinda of the point," Kate laughed.

"You are radiant," Hanna said.

"Ready?" Kim asked once she had the pictures she wanted. Kate nodded. "Okay, see you outside in forty-five minutes, ladies," the photographer directed the bridesmaids.

Kim, Kate, and her mom headed out. They took some individual pictures of Kate, and she had a first look with her dad that was super sweet. He cried and told her how beautiful she was. The bridesmaids came out when it was time, and Kim got some fun shots with everyone before taking a few family photos.

"You are beautiful," Sky said, giving Kate a hug.

"Thank you," Kate beamed, and Kim snapped a picture of them. Kate specifically requested some of her with Emmie Wren, Sky, and the Thomas kids. The pictures wrapped up about forty-five minutes before the ceremony.

It was about to begin,

Kate could hardly wait to see her groom.

Chapter Forty-Five

"You and Rett want to pray together, right?" Kim asked, and Kate nodded.

They positioned Kate safely in a hallway to wait for her groom. Within ten minutes, Rett's hand reached around the corner, and Kate took it.

He simply said, "I love you" before beginning his prayer. "Heavenly Father, this day is all about you and the commitment we are about to make. But that commitment can easily be broken if we don't lean on you. We pray that you will be honored and glorified through this day. We commit to serve you together for the rest of our lives."

As he squeezed Kate's hand, she continued, "God, we thank you for the opportunity to show people what your relationship with your church looks like in a visual way. We pray that someone will come to know you because of what we are doing today. We commit this marriage to you before it even begins, and we know that you know what the future holds. We love you so much. In your precious son's name, amen." Rett released Kate's hand and walked away—but not before she whispered, "I love you too." Their prayer was a powerful moment, and even Kim had tears in her eyes when it was over.

"It's our turn now," Caroline said when Kate came back into the bridal suite. The bridesmaids all formed a circle around her. Each of the bridesmaids and Emily prayed for Kate and Rett and their marriage. The Lord's presence was evident in the incredible moment the girls shared.

***

In the guys' room, Joshua was praying over Rett as the groomsmen gathered around: "Dear God, we thank you for this day and how special it is. We pray that you will be with Rett and Kate. Bless them today and always. May you be the center of their marriage so that they glorify you in all they do. Thank you for placing Kate in Rett's life and for molding them together. Thank you for Kate's grace in accepting every part of Rett. Teach them what it means to live in forgiveness and trust. In your precious and holy son's name we pray, amen."

Just as Joshua was wrapping up, Linda, the wedding coordinator, arrived. "It's time," she smiled, and Joshua, Rett, and Nathan got into place at the front of the sanctuary to wait for the rest of the wedding party to file in. Chad walked in first, hugged Rett, and handed him a golf ball, as did Sky, Houston, and Patrick. By the time the bridesmaids walked down the aisle, Rett's pockets were full.

Hanna was the first of the bridesmaids to walk in, followed by Abbie, Rachel, Caroline, and finally Emmie Wren. When the doors shut behind Emmie Wren, Rett's heart started pounding; he would be seeing his bride in a matter of seconds. The music changed, and the doors opened. As Kate and her father began to walk toward him, tears welled up his eyes. She was incredibly beautiful, and she was going to be his wife. Rett was beaming through his tears when she finally made it to him.

Joshua started the ceremony. "I'll never forget the morning Rett called me to ask if I knew a Kate Adams. I immediately knew something was going on. One day early in their relationship, Rett told me that he had never felt this way about a girl. I asked him to define his feelings, but he couldn't for over year. When he could finally put words to what was happening in his heart, he told me that Kate made him feel at home, and I knew he had found the woman he was going to marry. And that's why we're here—to join these two in marriage. So, who gives this woman to be married?"

"Her mother and I do," Charlie said. He hugged his daughter and placed her hand in Rett's.

"Ephesians 5:22–33 says, 'Wives, submit yourselves to your own husbands as you do to the Lord. For the husband is the head of the wife as Christ is the head of the church, his body, of which he is the Savior. Now as the church submits to Christ, so also wives should submit to their husbands in everything. Husbands, love your wives, just as Christ loved the church and gave himself up for her to make her holy, cleansing her by the washing with water through the word, and to present her to himself as a radiant church, without stain or wrinkle or any other blemish, but holy and blameless. In this same way, husbands ought to love their wives as their own bodies. He who loves his wife loves himself. After all, no one ever hated their own body, but they feed and care for their body, just as Christ does the church—for we are members of his body. "For this reason, a man will leave his father and mother and be united to his wife, and the two will become one flesh." This is a profound mystery—but I am talking about Christ and the church. However, each one of you also must love his wife as he loves himself, and the wife must respect her husband.' Marriage is a picture of the gospel and therefore is not something to be taken lightly. We are the example to the rest of the world, and I know that together will be a great example."

Rett and Kate exchanged vows and took communion while the Generations music minister and his wife sang. The song gave them a minute to just be together before they exchanged rings, and Joshua said a few more things about them as a couple.

"I now pronounce you man and wife," he concluded. "You may kiss your bride." Rett kissed Kate for a good five seconds as their guests cheered.

"I present to you Mr. and Mrs. Everett James Johnson," Joshua grinned. The newlyweds walked up the aisle as their family and friends clapped. When Kim asked them to stop for a photo at the top of the aisle, Rett dipped Kate and kissed her again. She came up laughing, and they followed Kim out to where they would take pictures of the whole bridal party. She captured pictures of the couple and the full bridal party as well as a few final family shots.

"You look absolutely beautiful," Rett whispered, kissing his wife. "I love you, Katie."

"You don't look too bad yourself. I love you, Superman," Kate answered as they headed to the reception at Doublegate—

A married couple, ready to celebrate with their family and friends.

Chapter Forty-Six

"Let's meet our bridal party," the DJ announced soon after they arrived at Doublegate. "Mrs. Hanna Daly escorted by Mr. Chad Borshkin." Hanna and Chad came in dancing. "Miss Abbie Johnson escorted by Mr. Sky Thomas." Abbie jumped on Sky's back to enter the reception hall. "Miss Rachel Johnson escorted by Mr. Houston Singletary." Houston spun Rachel and dipped her. "Miss Caroline Drews escorted by Mr. Patrick Whitfield." Caroline jumped into her fiancé's arms. "The matron of honor, Mrs. Emmie Wren Thomas, escorted by the best man, Mr. Nathan Daly." Emmie Wren bent down, and Nathan jumped over her like they were playing leapfrog. "And finally, let's give a warm welcome to the new Mr. and Mrs. Rett Johnson!" The newlyweds came in dancing, and he pulled her close to kiss her the minute they reached the center of the dance floor. "We'll kick off this party with the bride and groom's first dance," the DJ instructed.

Rett and Kate took the dance floor as Russell Dickerson's "Yours" played. Rett sang in her ear and spun her during every chorus.

"I love you." Rett kissed his wife as the song ended.

"I love you too."

Kate smiled as Charlie walked over for the daddy-daughter dance. Charlie pulled his daughter close as Heartland's "I Loved Her First" came through the speakers. "Rett's perfect for you," he told her. "I couldn't have asked for a better man to be your husband." Charlie spun her out; tears stinging Kate's eyes.

"Thanks, Daddy. I love you," Kate smiled. Charlie kissed her cheek as the song ended.

Rett and Esther were next, and they danced to Mark Harris' "Find Your Wings."

"You look so happy," Esther told her son.

"I am happy, Mom—happier than I've been in a long time," Rett assured her. They sang along to the song, and Esther laughed as he spun her out.

"I love you, EJ. Always have, always will." Esther was misty-eyed as the song ended.

"I know, Mom. I love you too. You are the best mom I could have asked for. Thank you for everything." Rett hugged his mom.

When the dances were over, it was time for everyone to eat. Rett and Kate led the dinner line and sat down at their table. They laughed and talked with friends until Charlie stood to make a toast. "Today has been perfect, and I know Rett and Kate are thankful you all are here because Emily and I certainly are. It's hard to believe that it's been four years since this young man showed up at the hospital and informed me that he was dating my daughter. I knew he was something special when he stuck around for a whole week, and we enjoyed getting to know him even better over the next summer. Rett fit into our family perfectly, and we knew that he and Kate would be together forever. This past Christmas, a very nervous Rett asked for my blessing as he got ready to propose, and I wholehearted gave it. I knew there was no one else for her. Rett has challenged, grown, and loved her in so many ways, and I can't wait to see how marriage looks on them. We love you both. Welcome to the family, Rett." Charlie lifted his glass and passed the microphone to Emmie Wren.

"I thought a long time about what I wanted to say tonight," Emmie Wren said as she stood. "Kate is my best friend, making the five years between us feel like five months on a good day. My husband, Sky, and Kate share a special connection that I didn't understand until Rett sat in my living room and let me interrogate him like any big sister would. Rett did not use the words that night, but they were written in his eyes—he loved her. And he proved it time and time again. When I thought about what memory I wanted to share, the one that came to mind was our trip to D.C. last year. That weekend, Sky and I were able to see Kate and Rett as a couple, and we loved the way they acted around each other and how comfortable they were together. Today is not the beginning for them; it's simply the next step in their relationship with each other and with the Lord. They have defined what it means to have God-honoring relationship, and I'm so thankful that the teenagers they are loving on at Generations have them as an example. Rett, I'm excited to get to call you my little brother. And Katie—welcome to this crazy ride called marriage." She raised her glass, and Nathan stood.

"Kate," he began, taking the microphone, "I know you're glad

Rett finally has a wedding band on, but I have to admit that I'm hoping jealous Kate will still rear her head every now and then; she's pretty fun to watch. But in all seriousness, God knew what he was doing when He placed you in Rett's welcome group four years ago. You have been the biggest blessing—not just to Rett, but to everyone around him. Rett is a different person since meeting you, a better person. He's always been the one to turn heads with his devilish good looks, but he's never looked at girl or talked about a girl the way he looks at and talks about you. Rett has been like my brother since we were six years old, and while Rett was in Israel, you became like a sister to me. It felt like our family grew. I hope that as the years go on, you and Hanna will become like sisters, too, because I'm not going anywhere.

"Rett, from the minute you met Kate, you were smitten. I was pretty sure you were going to start writing her name on all your notebooks," Nathan teased as he went on. "You treated her with respect, and I watched you fall deeper into love with her as she responded in kind. You planned surprise after surprise for her, and I was always amazed that she put up with them. Then I realized that she actually liked them, and that's when I knew you had the right girl. You love her, but she loves you with more grace and strength than I could have ever imagined. But then, I guess someone else had to be able to put with all your ridiculousness. You are the best friend I could have ever asked for, and I'm thankful that you found the girl who makes you feel at home. Congratulations to the newlyweds." Nathan raised his glass to finish the toasts, and it was time to cut the cake.

"You ready?" Rett grinned as they headed to the five-layer white cake with pink roses cascading down the left side. They cut a piece off the back, and Kate giggled as she smashed it onto Rett's face. He did the same, and she felt the icing on her cheek.

"Y'all look at me," Kim laughed, and Kate smiled before Rett helped her clean her face. For Rett, there were red velvet cupcakes in the shape of the Superman logo, and they fed each other a bite of one of them—this time with no shenanigans. After they cut the cakes, the DJ opened the dance floor. They danced and talked to their guests until it was time for the bouquet and garter tosses.

The DJ called all the single women to gather at the front of the room. When the photographers were in position, Kate tossed her bouquet over her shoulder. As it went flying through the air, the girls all reached for it, and fell into the hands of one of the many high schoolers. With much laughter, Kate sat down in the chair for the garter toss, and Rett winked at her. He reached under Kate's dress, pulled her garter off, and threw it casually over his shoulder. In stark contrast to the girls, the guys seemed to jump away from the garter rather than towards it, but as they all goofed around, eventually one of them picked it up and posed for pictures with the girl who had caught the bouquet.

"Ready to go?" Kim asked the newlyweds as the group dispersed.

"Our families want to pray with us before we leave," Rett told her.

Kim gathered everyone in a quiet spot, and each member of the family had a chance to pray. After a moment of silence, Dale wrapped it up. "Father God, we thank you for Rett and Kate and what they mean to you and to each other. We thank you bringing them together, and we pray that you will bless them as they begin their life together. Give them understanding when things get hard and the ability to forgive each other on a daily basis. May you always be at the center of their marriage. In Jesus' name we pray, amen."

Rett's eyes shone with unshed tears, and Kate gently touched his face; she knew there were still more tears to come tonight.

"Now we're ready," Kate told Kim, and everyone gathered to send off the couple. Once Kim and Jacob were in place, Rett and Kate took off running through the sparklers their guests held out. They kissed before getting in Rett's decorated car. The groomsmen had really turned it into a sight to behold.

"I love you, Superman," Kate said, kissing him across the console with a long, lingering kiss that begged for more.

"I love you too, Katie," Rett responded when they broke the kiss. He looked at her with loving eyes.

"Are you going to tell me anything about our destination now that we're leaving?" she asked as they pulled out of the drive and waved goodbye to their guests.

"I'll tell you this—we're not leaving until tomorrow. We're spending the night at home," Rett told her, and a smile spread across her face. Rett knew she was happy with the decision, and he was grateful that they could take their time their first night together. He reached for her hand and brought it to his lips.

"Home," she breathed. "It's our home now, officially." Kate bit her lip; this was it. Rett couldn't help the laughter that escaped his throat. With the sound, the tension between them seemed to dissipate. They pulled up at the house, and Rett helped her get everything out of the car. Rett walked in, expecting her to follow him.

"What you are doing?" he asked from the entry when she didn't come in.

"You're forgetting something." She stood there unmoving until it dawned on him. He took the bags from her hands before turning to pick her up and carry her, bridal style, over the threshold.

"Welcome home, my beautiful wife." He kissed her.

As they pulled away, she blushed. "I know that this is weird, but I want to get ready and change—but there is no way I can get out this dress by myself," Kate admitted, biting her lip. She had painstakingly picked out what she would wear for this night.

"It's fine." Rett sat down behind her and set to work on the dress. "You weren't kidding," he laughed as he struggled to get the dress undone. "Okay, I think I got it," he finally said. His hands were shaking at the sight of her bare back, and he ran a finger over her scar.

"Thanks. Give me ten minutes, and I'll be ready." She walked into the bedroom and let the dress fall to the floor around her feet. She stepped out of it and gathered it to gingerly lay over a chair in the corner of the room.

Then she put on the new lingerie she had chosen especially for that night and wrapped herself the robe she had hung in the bathroom earlier. When she opened the door and Rett walked in, Kate wasn't able to read his face.

"I love you so very much," Kate told him, trying to reassure him. She knew he was nervous about showing her his scars for the first time. He blew out a breath and shrugged out of his suit jacket.

"It's pretty ugly, Kate. You might change—"

"Don't talk about my husband that way, please," Kate whispered. She was going to give him all the time he needed for this moment, but she refused to encourage his negative thoughts. Rett unbuttoned the dress shirt, his tie long gone.

"I . . . Katie." He looked at the floor. "I don't know if I can do this." If Kate hadn't been so close to him, she might not have heard it.

"Rett." She reached for his hands. "EJ," she said tenderly, knowing it would get his attention. He looked at her for the first time since walking into the bedroom. "I'm here. I'm not going anywhere. I love you." He swallowed, nodding as Kate reached up brush away the tears that were glistening on his cheeks. They stayed that way for a long moment until he was ready. When his breath was steady, he backed up slightly and turned around to pull his t-shirt off. He stood with his back to her, and Kate fought sobs for a minute before she stepped forward and began to trace some of the deeper scars. Then she grew bolder and began to kiss a few of them. Rett turned around, and her finger traced the scar on his stomach that ran from just above his belly button to just below his sternum.

"I love you, and there is nothing that can change that. *Ever.*" Kate kissed Rett with all the love she held for him. His legs nearly gave out as the love of God and Kate's love washed over him.

With complete assurance, Rett knew he was home as long as he was with Kate.

Acknowledgments

I've been working on this book since I was in high school so I have A LOT of people to thank. YOU'VE BEEN WARNED:

Megan Lawrence, Thank you for being the best editor and working with me to make this story the best possible. You have stretched, challenged, and guided me through this process. I don't know where this story would be without you.

Kim Russell, Thank you for the headshots and beautiful cover photo and for walking me through a wedding day without a bride and groom doing a first look.

Madyson Chambers and Joshua Kendrick, Thank you for being willing to be on the cover. I cannot thank you enough.

Abby Welch, I know you didn't sign up for cover design but I'm so thankful you and your work!

Anna Sanders, I know you probably don't recognize much but I hope you can see your handiwork in some of the pages. Thank you for sharing your Mexico experience with Rye. And for starting this journey with me to help this dream grow and flourish into a reality.

Samantha Nelson, I'm pretty sure this book wouldn't exist without you editing that first full draft so I owe you a giant thank you.

Anna Lynne Schaeffer, *Ding. Thank you for being my writing buddy and my sounding board. Your help and friendship have been the biggest blessing. You have left your mark on this book in more ways than one. #alwaystheburger

To everyone who read a version of this book, I cannot thank you enough. You were a vital part of this process.

Bethany Cromie and Rachel Janes, Thank you for letting me talk things out with you when they wouldn't get out of my head and all the naming advice.

Heather Kinnebrew, Thank you for walking me through the Journeyman process so that I would get it right for Rye and for all your encouragement.

Elizabeth Walters, Thank you for your words of wisdom about the foster care system and helping me make sure that I was on the right track with telling Rett's story truthfully.

Bailie Cook, Thank you for your help with the break in scene and how the police would handle that situation.

Aly Driver, Claire George, Caroline Kirby, Abby Minshew, Thank you for being my teenage sounding board and helping with Abbie.

Señora Joy Joiner, who is the reason that Kate becomes a Spanish teacher. I might not have been as determined as Kate was to study Spanish but I'll forever be thankful God placed you in my life.

Sherwood Baptist Church, when I needed a name for a church in Albany that would basically be Sherwood I didn't have to think about the name at all because it was ingrained in me a long time ago that "Whoever wants the next generation the most will get them." I'm so grateful for the place that grew and nurtured my faith and the countless people who have influenced me because of that special place.

Bay Leaf Baptist Church, I didn't know what truly meant to have a church family until I became a part of Bay Leaf. I've grown in my faith and understand fully what it means to volunteer in youth ministry and live out my calling. Thank you for the opportunity to put into practice so many of the things that Rett and Kate get to do.

Mama and Jim, We made it. I finished my first book. I cannot thank you enough for all your help and support. And of course, a special thanks to Jim for the most important contribution to this book: Chad's last name.

Daddy and Piper, I'm so incredibly grateful for your support, thank you for everything!

Joshua and John, I know y'all probably won't actually read the book but I love you anyway. And John, for naming Houston Singletary and giving me a clear vision who that character was.

My Grandaddy, Charlie Lewis. Thank you for teaching to always go after my dreams. I miss you and love you. (KK, I hope you can see him on the pages of this book. He's the whole reason Kate's dad's name is Charlie)

Mimi, I did it, you get to hold an actual copy of a book with my name on the cover. I cannot express just how much your words of wisdom and encouragement have meant to me. I'll forever be grateful for you and Pipi supporting me in my education and helping me go to the college of my dreams, Samford University.

Gram, You continue to teach me strength and grace. I know how proud you are that you get to share this book with all your friends. Paw Paw, I miss you and I love you, you always believed in me even when I didn't believe in my self, thank you.

The rest of my family (Addi, Shanna, Curt, Jason, Kasey, Annabelle, Luke, Susan, Nathan, Collins, Clara, Ty, Uncle Charlie, Aunt Kelly, Uncle Brooks, Aunt Jolee, Uncle Richie, Aunt Amy, Mallory, Erika, Susannah, Jacob, Julia, Jackson, Tori, Hunter, Carter), Thank you for supporting this dream that I've had for so long.

Natalie Dixon, Susan Sanders, Beccy Clark, Phyllis Rogers, Wendy McLeod, Leah Glow, Mitzi Adkinson, Lesli Todd, and the rest of my mom's friend group: My second moms who have spent time praying over this book, I cannot express how thankful I am to have you in my life and in my corner.

My Samford friends, especially Jackie Carman and Melissa Denning, your support and encouragement have meant the world to me and I'll forever be grateful for the college experience that shaped so much of this book.

My Small Group (Bobby, Leslee, Bailee, Lilly, Ryan, Diana, Eleanor, Bryce, Casey, Jennifer, Gabriel, Christopher, Mrs. Cindy Bush, Taylor Sapp), You have been so wonderful, encouraging, and supportive. You have prayed with me and for me every step of the way and I will always be grateful.

My Bay Leaf Girls, your kind words of encouragement have meant so much. I hope y'all LOVE the finished product.

Ashley Sanders, Megan Beam, and others from the small little writer's community that I happened to stumble across, I'm so grateful I found you. You have strengthened my craft and taught me so much.

I've been working on this book for over 13 years so I'm sure there are people I forgot to thank--it was not intentional, I promise. I have been so encouraged by every text, like, comment, prayer, and everything else that has been made or said so that this book would actually become a reality—may the journey to the next one be shorter.

"Now to Him who is able to do immeasurably more than all we ask or imagine, according to His power that is at work within us, to Him be glory in the church and in Christ Jesus throughout all generations, for ever and ever! Amen." (Ephesians 3:20-21)

About the Author

Ruth Anne Crews holds a Masters of Divinity from Southeastern Baptist Theological Seminary and a Bachelors in Journalism and Mass Communications from Samford University. When she's not reading and writing, she's hanging out with middle and high school girls teaching them about God's love for them. She loves all things pop culture and superheroes. She currently lives in North Carolina but is originally from Albany, Georgia. Follow along with all her adventures on Instagram @ruthannecrews and on her blog, ruthannecrews.com